SPARK THE FLAMES

ALSO BY IVY ASHER

The Osseous Chronicles
The Bone Witch
The Blood Witch
The Bound Witch

The Lost Sentinel
The Lost and the Chosen
Awakened and Betrayed
The Marked and the Broken
Found and Forged

Shadowed Wings
The Hidden
The Avowed
The Reclamation

The Sept
The Hunt

The Eerie
Into Their Woods
Into Their Den

Hellgate Guardian Series
Grave Mistakes
Grave Consequences
Grave Decisions
Grave Signs

Standalone Novels
Order of Scorpions
Conveniently Convicted
Rabid
April's Fools

SPARK THE FLAMES

SECRET OF THE SYPHON

IVY ASHER

Podium

This is a work of fiction. Names, characters, places, and incidents are either products of the author's imagination or used fictitiously. Any resemblance to actual events, locales, or persons, living, dead, or undead, is entirely coincidental.

Cover design by David Gardias, Best Selling Covers

ISBN: 979-8-3470-3167-2

Published in 2026 by Podium Publishing
www.podiumentertainment.com

For Sanaiya.
Every badass I write is for you.

Dear Reader,

I'm so excited to welcome you into this world of magic, mystery, and mayhem. Every story I write begins with a spark of an idea. Sometimes it's a flicker of a world, a flash of power, or the gleam of a character that ignites my imagination and sets everything ablaze.

This story found its voice in stolen hours, late nights, and messy notes scattered between real life and fantasy. After all the revisions, edits, and self-doubt, I discovered a book that was more of a battle cry for every reader who has lost everything and clawed their way back.

Publishing with Podium has been an incredible journey. Their belief in this story and in the power of storytelling means the world to me. Whether you're reading, listening, or both, none of the magic in *Spark the Flames* would exist without you. Every page you turn, every moment you lose yourself in this world, or find yourself in the characters, you become the heart of it all.

I hope these characters stay with you long after the last page. I hope this story consumes you in the best possible way. And I hope you know how grateful I am that you've picked up this book and breathed life into everything that it is.

Love and tackle hugs,

CONTENT WARNING

In this story there are incidences of, and references to: torture, physical assault, starvation, sexual assault (reference only), attempted suicide, murder of adults and children, kidnapping, graphic language, graphic violence, and graphic sex and sexual content. Please be aware that there may be other unidentified triggering content that is not listed here.

ASH BARREN
TALON'S REACH
FOUR TIERS
BURNER KEEP
RENDER KEEP
CHANNELER KEEP
THRASHER KEEP
PARAGON CITY
THE DIVIDE
THRASHER TERRITORY
SOUTHERN TERRITORIES
THE SCORCH
DEADLANDS

DRAMERIC
BONE ISLES
BURNER TERRITORY
RENDER TERRITORY
CHANNELER TERRITORY
LAIRWOOD
NEWDEN
THE DIVIDE

SPARK THE FLAMES

CHAPTER 1

My bare feet pound against the frozen, unforgiving ground as frigid air scrapes its icy claws in and out of my lungs. I dash through the clouds of breath that puff from my mouth like smoky beacons intent on betraying my location. Frost-tipped pines streak by as I dart through an endless maze of trunks.

"Too slow," I pant at myself, pushing even harder, trying and failing to move faster.

I don't hear them chasing me yet, but time is slipping away too quickly, and there isn't nearly enough distance between where I am and the cell they've been holding me in.

My steps and breaths are too loud. Any second, the alarms are going to go off and they'll know. They'll start hunting. Desperation mists my every exhale, and my chest aches from exertion.

"Move, Ever!" I command, agitation and dread skittering up my spine, begging me to go faster, farther, but I'm so fucking weak and already pushing my abused body to the brink. I wish there'd been more time between when they last bled and beat me and this lucky break. If I'd had a chance to recover, to heal even a little, I'd be in a much better position than I'm in now, but I know I won't get another chance like this. It's now or never.

My lungs are tight, protesting the desperate pulls of oxygen my atrophied muscles are screaming for. Four months ago, a run like this would have been nothing more than a warm-up. I would have thrown my hair up, put on my favorite running bra, and gone full out for hours without breaking a sweat or even getting winded. Now, thanks to the blood brokers, those days are gone, and I'm painfully aware that if I don't figure out how to get the hell away from here, they're never coming back.

Frantic, I look around, hoping to get some sense of where I am, but all I see is a dark, endless forest. One that could be anywhere. When I was moved to this new location, the Tainted spelled my senses again. I have no idea why they still bothered with a blindfold and a thick, abrasive bag over my head, but despite all their precautions and efforts, I could still feel that the air is different here—wherever *here* is. There's a distinct weight to the atmosphere, a press of moisture all around me that didn't exist in my last prison. Not that knowing *that* particular detail is helpful. Sweaty air isn't exactly the road map to escape I desperately need right now.

I hate cities, but I'd give anything to be in one right now. A place packed with buildings, busy streets, and people. Somewhere it'd be easy to turn a corner and just disappear. A campground filled with hunters all armed to the teeth and ready to defend a poor defenseless woman could work too. But I'm not that lucky, so instead, I find myself sprinting through a sea of hills and mountains covered in an infinite span of towering trees and patches of snow. There's nowhere to hide. Nowhere to blend in or cower until the danger passes, nowhere to hole up and heal so I can try to fight my way out.

Basically, I'm screwed.

Well and truly fucked.

The piercing wail of an alarm slices through the placid night, and my gut sours.

Fuck! Time's up.

My heart hammers even harder, and I beg my limbs to push past the pain and fatigue. Distant shouts sound off somewhere far behind me, but they're not nearly far enough, and I can hear my doom on the wind.

They're coming for me.

A mocking moon hangs high in the sky, the stars watching the show far below like apathetic spectators. The tall trees all around me start to thin as I sprint through their cover and race uphill. Every muscle I have burns in protest.

Maybe I can find a road. A road could lead to a concerned motorist, someone who might speed me away. Screw the campground full of hunters; I was being greedy. A sole hunter prowling through these woods is all the good fortune I need right now. I scoff at the thought. Good fortune has never been on my side, hence the reason I'm here, running from a bunch of blood brokers and the tainted sorcai who employ them.

As though fate itself wants in on my mocking, I break through the foliage and run into a clearing, where I'm forced to skid to a stop. And just like that, the fragile flame of hope I've been carefully tending becomes nothing more than a slip of smoke escaping my white-knuckled grasp.

Gone are the palatial trees and frostbitten bracken. In their place is a sea of stars nestled in a cold blanket of dark, desolate night and a rocky cliff jutting toward it all like some sinister runway to oblivion.

A fucking cliff.

Of course that's how this all ends.

I open my mouth to scream, to bellow a protest I'm pretty sure will sound more like a lament, but an incredulous laugh spills out instead. I stare out into the heavens and shake my head. I've lasted this long. Survived everything these Tainted fucks have done to me, taken from me. I've finally managed to escape, only to be stopped by Mother Nature.

What a heartless cunt.

My laugh takes on a tinge of hysteria. I slap a hand over my mouth and pull in a frosty breath through my nose, needing to ground myself and get my shit together.

It's not over yet.

Looking behind me, I retrace my path, wildly searching for a solution, for some other way out. All I find are dots of floating light flickering in the distance. The glowing balls draw closer as the conjurers holding them search for me. I hear them, my captors relaying instructions and coordinates back and forth, their voices grating on the last of my self-preservation.

My mind releases the floodgates on thoughts I've been holding back from the minute Renatta and I were ambushed.

I won't let them take me again.

I won't spend another second being tortured, bled, and sapped of sanity.

I have to escape . . . one way or another.

In a last-ditch effort, I seek out my dragon. I search everything within me for the only thing that might save me now. It only takes a few seconds to know the suppressors the tainted sorcai have been dosing me with are too strong. I haven't felt my other side in . . . I don't even know how long. And even if by some miracle I could sense my other half, could tap into that power, some other cruel twist of fate already has it under lock and key.

It's all thanks to a curse that helped kill my people, my family, and now, it seems, will ultimately kill me too.

I was forced to watch in silent horror as magic stole my kith's ability to transform into their dragons. Watched as my kindred were slaughtered, one by one, like helpless fawns instead of the fearsome, mighty dragons they were. I wish I could crawl back into my father's armoire, like I did that night so many years ago, and hide from what's happening to me now, but it won't save me like it saved me then. Cowardice has a shelf life.

Frustrated and running out of time, I push my fingers through my hair, only for them to get stuck in the mats and tangles that dominate the flame-colored locks. I can only imagine the state I'm in now. I've lost weight and muscle. My pale complexion is pallid at best, and my jade-green eyes are probably nothing more than bloodshot pools of desperation.

Crisp night air steals all the remaining warmth from my limbs. I rub my arms, ignoring the neat lines of scars I now feel there. I'm dirty. The black tank top and shorts I was given weeks ago are creased and wrinkled with dirt, dried sweat, and blood. I wouldn't be surprised if the blood brokers are tracking me by foul smell alone.

"Shit!" I hiss as the voices in the distance grow louder and more animated. They sound like hounds that just scented prey.

I take in the expanse of mountains in the distance and then look up at the sky, as though the man in the moon is going to reach down and pluck me from this nightmare. But there's no saving me from this. I realize that now. I thought if I could get away, if I could just run, that somehow it would all be okay.

Stupid.

I was so bloody stupid.

Pulling in a deep, biting breath, I close my eyes and try to calm my racing thoughts. I give myself a second, a moment to mourn the hope that's carried me through the last 117 days. Faces and memories swarm me, unbidden . . . my sister . . . my Flight.

Are they still looking for me, or did they give up?

Will they ever know what happened to me and Ren?

A fist tightens around my heart as I think about all the things I thought I'd do before I died. I thought I'd find a way to break the curse. That I would lead the charge for retribution and give what's left of my kind a life out of the shadows, one filled with more than suffering and sorrow. It'll be up to the others now.

A sob lodges in my throat at the realization of everything I'll lose, everything I'll miss out on.

Before my emotions can force me to rethink what I'm about to do, I shove them away, burying them so deep it's like they were never there to begin with. Hardening my resolve, I exhale the trepidation tightening my lungs and pull in a bitter, fortifying breath.

I won't let them corner and catch me again.

I won't let them use me to get to the others.

With a determined shake of my head and hardening of my soul, I back up twenty paces, and then I start to run again. I pump my arms and my legs as hard as I can. Silent, hot tears spill from my eyes, stinging my cold cheeks. The rocky edge of the cliff speeds closer, but I ignore the panic that surges through me and begs me to stop.

"I'm sorry, Enslee," I whisper as the ground disappears from under me and I leap away from the cliff's edge.

Dread congeals in my veins, but with it comes an unexpected rush of release. A ripple of tranquility surges from my center as a whip of wind catches me. For a second, I can almost pretend it's going to whisk me away. I float for less than a breath, and in that short, stolen moment of time, I can imagine all too well what it would be like to shift into the mighty dragon I'm meant to be.

My soft skin would harden into an armor of scales. Great leathery wings would bud from my back and formidable fangs drop from my mouth. My size would dwarf the moon itself, and I'd ride the gelid currents back to the blood brokers and sorcai that hurt me, and I'd make them fucking pay.

But none of those things happen. Gravity yanks me from my wishful imaginings and shoves me cruelly back into my plummeting reality. Finality overwhelms my senses, and when my fall doesn't miraculously explode into flight, my heart drops even faster than I do.

My dragon is as trapped as it's always been, but for once, maybe that's a good thing. Maybe it's better that the curse will claim me too.

If I had my dragon, even if just a part of my power managed to reveal, I might survive this, and I need to *not* survive this.

Death isn't the escape I was hoping for, but it will do. At least I'll go hugging the sky and kissing the wind, knowing the others are safe. Protected.

Knowing I didn't break.

Alarmed shouts spill over the cliff's edge I just jumped from. I smile at the sound of their distress and close my eyes, greeting the end like the long-lost family I miss so much.

Fuck the Tainted.

Fuck the blood brokers.

And fuck The Horde. I hope the betraying bastards all die writhing in pain and become nothing more than forgotten ash on the wind.

Menacing rocks and an unforgiving ground draw closer. My heart bludgeons my chest so hard it feels like it'll break through at any moment.

I wish it would.

It would probably be a less painful way to go.

I wait for one more glimpse of my life and loved ones to flash before my eyes, but it doesn't come. All I see is vast wilderness and a ruthless, taunting fate rushing up to meet me.

Then we collide.

And I do my best to die.

CHAPTER 2

Woolen and heavy. Everything feels too soft, too feathery . . . my body . . . my mind. And yet the panic in the reedy feminine whisper pierces through the murky depths I'm shrouded in like a hot lance through dandelion fluff.

"A dragon. They have us tending to a dragon, a *female* dragon, like that's just some normal, everyday, no-big-deal thing."

"It's only an issue if you make it one, Gina."

"Everything about this is an *issue*, Pete. She's a dragon. You know, the kind that burned half the planet in the Fae Wars and then declared themselves rulers of everything that didn't go up in smoke."

"I'm pretty sure they call themselves drakes when they're in this human-ish form. And they saved our asses after The Bearing. We'd all be slaves to the fae right now if the dragons hadn't done what they did."

"I don't care what they call themselves. I care that we have one of their females unconscious in the bed behind you, which means The Horde is going to come down on all of us. You know how they are. They're ruthless when they think they've been wronged. Just ask the wyverns. And if there's one thing that's guaranteed to incite their wrath, it's messing with one of their females. I've never even seen one before. That's how psychotically protective they are of the few that are left."

My muddled mind tries to make sense of what's going on, but when I reach for clarity, my cumbersome limbs can't seem to find it in the foggy haze all around me.

"Shhhh, Gina! You're getting yourself worked up for nothing. The Horde isn't going to show up and burn the town to the ground."

"And how do you know that?"

"One, because not all of them breathe fire. Different subgroups, or kiths as they call them, have different abilities—"

"Pete, spare me the lecture. The Dragon Horde is not going to send us their Healers or the dragons that grow flowers and talk to trees. They're going to send the Thrashers, their punishers and trackers. You know, the massive, scary ones who hunt down the troublemakers and show the rest of us why messing with the top of the food chain is a bad idea. Again, do you really need this history lesson after what they've done to your own people?"

"This female was brought here because we were the closest trauma center. We didn't hurt her, Gina. We saved her. And before you go throwing *my people* in my face, the sorcai that rebelled with the wyverns were dealt with. Rightfully so. That's the Arcane way. I know you humans like to think you're entitled to things the way they were before The Bearing, but you morons were the ones who started shit with the fae and almost got yourselves wiped out. The Arcane intervened, like you begged us to, and now you get to fall in line like the rest of us."

I try to swat away the hissed conversation that's buzzing around me like a pesky mosquito, but I still can't get my arms to work like they're supposed to.

In fact, nothing seems to be working. I'm pretty sure I'm wrapped in cotton and trapped in sand, and it's making everything too slow and yet somehow too fast.

I do understand one thing though—I should be dead.

I should be, but I'm not.

"Gina, if your prejudice is going to keep you from doing your job, you need to go notify shift lead so they can send someone else in here who can help. We are required by law to report any cases that even faintly look like they're linked to blood brokers. The fact that the victim is a dragon doesn't matter. The Horde is sending a team to investigate and collect her, and we need to get her cleaned up so that they don't fly into a rage and burn us all alive when they see the state she's in. Now, get to work or get out."

"Thought you said they don't all breathe fire," the woman grumbles quietly. "Can't you just bibbity bobbity boo her clean with all your superior sorcai magic? I know you're licensed for it. Why do you even need me?"

"They found some sort of strange magical block in her blood when they were testing it to figure out what she was. Even the higher-ups don't recognize what it is or why. They don't want anyone messing with it more than they already have, which means no more unnecessary magic around her. We get to do things the old-fashioned way today. Now, get to work."

A cold cloth brushes against my forehead, and I groan a weak protest, not liking the chilly touch. A squawk of fright sounds off next to me, followed by the scuffle of feet scurrying around. Harsh, worried whispers press in against me like a scratchy quilt, but I lose track of the noise and time as it all grows too fuzzy and too fragile to hold on to before growing quiet.

The sand I'm trapped in pulls me deeper, disarranging my senses even more. I float, both light and heavy for a while, neither here nor there. Until the long-past-hazy conversation comes back and I manage to cling to a part of it that feels important. The statement tries to escape my grasp. It wiggles and writhes like a slippery fish, but I hold on tight, forcing the words to replay in my mind over and over again.

The Horde is sending a team.

The words are weighted. Heavy. But I'm still floating all over the place, and it's hard to connect the dots into a picture that makes sense.

The Horde.

My heart rate picks up, and the murk starts to clear.

The Horde.

And then my mind seems to reboot, and it all clicks together.

The. Horde. Is. Sending. A. Team.

I pull in a sharp, steel-edged breath as adrenaline floods me, and I sit up, ignoring the cords attached to my body that strain against the sudden movement.

Shit. *Shit!* I can't be on The Horde's radar. The blood brokers and the Tainted were bad enough. *The Horde* is the equivalent of jumping from the frying pan into the mouth of an angry, churning volcano or—you know—a fucking fire-breathing dragon.

I force my eyes open, blinking furiously against the sudden light that overwhelms me.

Sunlight.

Something I haven't seen or felt for months.

Operating on pure panic, I give myself no time to marvel at the bright heat. My eyes immediately start to water from the staggering illumination. I wipe at them with a shaky hand as I try to decipher the blurry images surrounding me. The first thing I can make out is the plastic tubing leading away from my arms. Fear instantly throttles me at the sight, and my mind transports me back to my cell despite my other senses telling me I'm not there anymore.

Fright crawls up my throat and I claw at it, desperate to keep it at bay. I frantically search for Wistan. I know that evil bastard is lurking somewhere nearby, just waiting for me to be conscious enough to carve new tally marks in my skin. I don't see him anywhere and confusion sweeps in, followed quickly by relief when I recognize that I'm in a room. A sterile-looking room. Alone. Which is odd, but it's not a cell. Not a cage. I'm not tied down. They always tie me down when they're going to bleed me.

I expand my senses, searching for dampeners in the room or anything else designed to weaken me. That fucked-up brand of magic has been a staple in every cell the blood brokers have kept me in from the moment I first woke up in one, but I don't sense anything here.

My gaze darts back down to the cannulas in my arms and the small tubes attached to them. More ease trickles through me when I realize they aren't robbing me of blood, but rather feeding some kind of clear fluid into me. I take in the silent machines to my right and left, the bed I'm sitting in, the simple sheath covering me, and belatedly I put it all together.

I'm in a hospital.

I've seen them in movies, and a few members of the pack we trade with back home have talked about being treated in one, but I've never experienced it myself. I've always been careful not to go anywhere where my blood might be exposed.

I connect the clues of my environment with the whispered, fuzzy conversation I was in the middle of earlier, and my heart simultaneously leaps and plummets.

Somehow I survived my fall.

The blood brokers don't have me again.

And The Horde is on their way.

A brittle, groggy groan slips out of me, and I force myself to swallow down another as I swing my feet around to the side of the bed. Surprisingly, I don't hurt anywhere. Where there should be agony, there isn't so much as an ache. For someone who smashed through too many layers of branches to count and then shattered themselves against the hard ground of a merciless mountain, that shouldn't be the case. I should be suffering from debilitating pain, and yet all I am is stiff.

Probably because I've been lying in this bed for too long and now my bones are in no hurry to leave it. Aside from that though, I feel surprisingly okay. Nowhere near as strong as I was before I was taken, but certainly more robust than I have been in months. Then again, I felt closer to death in my cell than I did falling off a cliff, so that's not saying much.

"There's our fighter," an animated voice warbles as a lanky man strides into the room.

I startle, shocked by the invasion of noise and the sudden appearance of the stranger. My alarmed thoughts shoot straight to *The Horde*. I was very young the last time I met a dragon male face-to-face. They're colossal. Something this guy is not. So unless The Horde recently stopped wearing scale armor and started wearing baby-pink scrubs, this guy isn't one of them. He must work here.

The male's bright brown eyes twinkle softly with intelligence as his gaze bounces from me to the flashing machines standing sentinel on both sides of the bed. I scent his magic before its tepid touch brushes lazily across my senses. It's not dark, it doesn't smell spoiled, he's not Tainted, but he's—without a doubt—sorcai.

The presence of any kind of Arcane magic has my instincts and reactions once again at war with my rational mind. Without second-guessing why, I leap at the stranger. Before he can so much as gasp in surprise, I yank the IV from my inner elbow and wrap the tubing around the male's neck. I pull as hard as I can until he's grasping frantically at the coiled plastic, his face turning a welcome shade of deep red.

My arms tremble with the effort, even though this puny sorcai is making his death far too easy. I feel better than I have in ages, and yet I can still feel the effects of what the Tainted have done to me over the last four months. I pull even harder on the IV tubing, but all too quickly, the fight and strength start to drain out of my limbs.

I growl in frustration, angry that underneath the burst of strength and adrenaline I just had, I'm still frighteningly frail, still so hollow. I search for my dragon as I force the sorcai to his knees. His long fingers desperately claw and slap at my arms as pained gurgles bubble out of his mouth.

Worry plumes through me when I still can't reach even the faintest hint of a dragon inside. I'm accustomed to being blocked from the power and the ability to transform, but I used to be able to at least sense it stretching under my skin. Now there's nothing. It's been like that since I was taken, and I worry I've been cut off for so long that it's gone for good, and I don't know if it can come back.

Maybe only part of me survived the last four months.

A sizzle of electric power fills the air before a bolt of magic slams into me from behind. I'm thrown from the sorcai's back into a wall as streaks of magic strike painfully all around me.

"What is happening in here?" a woman demands, her hands held threateningly in front of her as more strands of bright yellow power flicker between her readied palms.

The sorcai I was choking shakily pulls the IV tubing from his bruising neck, his loud coughs bouncing off the walls of the room as another man comes running in. He's a shifter, predator class, although I can't immediately tell what animal since it's not one I've come in contact with back home. He's not in scrubs, but the stethoscope hanging off his neck tells me he's probably a Healer.

I scent the air for the telltale sour fetor that all Tainted carry. They try to hide it, but I can always sniff it out. Just like the sorcai I was trying to strangle, this shifter's scent isn't rancid, meaning he hasn't been in contact with anyone I'm running from. The room still smells sharp and clean with a hint of burning ozone that's growing stronger as the woman just inside the doorway continues to eye me angrily, her yellow magic and her unanswered question still flickering in the air.

"Where am I?" I demand, the question friable and frail as it scrapes out of my throat like fine-grit sandpaper.

The unexpected hit of magic has my legs wanting to buckle, but I lock my knees and lean against the wall, refusing to go down. I may feel like I've got tissue paper for limbs, but I sure as shit am not going to announce that to any of them.

The shifter healer moves to a machine that's flashing red and presses a few buttons until the lights fade to a soft, complacent white once more. "You're in Lairwood. Hikers found you in Newden. You were transferred here when your injuries were more critical than their facilities could handle. You're lucky to be alive."

"Newden?" I croak as shock rings like a gong in my head, making everything go quiet before it gets loud again.

I was on the other side of the divide when I was taken. Ren, our Flight, and I were tracking a Relacour in vampire territory. I didn't sense the trap until it was too late. I didn't think the Tainted would risk moving me through so many territories. Looks like the branches of their network are farther-reaching than we realized.

"You've been here for several days. We didn't know if you'd wake up," the shifter tells me as the woman helps the man I attacked to his feet.

He rubs his throat as he looks at me, his pink scrubs now ripped in a few places and disheveled. I'm surprised by the contrition I find floating in his stare. "I didn't mean to scare you. I'm very sorry," he rasps, his voice almost as coarse as mine.

I stare at him blankly, dumbstruck by the apology. Maybe I've taken one too many blows to the head while I was held captive, but I attacked him and *he's* sorry. That's not how things work where I come from. He watches me expectantly, like he's waiting for my pardon, but the only thing sitting on the tip of my tongue is unease. I don't know what to do with his *sorry* other than not trust a breath of it.

I look around the room and I don't know if I'm searching for answers or an escape. I need to get out of here. I need to get home.

Home.

It dawns on me that home might be even more impossible to get to than I thought. The realization comes like a kick to the chest, and it's all I can do not to stagger and sink to the ground. Enslee might have closed the wards to me and Renatta after we were taken. Our Flight would have told her what happened, and she'd have acted accordingly. Which means I may not be able to get back in.

Certainly not if The Horde is on to me. That would bring death right to the hidden front door of the others. I'm sure the Burner king would like nothing more than to discover there are survivors of his successful coup d'état all conveniently gathered together. That would definitely make it easier for him to wipe us out once and for all.

We've been successfully flying under the radar, biding our time while we figure out how to break an unbreakable curse. But until we're free of it, we need the world—and especially the king and The Dragon Horde—to continue thinking that the Syphons are all dead.

A tremor moves through my hands, and my breathing speeds up. The need to run and hide builds in my blood, and I fight the urge, knowing I'll get nowhere fast without some sort of plan.

I need to get out of here. Then I need to find a communicator—not one in the hospital though. I can't risk The Horde discovering that I contacted anyone, and they'll scour this place first. I can't chance a missing communicator being noticed.

I try to think through what's coming my way. If I'm lucky, they'll only send one operative team, or Flight, as dragon hierarchy classifies them. Unlike my rag-tag Flight back home, The Horde will have the best of the best. Burners, Channelers, Thrashers, and Renders. But it's the Thrashers I'm most worried about in this case.

Physical threats in every sense of the word, from their impenetrable skin to their offensive abilities, Thrashers are also the best trackers of our kind and renowned tacticians. It's possible that the Flight they send might not have one, but it's not likely, which means I need to get as far ahead of them as I can, and fast.

Fragile threads of a plan in place, I focus back on my surroundings and realize the other two sorcai left the room. The shifter is the only one still here, and he's apparently talking to me. I tune in, barely catching the last of what he's saying.

"We've given you a concealment charm to help with the scars. It will hide the look and feel of them while you wear it. The charm should last around a month before you'll need a new one," he declares, gesturing to a silver band that fits around my right ankle.

My gaze drops to the innocuous circlet. It could easily be mistaken for a trendy piece of jewelry, but I can feel the hum of magic against my skin. The spell work is refined and potent. Whoever did it must have been very expensive. I want to immediately rip it from my body, but when I reach for it, the smooth skin of my arm gives me pause.

I stare at my limb, at the expanse of pale skin that's no longer carved up and tally-marked. I turn my arm over, seeing the underside is just as smooth. A confusing mix of emotions rushes through me. Pain, relief, shame, anger—everything swirls together and mixes into a whirlpool of turmoil and wonder. I reach behind me and run a hand over my smooth upper back. I don't know what to think about the absence of scars. I know they're there—they were gouged just as deeply inside as they were outside—but the shifter is right, I can't see or feel them.

For a second, I can almost pretend I was never taken.

My blood wasn't stolen and sold off to the highest bidder.

Renatta wasn't tortured and killed in the cell next to mine.

If I never remove this spelled band, I can make believe all of it was just some horrible nightmare, a fucked-up figment of my imagination.

If only I couldn't still hear Ren's screams or the way she begged at the end. If only the magic anklet could erase every memory I have of being bled as Wistan laughed and carved a tally into my skin solely to commemorate my inability to stop him.

Anguish squeezes my chest, but I refuse to acknowledge it. I have bigger things to worry about right now, The Horde being at the top of that list.

"We would greatly appreciate it if you'd wear the charm until after The Horde's retrieval team talks to you. I hope you understand, but we need to prepare them for the magnitude of your injuries. Our facility and town won't hold up to a dragon's temper," the healer concludes, his last statement more of a plea than an assertion.

Despite my efforts to remain outwardly calm and collected, one of the machines next to the healer starts flashing red, betraying the rapidly increasing thrum of my uneasy heart. He hurries to press a bunch of buttons to calm the disgruntled tech, and I start pulling wires and tubes off of me to help the process.

"We didn't know that you were a dragon when you came in," the healer nervously rambles. "You didn't have a dragon mark or any other kith designations, and for some reason, you don't smell like a dragon, but when your blood work came back—oh no, don't do that!" he yelps when he turns back to find me yanking another electrode from my body.

The shifter moves closer to try to stop me, but a warning growl rumbles out of me, and he instantly freezes in his tracks. He lifts his hands in a placating gesture, his eyes widening with even more worry when I glare at him and continue disconnecting myself from all of the machines and IVs.

"Please get back in bed, dragoness. You need to rest. Your body has been through a lot, and healing it isn't going to be a quick process with the fall you sustained and with what . . . " The healer hesitates for a moment before soldiering on. "With what was done to you before that."

I try not to roll my eyes at the clumsy way he tiptoes around the horrid condition I know I was in when I was brought here. Not to mention the magical block suffocating my abilities that they discovered but don't understand. I'm sure his imagination has provided him with a laundry list of fucked-up things that probably happened to me, things too awful for him to even whisper, and yet, I lived through them.

It doesn't matter though. There will be plenty of time to revisit all my traumas, but I'll do that far from here and far from The Horde. Irritated and anxious to get going, I run my fingers through my hair as I start to pace. A flicker of shock moves through me when my fingers rake all the way through without getting caught on a single snarl. My hair is clean. Such a simple, benign thing finally makes everything really sink in.

I'm free.

I'm actually free.

I escaped Wistan and his band of blood-stealing bastards.

Now I just need to get somewhere safe.

The healer watches me warily like he's debating whether The Horde will flay him alive if he dares to try to restrain me. I study him for a moment and realize I'm going about this all wrong. I need to be artful, not an asshole, if I want freedom. I can't muscle my way out—I'm not strong enough—and these people are way more scared of The Horde than they are of me. I need them to let their guard down so I can sneak out from under it, which means I need to be a good little dragon and pretend I want to be rescued.

Forcing the mounting tension from my body, I adopt a contrite and compliant mien. I nod my head at the healer, slumping my shoulders like I'm suddenly too exhausted to move, and start to drag my feet back toward the bed like he wants me to.

"You're right. All of this has just been a lot," I tell him, gesturing around the room and batting my eyelashes like I'm fighting back poor-little-girl tears. "Thank you for saving me, and thank you for helping me get back home."

The shifter blows out a breath, and the strain in his posture instantly melts. "Of course, dragoness. We're happy we could be of service. I'm going to get you some new lines," he quickly announces, like he's eager to escape before I can change my mind and start being difficult again. He waves a hand at the pile of electrodes, wires, and plastic tubing on the ground. "Once everything's reconnected, we'll make you as comfortable as possible until your people arrive."

"Of course. But before you go," I rush, stopping him as he turns to leave, "is there somewhere I can clean up before they get here?" I do my best to look and sound fragile and cooperative.

I watch a flash of hesitation sweep across his face, but I'm hoping what I am, and what's about to be thundering through the halls of this facility soon, overrides his sense of authority so he gives in to what I want.

Female dragons are watched over and protected like the rarest treasure—and there's nothing a dragon likes more than treasure. Fighting and fucking are high up on the list, but claiming, whether that's a territory, a Flight, a Wing, or some priceless precious dragon commodity, *that* is a key tenet of our species.

"You're right. Neither you nor this facility deserves The Horde's wrath," I press when it looks like he's about to decline my request. "It would probably be best if I'm a little less . . . disheveled when the others get here."

I offer him a small smile after slipping a little regal affectation into my tone, one that suggests I'm not used to hearing the word *no*. The healer's eyes dart nervously toward the door, like he can already see a team of angry drakes storming his way, ready to punish him for daring to deny me anything.

"Of . . . of course," he stammers. "There's a washroom there." He points toward a doorway that's behind me. "I'll have an orderly bring in some spare scrubs while I get new lines for you. Anything else you need?" he adds, the sharp tang of fear suddenly filling the room.

"No, just freshening up will make a world of difference."

The shifter nods quickly and starts to rush out. His shoulder clips the frame of the doorway hard. I wince, but he doesn't so much as pause or rub at the bruise that has to be blooming as he hurries away.

I suppose there are some perks to being at the top of the supernatural food chain, regardless of whether or not I want to be there.

Anxiety churns in my gut, and the need to move, to get going, nips at my limbs.

Now . . . to get the fuck out of here.

CHAPTER 3

My too-big shoes squeak against the vinyl floor of the hallway. I have to stop myself from glaring down at the footwear that's doing its best to make my attempt at an inconspicuous escape as conspicuous as possible. Luckily, the corridors I've been slinking through so far have been empty. I don't know if I feel relieved by that or dismayed.

I keep my stride even and purposeful, acting like I walk these halls every day. I need anyone who might look my way to think that I've got somewhere to be and a job to do just like everyone else. Business as usual.

I didn't leave an orderly and a healer unconscious and tied up in a bathroom.

Nope.

I didn't don the scrubs said orderly kindly brought me and then promptly steal her shoes.

Not me.

I'm just another worker on my way to do whatever it is the people in bright blue scrubs do here, not a drake running for her life. I smooth my hand over my hair, hoping the tight bun I twisted it into helps it to be less noticeable. I can't do anything about disguising the color. I'll just have to hope it's not as unusual here as it is in the south.

Adrenaline tries to encourage my feet to move faster and my hands to shake, but I don't allow either to happen as two people round a corner and head my way. They're locked in an animated conversation as they pass by, and I casually let out a puff of relief when neither even glances my way.

I sidestep a transport drone and the large floating bouquet of flowers it carries, my stolen shoes mercifully silent as I avoid the speedy magi-tech bot. I've seen a few flying around, doing one job or another. If my situation wasn't as close to fucked as it is, I'd be tempted to grab one or two and take them home with me. Not that The Scorch has enough Source magic to keep the tech functioning, but if we could modify them, they could come in handy.

I shake my head to help dislocate the direction of my thoughts. I'm used to capitalizing on unexpected opportunities, taking advantage of luck when it leans my way, but I remind myself that this isn't a run for supplies or recon. The stakes are much higher, and I need to stay focused on what's most important: getting away.

Traversing another corridor, I follow the signs directing me to the elevators. I wind down another hallway and spot my goal at the same time I spot an adjacent nurses' station.

A very busy nurses' station.

My stomach tightens when I notice a security guard in the corner, although fortune may be in my favor because he happens to be busy chatting up a pretty woman in pink scrubs. I keep my pace steady and my face blank. I may be out of my depth when it comes to a hospital and how it operates, but I'm not out of my element when it comes to sneaking.

Experience has taught me that if you act like you belong somewhere, others don't usually question it. It's an actuality that's served me and my Flight well when we've had to leave the safety of our home wards to acquire or kill one vital thing or another out in the world.

Different lab coats and scrubs create a kaleidoscope of colors as staff flit like diligent little worker bees in and around the nurses' station. I'm worried one of them might recognize me, but no one looks over as I approach. A receptionist glances up as I walk past her desk, and I offer her a small friendly smile. She quickly returns it and then busies herself with something.

I try not to hold my breath as I close the distance to the elevators and press the button to call the car before stepping back to wait. I didn't actually think it would be this easy, but I'm not about to invite trouble my way by questioning it.

I wait for what feels like eons, but an elevator doesn't arrive to quickly and quietly whisk me away. I press the button to call it again, the airy hope for an easy escape I was just floating on disappearing like a popped balloon.

I stare at the button and then at the opaque list of floors above the elevator doors that should light up as a car approaches, but once again nothing happens. Nothing flickers to life on the panel. There's no whirring of machinery telling me a car is darting to the floor I'm on. I casually look around, searching for another button or panel to try since this one seems to be broken, my heart picking up speed at the unanticipated impediment.

"Ma'am . . . " someone behind me calls out.

I ignore the polite summoning, hoping it's aimed at someone else, and impatiently press the button in front of me for a third time.

"Ma'am . . . " a female calls again.

Shit.

The stairs are probably nearby. Maybe I can plan B it in their direction.

"Ma'am!" the persistent woman behind me barks again, and I can practically feel eyes turning in my direction and settling on my back.

"I think she's talking to you," a male about my size, wearing green scrubs, declares as he sidles up next to me. He smells like wolf, but there's an undercurrent of selkie too, and I'm not sure which is his.

I tense. "Oh," I chirp with faux surprise at his comment, turning to find the receptionist leaning over her desk, her stare trained on me.

"Try your card one more time," she instructs, gesturing to the elevators. "They just updated the system again, and it's being glitchy." She gives me an apologetic look, and it helps to stave off my panic.

"Got it," I answer, trying not to fumble as I dig into my pocket for the ID card. The one I took off the healer before I knocked him out and tied him up with his own stethoscope and the lines he brought to reconnect.

The male next to me is steadily tapping on his com bracelet, but I pretend I don't notice the device I could desperately use right now. Instead of ripping it off his wrist and making a desperate run for it, I step forward to swipe the pilfered badge against the black square of glass on the wall that I assumed was a camera until now.

"Mine goes on the fritz too every time they admit someone high-profile on the floor and update the clearances," the guy next to me volunteers, nodding at the card I tuck back into my pocket. "I think I spend more time talking to the magi-tech team about my access than I do actually doing my job."

A chime goes off and the elevator doors finally slide open. I step into the car, and the male in the green scrubs follows.

"I heard some nurses whispering about a dragon that was admitted," he offers conspiratorially as the elevator doors shut and it starts a painfully slow descent. He runs his hand quickly through his golden hair as though ensuring it's sitting the way he likes.

Agitation prickles through me, but I keep my face neutral and shrug indifferently at his revelation. "That's none of my business," I respond, courteous but dismissive.

My nerves start to settle and the taut apprehension that's been sitting in my stomach like an anvil disintegrates into an eclipse of ruffled moths. I bite back a sad smile at the thought. That's what Ren always called the uneasy feeling that flutters in your stomach when you're worried. She always said butterflies are for good things, moths are for situations that could go one way or the other, and wasps are when you know you're fucked.

"You've seen her, haven't you?" the male demands excitedly, pulling me from my thoughts.

I tuck away the loss that unfurls at the thought of Ren and focus back on my unwelcome elevator companion. The car suddenly slows and comes to a stop. The doors slide open and in floats a cart. I move to the side to make room, studying the contents of the new arrival as the doors once again shut and the elevator resumes its unhurried, sloth-like descent.

A jolt of excitement perks me up when I realize that the bot that just joined us is packed with food. There are rows of covered plates and a basket of what looks like wrapped sandwiches, with drinks tucked into a nook at the back.

"I knew someone important had been admitted. They cleared out the entire east wing of the floor, and everything has been very hush-hush. I've only ever seen them do that once before, when one of Lord Quall's guests was sick and his personal Healer was unavailable. But, wow, an actual dragon . . . here," the male marvels, oblivious to the fact that I'm too busy calculating whether I can consume this entire food cart before the elevator reaches the lobby to give a flying shit about his dragon fixation.

"Just tell me if it's *actually* a female dragon," Green Scrubs pleads. "The nurses were whispering about it, but I didn't actually think . . . Is she as big as the males?"

The car slows once more, approaching the floor the guy selected and saving me from having to answer him. Or at least I thought it would, but when the doors open, Green Scrubs doesn't get off the elevator. Instead, he presses a hand to the door and gives me a dogged stare that tells me that he has no intention of moving until I answer him.

I debate once again denying that I know anything at all, but I obviously didn't do a good enough job of lying in the first place or I wouldn't be in my current hostage situation with Green Scrubs. I level him with an exasperated look, careful not to let the sudden violent nature of my thoughts bleed through at the way he's cornering me. I can tell he's not going to budge unless I give him something, and as much as I'd like to give him a broken jaw right now, time is of the essence and I need to behave.

I sigh and roll my eyes, not having to fake the irritation I feel at giving in to his inappropriate demand. "She's huge, ugly as they come, and a bitch."

A smile quickly stretches across his face, and he nods like I've just imparted some great pearl of invaluable wisdom.

"I bet that's why they never let the rest of us Arcs see their women. They're probably uglier than bog goblins," he whispers and then laughs while finally stepping out of the elevator and letting the doors go.

"Worse," I call after him as the metal doors cinch closed. I chuckle, amused.

Let the gossipmongers feast on that.

Fingers crossed it will help with my head start. That asshole will be busy spreading misinformation, and when they finally realize I'm gone, the staff will be looking for a big, snarling, repulsive bitch drake instead of me.

I focus back on the cart floating next to me, looking up at where I suspect cameras are hidden in the ceiling of the elevator car. I know they'll eventually check this footage, but I don't technically need to be invisible here. What's a little food theft on top of what I'm already up against?

Deciding it's worth the risk, I grab two wrapped sandwiches and a large container of water. No alarms go off when I relieve the cart of some of its bounty, and I internally fist pump with satisfaction. The elevator stops on floor three, and the cart floats out while I expeditiously scarf down one full sandwich and wash it down with a third of the water.

Thankfully, no one else interrupts my ride down to the first floor, and I step out into a bustling beige lobby. Late-afternoon light glitters on the floor and walls, and I step into the heavy foot traffic, aiming for the wall of windows and the two sets of sliding glass doors that whoosh open and closed as they admit and expel visitors and employees alike.

Slipping out of this place has proven to be even more anticlimactic than I thought it would be. I should be relieved by that, but all it does is stoke my worry. Looking around, I expected an alarm to go off or a herd of security guards to be running my way. I figured someone would have found the employees tied up in my bathroom by now, or they would have managed to get free and sound the alert that I was making a break for it, but nothing happens. I unwrap the second sandwich and consume it at a more reasonable pace while I practically waltz out the front door, feeling lighter and more hopeful than I should for someone who has no money, no communicator, and no clear way to get home.

I'm not a sitting duck for The Horde anymore though, and that's something at least. They'll be on my ass soon enough, but one thing at a time.

A wave of heat sweeps over me as I step out into the sun. The sweltering warmth clings to me in a familiar sticky way, but the tidy grasses, full trees, and rainbow of colorful flowers planted all around are a far cry from the cracked, sunbaked terrain I grew up in.

The only things that thrive in the harsh, arid air of The Scorch are cacti, tumbleweeds, and a rousing call for retribution from the castaways that are forced to call it home.

I've visited a number of southern cities in my lifetime, but with zero access to jump portals, I've never been able to travel far from the cloying reach of the desert. Not until now anyway. I wish I had time to marvel at how different things are on this side of the divide, but every second I waste admiring the plants and flowers is a second that brings The Horde closer. However, it's harder than I'll admit to tear my attention away.

Learning about the lush, fertile lands that grow around a Source and seeing them are two very different things. I've always known just enough to understand exactly what I was missing being raised in the harsh and unforgiving Scorch.

Lairwood isn't a Source City, but judging by the look of things, it's not on the fringes either. Definitely far from the deadlands I've called home.

Finishing my sandwich, I down the rest of the water and drop the trash in a compactor as I get the lay of things. I'm surrounded by a cluster of tall buildings, each about thirty stories high, give or take. Glancing up, I take in the wide, distant airway, teeming with traffic that surrounds what I suspect is Lairwood's city center.

Air gondolas, atmo coupes, and other sky craft zip around the airway and then breeze down the smaller windways that twist between the tall buildings. The map of windways above is mirrored on the ground by flyways for smaller, single-user vehicles, cycles, and public airtrams. They're bordered by throngs of pedestrians on sidewalks and smaller buildings that are a mix of apartments, shops, restaurants, and a myriad of other random businesses.

I start walking, picking my way down foreign streets with no other goal than to get away. Away from the hospital. Away from The Horde. And away from everything that's happened to me over the last four months—although I'm sure the last one will linger for far longer than I'd like.

I put more distance between me and what I'm running from, but instead of feeling relieved or reassured, I find myself feeling hunted. I nonchalantly look around, but I can't identify anything that could be directly responsible for the feeling. And yet with each step I take, I feel more and more exposed.

With a creeping dread, it dawns on me that I've been so focused on trying to get away from The Horde that I haven't given much thought to the Tainted and their blood-broker goons.

The guards that chased me saw me jump. They more than likely assumed the same thing *I* did when I flung myself off that cliff, that I'd die. But if word got back to them that I made it, I don't know if they'd try to take me again.

I'm not sure exactly how long I was unconscious at the hospital, but it's not like the healers and staff were tight-lipped about my existence. Now that I've abandoned the safety of the healers and nurses, have I made myself an easier target?

I slow my stride and carefully start studying the faces of those around me. My chest constricts with anxious anticipation, and my heart kicks up a beat.

Do I recognize any of them?

Could the stranger walking next to me be someone who dragged me out of one cell just to throw me in another? Could that shop patron be the guard who liked to dump my food just out of reach?

Subtly I search the faces of the unknown pedestrians around me, looking for anything that sparks recognition. Several males that wander by are wearing suits, but none of them have the expensive flair that fucker Wistan favored.

Stupidly, I wrote the bastard off as a threat the first time I met him because of his perfectly tailored suit. He oozed old money and prestige, and because of that, I assumed he wouldn't be the type to get his pretty little manicured hands dirty.

Fuck, was I wrong.

I rub a hand over the scars on my arm, forgetting that the charm on my ankle has temporarily magicked them away. A tendril of fear tries to flicker up the back of my neck, but I shake it off while I look around for any sign of Wistan's aristocratically angled face. I don't spot even a hint of his flawlessly styled sorrel-brown hair or the weaselly mustache I used to dream about ripping off his face.

He could torture me for days and still look as fresh and clean as he did when he first walked into my cell. In the hours between pain and oblivion, I often tried to puzzle out if he wore a spell to keep from getting dirty or if he was just so proficient at torment that he expertly knew how to avoid the messes he loved to make.

A cold understanding settles heavy in my gut. If Wistan knows I survived, he's not the type to let me go. Being bested by the likes of me would be unacceptable to him. He would do absolutely anything to get me back in a cell and once again at his mercy.

I've been worrying about what would happen if the dragons got their hands on me, but Wistan could be hunting me right now too, and for a chilling, breathless moment, I don't know which fate would be worse.

CHAPTER 4

The hot afternoon finally releases its grip on the day, and the conceding sun dips behind the tall buildings. Hints of orange and pink begin to flirt with the bright blue of the sky, but I keep my head down and focus on putting as much distance as possible between me and downtown Lairwood.

I've made solid progress so far. I've done a good job of doubling back through the maze of streets, compounding my scent, and leaving what false trails I could. A good Thrasher will work through it, probably faster than I'd like, but it should buy me some time.

A group of ourocycles zooms down the flyway next to me. The magi-tech that powers the speed bikes snakes around the front and back of the engine, creating a glimmering figure eight that I find strangely hypnotizing.

I would do a lot of fucked-up things for something that nice back home.

Wind whips past me in the wake of the cycles, and the faint hum of magic that always accompanies them fades as they get farther away. An airtram blows a warning horn as it picks up passengers before lifting off and puttering away.

Just like during my other forays into bigger towns and cities, I find myself quickly overwhelmed by the sounds, sights, and scents of this place. I never realize how quiet the deadlands are until I visit more populated places and am bombarded by everything that moves, makes noise, or smells.

Joining a group of people waiting patiently at a crosswalk, I keep my gaze focused on the sign that will light up when it's my turn to walk. I try not to do anything that will paint me as out of place. I'm sure the hospital knows I'm missing by now. Someone would have found the orderly and the healer I tied up, and I keep expecting a stranger to notice me and then loudly declare that I'm the dragon everyone is looking for.

It doesn't happen, of course. People barely glance my way, too caught up in their own minds and issues. The few who do notice me don't give me more than a cursory perusal. It should calm my nerves, and yet they're still strung taut as a mech bow.

The crosswalk chimes and I follow the crowd across the street. I decide I'm far enough away from the center of Lairwood, and I've done enough to throw anyone off my trail. It's time for the next phase of my plan.

A door swings open just ahead, and I observe a small cluster of people pouring out of what looks like a noisy bar. It must be happy hour, not that I've ever been to one. The group laughs and jokes and carries on as they file past me, and I make a split-second decision to grab the door to the bar as it starts to swing closed.

I stride in, deciding that this is as good a place as any to blend in for a bit while I work through my checklist to get the fuck out of this random city. With practiced efficiency, I quickly scan the interior as my eyes adjust to the dimmer atmosphere.

There's an outdoor beer garden that's full and a bunch of tables inside hosting a few large groups. I head to one of the long bars that run down each side of the establishment, pulling out a stool and plopping down onto it. There's an older man seated on the far end, but he doesn't even look my way. Neither does the bartender as he continues to mix a couple dozen drinks. A handful of his prepared concoctions suddenly lift from the bar top of their own accord before darting over to a high-top table out in the beer garden, not one drop spilled.

Shelves of liquor gleam like polished gems under the dusky mood lighting of this place, but I'm more interested in the bright neon board that's flashing what forms of payment are accepted here. The universal sign of a numbered bracelet is first on the list, indicating that they take credit transfers, and a glowing red drop of blood declares that direct donation is an option too.

My eyes land on the ticker flashing today's rate for the different species of magic. A drop of dragon's blood could probably buy this whole block. Not to mention it will definitely flag The Horde and a blood broker somewhere, so I absolutely won't be pricking my finger for some overpriced bottle of microbrew.

I run my hands down my bright blue borrowed scrubs. They're a few sizes too small and a little too tight on me, but I doubt anyone is going to pay much attention to that in here. Folding my arms on the bar top, I lean forward and focus on a vid screen feed playing in the corner. It's one of many on the far wall, each of them displaying all kinds of different programs. Stare at any one of the holovids long enough, and it'll filter the sound directly to you.

I home in on the one with a man and a woman sitting behind a crescent-shaped desk, both dressed smartly and staring at the camera while they prattle on about whatever the powers that be consider newsworthy.

"Paragon City is busy with arrangements for the upcoming four hundred forty-third Liberation Day," the blonde woman chirpily announces as the sound sifts to me. "With celebrations fast approaching, Arcane leaders of all kinds are getting ready to flock to the city for the festivities, and, of course, the annual Blood Rite. Let's go to Florent for more details on what King Noctis and the dragon clans have in store for us this year."

"That's right, Dani, planning and preparations are well underway, but what everyone wants to know is how will the Crown top last year?"

A tired-looking bartender steps into my line of sight, and the sound of the news program quickly fades away. His leathery skin and scruffy salt-and-pepper hair give him a grizzled quality. The lines around his silver eyes and frowning mouth tell me that his scowl is a permanent fixture and not personal. He quirks a dark eyebrow expectantly, and I hesitate. I can't buy anything, but I know I need to if I want to keep sitting here.

"Do you charge for water?" I ask tentatively, immediately regretting the stupid question, but it's out there and there's no taking it back now.

You can't get a *fuck you* from someone for free in The Scorch, but maybe a place like Lairwood is a bit more civilized. If not, maybe he'll take pity on me. I look better than I have any right to—thanks to the healers and the charm they gave me—so if pity doesn't work, I can try to flirt my way into sitting here for a bit longer.

I survey the grouchy male again, fingers crossed on the pity option.

He looks me over for a moment and then shrugs one shoulder. "Is that all for you?" he asks, a glint of annoyance in his overworked gaze.

"Yes, thank you," I offer, hoping a small dose of manners might get me a second glass if needed.

He doesn't say anything else as he plucks a cup from a stack and fills it from the tap. The water is cloudy and a bit more orange in color than is probably healthy, but I keep my mouth shut as it's set down in front of me. The bartender trudges away and I stare at the glass of liquid and the sediment already settling on the bottom.

Eh, I've drunk worse.

Lifting the cup to my lips, I force myself to sip the contents instead of chug them like my instincts are telling me to. It's a silly reaction, especially since I'm not even thirsty. It's more the fact that I can ask for water and get it, that I can drown myself to my heart's content and no one will stop me—well, no one aside from the pissy bartender, that is.

"Are you on call?" a nasally voice asks.

I turn, looking for the owner of said voice, not seeing anyone until I look down. He's about hip height and built like a wine cask, with wiry, sandy-brown hair and a long, thick neckbeard that's a shade darker. I have zero interest in talking to him, but the credit band on one wrist and the communicator on the other keep me from telling him to kick rocks.

He gestures to my murky drink and then at my scrubs with his stumpy hand as though the gesture provides all the context his question needs.

"On call?" he asks again as though I must not have heard him the first time.

"Something like that," I answer vaguely, careful not to outright lie. I don't think gnomes can smell them, but just in case they're one of the few Arcane—or Arcs, as they're often called—that can sense or scent deception, I proceed with caution.

The gnome's eyes spark with interest. "I always wanted to be a healer," he tells me, climbing up on the stool next to mine and making himself comfortable. "I had the mind for it but not the talent," he continues, wiggling his fingers in the universal sign of magic.

I open my mouth to say something, but he just keeps going as though my participation in the conversation isn't needed.

Fine by me.

"I like to think I save people in other ways. Not many file clerks will say that out loud, but how can you expect people to cheer for you if you don't cheer for yourself, ya know?"

He flags the surly bartender, and I take another sip of my water while studying my new companion, or rather his com and credit bracelets. He's on the taller side for a gnome. His plaid shirt and khaki pants are far from the latest fashion, but many Arcs don't do well with change. Some of them cling to the past so tightly it's like they're hoping it will snap forward and they'll be smack-dab in the middle of it again. It doesn't make a lot of sense to me, but most of my life has been "adapt or die." Being resistant to change has never been an option.

The Fae Wars and The Bearing were long before my time, just under 450 years ago, but from what I've heard, life wasn't so great for our kind back then. Not that I can say life is so peachy for me right now. Actually, when I think of it, it bears a strange resemblance to life before humans knew we existed: sneaking around, hiding in the shadows, hunting in the dark recesses of society.

"It's like strands of fire," the gnome exclaims, pulling me back to his one-sided conversation when he points to my hair. "The different tones of orange are really captivating. Is it natural, or do you spell it?"

Aaand the gnome's a presumptuous asshole.

"Going to ask me if the carpet matches the drapes next?" I sardonically query, lifting my water for another sip.

A green blush colors his cheeks, and he stammers, pushing his glasses farther up his nose. The thick lenses make his eyes look even beadier than they already are. While he collects himself, I debate the best way to lift his com off his wrist. I'd love to snag his credit band too, but some of them have anti-theft tech now, and I don't want to risk an alarm or an offensive spell I'm not in a position to deflect.

I vacillate between cozying up to him for the grab or doing the ever-effective bump and run, when the gnome unknowingly decides to do all the heavy lifting for me.

His hands come up in an apologetic gesture and somehow he smacks my drink right out of my hold. If I didn't know better, I'd think this ridiculous act of clumsiness was his attempt to pick my pocket, but I don't have anything worth stealing.

I gasp and jump up, eager anticipation sparking in my veins as I skillfully slip a finger under the clasp of his com bracelet and flick it open. At the same time, I *accidentally* bump into his stool with my hip, making it teeter while I knock his glasses askew.

The gnome yelps and grabs for his specs before they can go flying off. He then seizes the bar to save his balance on the stool and unknowingly jerks his hand out of the unclipped band of his com.

I close my fist around my prize, hiding it as I dramatically gasp and start wiping at the water that spilled down my front and all over the bar and the gnome. A cleaning drone swoops over and immediately starts suctioning up the liquid on the bar top. Flustered, the gnome tries to dry his glasses using his wet shirt, all while waving off a second cleaning drone that's trying to dry the stool he's still sitting on.

"I'm so sorry," he stammers, squinting in my direction, but his eyes are focused a little too far to the left of where I'm actually standing. "Pretty girls make me nervous."

The endearing comment nurses a flicker of remorse in me, but I quickly bat it away and make a show of looking down at the wet spots on my scrubs.

"It's okay," I offer, fighting back a laugh as one of the cleaning drones vacuums too close to the end of the gnome's neckbeard and starts to suck it up. "I'll go get dried off and be right back."

I leave the poor guy fighting to reclaim his facial hair and head for the bathroom. Exhilaration quickly dams up all the stress, worry, and heartache I've been wading through. Just like escaping the hospital, that was easier than I thought it would be.

I have to keep myself from running for the bathroom as I slip the pilfered com bracelet onto my wrist. The door to the ladies' room squeals noisily when I pull it open, and by some small miracle, there's no one else inside. Hastily, I open the closest stall, my heart hammering as I lock the flimsy door behind me and tap open a line on the com screen.

A transparent keyboard floats above the magi-tech on my wrist, and I hurry to scribe in the number I've repeated to myself like a mantra for the past four months, hoping one day I'd be calling it again.

The keypad disappears and a holoscreen flashes into place. Three dots appear in the center as the call tries to connect, and I start to pace in the stall.

Two steps, turn. Two steps, turn.

Pressing a shaky hand to my mouth, I breathe through the rush of desperate anticipation that floods my system. The com screen disappears and the keyboard pops back up in its place, indicating that the call wasn't answered. I rush to dial the number again, my heart feeling like it might explode in my chest when the three dots on the screen appear once more.

"Come on, Enslee. I know you don't know the number, but answer it anyway."

For a second time, the com screen drops away and the keypad appears. I swallow down a frustrated growl and just barely stop myself from punching the metal wall of the stall. Reining in my temper, I scribe in the number one last time, my mind whirring with what to do if she doesn't answer.

The next phase of my plan relies heavily on someone picking up the burner com and helping me navigate a way to get back. Something, I'm realizing now, that might have been a bit delusional. I know better than anyone how careful we have to be.

It would be one thing if there was a Flight out in the field; a call from an unknown number might be expected then. But I guarantee that Enslee's locked everything down after my Flight was ambushed. If she's given up hope on me and Ren, they'd have no reason to be monitoring this line.

My chest aches as I watch the three dots on the screen. They do their rhythmic little dance as the call waits to connect, but it all feels like some cruel taunt. My stomach drops, knowing the screen is going to disappear at any moment, the call once again unanswered. My eyes start to sting as I wait for the keyboard to pop back up when suddenly the com screen chimes and a face appears.

"Who the fuck is this?" a gruff, no-nonsense voice barks, and as much as I try to stop it, emotion overwhelms me.

There were so many times I wondered if I'd ever hear any of their voices again, see their faces. He looks the same. Dark skin, black hair that's twisted back from his face, scar bisecting one side of his hickory brown gaze.

"Craith," I croak, my throat suddenly dry.

"Who the fuck is this?" he asks again, more menace in his tone as he leans closer to the com screen.

I realize that my video is aimed at my chest, and I quickly twist my wrist so the camera on the bracelet can capture my face.

"Craith, it's Ever. I need Enslee," I rush to tell him, fighting back all the sentiment trying to rush me even though there's no time for it.

Craith's eyes widen and he reels back from the screen like it's threatening bodily harm. "Can't be," he whispers hollowly. "You're dead."

"Do dead people tell you to go fuck yourself?" I ask wryly, but there's a flutter in my tone exposing the effect his statement has on me. I assumed they would think the worst. I guess I wasn't as prepared to have my conjecture confirmed as I thought I was.

My response seems to slap Craith across the face with authenticity, and he rallies. "Get the queen," he shouts at someone off-screen.

He must decide that's not good enough, because he starts running, the com screen bouncing around as he sprints to wherever Enslee must be.

"Where are you? Are you okay? Is Ren with you? Are you compromised? What happened?"

I blow out a grateful breath, relieved that Craith is taking this seriously, that help isn't as far off as I feared. I open my mouth to answer the barrage of questions, and then it hits me: I need to be very circumspect in *how* I answer them.

I had a lot of time to think while I was stuck in a cell. Hours upon hours spent ruminating over how we were attacked. Endless minutes devoted to scouring through every detail of the night my Flight was taken by surprise and Ren and I paid the price. The only conclusion I've ever been able to come up with is that we were betrayed.

I've spat the vile taste of such a notion from my mouth more times than I can count, but the more I question it—the more I try to reject it and see some other possibility—the more reality sinks its razor-sharp talons into me.

We were set up.

What's worse is that it would have been by someone very close and very trusted. Someone part of the inner circle. Someone whose loyalty is without question. And the problem is, I can't figure out who, let alone why.

"Blood brokers," I finally answer, addressing his last question first. The one he already knows the answer to but wants confirmed. "We were taken by a group of sorcai. I'm in some town called Lairwood, and . . . I've been better."

I purposely don't tell him about Ren or the Tainted, unsure if it's safe or not, if *he's* safe or not. I shake my head and swallow down my fury, knowing it's not the time or place, but the way all of this is going to make me distrust and doubt people who are like family just might be worse than anything that's been done to me until now.

"What is it, Craith? What's wrong?" My sister's worried voice fills the call, and hearing it is both a soothing balm and a tightening fist around my heart.

Craith's garbled response is met with a shocked gasp, and then the com screen whirls and tilts until familiar flame-colored hair and jade-green eyes are staring back at me like they've seen a ghost. Enslee's pale skin looks even paler, and exhaustion and grief sit heavy in her features.

"Is this real?" she whispers, pulling the screen closer. "Tell me this is real," she demands with a pained wail.

"Hey, Ens," I greet, my voice cracking with emotion as tears well in my eyes.

"Ever!" she cries in answer, her own tears spilling freely down her face. "Where are you? Are you hurt? We'll come get you right now. Is Ren there?"

Enslee starts barking orders like the born leader she is, and I can hear scurrying and running in the background as people rush to follow her commands. Swiping at my eyes, I clear my throat, trying to get a hold of my runaway emotions before they veer off even more than they already have. As much as I'd love for Enslee to come roaring to the rescue, it's not that easy.

"Ens . . . Ens!" I snap, needing her to focus back on me.

Jade-green eyes once again meet mine, and something in my face thankfully stops Enslee in her tracks.

"I don't know how much time I have, and I need you to listen, Ens. Renatta's gone. They killed her. I got away, but I was hurt. I ended up in a hospital in Lairwood, and they called in The Horde. I'm going to try to shake them, but if I can't . . . "

"Oh, Ever," Enslee murmurs, distraught, her face falling as the shock of everything I just threw at her settles. "Ren . . . " The name is a broken lament I feel in the depths of my soul. "Fuck!" Enslee roars, and I can tell it takes all of her effort not to throw the com in her hands as rage takes over. "Someone tell me where the fuck Lairwood is!"

"It's on the other side of the divide, Ens," I tell her flatly, refusing to let any of the despair I feel bleed into my voice.

"The Horde?" Enslee asks, like she's hoping somehow that she misheard.

I nod solemnly. "They were on their way when I snuck out of the hospital. If they're not there already, they will be soon."

Paper rustles in the background and I can just make out someone spreading an old map. I can picture the others all frantically scouring it, and Enslee's focus drifts from me as several people start to talk and strategize. I listen carefully, hoping to hear something—anything—that might help me.

"Can you get to Feyer?" a deep voice asks, and my throat gets tight when I recognize whose it is.

"It's good to hear you, Vero," I tell him, a small smile sneaking across my face.

"Not as good as it is to hear you," he replies, his tone growing thick. "If you can get to Feyer, I can send your Flight to get you from there. Mizzen Pass is your best bet, but you'll need supplies and you'll need—"

The door to the bathroom opens with a squawk. I search for the mute button on the com bracelet, but I don't immediately see it and instead press a finger to my lips. Vero instantly goes quiet, and I hold my breath as my pulse starts to race.

"Korinne is so full of shit. She just has to be the center of attention," a woman sneers, the sound of multiple pairs of heels clip-clopping across the floor filling the bathroom.

"Dragons? Is she serious? I'd believe she hitched a ride over here on a fucking unicorn faster than I'd believe she saw a bunch of dragons in Lairwood."

Like crashing waves against a sandcastle, the stranger's words pulverize all the time I thought I had. The moths that have been flitting around in my stomach suddenly turn to wasps.

Snide laughter bounces around the bathroom, and someone enters the stall next to mine, closing the metal door behind them with a thunk.

"'I swear, guys! There were over two dozen of them. They stepped through a jump portal that appeared out of nowhere, got into lirocars, and sped off,'" another girl mocks, and everyone starts tittering again.

"Like she's ever seen a lirocar in her life! Those airboats cost more than this whole territory. But of course, Gio and Hurley are eating out of her hand, just lapping her shit up. Stupid simps."

I feel the blood drain from my face as I tune out the rest of the gossiping and lock eyes with Enslee. Tears shine in her stare and she shakes her head like the movement itself will erase everything we both just heard.

The Horde is here.

I keep silent as the women piss, bitch, and wash up. Enslee mutes the line from her end, and I watch as she snaps and snarls at her advisors. My stomach aches with simmering fear and frustration, and it starts to boil over into my chest. When the bathroom door screams again in protest and the herd of haters exits, Enslee's now alone in what looks like her private quarters, and there's a hard look of resignation in her light green gaze.

"If The Horde doesn't have a Thrasher . . . " I start, and Enslee closes her eyes, a tear slipping down her face.

"They'll have a Thrasher, Ev. If they're anything, it's prepared. They're probably already tracking you."

It's my turn to shake my head as I resume my pacing in the tight space of the stall.

"They're going to catch you—"

"No," I cut her off, slashing a hand through the air. "I'm ahead of them. I can *stay* ahead of them. I can cover my tracks and make it to Feyer. The Horde can't sense me. I don't smell like them, which will make sniffing me out harder. If I can stay off their radar long enough, they'll probably think this is all some hoax and punish the town for making up some bullshit sighting."

Enslee's features soften as she studies my face. "Do they have your blood, Ev?" she asks simply, and I can see by the hopelessness floating in her eyes that she knows they do. The hospital took mine while I was unconscious; it's how they knew what I was. There's no other way to identify us.

A tear slides down my cheek, followed by another, and I let them drop unchecked as Enslee wipes at her own.

"They're going to catch you, Ever. They're going to take you back to Paragon City, to Four Tiers, and they're going to find out what you are," she tells me gently, like she knows it won't take much to shatter me, so she has to be careful.

"They're going to kill me," I declare flatly.

Enslee's tear-streaked face hardens back to familiar steel as a dogged determination alights in her green eyes.

"Not if you can give them a reason not to," she counters, her tone tenacious. "They'll know what you are, but they won't know how or what it means. The Horde is greedy. You can use that, Ever. Use it to gain access to what we've been searching for all this time. They have to have records somewhere tracking the Blood Crafters, and if you could find them, access them . . . this could be fate clearing our path," she hedges cautiously, like she already knows this line might not be as secure or private as we think it is.

I snort an incredulous laugh. "Fuck fate," I whisper, and Enslee gives me a brief smile before it falls away.

"Fuck fate," she agrees, her gaze searching mine. "You can do this, Ever. If anyone can, it's you. You survived the massacre that killed our kith and our kindred. You survived The Scorch and that run-in with the chimeras. You survived the blood brokers, for fuck's sake. You can survive The Dragon Horde."

I shake my head but don't say anything. We just sit there in silence for a moment even though we both know the clock is winding down all too quickly.

"They're going to kill me, Ens," I repeat, needing Enslee to really hear me, to truly understand the most likely outcome here and what it means for all of us.

The burn of this truth isn't as harsh going down the second time. Then again, I was ready to die to protect my family from the Tainted, and now I'll do the same to protect them from the dragons.

"Even if I can convince The Horde not to slit my throat the minute they find out who I am, whoever helped the wyverns and the sorcai kill our family *is* going to come after me. They wanted all of us dead for a reason. If it's King Noctis, like we suspect . . . "

"If The Horde thinks they can use you, they won't let anyone hurt you," Enslee argues.

"Ens, the entire Horde could be responsible for slaughtering the Syphons. For all we know, *every* dragon clan—the Burners, Thrashers, Channelers, and the other Renders—was involved. We have no idea who to trust."

"No, we don't, but you know what to look for. You know how to play the game. So play it, Ever, because I refuse to let this be goodbye. I *will* see you again. We will ride into the fray together until glory is ours. I command it."

I huff out a weak laugh at her dramatics and shake my head. "Yes, Your Majesty," I mock, but there's no real bite to it.

"You know I always get what I want," she teases softly, but the tears and the glint of agony in her stare betray her.

I pull in a shaky breath and nod once, doing my best to compose myself. She may not want it to be, but if this is the last time I ever see her, there are things she needs to know, things she needs to do to protect herself.

"You have a snake in your nest," I offer as cryptically as I can in case anyone else is listening.

Enslee's green eyes harden. "I know. I'm working on rooting it out, but it's proving difficult. Any light you can shed on our shadows?"

"Unfortunately, no. But don't let anyone leave the wards, it's too dangerous. No missions. No supply runs. Not until the slithering coward is missing their head for selling us out."

Enslee gives me a solemn nod and pulls in a deep breath. "I don't want you to go, but you should get a move on. Give those Horde fuckers a run for their money."

Choking down the sorrow that tries to escape, I harden my resolve and blink back tears as I take in Enslee for what might be the last time. I'll do everything she asks. I always have, but it doesn't mean I'll end up anywhere other than skewered through with a pike before I'm ripped limb from limb and burned to ash for good measure.

"I'll see you soon, Ens," I lie, and she smiles and pretends she believes it.

"Soon," she repeats, her voice cracking under the deluge of anguish I see rising in her gaze. "Spark the flames, Ever."

"Ignite the infernos," I answer automatically.

"Ash the embers," we both say at the same time, a small chuckle escaping us as we finish the chant we've exchanged back and forth since we were kids.

I tap a button on the stolen com bracelet, and Enslee's face disappears as the call ends.

"Goodbye, Ens," I whisper again, and then I pluck the com from my wrist, crack it in half, and drop the tech in the toilet before flushing it away.

I step out of the stall into the quiet bathroom and catch my reflection in the mirror. I look almost as bad as my twin. My pale skin is blotchy from crying.

Exhaustion sits heavy in my features, and my jade-green eyes are so bright with emotion they look like they're glowing. I fluff my flame-colored hair and fill my lungs with a fortifying breath before moving for the door.

The Horde is going to kill me. I have no doubt, regardless of the false hope Enslee tried to rally, but she is right about one thing—I sure as shit can give them a run for their money.

CHAPTER 5

I exit the hallway that leads to the bathrooms and step out into the main part of the bar. Instantly, I know something is wrong. The quiet murmur moving through the previously rowdy space has the hair on the back of my neck rising. Carefully scanning the crowd, I notice that they're all staring at something outside, and I have a sinking suspicion I know exactly what it is.

Maneuvering myself until I'm able to peek between two tense patrons, I see what's set everyone on edge. A matte-black lirocar is floating just outside the building. If there were any doubt as to who's inside, the flags with two intertwined dragons surrounding a singular flame are a dead giveaway.

I'd love to see the look on the faces of the doubting women from the bathroom. I bet the friend claiming she saw dragons earlier is feeling smug as shit right about now.

Alarm seizes every muscle I possess as I study the hovering vehicle. Ren was right—lirocars really do look like fancy airboats with a stabby front end. I try not to panic, reminding myself that freaking out will get me nowhere.

Hurriedly, I scour the interior of the bar for another exit. I know there is one at the end of the hall by the bathrooms, but I'd bet the other stabby airboat the haters in the bathroom were talking about is parked back there. I know if I were trying to corner prey, the back exits would be the first thing I'd cover.

The lirocar hums with magic as it sets down on the pavement out front, and four doors immediately slide open.

Instantly I freeze, and despite my best efforts, panic starts to win.

My pulse thunders in my ears.

Wasps riot in my stomach.

My even breaths become faster and faster.

I try to get a hold of myself, to not let fear override me. A lesson everyone in the bar could heed, judging by the reek of terror that's now overpowering this place. It's clear I'm not the only one who thinks dragons equal death.

That's when it dawns on me. Maybe I shouldn't be fighting back the dread . . . maybe I should be encouraging it. And not just mine, but everyone else's. Because if there's one thing you can count on when it comes to the Arcane, it's self-preservation.

A large, boot-clad foot steps out of the lirocar outside, followed by a toned calf and thick thigh covered in black scale armor. I don't wait to see which giant of a drake the leg is attached to. Instead, I open my mouth and let loose a terrified, bloodcurdling scream.

"They'll burn us alive! Everybody run!"

The bar explodes into action, and I'm a little shocked that my impromptu Hail Mary is actually working. Screams and the sounds of splintering wood and shattering glass fill the air, and like a herd of frightened lemmings, the crowd writhes and surges as people scamper for a way out. I'm enfolded into the distressed crowd as another group of Arcs shoves down the back hallway behind me in search of an escape. The front door of the bar crashes open, and a flurry of fearful patrons pour out onto the street.

Barked commands to *stop* pepper the panic, but there's no stemming the flood of terrified people and their all-consuming, desperate search for safety. Cool evening air washes over me as I ride the tide of alarm out of the bar. Outside, everyone branches out into different directions, and I run with them, rapidly trying to figure out where to go.

Unfortunately, the scared citizens of Lairwood have one up on me, because they have homes and other places they can flee to, whereas I have shoes that are too big, scrubs that are too small, and zero options.

My gaze catches on the bright white *Lairwood Memorial* emblazoned on the chest pocket of my top. I might as well be holding a flashing sign that says *Here I Am!* while doing a little jig for attention under a spotlight.

Shit.

I need to ditch these scrubs.

Veering to the right, I stay on a main road, running down the street while I look for a shop or someone drying some clothes out on a balcony I can steal. At first, other pedestrians are confused by the swarm of runners coming at them, but all it takes is a few horrified shouts of "Dragons!" and the panic catches like a brush fire.

Clothed mannequins in a window catch my eye like an SOS flare going up in the middle of a moonless night, and I race across the street toward the store. The buzz of an engine and accompanying hum of magic immediately remind me of why it's stupid to dart out in the middle of a flyway. Instinct screams a warning and I leap back just in time to narrowly miss being decapitated by a speeding ourocycle. The rider swerves belatedly and then recovers, yelling something at me

I can't make out thanks to his helmet, but I don't get the impression he's asking if I'm okay.

More carefully this time, I pick my way across the road, avoiding any more idiotic mishaps before tumbling into the clothing shop, breathing heavily and looking like I'm stricken with terror.

"Dragons," I shout in warning. "We need to hide!"

My fearmongering isn't as instantaneously effective as it was in the bar, and the two shop clerks stare at me like I'm crazy, while a handful of customers look from me to the workers and back again, confused. Thankfully, that's when a crowd of people outside goes screaming by, and everyone in the store finally stirs with concern.

A shop worker hurries over to the front windows to see what's going on, and some of the patrons drop the clothes they were looking at and start to leave. I just keep repeating "Dragons!" and "Everyone hide!" until I whip up an appropriate amount of panic. Meanwhile, my gaze is spinning as I assess what clothes I can quickly grab and slip into.

I almost groan when I realize I've stumbled into what looks like a high-end store. Everything is the structured, overexaggerated, stiff crap favored by Arcs with too much money and not enough sense. Nothing looks practical. It's either straps that barely cover anything or square shoulders with geometrically shaped sleeves and bottoms that flare out wider than I am tall.

Finally I spot a light gray sleeveless top with a cowl big enough that I could pull it over my hair, and I yank it from a hanger. A matching skirt is on display just below the tops, and I waste no time grabbing it too. I slink toward the dressing rooms, but a worker is hurrying everyone out of the individual stalls. I debate just grabbing the clothes and making a run for it, but I need to actually be wearing them if they're going to work as effective camouflage.

The other shop employee is frantically shutting and locking the display cases around the register, and it takes me half a second to decide *fuck it.* I duck down, trying to be as inconspicuous as possible and kick my stolen shoes off before scrambling to get out of my pants. I tug the skirt on and then rip off my top just as someone comes sprinting down the aisle. She almost trips over me but luckily catches herself and continues to dash for the door, fear encouraging her to focus on getting out of here and not on the weirdo stripping in the middle of the store.

I pull the top on, straightening as I kick my discarded clothes and footwear under a table. My eyes rapidly search for replacement footwear as another customer rushes by, and I tug my new clothes in place. The top is tight and shorter than it looked, cutting off above my waist. The skirt sits low on my hips and doesn't leave much to the imagination, but it at least drops to just above my knees, and there's give to the fabric so I can move in it.

I just spot a wall of fancy heels and shoes when someone slams into me from behind. I catch myself on a display and turn to find the worker who was clearing out the dressing rooms.

"What are you doing?" she snaps.

At first, I think she's referring to the stealing that's currently going down, but she's flushed with fear, and her eyes keep darting to the windows at the front of the store and then back toward a door that's marked *Employees Only.*

"You can't stay here. You have to get out," she continues, confirming that she just wants me gone so she can go too.

"I can't find my shoes," I whine, a little too dramatically, but she's thankfully unfazed by my crap acting.

She takes one look at my bare feet and grabs a pair of black boots from a display, chucking them at me. "Those should work. Now leave!"

Well, okay then. Don't need to tell me twice.

I speedily buckle the boots on and grab a pair of sunglasses from a rack, slipping them on as I race for the front door. The worker standing there doesn't say shit to me as she frantically waves me out, pulling the door shut behind me and promptly locking it. I'd be offended by the way they just threw me out if it wasn't exactly what I needed to happen.

The commotion on the street seems to have calmed slightly, so I keep my pace brisk but not urgent. I smoothly pull the cowl of my newly acquired top over my head, making sure all my bright hair is tucked back and hidden. I round a corner and then another, breathing easier with each block I put between me and the shop and the bar.

I'm tempted to try to find somewhere I can hide and hole up until the mayhem passes, but my gut is telling me that's not a good idea. I'm up against a skilled tracker, judging by how quickly The Horde found me at that bar. I thought I'd given myself a bigger lead, but I need to be even faster. Maybe I can—

"Oof," I grunt as I slam into what feels like a hard wall.

Hands catch my shoulders as I stumble back, but I'm quick to slap them away as I catch my footing.

"Watch where you're going," I warn whoever just bodychecked me.

"With all due respect, you ran into me," a deep, amiable voice counters.

Warning pits my stomach, and I look up . . . and up . . . and up before landing on the probing stare of the *brick wall* I just crashed into.

Oak-brown eyes sweep over me, set in a face that's too pretty to belong to the monster standing in my way. A faint breeze plays with a few strands of his sun-bleached blond hair, and I don't need to see his dragon mark to know he's the one controlling the element that's suddenly teasing around us. I also don't miss how he's using that same ability to pull in a good whiff of me.

His brown eyebrows furrow with curiosity when he doesn't seem to smell what he expects, and he tilts his head like he's perplexed.

"What are you? I've not come across your scent before."

I will my heart to beat steadily in my chest and keep my breathing even, calling on every ounce of training and experience I have in getting out of sticky situations. This drake is a Channeler, not a Thrasher. There's still hope I can walk away from this.

"Frilled Lizard," I answer, stepping to go around him and doing everything in my power not to groan and roll my eyes at myself.

Frilled Lizard? Really, Ever?

Of all the options I've rehearsed and used, I had to go with the one that was only supposed to be a running joke between me and my Flight.

"Frilled Lizard?" the drake repeats, stepping in my way again so I can't move past him.

His scale armor looks black in the shadows of the small side street we're on, but I suspect it's really some dark shade of green or blue, as Channelers typically sport armor in one shade or the other. I don't see any evidence of weapons strapped to him or tucked anywhere on his body, not that he needs them when he *is* one big, giant weapon.

Another drake appears from a side alley less than two dozen feet away. He's, of course, just as big as the one in front of me, but this one has long red hair that's pulled back in battle braids. His gray eyes are shrewd as he looks around. They must be canvassing blocks one by one.

Please don't be a Thrasher. Please don't be a Thrasher.

Red spots Blondie and starts moving toward us. Once more, I try to move around the Channeler, only for him to block my way again. I bite back an annoyed sigh as I return my attention to the big blond fucker, my features a mask of indifference while my insides are liquifying with dread.

"Can I go?" I huff at the Channeler. "I'm not who you're looking for."

His brown eyes narrow slightly at that statement, and I internally want to kick my own ass.

"Who said we're looking for anyone?" Blondie asks, studying me a little too closely for my liking.

I roll my eyes, then realize he can't see it behind the dark lenses I'm wearing. The sun's set just enough that eyewear really isn't necessary anymore, but I'm hoping the walking, talking brick wall doesn't think twice about it.

"Why else would The Horde be here?" I counter.

The gleam of suspicion in his gaze dims as he looks me over and scents me again. My logic seems to register to him, supported by the way I look and the fact that I don't smell like a dragon.

Did the hospital not explain that fact to them?

The redheaded male is less than ten feet away, and the need to be on the move before he fully closes the distance hammers my insides.

"Besides, I just saw someone else in armor like yours chasing a woman in blue scrubs with orange hair," I supply, pointing over my shoulder at the main road. "She looked scared," I add as the drake's focus snaps to the road behind me.

I try not to hold my breath as I wait the second it takes for Blondie to take my bait, but my heart kicks up against my will when he steps around me, all his attention back on the beloved hunt and not on our trivial exchange.

"This way, Ogdan," he calls to the other drake, and I refuse to track them with my eyes as they start to jog down the lane, my existence all at once long forgotten.

It's almost impossible not to run, knowing two members of The Horde are less than ten feet away, but somehow I keep my strides unhurried as I continue with my nonchalant skedaddle. I'm almost to the mouth of an alley half a block down when a command comes from behind me.

"Stop!"

I dare a glance over my shoulder and immediately regret it when I see Blondie and Red swiftly marching back in my direction.

"Take your glasses off and pull your hood down," Red orders, his stern face now locked on me and teeming with indictment and a hard glint of determination.

Fuck.

With zero hesitation, I dash for the alley, sprinting with everything I have down the darkening narrow path between tall buildings. Behind me, the pounding footfall of the drakes drowns out the frantic cannon fire of my pulse. They shout commands at me that I ignore and quickly relay their location to someone else, calling in reinforcements.

I run full out, winding down thinning lanes and barreling around corners, but the two big bastards keep on me. I rip the glasses off my face so I can see better, and my cowl slips off my head, letting my flame-colored locks stream behind me like some taunting flag to a pair of enraged bulls.

The drakes announce my description to whoever is on the other line of their coms, and when they get confirmation that I'm who they're after, their pace alarmingly picks up, like they were taking it easy and toying with me before.

As I tear down another back way, the foreboding I've been keeping at bay crests when I see a two-story metal fence cutting off the far end. The drakes behind me slow a little, like they expect me to realize I'm caught and give up, but a little chain-link obstacle won't be my downfall.

I leap for the barrier, trying to get as high up on the fence as I can before I start to scramble up the rest. One of the drakes curses, just as a lirocar speeds to a stop on the other side of the barrier I'm scaling. A large body slams into the chain link below me, and I almost lose my footing.

"Give it up now, lass. We've got you surrounded," Red barks as he climbs after me.

I'm tempted to flip him off, but instead I flip myself over the top of the metal fence. The bottom of my skirt catches on the sharp tip of a link and rips up the side, but flashing a little cheek is the least of my problems right now.

I don't even pause as I use the fence for leverage and leap onto the roof of the floating lirocar now below me. More swearing explodes at my back, and I scramble to keep my footing on the slippery surface of the fancy floating airboat. I slide down the dark windshield, picking up speed as I ride the sleek, aerodynamic shape of the matte-black car until I reach the front where the vehicle comes to a sharp point—allowing it to cut through air like a hot knife through butter.

The car starts to drop, clearly trying to land, but I have no illusions that whoever is driving is trying to help me get down safely. No, whoever's inside wants out, and the doors probably won't open while the vehicle is suspended midair.

Gravity continues to work in my favor, and I slide right off the front of the lirocar and land on the ground with a pained grunt before pushing myself up and bolting away.

I want to crow with elation that my body isn't giving out on me yet. I know the healers went to work fixing everything they could—and I'm currently feeding off of straight adrenaline and fright—but I'm not a fraction as bad as I was when I was running from the blood brokers before, and that feels like a miracle.

The alley I'm in spits me out onto a larger main road, and I race down the sidewalk, dismissing shops and restaurants as places I could slip in to try to lose The Horde. I spot an airtram down the way but quickly reject the slow, floating public transport as a getaway car. If I could steal an ourocycle though . . .

I almost dismiss the idea, more likely to end up splattered on someone's windshield than I am to get a driver to stop and let me hijack them, but then I see another lirocar speeding up the flyway, headed right for me. In a split second, I decide splattered against someone's windshield is a more humane way to go than what the drakes will do to me when they find out what I am.

Abandoning all good sense, I dart out into streaming traffic. Bellows of objection and frightened screams fill the air along with the whoosh and mechanical shudder of airbrakes being engaged as drivers try to avoid the lunatic who just ran out into the flyway.

I have half a second to regret my decision as a small aircar barrels toward me, our collision imminent. I don't close my eyes; I stare death right in the face as it shrieks toward me. Finality is a blink away when, out of nowhere, a wall of wind slams into the car, sending it hurtling away at the same time someone tackles me from behind.

I'm pulled against a hard chest as massive arms wrap protectively around me. My unwanted hero and I go tumbling, momentum churning us around and around. But I don't feel the pavement bite into me like it should, and nothing else gets past the crush of muscle and sinew that's encircling me. Whoever grabbed me takes the brunt of our careening crash before we finally skid to a stop.

Noise and chaos erupt all around us, and I find myself splayed on top of a dark, menacing nightmare. Jet-black scale armor comes into focus as I try to catch my breath. Then I see the tactical bands on the mountain's arms. Bands with symbols signifying that the imposing monolith under me is a member of the Royal Wing.

Under his inky armor, a dragon mark of onyx fire crawls up an alabaster throat that's expanding and contracting quickly, its owner breathing hard. Angry. The tips of the dragon mark's black flames frame a sharp, masculine jaw that's brandishing a hint of dark stubble. Full lips, a perfectly straight nose, and the bluest eyes I've ever seen glare up at me.

"What the fuck were you thinking?" the dark menace growls, his bright blue eyes like two hard gems sparkling with disapproval.

"I had a craving for road pancakes," I rasp, trying and failing to push away from him.

Two massive hands anchor my hips in place and keep me from moving away. The drake sits up and it forces me to slide down his impressive torso into his lap, where I try and fail again to scramble off of him.

"Why didn't you shift? You could have been killed. And for what? We're not trying to hurt you."

"Oh, right. Was I supposed to get that message before or after all of you started chasing me? That's not exactly an invitation for tea and cookies."

"No, just road pancakes, it seems," he grumps, his gargantuan arm muscles flexing to keep me in place when I try to wiggle away again.

"Let me go," I demand, all too aware of our compromising position and the distinct lack of clothing over parts of my body that are in direct contact with parts of his. Straddling the enemy is not how I'd prefer to die.

"Why? So you can display your complete lack of survival instincts and run into oncoming traffic again?"

"Aeson, are you okay?" a male demands as he comes running over. He's all tones of brown, his carob-colored armor, his tan skin, his dark chocolate hair, everything except for his hazel eyes, which lean more moss green than brown.

"I'm fine, Jori. Take her," the Aeson brute orders, lifting me off him and handing me to Jori like some naughty pest he just found rummaging through his garbage.

Jori looks slightly apologetic as he takes a hold of me. Thankfully, I'm set on the ground next to him instead of thrown over his shoulder or some other equally barbaric thing. Aeson pushes off the ground, dusting himself off and running a hand through his short black-brown hair. I take that opportunity to twist out of Jori's lax hold and make a run for it.

Jori barks out a warning, but I only manage four strides before skidding to a stop. Like Scorch mirages come to life, more than a dozen drakes surge toward me, forming an impenetrable ring of scale armor and bulk. Dark jewel tones of armor draw my eye, and I quickly catalog what kiths they could belong to as I spin, desperate for a way out or a weak link that will lead to one. The drakes anticipate my efforts and rush to close ranks, penning me in but not coming any closer and risking what might happen if I feel cornered.

A lirocar sets down on each end of the road, bookending the standoff and leaving me nowhere to go.

I'm trapped.

A warning growl rises in my chest as I back away from the drakes all around me.

"Come now, Frills, is that really necessary?" the blond I bumped into earlier asks as he steps forward.

"Frills?" the redhead with the battle braids questions. I think his name was Ogdan.

"The little minx tried to tell me she was a Frilled Lizard," the blond announces, and several chuckles move around the ring of drakes.

My gaze narrows at their easy banter. Apparently, my life teetering on a knife's edge is no big deal to them. Then again, did I really expect anything different from The Horde?

"Maybe she *is* a Frilled Lizard. I don't smell a dragon," a male with dark skin and eyes observes, and then all of the dragons cornering me pull in a deep breath, scenting me.

Apprehension tightens my chest. If they index my scent, it could be bad for the others. For the first time in my life, I wish I were a thoon and could spray a terrifyingly offensive musk at anyone who got too close, just like the floppy-eared desert rodent I learned to avoid growing up.

"Definitely doesn't smell like a dragon, but that won't stop you from trying to talk her out of her skirt," another male teases, and I tense.

"Enough!" a resonant command sounds from behind me. Aeson, the dark storm who tackled me, strides forward, and the others shut their mouths and straighten up. "This is neither the time nor the place. The *mystery meat* will be escorted back to the rally point, and First Flight will decide what to do with her from there. Fall out."

My head snaps in Aeson's direction.

Mystery meat?

The cocky smile stretched across his face heats my blood, and I force myself to pull in a deep breath to calm the rising tide of anger simmering in my gut. Unfortunately, the overwhelming stench of male dragon does nothing to soothe me, and the growl still reverberating in my chest grows louder.

"I think she likes you, Aes," Jori quips, moving closer despite my body language and snarl warning him against it.

He reaches for my arm like he expects me to offer it up for the taking, so I grab his wrist and yank him forward and down so I can knee him in the face. Unfortunately, my strength is waning and he's huge, so my knee never connects with anything vital, but he does stumble a bit, and that feels like some sort of victory. Small as it might be.

"She's a spicy lizard." Ogdan whistles, approaching from my other side. "We can do this the easy way or the hard way, lass, but one way or another, you *are* coming with us."

There's a lilt to his voice that speaks of a world long forgotten. A place of fairy rings and fair folk and an island once painted in innumerable shades of green. One that's now nothing more than ash and rock. There was a wyvern I once knew who sounded a lot like him. She told the best tales about the old worlds and the times before.

"What's the easy way?" I ask with a glare before once again glancing around, hopeful for some surprise way out. There still isn't one.

The impenetrable ring of dragons has dispersed, but I'm boxed in by a wall consisting of Aeson, Ogdan, Jori, and Blondie, whose name I haven't heard yet. Other drakes have taken it upon themselves to direct the traffic we're disrupting to move around us, while people are standing on the sidewalks watching what's happening. However, as soon as they spot any approaching drakes, they scramble off, their curiosity instantly cured.

"The easy way is I ask you nicely, and you do as you're told," Ogdan answers smoothly.

"And the hard option?"

A smile teases one corner of the large male's lips. "I ask you nicely, and then I *make* you do as you're told."

I take a moment to weigh my options. I'm tempted to choose the hard way. If it would gain me anything other than embarrassment, I just might—for no other reason than to be a pain in the ass—but my adrenaline is crashing and my limbs already feel the toll of my mad dash through the city streets.

I want to fight, but I'm not stupid. For now, the drakes aren't trying to kill me, which means I should save my strength for when that changes . . . because it most definitely will, and probably soon.

CHAPTER 6

The easy way, I guess . . . for now," I concede, crossing my arms over my chest and scowling up at the redheaded male in black scale armor, who's finding this exchange entirely too amusing.

It's unsettling. I always figured The Horde had one setting, arrogant and severe, but the playful air about this drake has me off-kilter when I really can't afford to be. Ogdan's smile grows wider and he waves a hand in the direction of the onyx lirocar to the left. Five drakes stand around it as though they're waiting on me to load up.

I notice there's a drake that's half a foot smaller than the others. Initially I discount the detail as unimportant until they turn around and I realize it's a female. Her black hair is buzzed close to the scalp, making her pretty bronze face look harsher. Well, that and the *don't fucking talk to me* air about her. Her scale armor is a deep green, and while smaller in stature, she's as fit and formidable as the males around her.

Despite myself, I'm instantly curious about how she's here and why, but I tuck all my questions away and move toward the vehicle as ordered. Ogdan falls into step next to me, his gray eyes studying my every move. I can't tell if he's being curious or cautious. Probably both.

We approach the vehicle, and the agitation I'm attempting to ignore—because I can't do shit about it—only grows. I've never been in a lirocar before. The autos and sandcycles we drive in The Scorch are nothing more than scrap that's been pieced together with a blowtorch and a death wish. This vehicle, however, is more like a piece of art. I'm hesitant to even touch it.

I peek inside the airboat, unable to help myself, and find the interior is as lush and spacious as you'd expect. There are wood accents, buttery soft–looking seats, and a clear disregard for practicality, because everything is done in tones of cream and taupe. I'm pretty sure I'm staining things just by looking at them. Lucky for me, people who drive shit like this don't care about paltry things like dirt. They'll just get the interior redone at the first sign of soiling, or better yet, throw the whole car out and buy a new one. The haters from the bathroom sure as shit got one thing right—these things cost more than the GDP of most territories.

I stand there awkwardly and continue to just stare. I know I'm supposed to get in, but I have no idea where to sit now that I'm looming in the open doorway of this behemoth. There's a bank of three seats that back up to a privacy screen I assume is separating us from the driver and front passenger. Another bank of three seats butts up against the back, and there are two captain's chairs in the middle that face each other from opposite sides of the vehicle.

Picking up on my obvious discomfort, Ogdan brushes past me and climbs in first, showing me how it's done. I pull in a deep breath, blow it out, and then move to follow, ignoring everything inside of me screaming not to.

"Into the mouth of the dragon," I mumble under my breath as I step into the luxurious leather and teak interior.

A low chuckle from behind me tells me my comment hasn't gone as unnoticed as I thought it would. I look back to find the blond climbing in. Light from the interior dances across his scale armor, and I discern that it is, in fact, dark blue.

"Not quite, Frills, but I'd be happy to introduce you to all the pleasures that can be had in the mouth of a dragon if you're interested," he offers with a naughty smile and a cheeky wag of his eyebrows.

"Chastain! Unless you want your tongue ripped out, you will not speak to her like that again. Understood?"

Chastain's back snaps straight and his mouth clamps closed. "My apologies, Commander. I'm used to teasing Tove. Won't happen again," he shouts, military sharp, saluting Aeson as the dark drake strides closer to the open doorway. He stops and leans toward the blond.

"Tove is Tove. Lorn will gut you if he hears you talking like that, and I'm not far off from doing the same. Get your shit together. We don't even know her."

Chastain nods apologetically at Aeson and then climbs into the lirocar, plopping down into a seat at the back.

I decide on one of the captain's chairs, not wanting to be close enough to touch any of the drakes piling in. I settle and look up just in time to see Commander Aeson drop down in the seat opposite me.

My stomach constricts with apprehension.

His long, stout legs almost touch mine, his large frame managing to crowd me even from the other side of the car. I get the distinct impression he's purposely trying to prod at my limits to see how I'll react. It doesn't feel antagonistic or like a display of dominance one might expect from a large, virile male dragon. It feels . . . calculated . . . measured. He's testing me, but I don't know why.

My eyes once again land on the bands on his arms and the symbols etched there. There's something about them or him that's pecking at my intuition. I can't pinpoint what though. He's obviously in charge and respected based on the way the others respond to his authority. The relaxed banter and easygoing exchanges happening back and forth speak to a deeper connection and admiration between him and the others.

It reminds me, surprisingly, of me and my Flight. And while that should be something that offers a little comfort in this nightmare of a situation, I find the exact opposite is true. It's unsettling.

"See something of interest?" Aeson asks, the resonant gravel in his tone yanking me from my thoughts.

I look up and find the commander watching me. He dips his chin toward his arm, at exactly where I was staring, and lifts a single eyebrow in inquiry.

I glare at him in answer.

Instead of being bothered by enmity, amusement flickers in his vivid blue eyes.

"Who's buying the first round when we get back?" Chastain solicits, a carefree grin once again stretched across his pretty-boy face.

"Mission's not over yet," Ogdan rebukes. "You know better than to jinx it, airhead."

"I'm just glad there's actually a female to retrieve and this wasn't the elaborate trap we thought it might be," Jori observes, kicking his legs out and making himself comfortable.

"It could still be a trap," the female Horde member grumbles as she climbs into the car. She kicks Jori's legs until he retracts them, and the commander swivels to the side so she can pass between us, claiming a seat at the front. "In the wild, the prettiest things are often the deadliest," she adds, staring right at me.

"Spoken like a true Seeder," Ogdan taunts, and the female flips him off.

I make note of her designation and the vine-like dragon marks she has winding around her fingers and crawling up both hands before disappearing under the scale armor covering her arms. They've got a plant whisperer and an air tamer, I observe, looking back at Chastain, the brick wall I first ran into.

There's at least one more Channeler in this group, and Jori's carob armor tells me he's a Render. My guess is he's the Flight Healer, with the way he rushed to check on Aeson after the bastard rescued me against my will. Both Ogdan and the commander across from me are Burners, but I don't see a Thrasher piling in with us.

The lack kindles the smallest ember of possibility that I might be able to get away if I just bide my time. Then again, I can't see the driver or front passenger beyond the privacy glass, so I probably shouldn't hold my breath.

"Tove doesn't mean anything by the deadly thing," a male I haven't encountered yet informs me as he climbs into the airboat. "That's just her winning personality shining through," he teases, reaching toward me like he's going to pat my shoulder.

Reflexively, I smack his hand away. "Don't touch me," I warn, danger dripping off my tone.

Wide-eyed, the male lifts his hands in a gesture of surrender. "My apologies," he offers, moving quickly away from me toward the back.

Everyone in the vehicle is quiet, like my reaction set them all on edge.

Good. They can join the club.

Six of them have piled into the fancy airboat now, and I can feel them watching me as closely as I'm watching them. It makes me antsy, prickly. I want to scrub the stares from my skin.

The airboat doors suddenly hiss closed, and the lirocar starts to rise off the ground. The gradual lift is accompanied by a magical hum that grows louder as the vehicle spins until it's facing the direction it wants. With zero warning, it shoots forward and I gasp at the shock of speed achieved in no time flat. I grab onto the seat beneath me to keep from tumbling sideways into Chastain's lap.

We cut through the flyway like a perfectly honed arrow that's been let loose by an expert archer. Buildings blink by in a flash, and the ride is smooth, speedy, and annoyingly . . . fun. Ren would have gotten a kick out of this, even if *death by dragon* was at the end of the excursion.

An ache starts in my chest, and I try to ignore it, focusing on the city of Lairwood as it disappears behind us. The sun finally decides to set, blues and purples blooming across the sky and chasing away the other pretty colors. I try to lose myself in the scenery out there instead of concentrating on all of the brooding dragons in here, but the windows around the lirocar suddenly shift from translucent to opaque, robbing me of the welcome distraction.

I guess I'll just have to imagine what it looks like out there—a skill I've gotten quite good at over the last few months. It will probably be dark the next time I set foot outside, and I wonder if I'll get a chance to see the stars before they rip my head from my body.

Enslee's voice rings in my mind. *"You can do this, Ever. If anyone can, it's you."* I try to let her faith buoy me, but everything is crashing in, and I feel like it's only a matter of time before I'm pulled under and drowning.

I run my thumb down my inner forearm, an unfortunate habit I've picked up in the past month or so. But something about counting the scars there helps to calm my mind. It definitely helped to anchor me to reality in that cell when I felt the tethers of my sanity on the verge of snapping.

Unfortunately, thanks to the charm still sitting on my ankle, I don't feel the scars.

All I feel is lost.

"The healers mentioned that they thought you'd spent some time with blood brokers. Is that true?" Aeson asks, his question invading my churning thoughts and my attempt at calm.

I deliberate if there's anything to gain by snubbing his question. I dart a quick glance at the others surrounding me, my gaze pausing on Ogdan for a beat before settling back on the commander. Guess it's time to try to do what Enslee ordered and play the game. I chose the *easy way* already—might as well ride it out a little longer.

"I don't know that *spent some time* is the phrase I'd use for it," I finally answer, hating that speaking to them at all is my best chance for survival.

"How long did they have you?"

I study the commander's face, trying to read the intention behind this line of questioning right now, but the emotionless mask he has in place is solid. My gaze dips to the dragon mark on his throat before I look away.

"By my last count, one hundred seventeen days, give or take a few I might have been unconscious for," I offer nonchalantly.

A low rumble of anger rolls through the car, instantly ratcheting up the tension. A few of the drakes adjust their positions like they suddenly can't restrain their restlessness, but one look from Aeson and the noise and furious fidgeting stop.

A heavy silence settles between us, and I find myself wondering if their reaction is because they hate blood brokers or if it's because they're Horde and a slight against one dragon is a slight against all dragons. Something they can't allow or they risk looking weak and opening the door to having their reign challenged.

"How did they get you?" Chastain asks.

My eyes dart to the blond Channeler and then back to Aeson, trying to gauge how the commander feels about the other's uninvited insertion into the interrogation. There's no hint of annoyance or reprimand in the commander's gaze. Maybe this is a thing they do to throw their captives off guard. They act all friendly and curious, making the unsuspecting victim feel comfortable, and then they strike.

I suppose it's good I'm not unsuspecting.

I find everything they do suspicious.

"How they get everyone," I reply with a shrug. "Wrong place at the wrong time."

"But where's your family, your kindred? Wasn't anyone protecting you?" the male whose hand I slapped away earlier questions.

I eye him and his rich purple scale armor. I originally pegged him as a Channeler, but the glyphs of his dragon mark tell me otherwise. He's a Render, a Shield, more specifically. I want to study the lines and circular shapes on the side of his neck, but I stop myself and look away.

"Gone," I reply after a beat. "And, recent circumstances excluded, I can usually protect myself."

Incredulous huffs puff out from more than one of the drakes surrounding me, and I roll my eyes.

"Not everyone has to be part of the big bad Dragon Horde to get by in life," I point out.

"Said by someone who clearly doesn't know what it means to be part of The Dragon Horde," Tove retorts, and I glare over at the female.

"Think you've got me pegged, Seeder?" I prod, unable to help myself.

She matches my glare with one of her own.

"No, little lizard, I just know bullshit when I hear it."

I swallow down a groan at her jab. I'm never going to live down the lizard thing if I survive this. It's probably good that the odds aren't in my favor. My Flight back home would be dying if they knew how badly my brain betrayed me when I needed it most.

"I guess you've got it all figured out, then," I counter, sitting back in my seat and purposefully shutting my mouth.

This does earn a flicker of annoyance from Aeson, who levels her with an unhappy look. Tove drops her eyes in a gesture of submission, her body language and immediate silence contrite.

"Well, *I* don't have it figured out," Jori announces. "I can't even tell if she's one of us or not."

"She's a dragon," Aeson declares confidently, leaning back in his seat and crossing his arms over his chest. I try to study the expression on his face, but his new position dips his features in the shadows of the dim interior, and I can't get a good read.

I'm tempted to ask him how he's so sure. I know I don't smell like one to them, and none of them have magically tested my blood, but I keep my lips sealed.

"Should we take bets, Commander?" Chastain gibes.

"If you're stupid enough to go up against Aes, I'll gladly take your credits," Tove taunts.

"She's not scared," Aeson announces, the statement cutting into the easygoing revelry and instantly silencing it.

My heart stutters when he leans forward again, his blue eyes fixed on mine like he's excavating my soul in order to unearth my secrets one vulnerable layer at a time.

"She's frustrated, reckless when cornered, savvy, and weaker than she wants any of us to know, but she's not terrified."

Anger flares through me, tensing my muscles and settling in the look I aim at the commander like daggers eager to draw blood and maim.

"I am not weak," I tell him, my tone an open invitation for him to test me and find out for himself. It doesn't matter that he could burn me to a crisp in two seconds flat and I couldn't do a thing to stop it, or that he'd heal from any injuries inflicted in a fight and I wouldn't. I don't care that he's Horde, or a member of the Royal Wing, and I'm nothing more than some sand-stamped lostling; I'll spoon-feed him those words if it's the last thing I do.

He stares at me as though weighing my mettle right then and there. "No. Not weak," he agrees after a long pause where the tension in the car grows so thick and heavy I'm surprised it doesn't force the airboat to fall out of the sky from the sheer weight of it. "I didn't mean it like that. I meant hurt. You're hurting and you don't want us to know."

Shock shoves at my fury and scrapes at parts of me I thought I was an expert at hiding. I batten down the hatches on my secrets and tuck my trauma more firmly against me.

Aeson gives me a look I can't decipher, and then his eyes dip down my body. Warily, I follow his gaze until it lands on my naked thigh, exposed through the tear in my skirt. I notice for the first time a long, shallow scratch there that's barely weeping blood. I have no idea when it happened.

I stare at the scrape, somehow not convinced that's what the commander was truly talking about. I feel alarmingly wounded by his well-aimed words, but did he get off a lucky shot, or is he a skilled marksman?

Unease ripples through me and I'm unsure if I want to lash out at whoever this Commander Aeson is or hide from him for my own safety.

"When was the last time you met an Arc who wasn't afraid of us on some level? And yet here she sits, not a whiff of dread coming off her," the commander concludes, resting his case and once again relaxing back into his seat.

The raw intensity winding between us shatters like winter ice against the first touch of spring. Internally I shiver off whatever the fuck just happened and rally. Double-checking my defensive mask is right where it needs to be, I shake my head and smile at the commander like he's got it all wrong.

"That's quite some ego your neck is supporting, *Commander*," I taunt. "Explains why you're so big though—gotta have plenty of room for all that shit you're full of."

I hear a low hiss of affront from one of the drakes, and Ogdan starts to choke on either his shock or amusement. He coughs, pressing a fist to his chest to help clear his airway.

"You are right about one thing. I'll give you that at least," I concede, my gaze growing venomous. "I'm not scared. But not for the reasons you might think. I'm just not afraid to die."

I expect the commander to take offense at my jabs, but he once again surprises me when his only reaction is a satisfied smirk.

"And that's where this is leading . . . your death?" he asks evenly, like he's got me right where he wants me in this complex web he seems to be weaving. "What makes you so certain?"

My answering chuckle is hollow. "Because that's what The Horde does. You can pretend otherwise, but we all know if you can't claim, control, or comprehend something, you kill it."

"And which category do you fall under?" he presses, his gaze glittering with ardent interest.

Tired of this game already, I rest my head back against the seat and close my eyes with a smirk. "All of them."

CHAPTER 7

I'm not sure how long I pretend to doze before the car starts to drop. We've reached our destination. I keep my eyes closed, not caring to discover where we are. Wherever it is, I doubt I'll be here for very long.

"The other Flight is already back. Guess they didn't find anything," someone observes, but I can't match the voice with a name.

"Let's go, dragoness," Ogdan orders, kicking at one of my boots to get me moving.

"You go on ahead, I'll catch up," I mumble and wave a dismissive hand at him.

His answering laugh is vexingly warm. "You opting for the hard way already? And here I thought you'd hold out for a little longer. Don't make me lose the bet to Tove; her coffers are plenty full already."

An amused snort slips out of me before I can stop it. Thankfully, a sudden onset of irritation swiftly drowns out any lingering mirth.

I will not like this drake. He is not funny. He'd slaughter me without a second thought if given the order . . . they all would.

Cracking open my eyelids, I sit up and find the car almost empty. Aeson is standing by the open door, and Ogdan and Jori are both looming over me. All of their demeanors are more serious than they've been up to this point, so I lock down my innate desire to do the exact opposite of what they're telling me to and instead get up.

I'm escorted out of the lirocar into the waiting night. Stars wink down at me from above, just like I expected, and a pang of longing for home splinters through me. It may be brutal and desolate where I'm from, but nothing beats the view of the heavens from The Scorch.

It's quiet, wherever we are. Remote. I'm sure that's not by accident, and it has me buzzing with uneasy anticipation. I'm led toward a large metal building with two massive sliding doors, one of which is open. Light spills past the threshold, and bugs fly around in a frenzy, searching for the source. Bats feast on the mania, swooping down through the melee to eat their fill. Three towering males step out of the building, their presence instantly chasing the feast and feasters away.

"Is this her?" one of them asks, and I can feel his eyes raking over me even though his face is hidden in shadow. "She doesn't look in bad shape."

"Typical healers, always getting hysterical over nothing," another male I can't make out grumbles. "We'll take her in, Commander. Lorn asked that you and your Flight do a security sweep before you debrief. He'd like to leave within the hour."

Ogdan stiffens infinitesimally, but Aeson simply nods and gestures for Jori and Ogdan to follow him. Alarms blare in my head, and every sense I possess goes on high alert. I watch the group of dragons that brought me here stride off into the dark, and even though they're Horde and ran me down in the street like a dog, I can't help feeling like they're the safer option compared to the trio before me.

The strangers step from the shadows and silently surround me. They don't say a word as they start to walk, apparently expecting me to fall into step simply because they will it. I play along—not that I have much choice—but this new group of drakes doesn't know what to expect from me, nor I them, and it might be wiser to keep it that way for the time being.

I squint against the bright interior as I'm herded inside the building. The first thing I notice is the tall arch of a jump portal and the two sorcai standing at attention on each side of it. I don't get much time to marvel as my eyes are drawn to the dozen or so gigantic drakes all lining the perimeter of the other half of the structure.

However, it's the single empty chair, waiting like the open maw of a shark in the middle of the group, that has the wasps in my stomach stinging the ever-loving shit out of me. My flinty stare skips from the chair back to the surrounding Horde, snagging on an alarmingly familiar male.

Neatly trimmed, stark-white hair. A handsome face steeped in arrogance and entitlement. Offensively gigantic frame. And a set of bright blue eyes that, before today, I would have said were the brightest I'd ever seen. That was until I met Commander . . .

My brain stalls as I make a connection that should have been obvious but didn't bite me in the ass until right this second.

Fuck.

Kill me now.

How did I not piece together who that big fucker Aeson was? Did the chase and mounting adrenaline fry my fucking mind? Because there's no doubting it, not when I'm staring at his brother, Scion Lorn Noctis, firstborn son of King Kathal Noctis and Crown Prince of The Dragon Horde.

What the flying fuck are he and his little brother, Aeson Noctis, doing here?

Trepidation and shock ice my insides, but my gait is smooth and my mask firm as I'm guided toward the single chair. The scion approaches the Throne of Doom at the same time I do, and I'm unsure which of us is supposed to sit in it. A hard, unyielding hand presses down on my shoulder, indicating that it's my ass that's expected to occupy the hot seat, and I'm too rattled to fight or even object to the unnecessary and rude manhandling.

My thoughts reel, spinning turbulently in my head as I try to make sense of this disturbing development. The heir and the spare, far from home just to investigate a lone female?

Not a chance.

They have people who have people for that kind of thing, or at least I thought they would. Not that I've ever heard of anything like this happening before. Random dragon females aren't just dropping out of the sky, much to the disappointment of The Horde.

Then again, Enslee and the rest of us operate on dated news and questionable gossip way out in The Scorch. We have our own spies working for our best interests in Paragon City, but their reports are understandably few and far between, and they're usually focused on bigger issues and threats.

This scenario, however unexpected, seems out of character for the Crown. Why would the king chance it? Why would he risk his sons?

"I can see you know who I am," Lorn observes, his voice infused with authority.

So much for my impenetrable mask.

"Good. That makes things easier," he continues, stepping away from the two drakes he was speaking with, guards probably, and moving closer to me. "With one half of the introductions done, let's get right to what everyone wants to know. Who are you?"

Wariness moves through me like a rising tide, and I fight the need to stand up so that Lorn Noctis can't tower over me the way he wants. He approaches me slowly, and hundreds of different scenarios play out in my mind of how carefully I need to navigate this. I pause, realizing that this time, I actually don't need to be cautious.

It's too late for that.

I didn't run into The Horde by accident. I don't need to throw them off my trail so I can slink away unnoticed. There's no escaping this. It doesn't matter what I do or say now; I'm caught, and no sleight of hand or witty retort is going to undo it.

It's a liberating thing to realize that I don't have to watch my tongue or perform any mental gymnastics. Too bad that big helping of freedom comes with a side of completely fucked.

The prince of dragons stares at me expectantly, his bright blue eyes telling me he'll wait all night if he has to, but he better not have to.

"Ever Tenebrae," I answer after a lengthy pause.

Just as I expected, the scion's blue eyes narrow. He inhales deeply, scenting me for deception, and then his gaze flicks to a male with black hair, bronze skin, and deep red scale armor.

A Thrasher.

The subtle nod of his head confirms he's a tracker, one who's currently searching the air for lies.

"Your surname is an unusual one . . . rare," Lorn Noctis observes, his gaze growing slightly more intense as he studies me.

"It didn't used to be," I goad, and an immediate edge nicks through the room.

"No, it didn't," Noctis agrees, clasping his hands behind his back as he starts to orbit me, forcing me to track his every step like prey would a predator.

It's a tactic I've used myself when trying to unsettle someone I need information from. I never realized how fucking annoying it was until now.

"I'm going to cut to the chase, Ever. It's been a long day and I'd like to get back to Paragon City sooner rather than later. We heard the whispers coming from the Channeler clan about King Noctis and some of his decisions recently. If this is Lord Quall trying to make a move on behalf of Duke Dowzer, he lacks the numbers and overall strength and intelligence to pull it off. Why else would he set up such an obvious trap in his own territory? King Noctis will pardon your involvement in such idiocy, but only if you reveal *every* detail of what the duke and the lord hope to accomplish and how."

I'm taken aback by the scion's little speech, filing away the helpful nuggets of information—not that I'll ever see Enslee again to tell her. We knew there were issues amongst the dragon clans and kiths, but the Crown is good at keeping the extent and details of their infighting quiet. Enslee and her advisors would be eager to know that King Noctis thinks a Channeler duke and lord are trying to overthrow him.

All eyes are on me, and I feel the press of their judgment and silent questions. I shake my head and blow out a breath.

Here we go.

"You can shove your pardon up your regal ass, or the king's, I don't particularly care which. For the record, I don't know anything about the duke or the Qualls or any plans they might have. I'm not working for them or any other members of The Horde. I doubt that means anything to you, since I'm certain you've already made up your mind and aren't going to believe me despite your Thrasher over there giving you the ol' nod of approval. Save us all the trouble of a monotonous and useless back-and-forth and just kill me now. I too am tired of being here and would be happy to leave sooner rather than later."

A rumble of disapproval ripples through the drakes around me, their dislike over my show of disrespect coming through loud and clear.

Good.

I'll do what it takes to protect the people I care about, no matter the cost. And I really am fucking tired.

The scion glances purposefully at the Thrasher, who nods even though he looks shocked to be doing so. The tracker pulls in another deep breath as though he's second-guessing his own affinity and double-checking for even the faintest hint of deception, but we both know it's not there.

"Do you want to die, Ever?" Lorn asks evenly.

I scoff. "No, but when has that ever stopped the likes of you?"

"So, you're not working with the Channelers, the duke, or the Qualls, and you want me to believe that your presence here isn't some kind of trap?" He pauses and studies me for a long, drawn-out moment.

I roll my eyes, which only serves to make him more intrigued.

"You don't seem to like me very much. Why is that?"

I tsk. "Come now, *Lorn*, I can't be the first person you've run into that thinks you're a prick."

A warning growl sounds off from behind me, and one of the large guards who escorted me in here steps closer, anger radiating off him. The scion raises a hand to keep the male from erasing any more of the minuscule distance between us, and I bite back a smile.

Excellent. I'm getting to them.

"You will address the scion with respect," another male orders, a fulminating glare aimed at me.

"If I respected him, I would," I snap back, matching his glower.

"Enough," Noctis commands, and several snarls quiet instantly. "You're baiting me," he notes, not nearly as annoyed as I'd like him to be. "How curious."

Apprehension tightens my throat at the flicker of intrigue that alights in his blue eyes.

Shit.

I wasn't trying to pique his interest, I was trying to piss him off so he'd rip my throat out and be done with it before they had a chance to torture me for answers.

"First things first though. Stanzin, give me your knife," Noctis orders, and the Thrasher steps forward, unsheathing a blade from his thigh and handing it, hilt first, to the scion.

A trill of fear resonates through me as Noctis strides closer, a wicked-looking blade in his hand. I press back in my chair despite myself.

"Hold her still. We need confirmation," he orders as he draws nearer, and several sets of hands press down on me all at once.

Dread crawls up my throat, and in a blink, I'm no longer in a metal building surrounded by the imposing Horde. I'm back in a cell, being held down by tainted sorcai as Wistan slinks closer, his greedy gaze roaming over my body as he decides where to draw blood from this time.

I scream as I fight the hands pinning me in place. I thrash and snarl, bucking against the bastards trying to keep me down. Somehow my feet are free, and I take full advantage, wildly kicking out and reveling in the pained gasp I elicit when I make contact with someone. Bedlam explodes all around me as more bodies pour into the cell, and I battle against their bruising efforts to incapacitate me.

"What in the bloody realms is going on?" a booming voice demands, the question and the command in it momentarily breaching my terror.

The sound of people running peppers my fear, clouding it with confusion.

"We need confirmation that she's the dragoness from the healing center. I went to get it and she's gone feral," an imperious male defends.

"No shit, Lorn. Did you not hear what the healers said? What the fuck did you think happened to her when she was with the blood brokers? Get away from her with that knife. Anyone touching her has two seconds to stop or lose their hands," another male roars.

I'm suddenly back in the metal building on the ground, a chair tipped on its side next to me. My heart hammers so hard it feels like a steady hum in my chest instead of individual staccato beats. A ringing sounds in my head, and heat pervades my every pore, from both fury and shame.

Large, imposing bodies scurry away, but all I can focus on is the white-haired scion and the knife still clutched tightly in his palm. My heart rages against my sternum, and my lungs are so full of panic there's no room for air. He retreats, but my trepidation doesn't go with him.

A towering body steps in front of me, blocking my view of the knife and its possessor. The face of an avenging angel looks down at me, his stunning blue eyes bleeding wary caution as they take me in. Black flames crawl up his throat, the tips getting lost in the dusting of dark hair across his jaw and cheeks.

Aeson Noctis.

The second-born scion raises his hands, palms out, and crouches down like he's trying hard not to spook me. I hate the whimper that escapes as I skitter back, disoriented and unnerved by what just happened. It felt so real. I know it wasn't. I know I'm not in the cell anymore, not physically, at least, but how long will it take before my mind leaves it, before it stops pulling me back?

"It's okay. No one is going to hurt you. You're safe," Aeson attempts to soothe, careful not to touch me.

I don't need to find the Thrasher in the surrounding drakes to know everything he just said is pure bullshit, but the falsehoods do help to chase away my alarm and draw me fully back to where we are and what's actually happening.

"Safe?" I challenge shakily, biting back the surging embarrassment that's starting to inundate the last dregs of my fear. Anger helps to dam my mounting mortification, and I scowl up at the dark, hulking scion in front of me. "Is a Syphon truly safe anywhere?" I seethe, and I feel everyone around me collectively go still.

"What did you just say?" Aeson whispers, the look on his face vacillating between disbelief and shock, so I hammer it home for him.

"I'm Ever Tenebrae, daughter of the slaughtered King Merik Tenebrae, and the last surviving Syphon of my massacred line. Trust me, Spare, I'm not safe anywhere, least of all with you."

CHAPTER 8

In a lifetime, there is an endless number of rights and wrongs that can stack up for or against you. The tallies on either side can haunt your memories, bolster your greatest accomplishments, or leave you standing in an uncomfortable puddle of ambivalence.

I don't have a track record for getting things wrong.

Mistakes, all too often, are a death sentence, either for me or for those I care about. The luxury to make poor choices isn't one I've had very often. But as I stare at the two scions, one a winter blizzard, the other a dark thunderstorm, I wonder if the winds have changed for me and wrong is now the only way I know how to step.

The Noctis brothers share a look, one loaded with silent communication, but I'm ill-equipped to decipher what they're wordlessly tossing back and forth.

It can't be good.

Then again, it can't be that bad either, because they're not setting me on fire or tearing me limb from limb. I was so fucking certain they would too, and yet here I am, skipping past wrong street, licking a wrong popsicle in the middle of what-the-fuck-is-going-on lane. What's worse is I can't seem to escape this fucking place no matter what I do.

I was wrong about the ambush that got me and Ren taken. Wrong about whether or not I would survive my swan dive off a cliff. Wrong about my ability to run from The Horde. And now I'm wrong about these assholes killing me the second they discovered what I am.

A wave of restless energy ripples through the drakes surrounding me. Discernable impressions of shock, dismay, and suspicion are evident on some of their faces. Others have their reactions locked down tight. It's an impressive display of discipline. One I can't say I particularly care for at the moment, because it makes too many of them hard to read, and that makes their actions hard to anticipate.

Corrugated metal walls, chilly cement floor, and flickering lights are the perfect backdrop for my spiraling thoughts. The drakes around me look stoic, but I can feel their unease. It's as though they're waiting for me to rear up, use my affinity to steal all of their power, and then slaughter them where they stand.

If I could, I would, but they don't need to know, thanks to the curse, that I've never revealed my dragon, I don't have an affinity, and I can't do shit to any of them.

"A Syphon?" Aeson Noctis asks, his bright blue eyes breaking from his brother's and returning to me.

"The one and only," I bait somewhat flatly.

The skeptical look the spare is wearing tightens with unamused disapproval. The commander rises from his crouch in front of me, grabs the toppled chair I knocked over in my efforts to get away from his knife-wielding brother, and sets it back on all fours. "Sit," he orders before striding over to stand next to Lorn.

I scowl up at the brothers, fighting the sudden need to spend the rest of my life right here on this freezing floor now that I've been commanded to do the opposite. However, my ass is going numb, and I've spent way too much time in the last few months on the hard ground of a dank cell. I'm not going to make myself suffer when I don't have to.

I take my time getting up and brushing myself off before, once again, claiming the solitary seat offered to me. I cross my legs, and both brothers track the movement. Aeson's eyebrows dip infinitesimally when his eyes trace the long scratch still on my thigh.

"I find your claim . . . interesting," Lorn contends, studying me contemplatively. "King Tenebrae didn't have any daughters, only sons. And we would know, they were our friends."

I study the heir just as intently, but I don't discover the slightest hint of what he might be thinking. He's alarmingly calm—they both are. It's putting me even more on edge. After a moment, I nod in agreement. Not with the *no girls allowed* part of his assertion, but I know he and Aeson were close with my brothers before they were murdered. It wouldn't be a stretch to say that they knew my kindred better than I did.

My throat grows tight and I struggle with what to say, with how to explain. Habit has my mind whirring with ways I can skirt around sensitive truths I know won't be easy to swallow. It feels wrong to start spilling secrets after everything I've done to keep them under lock and key, but trying to keep things buried is pointless. I've been on a collision course with The Horde from the moment I woke up in the hospital. Now it's time to see what can be made of the wreckage.

With a sigh, I press my palms against my stomach to calm the eclipse of moths churning within.

"No. *Queen* Tenebrae didn't have any daughters," I correct. "But the king did. He had me."

Indignation undulates like a billowing sail in the room. The drakes around me remain silent, but I feel their offense nipping at my skin like hungry dogs out for blood. I'm no longer staring at stoic faces and censorious body language. Now their eyes scream *liar*, and fury strains the lines of their frowns. I don't blame them. If I were in their shoes, I'd question everything coming out of my mouth too.

"You want us to believe that you're the product of an affair?" Aeson counters, arms testily crossing over his chest while pique pulses through his clenched jaw. "Hate to break it to you, little *Syphon*, but we knew your father. He wouldn't have done that to his Bonded Mate."

I nod again, unexpectedly touched by the way the commander and many of the other drakes are coming to my father's defense, refusing to think the worst of him. I didn't expect that from a Noctis, much less any of the others.

It's . . . confusing.

"I'm not the product of an affair, and you're right, my father would've never disrespected his Bonded like that . . . not without her permission anyway."

Lorn shifts his weight as though uncomfortable with the burden of that revelation. His eyes flick to the Thrasher off to the side, the male sifting through my words and everything else he can in search of deceit.

I pull in a fortifying breath and square my shoulders, knowing I'm about to score a hit against The Horde, and dragons aren't the type to turn the other cheek. "For lack of a better term, I'm the product of a *breeding program*," I supply evenly.

Quiet wraps itself around my confession, and I try not to fidget or do anything else that might hint at my discomfort. I wait for the pieces of the puzzle to fit together and for the picture to become clear, but instead, the scions stare at me like I'm no longer speaking a language they understand.

I rub at my temples, trying to pacify the throb building there. All of this is too much. The Tainted, the blood brokers, the cliff, The Horde. I should be dead. None of this should be my problem, and yet here I am, stuck in the middle of all of it, despite every effort not to be.

"What?" Lorn demands after a beat, disbelief warring with confusion.

"The numbers of Syphons were dwindling dangerously low," I try again, attempting to connect all of the dots. "My father and the elders worried that unless drastic measures were taken, the Syphons would go the way of the Surgers and die out altogether. They went back and forth, desperate for a solution for a long time, but in the end, it came down to needing more births than deaths. So it was decreed that all Syphon males would procreate as much as possible in hopes of more births. Our females played their own part by bearing as many babies as they could . . . and, of course, looking the other way when their mates were called to do their duty. Like I said, a breeding program."

With that, anger and outrage ignite all around me, burning through the professional facades of the surrounding drakes.

"She's covering for the duke! Don't believe a word out of her mouth!"

"It's been over sixty years since the wyvern rebellion; where has she been all this time?"

"I don't see a dragon mark. She doesn't smell like us. This is a trap!"

"Female or not, she deserves to lose her tongue for such lies."

I level a challenging glare at the drake who spews the last comment, daring him to try it.

Lorn raises a hand, and all the hissing and accusations instantly stop. He searches my face carefully, methodically. At first, I think he's trying to gauge how batshit crazy I am, but then I realize he's looking for hints of my father in my features.

I meet his gaze head-on, knowing he'll find his proof in the shape and color of my eyes, the high angles of my cheeks, and the solitary dimple I have when I smile—not that he'll ever see that. Everything else is courtesy of my mother, but I doubt the scions knew her. We were only invited to the keep once. The day everyone died.

A small, sharp, almost imperceptible intake of breath alerts me to the moment Lorn Noctis sees the truth. It sits like a snare between us, one that can't be avoided, and yet there's no way around it either. No matter where any of us step from here, we're going to get tangled up in some shit, and people are going to get hurt.

He turns away after a beat and shares another charged look with Aeson. I've never wanted to be in anyone's head as badly as I'd like to root around in either one of theirs right now. Their lack of a murderous reaction to everything I'm saying coupled with the fact that they seem more intent on answers than persecution has me completely thrown.

Dragons killed my people. The wyverns and the sorcai played their part in it too, but the final blow, the one that sealed my fate, belongs to our kind. Even if the Burners weren't directly responsible for King Tenebrae's death or the wyvern rebellion, all of the clans have been picking off Syphons for ages.

It was the same for the Surgers. Syphons and Surgers were once part of the Render Clan, but dragons and other Arcs hunted both to extinction because they coveted our affinities or felt threatened by them. Surgers were sought after for their ability to either boost others' power or use it at will. For Syphons, it was because we could take away affinities both temporarily and permanently. Our kinds were collected and destroyed for no other reasons than greed or fear.

The weak always swipe at the strong when they think they can get away with it. That's our reality, maybe even the nature of most beings. They know it, and I know it. Which is why all of this is even more confusing. Why aren't the scions taking a swipe at me now, when they're outraged, I'm outnumbered, and I have no way to stop it?

Maybe executing me is above their pay grade? I suppose that might be something only the king can order. But if King Noctis was in league with the wyverns and the sorcai, like we've long suspected, why wouldn't his sons be in on it too? They were young when the uprising happened, but they aren't anymore. They'd have some idea of what their father's been up to, wouldn't they?

Unless we've somehow got it wrong.

Noctis was my father's second. He benefited the most from King Tenebrae's murder, but there are others who quietly celebrated the extinction of the Syphons. Far too many dragons eagerly stepped in to claim a slice of power when their competition was conveniently eliminated.

No, I can't rule out the king and his kindred just because they haven't ripped my head off like I expected. Only a small circle of dragons would have had access and the ability to organize and execute a coup. Kathal Noctis is, and has always been, at the top of that list.

"Where have you been this whole time? Why not come home before now?" Lorn demands, and I'm taken aback by the anger and frustration inundating his deceptively simple questions.

The indictment written all over his pretty face has me loading caustic words on my tongue. I take aim, prepared to make it crystal clear to the heir that The Horde isn't my home and never will be, but my rancor is immediately doused when a snarl shatters the otherwise quiet night.

The roar is so loud I feel it in my bones. It quakes the ground I'm sitting on and rattles the walls of the building. Another dragon bays a warning, but a jarring explosion cuts off the sound before magic shrapnel and bullets begin to rip through the structure surrounding us.

Chaos erupts everywhere, and I'm thrown to the ground by a heavy body. A blast of cold air tells me that the building protecting us has lost either some walls or part of the roof. Loud pops of weapons and detonating magic are almost drowned out by the drakes yelling orders to *reveal*, *open the jump portal*, and *kill whoever the fuck is attacking us.*

The sickening smell of compromised magic reaches me, and I bite back a heave of disgust and fear.

The Tainted.

The scent of their putrid power haunts my fucking nightmares, but none of the scrambling drakes seem to notice the rotten scent. I shove a hand over my nose and mouth to help block the stench and push up from the ground, needing to confirm my suspicions with my own eyes.

It doesn't make any sense. The blood brokers would have to be suicidal to try to take on The Horde, but that familiar reek and this level of firepower has my stomach tightening with trepidation.

A menacing growl sounds in my ear as I try to sit up before a large hand tugs me back under the body pressing protectively over mine.

"Think I'm going to let you flag your friends down?" a deep, irate voice accuses.

"Fuck you, Commander," I snarl, trying and failing again to push him off of me.

Why does he have to be so bloody big?

"What?" he snips. "No thank-yous for saving your ass?"

"The only thing you've done is make me a sitting duck," I grunt. "Get off me!"

Shock rings through me like a gong when Aeson actually listens, his profound weight and body lifting from my back. My surprise is quickly replaced with affront when the handsy asshole grabs me off the ground by the waist and starts carrying me through the mayhem, tucking my back to his chest like some weakling in need of his protection.

Alarmed shouts and outrage ricochet around the now dusty and debris-filled air. Two Shields are holding a massive translucent barricade around those of us still inside the building, both of their faces tight with strain. Bright yellow magic assaults the protective veil, viciously trying to burrow through it to get to us. Bullets hit the clear barrier, creating small ripples of warning with their impact, and outside the shield, drakes are revealing their dragons faster than I can gasp in shock.

A challenging roar rips out of the mouth of a red dragon as it streaks past a huge opening that's been blown into one of the walls. Acid sprays from the massive beast's open maw, and screams fill the air. The yellow magic trying to breach The Horde's protections instantly cuts off.

"Secondary protocols!" Aeson bellows, and the two sorcai I noticed when I was first led into the hangar scramble to open a portal. They pour dazzling silver magic into the gateway until a jump portal blooms at the center, unfurling quickly until it touches every rune-covered stone in the large arch. I barely get a peek at the destination on the other side. All I catch is a flash of blue before my view is blocked.

Drakes covered in various colors of scale armor surround Lorn Noctis and hurry him toward the now-open portal. Their scale armor has been fully extended to cover their heads and faces, making them look as though they're trapped half-way between drake and dragon. Horns and ridges on the armored faces hint at what their dragons look like when they're fully revealed. It'd be an intimidating sight if I wasn't envious as fuck right now.

Lorn's guards collectively press through the portal, the heir at the center of their circle of safety. Captivated, I try to watch the jump, having never traveled via gate before, but my line of sight is cut off when I'm set on my feet and then roughly spun around until I'm face-to-face with a very pissed-off Aeson Noctis.

"Are they here for you?" he growls, his armor-covered face inches from mine.

Thicker plates now cover the bridge of his nose in a herringbone pattern that rises up the center of his forehead. Small spikes protrude on each side of the V-shaped plates, growing bigger until they're cut off by two horns. The horns tilt back from his head, making his armored mask look even fiercer, and his angry blue eyes practically glow against the pitch-black of his scales.

He's an enigma. And for a second, I feel myself being drawn in by it like he's a black hole and I'm some orbiting ship with no choice but to succumb. I drop my gaze, unable to think or process when he's this close, glowering down at me.

Bodies of fallen drakes litter the ground. Pools of blood and gore now spatter the floor, painting a macabre picture that I'm alarmingly desensitized to. Aeson shakes me until my eyes once again find his.

"Did you set us up?" he barks.

His words take a moment to register, but when they do I recoil, his insinuation like a stinging slap.

"No," I answer, appalled. "They're not here for me. I want them dead as much as you do. More, even."

The horns, ridges, and scales of Aeson's inky-black armor begin to peel back, revealing his face. He kneels in front of me, strong hands grabbing my hips, and before I know what he's doing, the commander leans forward and licks the thin line of blood from the scratch on my thigh.

Heat blooms low in my stomach, and I try to jerk back from the searing touch of his hands and tongue. I don't get far before he's once again towering over me, grabbing my arms to keep me close.

"I have your blood now, *Syphon*, so don't even think of trying to run, because I *will* find you." He presses forward and I'm too stunned to do anything other than back up to make room for him. "I don't care who you are or what you're the last of—if you cost me any of my Wing, you'll beg for death long before I grant it."

The commander's features harden with the certainty of his promise, and something in my depths wants to rise and meet his challenge, maybe dole out a few threats of my own. Magic skitters over me like shards of ice, and I realize he's herded me toward the portal. Onyx scales climb up Aeson's throat, his cheeks, and then the rest of his face until he's once again wearing an impenetrable mask.

"You will shift and land where the others go. Do you understand me?" He doesn't wait for me to answer before he brutally shoves me.

Realization grips me too late as I fall back into the frigid magic of the jump portal. Horror slams into me like a tsunami, and I scramble for purchase, clawing at the commander's arms. His hard, slick scale armor keeps my desperate fingers from finding purchase, and all too quickly gravity rips me away, a scream spilling from my lips.

I fall.

Blue skies and creamy clouds surround me like a happy lie as I plummet. The portal I was just tossed through rapidly slips farther and farther away. On the other side of the magical opening, I watch as Aeson Noctis sprints fearlessly into the fray. One step he's a drake, and the next a breathtaking, bone-quaking black dragon tears free.

The bellow that thunders out of the scion promises death and pain. It resonates in every part of me, and for the first time since I was taken by the blood brokers, I sense the faintest call of my own dragon. It's nothing more than a slight, tingling surge, but I'd know it anywhere.

I can barely breathe with the shock of feeling it again. I've been trying not to think about the absence of this part of me, of what it might mean long-term, but it's back. Fast as a bolt of lightning, I wrap myself protectively around the weak flicker, terrified my dragon will disappear again. I will the weak glimmer to grow, beg it to consume me until this part of me finally claims its rightful place and my dragon fully reveals.

But like blowing too much air on the flames of a newborn fire, the fragile embers blink out and my dragon withdraws. I should have known better. I've been here too many times, trying to weld the broken pieces of myself together to no avail. No matter what I do, it never works.

Not for me.

Not for any of the other Syphons.

For the second time in a matter of days, I fall through the heavens with no ability to shift or save myself. I'd laugh at the fucked-up full circle of this moment, only this time, I know I won't be waking up in a hospital after this crash.

The portal, now far above me, is a night-filled gash in the middle of a bright cerulean sky. My rapid descent into another part of Drameric has the magical window turning into nothing more than a sliver as I drop too far to continue to see what's happening on the other side.

I twist and flip until I'm no longer facing the gate but staring head-on at the high-rises and keeps below, my death painted on their eaves and turrets. The last view I'll ever have spreads beneath me like a mocking grin. One I've longed to see again, but not like this.

Paragon City . . . we meet again.

CHAPTER 9

Air streaks past me so fast it feels like water shooting up my nose and into my mouth. The torrent steals my scream and I squint against the rush of atmosphere. Dread attacks my senses, but it doesn't matter how hard my heart bludgeons my insides or how much my mind clamors for a solution, the only possible upside to any of this is if I carve a decent path of destruction into one of the keeps when I crash.

Enslee did tell me to pave the way. I don't think that's what she meant, but it's the thought that counts, right?

Instinctively, I spread my limbs to try and gain control of my free fall. Shockingly, it works, and rage starts to drown out my terror the longer I plunge.

Who opens a gate in the middle of the sky?

But I already know the answer. It's a defense measure. A good one, if I'm begrudgingly being honest. It would stop anyone without wings from following The Horde into their stronghold—which is exactly what you'd want if you found yourself under attack like we just were.

I can't tell if I'm still breathing. I'm pretty sure my lungs have been ripped from my chest, and the rest of my organs feel as though they're trying to join them. But the longer I fall, the more I sedately accept my fate and take in the city beneath me as I plummet like a meteor toward it.

The sheer size of The Horde's citadel is even more daunting than I remember. I was six the last time I was here, and looking at everything now, it's obvious how much I've forgotten about the scope of what we're up against.

Paragon City is a mass of high-rises and congested airways. Vehicles buzz around towering buildings like bees circle flowers. Lakes and ancient trees are woven into modern architecture. And towering behind Paragon's crescent-shaped settlement are four different dragon keeps that sit like layers on a fancy cake.

Thrasher Keep is at the bottom, where The Horde's military barracks and training facilities are. Above that sits Render Keep, haven to the Healers and Shields. Channeler Keep is the easiest to identify on the second tier of the four.

The keep is equal amounts stunning fortress and greenery. I can't tell if the palace is made of plants or if the foliage is simply doing its best to take over everything.

Sitting white and gleaming on the top tier, like the finest jewel in the crown, is King's Keep, or Burner Keep, currently named for the clan that resides within. Two towering waterfalls spill down the back of the exquisite structure, and the mountain range bordering Paragon City and Four Tiers is known as Talon's Reach, but drakes often refer to the giant sleepy peaks as The Ancestors.

I stare at the crowning jewel, and I can't help but wonder how different my life would have been if I'd grown up within those walls like my father intended. I would have been raised among my kind, revered and indulged. I'd never have known hunger or terror. The cracked lands of The Scorch would be nothing more to me than a distant designation on a map. And I'd be soaring through these skies as a dragon instead of dropping to my death, the deadweight of a cursed drake.

Far below, groups of dragons are landing in a large clearing off to the side of Thrasher Keep. It must be Lorn and the guards that swept him off to safety. If only I led with the whole *I can't shift into a dragon* thing instead of explaining the ins and outs of the Syphon breeding program first. Then again, how was I supposed to know some asshole was going to toss me through a portal without discussing whether or not I was okay with it?

I don't know where Aeson thought I was hiding a dragon mark. The clothes I stole barely cover my tits, and my torn skirt is only hiding one and a half ass cheeks and a thigh. I was prepared to die at the hands of The Horde, so this really shouldn't piss me off, and yet my fury is simmering hotter and hotter because I didn't see it going down like this. I expected martyrdom, not mortification.

I do my best to try to angle myself toward a small body of water I've spotted in the lower part of Paragon City, but it's useless. Attempting to navigate myself anywhere without wings or a tail is beyond impossible.

The high-rises of Paragon City start to look like lethal spikes as I fall closer, and I know without a shadow of doubt coming face-to-face with them is really going to fucking hurt. Shoving that useless thought away, I grit my teeth as another growl grows in my throat. Every muscle in my body tenses for the impact that's less than sixty seconds away. My snarl morphs into a challenging scream as I prepare to go head-to-head with a building and lose.

Forty seconds.

Thirty.

Twenty.

Teeth clenched. Hands fisted. Mouth dry and eyes watering from the rush of air, I brace for impact.

Out of nowhere, a shadow falls over me. Talons wrap around my body unexpectedly, and suddenly I'm plucked from the sky like ripe fruit from a tree.

Violently, I slam against a scaled palm when it halts the trajectory of my fall. The hit knocks the wind out of me. I struggle to breathe, staving off the panic that's trying to rise from the sudden lack of air. I know it will come—any second now my lungs will recover from the rough impact and inflate—but it feels like forever before I wheeze in a desperate breath. Stars flicker in my vision as I gasp and recover, the dragon's grip almost punishing as it tightens around me.

I hate that I'm relieved.

I hate that I had to be rescued.

And by The Horde, no less, which adds insult to injury.

My body starts to shake from the dump of adrenaline in my veins. The pulse pounding in my ears thumps a distinct warning of *too close, too close*. The hard flap of heavy wings slows our momentum, and I can tell that we're coming in for a landing. I brace for a rough impact, but the final descent and touchdown is way smoother than I thought it would be.

Other large bodies set down all around us, and the faint sound of frantic voices breaches the dragon's fist I'm still stuck within. Light suddenly spills through the seams of the dragon's claws as it opens its hand and dumps me roughly on the ground. The impact is jarring, but I manage to keep the air in my lungs this time as an annoyingly familiar black dragon starts to shift back into his drake form next to me.

Cool grass caresses my cheek before I roll onto my back, reveling in the surprising development that I'm not dead. The clearing I was dropped in is teeming with busybodies, both of the dragon and drake variety, but I'm in no hurry to get up and become part of the mayhem. I should rally. I should be taking advantage of this time to study the shifted dragons and look for any anatomical weaknesses the Syphons might not know about, but it's been a long-ass day, and I feel like I've earned a moment.

"What the fuck was that?" Aeson snaps, his shadow once more crawling over me as he stomps in my direction. "That's the second time you put yourself at risk by not revealing. What is wrong with you? And I swear if you give me that road-pancake bullshit again, I'll take you over my fucking knee."

"Technically, it's the third time," I croak from the ground.

His answering snarl sends a warning shiver up my spine.

My temper rises to answer his call.

The commander clomps into view. I aim a seething glare at him, only for my fury to momentarily sputter out, because there's not one stitch of scale armor crawling up his body.

Nope.

For some reason, he's butt-ass naked. It probably has something to do with how irate he looks right now.

I know I should look away. I should lasso my retreating rage and go for the jugular. But the thick, corded muscle that's everywhere, the cut abs that dip down into a mouthwatering V, and the thick cock that's hanging low between a pair of beefy thighs have my tongue feeling like cement in my mouth.

His dragon mark covers his full chest and shoulders. The onyx flames continue down his burly upper arms, stopping just above his elbows. I can see hints that his back is covered. However, I'm not about to ask him to spin for me. Although a peek at his ass wouldn't go entirely unappreciated.

Parts of me, ones I refuse to acknowledge right now, clench at the sight of him. Need pools in my center, and I grow warm in anticipation of an offer that's not being made. I shove my unwelcome baser instincts away and focus on what he's snarling at me about.

"No more games, *Princess*. I want answers, now!" Rancor drips from the demand, and I look up into a mask of scorn. It's exactly what I need to banish any lingering lust and get a white-knuckle hold on my resentment.

He leans over me, the position meant to intimidate as he dangles his metaphorical and literal dick in my face. With that, I officially hit my limit of bullshit I'm willing to put up with.

I feint a jab toward his unprotected cock, and he reacts exactly like I hoped by dropping his hands to shield it from a hit. His misjudgment of what I'm actually aiming for leaves the rest of him wide open, and my fist meets his throat with a resounding thud.

"You want answers, asshole?" I growl, pushing up from the ground as he falls back on his ass, eyes widening in surprise and hands clutching his throat.

Too late, onyx scale armor wraps itself around his body, protecting him from any further attack.

"I can't shift," I snap, leaning over him, our positions now reversed. "I can't *reveal* because the sorcai who helped massacre my kind stole the ability. Or did you think all the Syphons just laid down and let themselves be slaughtered?"

Aeson claws at his throat, rage blazing in his gaze. It starts to morph into alarm when he opens his mouth for air but can't seem to pull any in. My indignation falters.

I must have hit him way harder than I thought.

Shit.

A wall of unforgiving air slams into me, tearing me away from the commander with the strength of a runaway tank. With a pained grunt, I go cartwheeling through the air and then skidding through the grass. I've barely come to a stop when my hands are yanked forcefully behind my back and something hard and cold is being clamped around my wrists.

Shouts for Jori ripple through the clearing. Everything hurts, but despite that, I turn my head in search of Aeson. A punishing hand wraps around my upper arm and hauls me up. My shoulder shrieks with pain, the joint threatening to abandon the socket as I'm dragged away.

I fight, but it's futile, and despite my best efforts, I'm briskly pulled from the clearing and the commotion.

I don't know if Aeson Noctis is breathing.

But what's bothering me even more than not knowing is why I care at all.

CHAPTER 10

I'm aggressively shoved inside an elevator. The hand still wrapped painfully around my bicep is the only thing that keeps me from tripping and landing on my face. I bite back a growl and swallow the bitchy retort I want to lob at the asshole manhandling me.

If my time with the Tainted taught me anything, it's that there's no point making things worse than they already are. Pissing off someone who enjoys lording their power over you always makes things worse. They'll get their hits in one way or another. It's better to take them head-on; it gives them less time to get creative.

My escort and I are followed into the metal box by another drake. I don't recognize either of them, but that doesn't mean anything. These two could have been part of the team that came to retrieve me, or it's just as possible that they weren't. What is apparent though is their pointed dislike. Whether that's because of the attack against The Horde in Lairwood or my assault on their beloved scion just now, I'm not sure.

One of the males presses his hand to a panel, and the elevator doors close. I expect the car to either rise or drop—like every other elevator I've ever been on—but it shoots off to the right instead. Unprepared to be zooming in any direction that isn't up or down, I go hurtling to the side wall. This time, instead of catching me and keeping me on my feet, the drake whose handprint is now bruised into my arm lets me slam into the reflective metal panel. Pain explodes in my cheek, and my bottom lip splits from the impact, but it's the quiet chuckle next to me as I slowly straighten that has me studying the drake more closely, learning his face, crafting a plan.

Anger scalds my blood, but I keep myself in check. I give nothing away as I sweep my tongue over my lip and clear away the blood. The elevator abruptly darts forward, and I fall back, hitting the hard panel behind me. My cuffed hands help to soften the blow, but my already-abused shoulders feel the hit keenly.

Done with the surprises, I bend my knees, dropping my center of gravity to try to prepare for the next startling shift in direction. It would have worked too, if only the guard didn't time his shove perfectly when the car bolted left and then down.

My head cracks hard against something—a wall, a fist, this asshole's audacity—I honestly couldn't say. This time, I go down with nothing but my knees and face to catch my fall. Warmth slowly trickles from my temple to my cheek, and black spots dance in my vision. I decide it's probably safer to stay on the ground for the rest of this funhouse ride, so that's exactly what I do.

By the time the elevator doors open again, I have no idea where we are in relation to Thrasher Keep. We could be above it, below it, or in the fucking mountains on the other side of Drameric for all I know.

I've never been sucker punched by an elevator before, but there's a first time for everything. I exit the car with a throbbing eye that will probably be black soon and some new cuts decorating the left side of my face. I don't think I have a concussion though, so there's that silver lining at least.

A familiar numbness sweeps in, claiming my limbs and consuming my emotions. I don't know if it's because I'm used to this kind of shit from Wistan and his Tainted or if it's because I've been waiting for The Horde to show their true colors. Either way, I don't give the dick responsible for my new injuries any reaction. I've gone head-to-head with scarier monsters than this prick. Assholes like him thrive on others' anger or agony; he'll get neither from me. Not on the outside at least.

Pewter eyes search my face for tears or any other sign of pain. I give him a wink and then proceed to act like he doesn't exist. As expected, my dismissal invites even more of the drake's ire, and he grabs me and pulls me down a short, empty corridor and into a large shadow-draped room. I'm dumped right in the center, the drake's footsteps loud in the empty space as he walks away to join the other male now guarding the doorless entrance.

Four softly shimmering walls shoot up from the ground, surging higher and higher until they hit the ceiling. I survey the lambent barriers that form my translucent cage, but don't bother testing the walls or trying to figure out if it's possible to escape them. I don't smell magic or sense any dampeners. The faintly glowing walls are completely silent, not lending me any auditory clues as to what they are either.

I have roughly a twelve-by-twelve square of darkness to work with, but there's no bed, bucket to piss in, or drain to allow for easy cleanup, so I doubt I'll be here too long. I take in the smooth floor and ceiling, both the same shade of milky tan. The earthen hue reminds me of the coffee that Kamay, my Flight's Tech Major, drinks nonstop—when we can get all the right ingredients, which is rare.

A spark of longing starts in my chest, but I douse it before it can grow into a flare of homesickness. From what I can see, wherever I am is made of a refined-looking, sleek stone. This place could double as a torture chamber or a great hall designed to host fancy balls and other opulent gatherings. Although, in my opinion, attending any kind of archaic dance would be a form of torture.

It's hard to assess the exact size of the space all around me. Anything outside of a fifteen-foot radius is pitch-black and impenetrable to my eyes. The only light in the room comes from my cage and the hallway that just barely illuminates the two guards bracketing the entrance, their backs now to me.

I exhale a tired but resigned sigh and then gingerly lie down in the dark center of my new cell. The cool floor feels good against my bruised cheek and the gash at my temple. My thoughts whirl, flapping around in my head like anxious birds that can't decide on a perch. They glide from my escape in the forest to my run-in with The Horde in Lairwood, pecking at everything I've learned and swooping around the gaps of what I don't know but need to.

Why the fuck would the Tainted try to take on The Horde? It's suicide. I knew my escape was going to piss Wistan off, but I figured he'd work through his anger issues with a good ol' killing spree. He'd certainly be doing the world a favor by getting rid of some of his lackeys. But to pick a fight with the dragons?

Blood is currency. Blood is status and freedom. Blood is an access point to magic, to power. Which means what's pumping through my veins is priceless. It made sense that Wistan and the blood brokers would keep me alive, that they'd use Ren to ensure my cooperation. Even when it was clear that one of our own had betrayed us, I figured it was for the same motivations: money, power, a chance to leave The Scorch behind. But the attack on The Horde has me looking past all of that and wondering if there's more to it, something I haven't considered, something I missed?

Worry flutters back and forth as I think about Enslee and the others. Are they safe? Will I ever make it back to them? I've never had the kind of patience something like the long game requires. I prefer a more direct approach. Something tries to kill you and you kill it instead. I'm not cut out for cat-and-mouse games, especially when I can't tell if I'm the cat or the mouse.

I jerk awake with a groan. I must have dozed off, or passed out, if the cold pool of blood I'm lying in is any indication. I'm freezing and, fuck, am I sore. For some reason, that makes me want to laugh, but I quickly swallow down the urge. My hands are still bound behind my back, and my arms are now numb. I try to shift my clothing around so it can protect more of my skin from the frigid nip of the stone beneath me, but I only seem to make things worse.

I can imagine Ren watching me right now and cracking up. She'd tell me I look like some sand grub trying to wiggle away from a bird only to be snatched up by a snake. She wouldn't be wrong either. I huff out a laugh at that and stop trying to rearrange my pitiful outfit when my top hikes up so high that the bottom swell of my boobs are peeking out, and the tear in my skirt threatens to rip all the way through the last few inches still managing to hang on by mere threads.

Now I just look like a sand grub with tits.

It's not funny. I know it's not, and yet I'm actively fighting off a giggle. My head swims and I realize that maybe I've officially lost it.

I survived Wistan only to be bested by an elevator.

I do laugh this time and then wince, because it makes everything hurt.

Why the bloody fuck do I feel drunk?

Maybe crazy isn't so bad if it comes with this sweet buzz.

Something sets off my internal alarms, and I realize I'm no longer alone in this room. I have no idea how long they've been there watching me, but someone's definitely there.

Several *someones*, if my instincts are right.

Discreetly, I draw in a deep inhale, hoping to scent my new company. But all I can smell is the puddle of blood I'm lying in.

I wait.

Something I've gotten very good at in the past few months—my Flight would be so proud.

The air around me starts to feel more and more oppressive, and the king's face appears front and center in my mind. I picture his regal features and wonder if the natural charm he always seems to exude via vid screen will be absent as he scowls down at me in my cell. Will he question me first, or will he do what his sons should have done when we first met—kill me with zero remorse or hesitation?

Will King Noctis be unnerved when he sees my face and finds pieces of my father staring back at him, or will it be just as easy to end me as it was to end his best friend?

The darkness is quiet and unnerving all around me. I watch it expectantly, but nothing happens. Just when I start to think my head wound might be messing with me, a large figure finally separates from the gloom and casually walks toward the front wall of my glimmering cage. It's not the Noctis I thought it would be.

"I figured you'd be wings-deep in canapés and cunt by now. Don't you have people to handle this sort of thing for you?" I ask, internally high-fiving myself.

Canapés and cunt . . . good one.

"Come now, Princess, must you be so crass?"

"'Princess Crass' does have a nice ring to it," I admit. "But, alas, the title is incorrect."

"Ah yes, my apologies. It should be *Scioness* Ever Tenebrae, unclaimed daughter of the fallen Syphon king."

I would roll my eyes at the posh intonation he's laying on a little thick, but my head hurts entirely too much, and it's creating an irrational worry that my eyes will get stuck facing the wrong direction. I already have the Frilled Lizard thing to contend with if I ever make it back to my Flight; no need to add backward eyes to the mix.

"Wrong again," I counter with my own snooty affect. "My father is dead, and like you said, I am unclaimed. Therefore, I have no title. So you can fuck right off with all that bullshit . . . respectfully, of course, Your Highness."

"We'll know soon enough exactly who and what you are. I'm here to verify your claims," he tells me, and it almost sounds like a threat.

"Oh goody," I snark in return.

Lorn Noctis steps fully out of the shadows, his black scale armor noticeably absent. In its place are fitted white pants that hug him in all the right places and a matching top that looks expertly tailored to highlight every plane and curve of his frame. The collar of his shirt is stiff and high, stopping just shy of his sharp jaw. Some kind of sparkling white embroidery licks up the chest and across the broad, structured shoulders of the shirt before plunging down the cape that drapes majestically down his back.

What he's wearing probably costs more than every drop of blood in my body. He looks rigid and unyielding, the white of his clothing matching the exact shade of his hair perfectly. His mere presence is magnificent, formidable, and I can't help but wonder if the heir ever gets to unwind and just let go.

Maybe if he gets close enough, my buzz will jump to him. Then we can both laugh about grubs with tits and undefeated elevators.

It's on the tip of my tongue to ask if his not-so-little brother is okay, but I'm not that far gone. I'm also still trying to convince my stupid brain that it doesn't care. I don't think I'm winning the argument though; my brain is a real stubborn bitch.

I smile at that and then wince as it pulls on the split in my lip. Lorn's brow furrows and he steps closer to the barrier, eyes piercing the dark interior of my cell to study my visage more intently.

"You're hurt," he states, surprised, like it's the last thing he expected.

"You should see the other guy," I joke. My head starts to pound harder, and I close my eyes. "Listen, Heir, the Tainted at least gave me some time to heal between my beatings. Can we reschedule this interrogation for tomorrow? I promise I'll be more fun then."

Lorn's eyes zero in on mine, and anger blooms in his cheeks. Suddenly he's striding forward, his features furious as he passes through the shimmering wall of my cage like it's nothing more than decorative air.

I stare, shocked.

Fuck me.

I should have tested these walls. If I could have just walked through them at any time, I'm going to kick my own ass.

The smell of my blood must hit Lorn as soon as he breaches the cell, because his pupils dilate and his lip lifts in an enraged snarl. "Get Zainab in here now!" he shouts over his shoulder before crouching down and reaching for me.

"Don't touch me," I growl, the sound filled simultaneously with threat and panic. I attempt to scoot away from him, but I don't get far, too stiff and cold to successfully scuttle.

He hesitates, looking pained and then pissed, but he thankfully drops his hands and maintains some distance. "Why are her arms still bound?" he seethes, head snapping in the direction of the two guards in the hallway. He calls for them, but I miss what he shouts because the cuffs on my wrists are suddenly released and the numbness in my arms and shoulders gives way to a needle-stabbing twinge that pulls an involuntary groan from my throat.

I roll forward, pressing my forehead to the floor as the feeling painfully returns to my mistreated limbs. A keen ache pulses through me, and I pant it out until the intensity starts to abate.

I'm lifted off the ground, and a fresh wave of pain washes over me at the unexpected and unwelcome movement. I turn to eviscerate Lorn for ignoring my direct warning not to touch me, but it's Aeson who's staring back at me, his face filled with rage.

"You," I puff in surprise.

"Me," he rumbles in agreement, repositioning me in his arms until he has me pressed firmly against his chest, one arm at my back and the other under my knees.

"What happened?" he demands as the walls of my cage fall like water from the ceiling and disappear back into the floor. He hastily strides toward the hallway, which is now sans guards.

This time, I do roll my eyes. Just as I suspected, I immediately regret it. My vision goes wavy and my head feels like it was dropped into a compactor, but my eyes don't get stuck.

"Did you just high-five yourself?" Aeson asks.

"It's for my eyes. I'm proud of them," I explain, but he looks even more confused.

"Aes, Zainab is already on her way. Where are you going?" Lorn calls to his brother's back as we practically race off.

"I'm taking her to Jori. He's closer," Aeson grunts, completely ignoring the censure in Lorn's tone.

"She's not clear to leave until we figure out what the fuck is going on," Lorn points out as he catches up to us, his cape billowing out behind him, which forces the other drakes following us to keep their distance.

Something about that makes me want to laugh, but I get a grip and stay quiet.

Why do I feel so warm . . . and weird?

I didn't pee myself, did I?

"We're not leaving, we're changing rooms. And you can just as easily ask her whatever you want in the infirmary. She'll be good, won't you, Claws?"

"I wouldn't count on it," I chirp honestly and then giggle.

Aeson looks down at me, concern floating in his gaze. I'm right there with him, because something is wrong with me, and it's not because I'm injured or in pain.

Pain, I know.

Pain, I can deal with.

This is something else.

"Tove, Ogdan, pull up the feeds and see what happened between the landing pad and the Warren," Aeson orders.

"On it," a husky, feminine voice replies from in front of us.

I turn my head to try to see the female I recall from my ride in the lirocar.

"Ooh, Tove, let me rub your head for good luck before you go," I call out.

Several chuckles sound off around me, but when I try to track them, the movement sends a spike through my temple, and I'm forced to close my eyes to stave off the tunneling my vision starts to do.

Fuck, I'm tired.

"No naps just yet, Claws. I want your eyes on me," Aeson barks.

"That's not my name, you bossy fuck," I snap and then titter when it comes out more like a drunken mumble.

"You tell him, Frills," Chastain encourages.

"That's not my name either," I whine, and it takes all of my focus to get my lips and tongue to form the words correctly. "What did you do to me?" I demand, suddenly confused.

"Ever, did you grow up near a Source?" Lorn asks out of nowhere.

I wave a finger at him and tsk. "Nice try, Heir, but you're not gonna trick me. Ooh, my mouth works again!" I declare excitedly when it doesn't feel like I'm talking around a pound of sand.

"I'm not trying to trick you. Source magic is a vital need for our kind. If you're depleted, being near a Source can have . . . an effect," Lorn explains, but I'm having a hard time focusing on his words and not the bright spots of light now dancing around his head.

How did lightning bugs get in here?

"I think you're Source drunk, Princess," Lorn tells me, flecks of amusement now dancing with the halo of lightning bugs.

I know what he just told me is of vital importance. It's setting off warning bells in my mind, and I should really care about that. But there's something else that's really bugging me, and the need to know is shoving everything else out of the way.

My eyes leave Lorn and jump back to Aeson. "Why won't you kill me?" I ask the commander, perplexed, but it comes out petulant.

Fiery blue eyes snap down to mine, shock and confusion blanketing his features. "Why would I do that?" he counters as though that's an answer.

It's not.

I hate when someone answers a question with a question. It's a dodge, a way to exercise control or reclaim it. It's another game, and I'm already so over playing them.

I don't know what Enslee was thinking. It's only been a couple of hours with The Horde, and I'm already fucking things up. Maybe the person I was before the blood brokers could have pulled this off, but I'm not her anymore. She was confident and capable, driven and focused. She would have had all these bastards eating out of her hand already.

I don't even know what I am now. Judging by how battered and broken I feel, whatever it is, it's not enough. Not anymore.

I huff out a sigh and rest my head against Aeson's chest, too tired to continue to fight to hold it up. "Why?" I parrot, shaking my head. "Because you killed my dad. Not you specifically," I correct with an amused snort as I nuzzle against him. "You would have been too young, your dragon too small. It was a bigger dragon that killed him."

We stop moving.

"What did you just say?" Aeson demands, his voice slightly strangled and a little too loud in the now-quiet corridor.

I bark out a laugh.

He asked that exact same question when I told him who I was.

I try to sit up in his arms, but my body screams a refusal. Aeson must see what I want and lifts me, bending his head so my mouth is closer to his ear.

"You think he was killed by wyverns," I whisper, captivated by the goose bumps that abruptly rise on his dragon-marked neck. "But he wasn't. I was there. I saw it. It was *dragons*. But don't tell anyone, it's a secret."

CHAPTER 11

Shock and disbelief fill Aeson's eyes. I pull my head back, our faces mere inches apart as what I just said settles between us like kicked-up mud in a pond.

"Dragons . . . " he repeats, like he needs to wrap his mouth around the words before he can wrap his mind around them. "Who?"

"Not here," Lorn interjects, reproach darkening his tone. He looks around the corridor pointedly, and Aeson straightens in understanding. We start down the wide hallway again, the clomp of heavy footfalls the only sound bouncing off the walls as we go.

Unease cloaks both scions, their furrowed brows and downturned mouths indicative of a typhoon of tumultuous thoughts. There's something oddly satisfying in the way my revelation has rattled them. It feels karmic and remarkably affirming to witness their struggle to process something that I, myself, have had a hard time coming to grips with. It's fucked up—I shouldn't wish my pain on anyone, but I can't find it in me to care. Betrayal is a nasty beast; why should I be the only one to wear its scars?

"We shouldn't take her to the infirmary," Lorn states, his mien contemplative and tense.

"The rookery is secure," Aeson supplies, but there's a splash of something in it that I can't identify, like he's unsure about that option but doesn't proffer a better one.

With a nod from big brother, Aeson changes direction. He walks right for what looks like a wall. A wall that suddenly slides open at the commander's approach, revealing another corridor, one that was completely hidden seconds ago.

I stare at the new opening, utterly gobsmacked. A queasy understanding clambers forward in my mind. On the off chance that someone escaped their cage down here and tried to run, they would never find the way out. It's diabolical, and brilliant, and it makes my blood run cold.

What the hell was I thinking coming here?

On my best day, I am out of my league in this place, and today sure as shit isn't my best day.

Aeson picks up his pace and we approach another elevator. I stiffen, nowhere near ready for round two. The commander must notice my reaction because his face dips and his eyes catch mine. Understanding dawns in his gaze, a keen comprehension I want to wipe away.

Why couldn't he be pretty and dumb? This would be so much easier if he was all package and zero substance. But no, it's just my luck that the fucker is clever, adept, and annoyingly observant.

Questions I have no intention of answering flash across the commander's face. I flatten my lips into a scowl and look away from him, making it clear I'm not going to tell him shit about why the elevator puts me on edge.

"Your secrets aren't going to be yours for much longer," he warns as the group piles into a much bigger elevator car.

"Maybe, but they're mine for now," I contend, ignoring the glimmer of challenge I see in his eyes.

This time, no one presses a hand to a panel or does anything else before the elevator doors close and the box starts moving. I look around the group, trying to discern which one of them is controlling this thing, but everyone looks stiff and focused, making it impossible to tell.

I recognize Chastain, the big blond brute I first ran into back in Lairwood, and another drake from the lirocar ride, the one with purple scale armor whose name I still don't know. A massive drake, the biggest I've ever seen, stands behind Aeson. His hair is black, his complexion tawny, and his scale armor is a rich dark brown. He's a Thrasher, and his solemn cinnamon-brown eyes are fixed steadily on me.

I meet the drake's stare, neither one of us offering a challenge or grappling for dominance. We simply take one another in, like we're trying to see where the other might fit in all the uncertainty and chaos that's unfolded today. I just barely notice the black glyphs and bands on his arms. They're almost camouflaged against the deep brown of his scale armor, but they irrefutably mark him as a member of the Royal Wing.

Chastain leans over and whispers something to him that I can't hear, and I spot another set of bands and glyphs that I know for a fact weren't on the Channeler's night-blue scale armor before. My gaze darts around the elevator, landing on one glyph-covered arm after another until I realize that they're all marked as members of the Royal Wing. It shouldn't be a surprise. I am standing in an elevator with the two Noctis scions, but it hammers home my precarious reality even more.

"Who is your mother?" Aeson asks out of nowhere.

The question spikes my adrenaline, which makes my head pulse even harder, but I pretend like nothing's wrong as I look up into a shrewd pair of sky-blue eyes. I get lost in the color for longer than is appropriate, and his hold suddenly tightens . . . almost possessively.

Why do I like that?

I study his face and find myself wondering things about the commander that I have no business wondering. This is my enemy. I shouldn't want to know what he looks like when he smiles, or care what his laugh sounds like. I sure as shit shouldn't be wondering what noises he makes when he comes.

A strange flutter starts in my core, and the oddest feeling washes over me. It's as though I'm no longer the only one looking out of my eyes. My first thought is that it's my dragon, floating just below the surface, taking everything in, assessing.

But somehow this is different.

The unfamiliar pressure doesn't subside, and an undeniable touch of cognizance tickles my mind.

Is Aeson doing this?

Or is this me?

Or maybe this is the Source's fault for getting me drunk?

I reach for my dragon, eager for contact or a sign that the cage separating us might be weakening, but, just like always, that piece of me is locked away and dormant.

Rattled and confused, I lean closer to Aeson, probably too close. I blame my scrambled depth perception and my fuzzy head, not this strange pull I suddenly feel toward him.

"I thought we weren't supposed to be talking about top-secret things," I whisper, purposely dodging his question, and his gaze drops to my lips.

"Is that top secret?" Aeson asks, his tone a gravelly taunt bordering on a deep growl that makes me think I just might know one of the noises he makes when he comes.

"I thought everything about me was top secret. Isn't that why you're sneaking me up to your rookery like some female your kindred wouldn't approve of?" I ask.

"You're not going to get anything coherent out of her until Jori deals with her Source issues," Lorn interjects.

I point at the heir's chest. "You have Source issues. You also have some dirt right there." I gesture toward his right pec. He swipes at his shirt irritably before looking down to find it's still pristine. I giggle. "Gotchya."

Lorn's scowl is icy. It's the perfect accessory to go with his white hair, wintry blue eyes, and cold beauty. The thought makes me giggle again.

"You have a dimple," Aeson points out, like I don't already know.

I gasp and cover the small indentation with my hand. "It's back?" I exclaim.

Aeson frowns at me, the look in his gaze perplexed.

"Don't scare it away!" I admonish. "I haven't seen the little guy in forever."

Aeson snorts out a laugh and then quickly cuts it off, like the show of amusement just happened against his will.

"It only comes out when I'm happy or having fun. Don't mess this up for me," I scold, and Aeson's amusement instantly dims.

Everyone grows quiet, and I bite down on my lip to keep any more nonsense from slipping out. I wince when I accidentally reopen the cut I forgot about.

"She's bleeding again," someone announces.

I wave a dismissive hand. "It's nothing, just my lip. I've had worse injuries . . . like way, way, way worse. Don't even worry about this one. It's not even a blip on the radar of the fucked-up things that have happened to me."

What the fuck am I even saying?

Mortification has me closing my eyes. I press a hand over my mouth as though it will stop the involuntary word vomit.

"Can someone just knock me out until we get where we're going? I don't know what the fuck is wrong with me," I plead, my voice muffled against the palm of my hand.

"We're almost there," Aeson assures me, and I nod and then regret that movement. "Now, back to your mom," he tries to redirect.

I groan and drop my hands back into my lap, irked.

"Stop being so obsessed with my mom; way to give a girl a complex." I open my eyes to give him a look, and freeze.

I'm surrounded by white dragon stone on the walls and floors. It has light gray and gold veins running through it, just like I remember. The arches are the same. The dragons carved into the stone of the walls, flying, hunting, living life, are different and yet similar enough that my heart lurches and my lungs try to quit on me.

Wasps get to work destroying my insides.

It's not the same. You're okay, I tell myself, but I instantaneously don't believe it.

I don't know why it didn't dawn on me that *this* is where they were bringing me. They said "rookery," and that could've only ever meant the towers of King's Keep. And yet, I feel like I've just been kicked in the gut.

I wasn't ready.

I don't know that I ever could have been.

"What's wrong?" Aeson demands, suddenly stopping so he can look at me, but my thoughts and memories are yanking me back to a time I'm all at once desperate to escape.

"King's Keep," I answer, my whisper a hollow shell of devastation, because the last time I was here, I watched my mother, my brothers, and my father being butchered.

My breaths grow shorter, and my heart rushes between beats until the cadence is one constant thrum of foreboding. Ants crawl through my veins, and I run a finger down my scars to try to ground myself, but they're still hidden by the charm, and that disconnect between what should be there but isn't—it sends me spiraling.

All at once, I can see it. Smell it. Hear it.

It's like I never left.

"No," I tell myself, clenching my hands into tight fists to quell the shaking. My broken and jagged nails dig into my palms, the small kiss of pain helping to focus my racing thoughts. "You're not there," I chant quietly. "They're not being torn apart. You can't hear them screaming. It happened already. It's over. You're not there."

But suddenly I am, and the horror of it all once again seizes me so fast I can't do anything but survive it all again.

Enslee burrows deeper into my lap, the fabric of my skirt helping to muffle her cries. They found our brothers. We thought they escaped, but the drakes are dragging them back into the room. The queen is screaming. Father is pleading. He's trying to bargain, to beg, but the armored drakes won't listen. Brooks is crying, he's so scared.

I should close my eyes.

I should look away . . . but I can't.

"I am not there," I chant to myself. "I survived."

Ronin and Novak scream when the drakes pull Brooks away. Their terrified wails join the agonized bellows of my father and the queen. My mother's lying in a puddle of blood just behind them. Her body has stopped twitching; she's gone still. I think she's dead.

Brooks screams, the anguish and agony searing through me, eviscerating everything I am.

I am not in that tower. I am not watching them die! I snarl at my mind, fighting back, refusing to succumb to the horror. Not here. Not now. It's not safe. I can't afford to be vulnerable. I can't show them my weaknesses.

I shove out of Aeson's arms, needing space, to be sick, to pace, to shatter . . . I don't know. I make it a few steps, but my blood loss and battered body put a quick end to my hasty retreat. My vision dims and my knees suddenly give out. A pair of capable arms are quick to catch me, to keep me from falling, and then I'm being cradled against a wide, hard chest.

A warm hand strokes my hair, and a sonorous voice picks up my mantra, repeating it back to me in perfect synchronicity. "You're not there," he whispers against my uninjured temple. "You're safe," he adds, over and over again until I can almost believe him.

I want so badly to believe him.

I whimper as the screams echo in my mind, but I refuse to look at the haunting specters of my family as they're ripped limb from limb. The smell of blood tries to fill my nose, but I hold my breath against the phantom invasion. I know it's not real. It happened, but it isn't happening now. Yet even with that certainty, it's so fucking hard to kick free of the violent torrent and find the surface.

I don't know how long I sit, murmuring in harmony that "I'm okay" when it couldn't be further from the truth. I tread through the trauma until I begin to find my way out. Slowly, my breaths grow even, my heart finds its proper pace, and my eyes adjust. The merciless memories are shoved back into their box and reburied within my tattered depths. I know they have no intention of staying there, they never do, but that will have to be tomorrow's problem.

I open my eyes, spent, depleted, but ready to face the world again. Chagrin colors my cheeks. I can only imagine what everyone around me must think. I feel alarmingly exposed and frustrated that I can't do anything about it.

I turn to face Aeson, not sure what to say, or how to even explain what just happened, but a different pair of blue eyes meets mine. Aeson isn't the one offering me comfort and coaxing me back from the dark.

The warm arms and gentle voice cradling me are Lorn's.

CHAPTER 12

Lorn doesn't say anything as I stare up at him. He also doesn't move me out of his lap or unwrap his arms from around me. We just sit there, watching each other, waiting. For what?

I don't know. Maybe he's waiting to see if I'll break again. To be fair, I'm wondering the same thing. I've never considered myself to be an overemotional person, but I guess forced captivity and torture can really change a girl. It's clear my time with the Tainted—and now being here with The Horde—is kicking up things best left buried.

Up close like this, I can see the lines and shadows of Lorn's dragon mark through the fabric of his stark-white shirt. The black flames start low on his torso and crawl up his ribs and chest, but only on his left side. More lines of onyx fire run from his wrist up his arm before that blaze meets the one on his chest, and the two pyres climb up and over his shoulder, but that's really none of my business, so I stop looking.

"Here, drink this," someone next to me orders.

I look over to find Jori. The Render from Lairwood, the one boasting shades of brown—from his hair to his sun-kissed skin, and even the armor protecting his body. He tries to hand me a cup filled with some kind of liquid. A look of confusion washes over his face when I don't instantly take it.

"It's just water," he reassures, his hazel eyes encouraging and his smile kind.

He tilts the cup so I can see the contents, before offering it to me again, as though I'm stupid enough to take his word for it.

I'm not.

An exasperated sigh slips out of Lorn, and he reaches over me to pluck the water from Jori's hand. He brings it to his lips, his eyes locked pointedly on mine, and drinks. His Adam's apple bobs in the center of his throat as he swallows a mouthful, and I suddenly find myself very thirsty.

"Just normal, everyday water," Lorn chirps. "It's not poisoned," he adds loftily, as though the notion itself is ridiculous. He takes another sip, humming with pleasure and overexaggerating just how good the poison-free water is.

I shake my head, unimpressed with the bad acting. "It might not be poisoned, but now it's got your backwash in it," I grumble as I begrudgingly take the drink from him.

An easy grin spreads across the scion's face, my words not ruffling his scales in the slightest. His hand flexes against my hip, and he relaxes under me like this interaction is completely normal for him. Maybe it is. He probably has females throwing themselves at him every hour on the hour, and this sort of intimate familiarity is commonplace. The same cannot be said for me.

I was raised by the last few surviving members of my mother's guard. They looked out for me the best they could. They shaped and sharpened me into a soldier they could be proud of, but I never found much softness in those battle-hardened warriors. They didn't hold and coddle me. They didn't talk me through my nightmares. Flashes of weakness called for more training, more honing. I had Enslee and the other Syphons, but they were nursing their own wounds, triaging their own trauma. I never wanted to burden them with mine.

I don't know why Lorn felt the need to comfort me. I don't know why I let him. Aeson did the same back in Lairwood, and I allowed it then too. I need to stop doing that.

I ignore Lorn's intense gaze as it roves over my face, and look around. We're in someone's rookery, but I can't tell if it's Lorn's or Aeson's.

The room itself could comfortably fit a few fully revealed dragons with plenty of space for them to stretch their wings without hitting the vaulted roof or the smooth walls. There's a fireplace, a living room area that could easily seat twenty, and a balcony that displays a breathtaking view of the mountains.

Lorn and I are sitting on a long bench that rests against the foot of a bed that's entirely too big for one drake or twelve. The bedding is ivory with fluffy pelts draped across the bottom. There are more pillows than any one person could ever need, and I notice images of dragons flying, fighting, and fucking carved into the tall headboard and all over the rest of the room.

With a jolt, I realize where I am. This is a mating suite. I don't know which of the scions it belongs to, but it's without a doubt a room meant for their Bonded Mate.

My stomach drops and I scan my surroundings again, pulling in deep breaths to determine if someone already stays here. I don't smell anything other than my blood and Lorn, but that doesn't mean anything. I look back at the heir, a multitude of implications fighting to get out.

Why would they bring me here *of all places?*

Is he bonded?

Is Aeson?

Why do I give a fuck?

Enslee warned me that The Horde was greedy, that they would want to use me. But they can't possibly think I'll fall right into one of their beds . . . can they? My heart kicks up in warning, but I dismiss the disturbed direction of my thoughts. I haven't revealed, which means I can't bond, forced or otherwise. I'm safe on that front at least.

That thought calms me, and then I recall the conversation in the hallway and realize I've read this all wrong. They needed somewhere secure, somewhere they could get answers and not worry about those answers being compromised or leaked, especially after that nice little bomb I dropped about King Tenebrae and who killed him. What better place than where they live, where they know they're safe and protected.

The problem is my father thought that about his rookery too, and look where it got him.

Subtle movement catches my eye by one of the colossal archways that leads out to the balcony. I find Aeson there, watching me. The big drake from the elevator, the one with dark brown scale armor, is standing in front of him, facing me.

I can't tell if the Thrasher is positioned to protect the scion or if he's there to keep the commander back for some reason. Aeson's stare is intense, but I don't know him well enough to discern what it means. I can't tell if he's trying to incinerate me with a glance, study me, or if he's simply ensuring I'm okay.

Why am I in Lorn's lap and not his? Does this bother him?

I drop-kick the useless thoughts away. It doesn't matter. I need to get my head on straight and stop being distracted by a pretty face and surly attitude. The other Syphons would lose their shit if they saw me like this.

"Please drink, dragoness," Jori once again encourages, and like a taut rubber band, my attention snaps back to the Render. "You've been through a lot today. You have to be hungry and thirsty. I've called for food, but that will have to wait until we get you all cleaned up and the Oric's come and gone."

I tense at the mention of The Horde's genealogist. I figured at some point they'd call one in to corroborate my claim. I've never seen one in action, but they sound like beings that strictly deal in the old ways of knives and ichor. I've had enough of that kind of shit to last me several lifetimes, but I don't say anything. My objections wouldn't matter anyway.

"Princess," Lorn rumbles, a note of rebuke in it.

I turn to glare at him. All too aware that I'm still in his lap and his hands are still on me. Now that my head is clearer and my thoughts in order, my instincts want me to get up and move away from him, but that feels too close to retreating, and I don't want to give him that either.

"Drink," he orders like the arrogant fuck he is, but it saves me from having to make a decision or trying to move when I don't know that I can.

You don't survive The Scorch without building up a good tolerance to some pretty nasty toxins and a wide range of poisonous creatures, so I lift the cup to my lips, flipping my middle finger up for good measure, and take a sip. I only intend to take a small drink, for the sole sake of proving to this peacocking prince that I'm not unreasonable or scared of what they might have done to it, but of course Horde water has to be the cleanest, most delicious, crisp mouthful of rejuvenating goodness I've ever had.

I empty the cup in two swallows and then hold it out greedily for more. A satisfied hum sneaks out of Lorn as a floating pitcher fills and then refills the cup four more times before Jori waves it away, cutting me off.

"You haven't revealed. Is that why you can't heal?" Jori asks, going right for the jugular of all my problems despite his sheepish intonation as he voices what so many of them must be wondering.

My gaze finds its way to Aeson. He hasn't moved from the spot by the window. His arms are crossed over his chest, and a muscle jumps angrily in his jaw. My cheeks heat when our scowls connect.

I turn back to Jori.

"No. I haven't revealed. I can't," I answer, doing my best to bottle up the simmering fury I feel with the admission, but some of it leaks out. "Whatever the sorcai did to the Syphons to keep them from shifting was apparently permanent."

Several drakes around the room fidget or shift their weight in a silent show of surprise and unease. I'm sure the idea that their dragon could be trapped and unable to escape is horrific. A few grumbled swears fill the air, and Aeson steps around the big Thrasher in front of him to move closer. The guard tenses a little as he does, but ultimately doesn't do anything to stop him.

I watch the strange interaction attentively. Is the Thrasher wary of what the commander will do to me if he gets too close or of what I might do to the scion if given the opportunity?

Over Aeson's shoulder, the sun is starting to set on this side of the continent, and the colors are slowly painting the room and its occupants in strokes of pale pink and gold.

"If you've never revealed, how do you know you're a Syphon?" Aeson asks, the rough timbre of his voice tickling across my skin and leaving goose bumps in its wake. I tear my eyes from the splashes of color highlighting the distant sky and stare back at the commander.

Lorn's hands tighten on my hips, and I'm suddenly reminded of exactly where I'm still sitting. I push out of his lap, needing immediate space from both brothers. The movement reawakens all my aches and pains, and despite the pitcher of water I just chugged, my head feels light and untethered.

I wobble, unsure if my feet are going to stay planted firmly on the ground where I need them, but thankfully, Jori steps in before either of the glowering Noctises can. He settles me gently on the velvety bench and thankfully not back into the waiting trap of Lorn's lap. With the tap of a few buttons on Jori's com bracelet, two med carts zip toward the Render from somewhere behind me and float to a stop on either side of him.

"If your abilities are damaged and you can't shift or heal, does dragon magic work on you?" Jori asks contemplatively as he starts opening gauze while unscrewing the cap on a bottle of something I can't identify.

"Maybe." I shrug. "Maybe not. I don't know any dragons to have them try, but the sorcai and shifter healers helped me after I escaped the Tainted. If their magic works, I assume yours might too."

"And how'd you get away from the blood brokers?" Lorn asks, rising from the bench and moving to stand near two drakes in dark orange scale armor. The stance he adopts—arms folded over his chest, frame taut, and intense stare honed in on me—mirrors Aeson's, and a twinkle of amusement moves through me.

"I jumped off a cliff."

A pin could drop and be heard loud and clear in the silence that consumes the room. The drakes stare at me, aghast.

"That explains how the healers got ahold of you in Lairwood," Ogdan observes, an impressed whistle trilling out of him as he raises his eyebrows and dips his chin.

I don't know when the redhead Burner and Tove rejoined the party. It must have been sometime in the middle of my breakdown.

"Lucky you survived that fall. I tracked the area where they found you. Were there any other survivors?" a drake with night-black skin and bloodred armor asks. He's leaning back against a wall next to Chastain and the drake in purple armor with long light brown hair.

I look around the room and give a derisive snort. "I don't know about *lucky*," I dispute. "But, no. I was the only one there."

I don't mention Renatta, not wanting to cut that wound open when I'm already triaging so many others.

"Answer my question," Aeson orders evenly, all eyes bouncing from me to him.

I try to remember what the hell he asked me, but can't. He seems to realize that, and with only a small dash of irritation, he repeats it.

"If you've never revealed, how do you know you're a Syphon?"

Jori reaches for my face and I automatically flinch away. He holds up some damp gauze in his other hand, silently communicating what he wants to do. I nod after a beat and force myself to stay still when he starts cleaning blood off my neck and jaw.

"I know I'm a Syphon the same way you knew you'd be a Burner before you belched your first flame," I answer, gesturing to the dragon mark on Aeson's throat. "Although, if we want to get technical, I'm nothing until I can reveal, which I can't."

Jori grabs my chin and tilts my head to get better access to my cheek and temple.

"So you've been keeping tabs on us? Watching us?" Aeson accuses. "You clearly know who we are."

"Don't flatter yourself, Spare. I know you and The Horde well enough to keep my distance, nothing more, nothing less."

"Oh, that's right, you think we killed your father."

"I don't *think*, I know," I snap.

"Wait. What?" Tove demands, striding closer, Ogdan right on her heels. Both drakes look as though someone just socked them in the stomach.

Jori presses something against the cut at my temple. It stings like a motherfucker, but I keep my face impassive and silently swallow the pain.

"So who was it, then?" Aeson demands coolly, doing his best to give Lorn a run for his money on the frosty-fucker front.

"I don't know *who* killed him. I only know *what* killed him."

"Anyone else confused?" Chastain announces, brushing his fingers through his perfectly tousled blond hair. He looks around the room as though he's searching for someone who will explain.

I huff out a sigh that morphs into a small hiss when Jori presses the same stinging shit to the cut on my lower lip. I fix my gaze on the dimming sky and toe a corner of my mind I don't like to spend much time in.

"I was born near The Wells and brought up there until my father called me and my mother to Four Tiers when I was six. He thought it was time to announce my existence and claim me as a Tenebrae, as kindred, before I got much older. The few other Syphons who'd successfully sired children outside of their bonds were going to do the same. It was supposed to happen after the Blood Rite that year."

"I'm done with that part," Jori interrupts, tossing a bloodstained strip of gauze into a waste bin on one of the carts. "If my magic works, it'll feel warm. If it starts to get too hot or uncomfortable in any other way, let me know."

I nod and hold my breath as Jori presses his fingers against the cut on the side of my head. It starts to warm, and then it tingles. For a moment, all I can do is marvel as the pain ebbs and my skin begins to knit back together.

"Holy shit," I gasp when Jori pulls his hand away.

He smiles and gives me a satisfied nod.

"You would have come in handy the last four months," I joke, dropping my gaze to my boot and the magic band it hides around my ankle.

It's on the tip of my tongue to ask the Healer if he can fix scars, but I don't know if they know about that, and I don't want to draw any attention to them if I don't have to.

Jori presses the pad of his finger to my lip and heals it too, before moving on to the bruises on my arms and wrists and then the scratch on my thigh. I shake off my awe and focus.

"They attacked the king's quarters," I continue, looking around the room as though it's suddenly going to morph into my father's. "It was late. I should have been in bed, but I'd been cooped up in the room all day, and I was having fun playing tag with my brothers. My father, his Wing, and a few of the other Syphons were sitting at a big table, going over the plan to announce me and the other children.

"The next thing I knew, insurgents were breaking down the doors. Everyone with a dragon immediately tried to shift, which is when they discovered the Syphons couldn't. The dragons that could grabbed the king and tried to escape with him, but the tower was being attacked from the outside too. We were trapped. Two guards grabbed Brooks, Novak, and Ronin, trying to get them out a different way. I followed, but the guards carrying them were moving too fast, and I got separated. So I did the only thing I could and hid in an armoire."

I don't tell them that Enslee hid right alongside me. That we held each other and cried, shushing the other when the sobs and terrified gasps echoed too loudly in the small, enclosed space.

"I saw the rebels kill my mother and attack my father. At first, it seemed like they wanted to take him somewhere. They were talking about transports and how to hide him, but there was an argument. Then, out of nowhere, one group of insurgents killed the others. After that, they went hunting for the queen and the scions."

I clench and unclench my fists, blinking away the emotion that tries to rise and blur my vision.

"They killed Brooks, Novak, and Ronin, one by one in front of my father and their mother." I clear my throat, trying to dislodge the lump that's forming there. "They saved my father for last."

The room is silent, like everyone's afraid to move or even breathe. I drop my head and force myself to get the rest out.

"Thrashers held him down. Channelers drowned him over and over again. Burners tortured him with acid and fire. Then they literally ripped him apart. A Shield warded the room to give them time and protection. Wyverns and sorcai helped attack the rookery, but it was dragons who barbarically and systematically snuffed out the lives of my kindred that night."

Condemnation and ire pervade the look I level at all of the drakes as I look around. My eyes meet Aeson's and then Lorn's, and for a moment, I let my mask drop. Let them see the full extent of the anguish and anger coursing through me.

I could tell them about all the hours Enslee and I have spent going through vid feeds and pictures, trying to identify which members of The Horde were responsible. If they only knew the way we've agonized over every detail, recounting each one to the other survivors until none of it even feels real anymore. But they've peeked through enough of my cracks for one night. It's time to retreat.

"In one night, almost everyone who knew I existed died. It saved my life. No one knew to look for me. No one knew I saw everything. No one knew I survived. I wish I could tell you who killed my father, but they were in full scale armor, their faces covered. I didn't grow up here and have no idea who they were. The Horde doesn't have a database showing what each dragon looks like in full armor. That's the only way I could try to find them."

I scan the different colors of scale armor in the room as I negotiate with my exhaustion, promising just a little longer and then I'll give in. I study one pair of bright blue, princely eyes and then the other as I wrap a thick layer of indifference around me and make myself more comfortable on the plush bench.

"Any more questions on why I've stayed away from The Horde all this time, or does that about cover it?"

CHAPTER 13

So where have you been for the last sixty-two years?" the drake in the bloodred armor asks.

"Who are you? Can I get some introductions at least before all of you continue to paw through every facet of my life?" I ask, aiming a critical look at Lorn. "You're being a shitty host."

He rolls his eyes at the gibe.

"That's Farrow," Aeson supplies, gesturing to the drake with the dark complexion and deep red armor. "Ogdan, Tove, Jori, Chastain, and Blay you met in Lairwood."

My attention moves to the Shield from the lirocar, the one in purple armor with long golden-brown hair and gray eyes. Blay. He gives me a friendly smile and doesn't seem bothered in the slightest when I don't offer one back.

Aeson waves behind him at a Channeler and then over to the big Thrasher guarding him. "This is Gatlin and Karis. I have two other members of my Wing, Herm and Sondar, who you'll meet when they return from assignment."

I find myself wondering what kind of *assignment* would have pulled two members of Aeson's detail away, but I let the question float off and settle somewhere else in my head when Lorn starts introducing members of his Wing.

"This is Nils and Urser," the heir tells me, nodding his head at the two drakes in burnt-orange scale armor that are flanking him. "That's Razeer and Atol." He gestures to another Shield and a Channeler. Both are positioned behind everyone else, their bodies angled to show that one is guarding a door over by the sitting area and the other is keeping an eye on the archway across from him. "You'll meet the rest of my Wing another time."

"See, that wasn't so hard," I snark while slinging an impudent glower at both scions. "I'm Ever," I offer politely and then look over at Farrow to answer his question. "Where I've been for the last sixty-two years is safe; the rest is none of your business."

The affable gleam in Farrow's black gaze gutters out. His countenance shifts to something that's more confrontational, and it's clear this isn't a male who's used to being denied or defied.

"The Scorch?" Aeson asks, but it sounds less like a question and more like a conclusion.

Shock pings through me, and my head snaps so fast in the commander's direction I feel and hear my neck pop. A satisfied little smirk slinks across the asshole's face, but I already know I fucked up and want to deck myself.

Rookie fucking move, Ever!

I school my features and study Aeson as he ambles casually from the archway toward his brother.

"Don't look so surprised, Claws. It wasn't that hard to figure out when you know what pieces to put together. We've been getting reports of wyvern activity in that area for decades. People still think there's a Reward for Capture order, so they call in sightings. It's never been worth looking into before now."

Raw panic pumps through my veins, but I don't react. We have strong wards in place that keep our camp hidden. No one, not even The Horde, has ever found it, and despite what Aeson's claiming, there are patrols out there who look.

The Scorch is a massive stretch of wasteland. The commander can send his best trackers, but it'll take them forever to pinpoint anything of value, and even if they do, they'll still never get inside. Enslee won't open those doors to them for any reason, not even me.

"You were with wyverns?" Chastain asks, the look on his too-pretty face a mix of bewilderment and disgust. "But they betrayed us."

I scowl over at him. "Not all of them."

"Enough of them did," Lorn argues.

I throw up my hands in exasperation. "I can say the same thing about dragons."

"Yes, your feelings about The Horde have been crystal clear, but I don't see that same level of resentment for the other Arcs who turned on the Syphons. Why is that?"

"Oh, there's no love lost between me and the Tainted, I promise you that, but I'm not going to condemn—"

"Who are the Tainted?" Aeson interrupts, and I draw back, stunned.

"Tainted sorcai," I answer, confused. "They're sorcai, but their magic is darker. It stinks like it's unnatural or going bad somehow. It changes them, makes them different. That's who I escaped from in Newden."

"I thought blood brokers had you?" Ogdan inserts, suspicion thick in his tone.

I let loose an irritable huff, confused as to how they're not getting it. "The blood brokers work for the Tainted," I explain, expecting the light to finally go off, but instead, I'm met with looks of uncertainty and puzzlement. Realization clamors like a gong in my head, and apprehension floods my system. "How do you not know about the Tainted?"

Lorn and Aeson share another one of those annoying cryptic looks, but I'm reeling too much to give a fuck about what it could mean. There's no way The Horde doesn't know about a psycho group of magic users who kill, kidnap, and drain Arcs? Their victims are the people the dragons are responsible for protecting. The Syphons have known about the Tainted for a while now. Are these dragons that out of touch with what's happening in their own territories?

A loud knock rhythmically thuds through the room. I look around, but I have no idea which of the surrounding four doors it might be coming from. Razeer strides to the one he's been watching and opens it. A statuesque woman practically floats in on a sea of ruffles. She gives a respectful nod to Razeer as she passes and then starts to glide our way.

She wears a round headdress made of blush-colored pearls and beads that makes her look even taller than she already is. Her pale pink dress is sleeveless and tight on her torso before cascading into a rippling mass of fluttering fabric that drops to midcalf before spilling into a long train of ruched pleats and tucks behind her. Her honeycomb-yellow eyes are fixed on Lorn, and with each step she takes toward him, my heart starts to hammer harder and harder.

Is this his mate? Am I sitting on her bench in her room and she's here to demand I give it back? I stand, prepared to do just that, but I have no idea where I'm supposed to go. So I do my best impression of a statue and freeze right where I am.

The ruffled goddess stops in front of Lorn and executes a smooth and polished curtsy that I couldn't dream of emulating even if I practiced it for years. The veneration in the female's actions and overall countenance helps to snap me out of my open-mouthed fascination.

"My apologies for the wait, My Scion. How may I serve you today?"

I bite back a snort at the stiff formality, but I must not stifle it completely, because both Lorn and the female look over at me.

"Your name?" Lorn asks emotionlessly.

"Tahir, My Scion," the female answers, even though they're both still staring at me.

Not his mate, then.

"Tahir, everything you see and confirm in this room will stay in this room. If it does not, your life is forfeit. Do you understand?" Lorn queries, but it's more command than question.

"Yes, My Scion. My silence and my discretion are yours to command."

The suggestion dripping all over that statement isn't missed by anyone standing around. A grin sneaks across Chastain's face before he covers it with a hand. And I swear I see a subtle quake of Blay's shoulders, like he's laughing, but his head is down.

Lorn doesn't look amused at all, or interested. "I need you to identify the breed and bloodline of this Arcane. Can you do that, Tahir?"

"Most certainly, My Scion. If it pleases you, I can begin now."

I'm taken aback as Lorn nods and Tahir begins to float in my direction.

This is the Oric?

Flabbergasted, I stare at the stunning female who can't be much older than me. I don't know exactly what I was expecting when Jori mentioned an Oric was on their way, but it certainly wasn't the ruffled vision before me.

I tense as she approaches, my mind going straight to the knives-and-ichor part of the stereotype I had in my head. It's not lost on me that Lorn didn't provide the Oric with any clues about who I am and what I claim to be, and it feels like a test he's hoping we both fail.

"May I read you?" Tahir asks as she draws even with me.

I look up at her and realize that what I thought was a headdress is actually her hair. It's piled on her head in a voluminous sphere that has pearls and other small jewels woven through. The layers of fabric that comprise her dress look as soft as clouds, and I almost have to slap my own hand to keep from inappropriately reaching out to touch it.

"What exactly do you have to do to read me?" I ask hesitantly, fighting the urge to finger comb the snarls out of my hair while trying to smooth the wrinkles out of my soiled stolen clothes.

Tahir reaches into the ruffles of her skirt and pulls out what looks like a thick wand and a porcelain box. She must have pockets hidden within the depths of her cloud dress. Maybe the over-the-top outfit isn't as impractical as I thought. She holds the thick wand up for my inspection.

"I'll scan your form with my sequencer first, and then I'll run a small sample of your blood through my centrifuge." She lifts the small porcelain box in her palm. "Both tests will compile data that will pinpoint breed markers and familial bloodline connections with ninety-three percent accuracy."

"Only ninety-three percent?" I tease, and Tahir smiles.

"Correct. We leave room for the natural evolution of species and also recognize that there might be unidentified genomes and bloodlines that we've yet to add to our records."

I nod as though all of that makes perfect sense. "How does your centrifuge procure my blood?" My throat tightens around the question, and my hands start to get clammy.

If she pulls out a knife, I can't guarantee that I'm not going to end up in someone's lap again for round three of *let's break the Syphon*.

"You just set your finger here." She points to a subtle divot in the surface of the box. "You'll feel a tiny prick and then a slight sucking sensation as the machine procures the sample, and then you're all done."

The bands of dread that were winding around me loosen, and I blow out a relieved breath. I can handle a tiny prick. I snicker at that thought and then get a hold of myself. I thought I'd gotten over my Source-drunk giggles, but maybe they're making a comeback.

"Okay. You can read me, then," I agree, and Tahir's smile blazes even brighter.

"Excellent," she chirps. "If you have any talismans, dampeners, charms, or other magic-imbued items, please remove them now," she instructs, and a pit forms in my stomach.

Tahir must see my face fall, because her honeycomb-colored eyes sharpen and go from vapid and congenial to astute and no-nonsense.

"Before you lie to me and tell me you don't have anything, the sequencer *will* pick up on it. We'll stay here as long as we need to get a clean reading. I'm certain the Royal Wing will happily assist as needed to ensure that happens."

Threat made crystal clear, I scowl up at the Oric before looking around at the determined faces of the surrounding drakes.

"Can everyone leave the room?" I ask, hopeful.

"Not a chance, Claws," Aeson immediately answers.

Tahir giggles. "Don't be nervous; you don't have anything that the scions haven't seen before," she offers sweetly, but I rear back like she just spat in my face.

"That's disturbing as fuck. Never say that again," I admonish. She just looks at me blankly. "I'm not getting naked. I just . . . " I flounder, unsure of what to say . . . how to explain. "If I ask you to turn around, will you?" I look at Lorn, hoping he'll be the more reasonable scion of the two.

"No," Aeson interjects, his blue eyes bristling with challenge, his bearing dark and stormy, like he's itching for a fight.

My glare is fulminating, but he isn't cowed as he squares off with me. Fury unfurls in my chest, but maybe that's a good thing. Maybe it's exactly what I need to face this.

"Fine," I snap, bending over to unlatch my boot. "I tried. If you fuckers lose your shit like the healers in the hospital were terrified you would, good. I'm going to enjoy watching you tear up your own shit."

CHAPTER 14

"What are you talking about?" Lorn demands cautiously, but I ignore him and keep my eyes trained on his arrogant asshole of a brother.

My boot hits the carpeted floor with a soft thud, and several of the drakes immediately pinpoint the magic charm on my ankle. I reach for it at the same time Karis and Gatlin step in front of Aeson, and Nils and Urser pull Lorn back behind them. I run a finger under the smooth metal of the charm until I feel the release. Pinching it, the formerly solid charm separates, and the magic that's been hiding my scars suddenly shatters and disappears as the anklet falls to the ground.

A shocked hiss is the first thing I hear as I straighten and face Aeson and the other drakes. I adopt the same *fuck you* stance that the commander was just aiming at me, ignoring the crescendo of outraged growls and the looks of utter dismay. The weight of their stares is laden with abject horror and distress as they take in the map of what I suffered at the hands of the Tainted.

Out of habit, I run my thumb over my forearm, sighing with relief when I finally feel the scars Wistan carved there. Aeson's thunderstruck gaze tracks the movement, and then a horrified understanding fills his eyes as they slowly lift from all the cuts and slashes marring my skin. My answering stare is razor-sharp daggers and icy contempt. I tell him with a single look exactly where he can shove the savage vehemence and pity now clouding his tempestuous face.

Rage simmers in his depths and smoke starts to stream from his nose. He takes a step closer, but Gatlin tries to stop him. Aeson rumbles a terrifying warning at the other drake, and Gatlin instantly freezes, dropping his gaze and tilting his head to expose his throat in a clear display of submission.

Pandemonium sweeps through the room as Aeson advances on me. Raw, undiluted power pulses out of him, and it sends the drakes already on the brink of a volatile shift careening past the point of no return.

"Who."

Aeson takes another step.

"Did."

And another.

"This."

Tahir scrambles back, and several drakes shout orders for everyone to move out of the way.

"To."

Blay charges. At first, I think he's going to tackle Aeson, but he streaks past, diving for one of the massive archways instead. A mountain-sized purple dragon erupts out of him, the beast launching itself off the outer lip of the tower. An enraged roar reverberates through the dragon-stone floors, walls, and ceiling as Blay's dragon streaks away.

"You."

Aeson is suddenly in front of me, waves of heat pouring off of him like morning mist off the waterfalls that flank this keep. I gasp as his power pools and eddies against me. The sensation is terrifying and somehow exhilarating. It's like holding on to a live wire, knowing it could incinerate me at any moment but not being able to put it down.

Smoke billows out of his nose and mouth with each heaved breath, and his eyes have morphed into the bright blue, predatory stare of his dragon. He reaches for me, but I slap his hand away, still riding the wave of anger his imperious bullshit has caused.

"Don't push him, Ever," Lorn barks in warning as Aeson snarls at my rebuke. "He's balancing on the edge of a frenzy. Don't tip him all the way over."

Instead of listening, I bare my teeth in a snarl at Aeson when he eliminates the space between us altogether. The warning growl rumbling out of me doesn't register in the slightest to the wild hurricane of a drake in front of me. In fact, it only spurs him on, and he answers my resounding threat with a thunderous one of his own.

His chest brushes against mine as he studies my face, drinking me in and swallowing me down. His rage confronts my own. My defiance baits his. We stand, two enemies on a battlefield, neither willing to cede to the other, and somehow, I've never felt more alive than I do right now. I've never felt more seen.

With a bellow that shakes the rookery, a dark blue dragon and then a bloodred one follow after Blay and go plunging off the railless balcony out into the dusky sky. The chandelier above me shakes and clangs, threatening to shatter, but it holds.

It isn't lost on me that the healers in the hospital were right to be wholly terrified of The Horde's reaction to my scars. These dragons don't know me. I'm nothing to them. And yet their response to what was done to me is undeniably visceral.

"How did this happen, Ever?" Lorn demands, his tone razor-sharp and surprisingly pained.

I'm taken aback by the heir's slip of emotion. My mind is warning me that I know better than to trust The Horde, but I'd be an idiot not to notice that there's more going on here than I'm capable of understanding right now.

Aeson reaches for me again, and this time, I let him trace the slashes on my neck with his unsheathed talons. I should probably be afraid. I've seen firsthand what the wrath of a dragon can do, how quickly it can tear the world asunder. But there's something about being in the presence of this primal, raw rage that calls to me. It's as though basking in the physical manifestation of what I can only *feel* inside is exactly what I need to be whole again, even if it's only for a little while.

Instead of my dragon surging forward and battering against the confines of the curse, the opposite happens. That part of me settles and calms, like it knows it's finally home . . . safe, and now it's time to heal and rest.

Aeson pulls me closer and I go willingly. He relaxes infinitesimally when our bodies press together, and he drops his face and rests his forehead against mine. Thick smoke wraps around us, but it isn't choking or cloying. It feels strangely protective, like he needs to shut everything else away and take a moment. As someone who's been there quite a lot lately, I get it.

Hot fingers stroke the scars on my neck and upper chest before dropping down to graze over the ones running down my arms.

I think he's counting them.

"How?" Aeson half rasps, half rumbles.

I sigh and close my eyes, wanting to lock his dragon out, but he nuzzles the tip of his nose against mine, and I give in and look up into his exacting blue eyes.

"Beatings—at least it started that way. He had this special kind of whip he liked to use. That's what's on my back," I explain, and Aeson's hands move from my arms to my shoulder blades, where he traces his way through my pain, one slashed scar at a time. "Eventually he got bored of that and started carving tallies into me. At first, he would do it every time they bled me, like he wanted to keep track of it on my skin. But after a while, it became less about the blood and more about lording his power over me. He'd carve tallies like I was his own personal scoreboard, a walking embodiment of his wins and my losses."

I shake my head and run a thumb over the lines and slashes on my forearm.

"I couldn't shift. I couldn't heal. I couldn't stop him."

My whispered confession mixes with the smoke floating between us. Aeson breathes it in, my pain anchoring his anger.

"Who?" he demands, the solitary word a threat and a promise.

I study him for a moment, taking his measure. I can't decide if he's worthy of my trove of wrongs and reprisals, if he can be trusted to bear the weight of them like I have. Maybe I should continue to hoard all of my hurts, keep everything to myself, but the temptation to share the burden, to put it down for just a little while, is like a siren's song rising through the haze of Aeson's smoke. I know I'm going to end up broken on the rocks for giving in, and yet, I just can't stop myself.

The fluttering in my stomach becomes its own frenzy, but I can't tell if I've trapped butterflies or wasps. My pulse races and my blood burns with rage, with heartache. Before I can change my mind or think better of it, I offer Aeson a broken sliver of myself, wrapped in the name of the bastard who tried to shatter me beyond repair.

"Wistan . . . Wistan Allaire."

CHAPTER 15

Aeson straightens, dropping his head back while sucking in a deep breath. It's as though my admission has freed him from a painful constriction around his chest and now he can properly fill his lungs and breathe again. He keeps me pressed tightly against him—not that I'm trying to go anywhere. A rumble of approval rolls out of the commander, the bolstering sound wrapping around my tormentor's name and carving Aeson's dominion across his destiny like a dooming slash cutting through the tallies of Wistan's future.

Aeson doesn't fill the nonexistent space between us with declarations of what he's going to do to the Tainted fuck who hurt me, or paint pretty promises of how he'll fix the unfixable. He doesn't need to. I know exactly what it means to hand over a name like this to a guy like the commander. The vow of reckoning is silent, but it's there all the same.

Part of me wants to get lost in the depths of that unspoken promise. It'd be easy to read into it, to wade around in the possibility that's suddenly swirling around us like Aeson's smoke. The appeal is most certainly there. I could turn my brain off and let my baser instincts slip lust-first into the haze of dragon pheromones and the dreamy defender-of-my-honor shit that's growing thicker by the second. But falling for a dragon, let alone Aeson Noctis, is about as smart as an injured gazelle sidling up to a lion for a cuddle. I'm, without a doubt, going to get eaten, and probably not in the way I'd enjoy.

No. I need to stick to the surface of what he's offering and not dive any deeper. People extend a helping hand for a myriad of reasons, and not many that make the list are completely altruistic. The commander is feeling protective, maybe even a little possessive, but that could have everything to do with him and absolutely nothing to do with me. Is it genuine interest, or is it just a carefully orchestrated and expertly executed plan?

For all I know, the hospital already told the scions all about my injuries and scars, and now they're using them to their advantage. It wouldn't be the worst plan: catch me at a vulnerable moment, then get me feeling all warm and fuzzy with the protective-dragon schtick. Aeson turns up the charm and taps into some of his undeniable appeal, but just enough to get me nice and chatty until I'm singing like a canary in pursuit of that dick.

If I don't fall for Aeson's tune, I suspect Lorn will step in and try his hand at playing me. The two have already started stacking the chips in their favor with the rescuing, the comforting, the touching, and the lap sitting. It's a good plan—I'd consider it myself in their shoes—but it's going to take more than a pretty face, a monster cock, and an unspoken promise of beating up the big bads in my life to get me to slice myself open and spill all of my secrets.

Aeson looks down at me, his dragon still staring out of his eyes. He lifts a hand from the scars he's been tracing on my back and pushes strands of my tangled hair off my shoulder. I'm tempted to tilt my head and see what he might do with better access to my throat, but whatever's at play here, I need to make sure it's working *for* me and *not* working me over.

It's time to meet fire with fire.

Deciding *if the commander can touch, I can touch too*, I lift my hand and lightly run the tips of my fingers up his forearm. Slowly, I trace each of the connecting plates of his scale armor, the hard ridges hugging the contours of his arms perfectly. I expect his armor to be cold, like metal, but his scales are warm, and there's a subtle texture to them that isn't discernable with the naked eye.

I'm not sure how sensitive the protective plating is, but Aeson must feel something, because a tremor moves through him as my fingers carefully explore. I want to ask him what it's like to wear it or call it forward. Does it feel the same in his drake form as it does when he's a dragon? Did it hurt the first time it appeared after he revealed? But I keep my mouth shut. If they know how eager I am for answers, or how little I know about dragons in general, they'll use it against me.

Aeson's fingers slip behind the back of my neck, and his thumb smooths its way across the line of my jaw. He gently tilts my head, the motion a demand for my eyes to leave the progress of my fingertips on his arm and focus on his face. His vivid blue stare burns with fervor, and his brow is drawn like he's trying to root out exactly what it is about me that has him so ensorcelled.

The stubble on his jaw proves entirely too enticing; I give in and run the back of my fingers across his prickly cheek. He closes his eyes for a breath, and when he opens them, his dragon has receded and I'm staring up into the bright blue gaze of his drake again. His nostrils flare and he scents me as though he's trying to catalog every thought and emotion I might be having while his rage and inner beast start to settle and calm.

Something new heats in Aeson's gaze as he appraises my face. His other palm finds its way to my hip, his hand so large that it skims across the small of my back and coaxes a small quiver from the muscles there.

I offer him a slow, knowing smile, and he watches my mouth like it's a precious flower blooming under the rarest of circumstances. I almost hate to ruin it, but I know I have to.

"Are you done with your mantrum now?" I ask, forcing my hands to my sides and refusing to acknowledge the itch charging through them to explore more of him.

Like ice water to red-hot coals, my question douses the building pyre between us. The growing need in Aeson's eyes sputters, and consternation quickly billows in.

"I thought the *Royal Wing* were the elite of the elite. A few scars shouldn't send the best and brightest The Horde has to offer into an all-out frenzy. You should be careful with that chink in your armor, or someone will use it against you."

Aeson's gaze is a full-blown glower by the time I stop running my mouth, and his hands fall away from my body as he takes a reluctant step back. My words work exactly as intended, which shouldn't bother me, and yet the regret that effervesces through me is unmistakable. Hastily I drop-kick the part of me that wants to reach for the commander's hands and put them right back where they were as he creates even more distance between us.

"Someone like you?" he queries cautiously, like he's being extra careful not to get caught on the sharp tips of my barbed words.

"No," I deadpan, not liking the accusation that flickers across his face. He's looking at me now as though *I'm* the one who invaded *his* space and got all handsy, not the other way around. "But not everyone is as stalwart as me," I add, my offended glare now mirroring his.

A derisive snort slips out of him, and his eyes once again dip down to my lips. "That mouth of yours is going to get you into trouble one day," he warns, but something in his eyes, in his tone, makes it feel more like an invitation than an admonition.

"One could argue it already has," I mutter more to myself than him.

The low hum of agreement he makes slips through my cracks and settles low in my belly. I swallow down the annoying butterflies that try to flutter from my stomach up into my chest and stop myself from running my hand over the scars on my forearm to help anchor me.

Someone purposefully clears their throat. The sound yanks me from the tunnel vision I've had on Aeson and shoves me back into the room with everyone I all but forgot about until now. Chastain, Blay, and Farrow are noticeably missing, but everyone else watches on with a mixture of emotion. I rifle through the upset and pity I see, make note of the fact that Razeer and Urser won't even look in my direction, and zero in on the way Tahir watches Aeson as he retreats until he's once again standing next to Lorn.

"Hey, Oric," I call out, for no other reason than I would like her to get on with the scanning and poking she's here to do so she can fuck off. If there's a little extra growl in my tone, it has everything to do with how tired I am and nothing to do with the way she's drooling over the commander like a fucking gor hound cutting a new set of teeth.

Tahir's head snaps in my direction.

"I'm ready if you are," I tell her, gesturing to the centrifuge and sequencer she's still holding.

"Excellent." She nods, the movement snapping her out of the lascivious thoughts she was obviously just thinking. "Are you in possession of anything else that could interfere with your scan?" Her honeycomb-yellow eyes drop to the anklet sitting on the lush white carpet next to my bare foot.

"Nope. The healers only gave me the one."

The Oric's gaze sweeps over me once, seeing for herself if I'm telling the truth. Her eyes pause on the other boot I'm still wearing. With a scoff, I remove it. Straightening, I cross my arms over my chest and arch an eyebrow in challenge. She swallows audibly before daring to step closer. She's noticeably more hesitant than she was before, but I have no idea if it's because she's worried she might spook me or if she's afraid to get too close, like my scars might be catching.

I hold my arms up when she lifts the wand-like sequencer. I don't know if I need to stand like I'm about to be frisked, but she doesn't correct me as she runs the tech stick around my frame. When she's done, she tucks it away into the mass of ruffles encasing her lower half and holds up the centrifuge.

"I suppose it must be some consolation that they didn't destroy your face," Tahir offers amiably as I press a digit to the box resting in her palm. It nips my finger and then sucks a small sample of blood from the pinprick of a wound, just like the Oric said it would. Thankfully, neither sensation triggers any kind of response in me.

For a second, I almost brush off the Oric's presumptive and rude-as-fuck comment, but curiosity gets the better of me.

"Oh, they fucked up my face plenty," I tell her casually, my gaze fixed on her vapid expression while my attention is keyed into Jori. "Turns out that my tears have healing properties and stopped me from scarring there. I tried rubbing them into other wounds, but the blood brokers caught on and stopped me from healing myself that way. Couldn't do much to stop the tears from touching my face though. Lucky me."

Ignoring Tahir's response, I glance over at Jori's pensive face.

Interesting.

Judging by the Render's expression, I gather that the magic-tears thing isn't a typical dragon trait. But it can't be a Syphon thing either, because all of my dragon perks are on lockdown—at least I thought they were.

I open my mouth to ask the Healer about it, but a high-pitched beep rings out from Tahir's ruffles where she stashed the centrifuge. She starts tapping at the rose-gold cuff on her wrist, and a screen pops up. Data that must mean something to the Oric starts ticking across the translucent display, and she studies it intently. After a beat, her brow furrows and her head tilts.

"That can't be right," she mumbles to herself before typing a few things onto the screen and staring at the new streams of data that start to roll across. Tahir's cheeks pinken to a hue that matches her over-the-top dress, and her frustration starts to spill over when she recalibrates the data a third and then a fourth time. Angry yellow eyes narrow in my direction, and an ugly vein perks up in her forehead as she whirls on me. "What did you do to mess with the sequencer?" she demands.

"I thought you said it could tell if I was tricking it?" I point out as the Oric's face grows even redder.

"It can, but—"

"Is it saying I tricked the sequencer?" I interrupt, waving at the screen still floating above her wrist.

"No, but you did. You had to, there's no other way—"

"What does it say, Oric?" Lorn demands regally.

Tahir flinches, shooting me one last scathing look before she turns to the heir.

"My Scion, please forgive me, but she's lying. The reading must have been tampered with somehow—"

"What does it say?" Aeson growls, his patience paper-thin.

A small, frightened squeak sneaks out of the Oric, and I almost feel bad for her. Then I remember that she just called me a liar after insinuating that my body was destroyed because of my scars. And just like that, every ounce of sympathy I might have evaporates.

"B-breed . . . " Tahir stammers. "Dragon, My Scion. It says that she's a dragon. But bloodline . . . her kith . . . " Anger hardens her features, and her gaze goes from honeycomb to a brittle-looking amber. "It's flagging her as a Syphon, My Scion. But that can't be—"

"Thank you, Oric. Your work here is done. I would remind you that everything you witnessed and confirmed in this room stays in this room, or else. You are dismissed."

Tahir's eyes grow wide and her mouth opens and shuts like a water-starved fish. Her shocked stare darts from Lorn to me to Aeson and back again.

"But, My Scion, you don't understand. It says she's a Syphon, but she can't . . . that's not . . . there's mo—"

"You. Are. Dismissed," Lorn decisively barks, the ice in his tone and eyes freezing Tahir's stuttered argument before more can slip out of her mouth.

Her lips clamp closed with alarm, and she flinches when Razeer takes a step away from Lorn's side, striding over to open the door before looking pointedly at the soon-to-be-ejected Oric. Tahir hesitates for another second before her head falls in defeat, and she dips into another smooth curtsy that makes me want to roll my eyes while coughing "kiss ass" at her.

"Yes, My Scion," Tahir submits solemnly, and then she all but sprints for the door, her ruffles swishing noisily in her wake. She shoots me one last vexed glare before disappearing through the doorway, and I quickly add her name to the ever-growing list of assholes I need to watch my back around.

The room is dead quiet as Razeer shuts the door and resumes his place next to Lorn. The drakes all around me look surprisingly dumbfounded. If I didn't know better, I'd say it was because they didn't believe anything I was saying until right this minute. Some of them are *way* better actors than I initially gave them credit for, because I thought a few were definitely on my side.

I sit down on the bench and stretch my arms across the back, making myself comfortable. "Is this a good time for a *told you*, or should I hold off a little longer?"

Lorn scowls at me, but a prickle of unease skitters across the back of my neck when Aeson's pensive gaze stays locked on the rug at our feet.

"Are there others?" Lorn asks after a beat, the question sounding more haunted than I think he realizes.

I shrug. "Maybe."

A palpable hope pulses through the room, one I rush to stomp out before it catches.

"If I survived, who's to say others didn't? But as far as I know, I'm the last of my kindred."

Lorn doesn't even glance in the direction of a Thrasher to confirm what I'm saying is the truth. Not that it would matter. I'm not lying.

I'm also not telling the entire truth.

I *am* the last-born daughter of the Tenebrae line. Enslee, my twin, was born exactly two minutes before me.

I'm not technically the youngest out of all of the survivors, but the other Syphons are kith, not kindred. A pivotal distinction the scions haven't picked up on.

Lorn shakes his head and pinches the bridge of his nose. "It seems the fates have been busy," he mumbles to himself.

"Fuck fate," Aeson and I both whisper angrily at exactly the same time.

Our eyes catch for the briefest of seconds before he looks away. His stare settles on one of the archways and the darkening sky beyond as though it's beckoning him, and I can see he's struggling not to answer.

An ache starts to spread through my chest, throbbing in time with my thrumming heart. I rub at it, drawing small circles over my sternum. A cavern reopens between me and the members of The Horde. They watch me like some apparition they're worried will disappear altogether or coalesce and attack. All of them but one.

His gaze on me shouldn't matter. My interest in his thoughts should be nothing more than a means to an end. His touch should be repulsive. And yet, none of those things are true. Which is a huge fucking problem, because I loathe everything he represents. A fact that should make loathing him and the others easy, but here I stand, my wrong popsicle dripping down my white-knuckled grip as I ponder if I was ever right about anything.

And if I wasn't . . . what the fuck does that mean for me now?

Lorn runs a hand through his white hair, brushing the locks back like he's daring them to disobey. He takes a step forward, squaring his shoulders and lifting his chin.

"Well then, Ever Tenebrae, last of the Syphons. On behalf of King Noctis and The Dragon Horde . . . welcome home."

CHAPTER 16

"Why are you on the floor?" a stiff feminine voice demands.

With an irritated groan, I crack a lid and look up to find Tove staring down at me. Her hands are on her hips, and her upper lip is curled with consternation while she observes the makeshift floor pallet I fashioned out of a fur throw and a super-soft blanket made of something I can't identify but am now obsessed with.

"Something wrong with the bed, Frills?"

My bleary attention drifts to Chastain just as he launches himself into the middle of the dragon-sized mattress and starts flopping around like a headless sidewinder.

"That's not my name," I grouse uselessly, knowing full well there's no escaping it now. I've made my bed and now I have to lie in it, or my floor pallet anyway. Waving a limp hand in the direction of Chastain and the horribly uncomfortable bed, I address both his and Tove's questions. "It's too soft," I murmur before pulling the fluffy blanket over my head and burrowing deeper into the lush fur beneath me.

"Oh no, you don't," Tove grumps, snatching my cozy treasure away and then hastily backing up until she's out of reach so I can't swipe it back. "You've been sulking in here for days. Enough is enough. It's a beautiful morning and we've got shit to do."

I throw an arm over my eyes to block out the bright light and groan. "It's called recovering, Seeder, not sulking. Don't you have a garden to weed or some trees to boss around?"

Chastain snickers and Tove chucks my blanket at him.

"Trees to boss around? Come on, *Lizard*, that's the best you've got?" Tove taunts, and I drop my arm from my face and scowl up at her.

"He laughed," I defend, pointing at Chastain, who's made himself comfortable on the massive bed that makes me feel like I'm slowly sinking in quicksand.

Tove's snort is derisive. "That's not the boon you think it is, Syphon. Chastain's idea of peak comedy is using his air affinity to make fart noises."

Chastain titters unabashedly, and I can't help the small smile that starts to tug at one corner of my mouth.

"Get out of that bed," Tove snaps at Chastain. "If anyone scents you in there, you're going to be a dead airhead."

The Channeler makes a face. "Who'd be sniffing the sheets?"

Tove tosses him a cutting look, and it must communicate something I don't get, because Chastain pales slightly.

"Point made," he promptly concedes, his eyes darting around like he's suddenly very concerned that he touched anything and isn't sure how to get out of the predicament he's put himself in without touching even more.

An unexpected burst of wind moves through the room. It lifts the Channeler out of the bed before blowing around the space to clear as much of the drake's scent away as it can. Chastain floats to where Tove is standing before gently dropping to his feet like a dainty little feather instead of the brick wall of a male that he is. The air once again grows calm and docile, but I look around warily like I expect it to try to sneak up on me.

"You're right, the bed is too soft," Chastain agrees. "But I thought you prissy dragonesses liked all that froufrou shit."

Tove and I scoff in tandem and then glower at each other, offended at the possibility that we might agree on something.

"This prissy dragoness is going to kick your ass in forms later," Tove deadpans, shoving Chastain when his only response is a lecherous eyebrow wag and a cheeky wink.

My ears perk up at the mention of forms. Do they have a gym nearby, or do they go down to Thrasher Keep? Ooh, I wonder if they have any of those fancy simulators I've heard about.

"Why do you look like that?" Tove demands, a guarded look entering her gaze as she surveys me even more shrewdly.

"Genetics," I snark, abandoning my makeshift bed and getting stiffly to my feet.

The floor was better to sleep on than the bed, but it's still a floor. I should be used to it by now, but I feel like that ridiculous girl in the weird bedtime story about breaking into people's houses and complaining about the oatmeal and beds not being right for her. Beggars shouldn't be choosers, and yet my body is whiny as fuck today.

"Not that." Tove rolls her eyes. "You got all cheery just now, why?" She watches me like she's caught me plotting something nefarious instead of seeing a brief flash of enthusiasm that I accidentally let slip through.

"Why are you two here?" I grump, changing the subject and heading for the bathroom.

Tove follows me. Thankfully, Chastain stays where he is.

"We're your guards . . . for now."

My huff of annoyance morphs into a growl of indignation when Tove pushes through the bathroom door before I can shut it in her face.

"I don't need your help taking a piss," I snap at the obnoxious female.

"No, but you must need help cleaning up, or you would have done it already," she claps back, her brown eyes narrowing at the tattered gray skirt and top I'm still wearing and the matted, tangled state of my hair.

I fold my arms over my chest, my irritation deflating until I feel like a pathetic, limp balloon. "I couldn't figure out how to turn the water on, and I didn't have anything to change into," I admit softly, nodding in the direction of the shower that has no handles, heads, or faucets. I even scoured the walls, looking for a control center or hidden screen, but couldn't find anything. I thought maybe it was motion activated, but no amount of jumping around, dancing, or begging encouraged the damn thing to cooperate.

Tove strides confidently toward the long vanity and the massive mirror floating behind it. She taps the glass, and a frame of bright blue and red command buttons lights up along one side. She enters a quick sequence, and a baby waterfall drops out of the ceiling of the large shower stall.

I glare at the falling water. Of course it was the mirror. I should have guessed the key would be in the one place I've been actively avoiding even though I put the charmed anklet from the hospital back on.

"Got it," I chirp, eyeing the control panel on the mirror like we're enemies.

"If you tap the wall to the right, a recess will open with everything else you need. There should be a detangler in there too," Tove offers, pointedly staring at the wild animal pelt that's supposed to be my hair. "You just pour it on and let it sit," she explains after a beat when it dawns on her that if I don't know how to turn on the shower, I probably don't know much about a lot of other things too.

I wish she was wrong. It'd be nice not to feel like a complete idiot around this caliber of tech and all of the fancy things here, but I don't remember any of this from when I was little. We sure as shit don't have stuff like this in The Scorch. We weren't in a position to waste resources or our time on things like vid screens where we could watch shows about how the rich and famous lived or see ads for all the things that might make life easier. Things that we could neither acquire nor afford. I've spent time traveling around the southern territories but never anywhere even close to as nice as this bathroom alone is.

"The Horde's best stylists will be arriving soon. They'll get your *nothing to change into* situation sorted. There's a robe for you there when you're done washing up," Tove tells me, nodding to a folded pile of midnight-blue silk sitting on the vanity.

The idea of a bunch of strangers invading my space with the sole purpose of playing dress-up makes my stomach clench. I wish there was a way I could get out of it, but I need access to Four Tiers and Paragon City, and I'm not going to get it naked—not the right kind of access, anyway.

Tove leaves without saying another word, and I start peeling myself out of my grimy clothes. I stare at the charm on my ankle for a moment, wondering if it's safe to get wet. After a beat, I decide to take it off, just in case. I know the magic powering the charm is going to fade at some point; no need to rush that along if I can help it.

Snubbing my reflection, I move past the mirror and the vanity and step into the shower. The stream of water is the perfect temperature, and I bite back a groan at how good it feels. Instantly I settle into the soothing heat, letting it relax me like this is my normal, everyday routine. It should feel unnatural, and while a lot of it is foreign, I can't deny how right it feels.

Endless food on call, soft blankets, luxurious living quarters, my own personal shower waterfall . . . I could get used to this. If I'd grown up here in Four Tiers, in the keep, like I should have, I *would* be used to this. I would be the scion everyone was curtsying and bowing to. It would be my ass they'd be kissing.

Ens and I would have been soft, cherished, pampered little scionesses. We would have worshipped our brothers and been protected by them. Our mom would have sung us to sleep and tried to keep us in line. Our father would have happily doted on us and spoiled his girls. We probably still would have been hellraisers. Ens and I had a knack for mischief even when we were young, but we wouldn't be killers. We wouldn't be the damaged, desperate survivors we are now. We would have been content, maybe even happy. Instead, our futures and our hopes were snuffed out and everything was ripped away.

And now I need to make sure it doesn't happen again.

I don't know how long I stand under the cleansing spray, letting my thoughts wander and weave around my predicament and what to do about it. Muffled voices on the other side of the bathroom door finally pull me out of my head and get me moving again. I tap on the wall Tove instructed me to, and sure enough, a panel slides open to reveal rows of cleansers, moisturizers, polishers, and a bunch of other things I've never even heard of.

I spot a bottle of detangler and dump half of it on my head. The instructions tell me that microbots in the solution will instantly work through the snarls and mats without needing me to do anything else, so I get to work scrubbing several layers of skin off my body. I pretend all the raised lines and ridges I feel almost everywhere are no big deal, that it doesn't bother me in the slightest that I can't scrub the scars off too.

When the detangler stops tingling, I rinse it out and then wash my smooth, tangle-free hair twice before sealing a repairing serum into the tresses. I force myself out of the luxurious water, even though it's tempting to spend the rest of the day here if for no other reason than to avoid the primping reality that's waiting on the other side of the bathroom door.

The room is thick with steam when I step out of the shower, but a fan kicks on and warm air quickly dries me and my hair while clearing the air of the thick haze. I move to grab the sapphire-blue robe off the vanity and freeze. I blow out a shocked exhale, and my warm, relaxed muscles instantly grow taut and tense.

I knew it would be bad, that it would be startling. I gave Aeson and the others shit for their reaction, but this . . . seeing it head-on with nothing to soften the blow, I instantly know how awful my cruel words and callous judgments were toward Aeson and his Wing the other night.

The familiar stranger in the mirror blinks. I stagger closer to my reflection, my stunned gaze skipping from line to line and row upon row of ruin. The scars are three-inch vertical gashes, all perfectly spaced and even. I wear a collar of them around my throat, and a starburst pattern of them across my shoulders and chest. The marks stop just above my breasts and start again right below. They're etched all the way down my torso, stopping at my hips. They encircle my arms in stacks and mar the entirety of one of my thighs. Wistan had promised to start on my calf the next time we spent time together, but then I got away.

I take in the places the bastard didn't mark, my bikini line, my ass, my boobs, knowing full well his brand of pain would have crossed those lines eventually. Wistan kept the others from touching and taking, but only because he lived for the mind fuck of making me ceaselessly wonder if today would be the day he finally went there.

I stare for so long my vision starts to blur. Not from tears, but because I can't seem to blink or tear my eyes away from what's been done to me. I'm covered in a fucked-up chain mail of torment, the pattern purposeful and planned. It could almost be beautiful if you didn't know the horror of what it was, how it happened.

But I do.

I'll never forget.

I turn to take in my back, catching just a glimpse of the destruction there before I gasp and quickly hide it from view. The scars on my front are methodical, a calculated claiming of sorts done against my will. But my back, that's what happens when Wistan loses control. That is raw fury and devastating havoc.

I'm marked by both aspects of the Tainted fuck, the calm control and the raging monster.

And now I'll never stop seeing *him* when I look at *me* . . . just like he wanted.

With a keening snarl, I smash my fist into the center of my reflection. The mirror spiderwebs from the impact and then shatters. My knuckles split on contact, and blood speckles the fragments of my ruined image before they go smashing across the counter and explode on the ground. I bite back the roar that wants to rip from my throat and close my eyes against the pain of needing to shift but not being able to. I would give anything to rip through this body and become a massive, enraged, terrifying dragon right now, and yet I'm forever fucking stuck with the horrors etched into the weak, fragile skin of my drake.

"What in the fae-cursed fuck is going on?" Tove demands as she throws the bathroom door open and storms in.

She takes one look at me, the broken mirror, and then my fist, and her anger quickly dims with understanding. She doesn't say a word as she grabs a towel off a shelf and hastily wraps it around my hand. She plucks the folded robe off the counter, shakes off the shards of glass, and then drapes it around me. I don't say anything as she carefully feeds my wrapped limb through a long sleeve that drapes almost to the ground. I slip my uninjured hand through the other arm before Tove belts everything together around my waist.

Glass crunches under her boots as she moves, and something about the sound helps me keep my shit together. It's as though I don't want to hear her stepping on the broken shards of my soul the way she's stepping on the shattered splinters of the mirror, so I keep my fractured pieces right where they are.

Chastain pops into the doorway, concern swimming in his brown eyes. "What happened?"

"Get Jori," Tove orders instead of answering his question.

"Don't," I cut in, and both of their agitated gazes snap to mine. "It'll stop bleeding soon. It's no big deal, and what's a few more scars anyway?" I add, but it comes out less carefree and more despondent than I mean it to.

Tove shakes her head and grumbles something unintelligible as she straightens in front of me, her determined stare demanding my attention. "I understand that help might be a foreign concept to you, but your stubbornness is only going to hurt you here."

I try to cross my arms in front of my chest, but the towel around my hand makes it awkward, so I abort the move.

"Statements like that only make me want to dig my heels in more," I tell the female.

"I know, which is why I'm going to do something I don't normally do, which is explain what you're up against instead of simply forcing you to comply for your own obstinate good."

Tove wraps another layer of the towel around my hand when she notices I'm starting to bleed through the one that's there. She nods at Chastain, who then lifts a fist to his mouth. A small vortex of air forms in the Channeler's palm, and he talks into it before blowing the tiny tornado off his hand and out of the room, probably in search of Jori.

"You need to understand some things about the world of dragons, Frills," Tove starts. "A lot changed after the wyvern rebellion. King Tenebrae's death rocked our foundations and destabilized The Horde more than the outside world knows. King Noctis has done everything he can to bring us back together, to give the illusion that there's still a united front amongst the dragons, but it hasn't been easy, and his position isn't nearly as secure as it should be.

"The minute you step out of this room, you are going to be in the thick of it. You're not facing off with the nobles just yet, but don't dismiss any interactions you have from here on out as unimportant. It may only be stylists and seamstresses in that room . . ."

She gestures to the open door and the quiet murmur of voices that can be heard through it.

"But each of them dresses and serves other kiths, and they won't hesitate to pass along whatever gossip they can collect about you to enhance their position or someone else's. If you walk out of this room injured, they're going to notice that you aren't healing.

"Your existence alone is going to rattle the powers that be, so don't let your pride or ignorance become a weakness they can exploit. Don't paint a larger target on your back than the one that's already there."

"Do they know who I am?" I ask, reaching for the charm on the vanity and bending down to re-secure it around my ankle.

"No," Tove answers evenly. "The king has called a Convocation for next week. I believe he intends to Name you there, but we don't expect your secret will last that long. We're not hiding you or what you are, but we're also not shouting it from the rooftops either."

"The fact that you're staying in this room should give the busybodies and spies plenty to scuttle around about for a few days," Chastain adds before flicking his wrist. All of the broken glass on the ground lifts off the floor and countertop and then rides a gentle breeze into a bin in the corner.

I marvel at the simple show of power, the vanity and floor once again clean and safe to traverse. "Show-off," I mutter, and Chastain chuckles.

"My affinity is good for more than just fart noises and blow jobs. You should see what I can do between your—"

Tove slaps the back of Chastain's head, cutting off whatever inappropriate thing was about to slip out of his mouth.

"What was that for?" he demands, rubbing the back of his skull.

"Do you have a death wish?" she asks with a glare.

"What? No," he stammers, once again looking confused.

"I swear, Wind-for-Brains, it's a good thing you're pretty and know how to follow orders. How you've survived this long in life is truly a mystery," Tove grumbles, just as Ogdan and Jori strut in through the bathroom door.

Ogdan's gray eyes sweep the room, landing on my towel-covered hand and the way Chastain is rubbing the back of his head.

"You punch him?" the Burner asks, amused, as he stops just inside the door and lets Jori pass him.

"No, she picked a fight with a mirror and lost," Tove informs him as she steps back to give Jori access to me.

I glare over at the prickly female. "And here I thought we were bonding."

She rolls her eyes.

"Come on, Tove," I tease. "You know you want to braid each other's hair and giggle about our crushes. You don't have to act tough just because the guys are here."

Tove shoots me an unamused look and runs her palm purposefully over her buzzed hair. "I don't giggle," she deadpans.

Jori huffs an amused sound and starts to unwrap the towel around my hand. He holds the blood-splotched cloth out to Ogdan, who takes it and instantly lights it on fire. I watch the red flames crawl up the edges of the towel, greedily consuming the bloody material until there's nothing but a small pile of ashes, which he brushes into the garbage to join the pieces of the broken mirror that Chastain already dumped there.

"Who's guarding the commander if all of you are here?" I ask, waving away the lingering envy I feel over the way they adeptly and all too casually use their affinities.

Ogdan tosses me a wide smile. "I'll let the commander know you're downright distraught over his safety, but worry not, Kindred, the rest of our Wing is with him."

I choke on air at the unexpected term of endearment.

"We aren't family," I insist, taken aback.

Ogdan's smile grows. "Aye, not by blood maybe, but us gingers have to stick together," he counters, flipping the ends of his shoulder-length burgundy hair, which is free of battle braids today.

My hand warms as Jori sandwiches it between his, the cuts on my knuckles already starting to disappear with the wash of his healing magic.

"The peanut gallery out there suspect anything?" Tove asks Ogdan.

"Nope. We were already escorting a last-minute addition up here when Chastain's summons found us. They're out there tittering and placing bets on who the commander's mate might be."

Once again the air gets caught in my throat, and I have to fight it to breathe. I cough and scowl over at the other drakes. Chastain mentioned something earlier about staying in this room and it giving the gossips something to gnaw on for a bit, but I got distracted by his affinity and didn't think about what he was saying until now.

I'm in a mating suite . . . Aeson Noctis's mating suite. The stylists probably think they're here to compete for the chance to make my wedding dress.

"Who's winning?" Tove inquires, a spark of mirth flickering over her features as I slap at my chest and gasp for air.

"Dasha," Ogdan says as he starts ticking off his fingers.

"Oh please, like Aeson would ever," Tove retorts caustically.

"Rosalin."

"Only if the king ordered it," Chastain harrumphs.

"And Priya," Ogdan finishes.

"Interesting." Tove hums thoughtfully. "I didn't know she'd thrown her horns in the ring."

"You can wash the blood off now. You're good to go," Jori announces, and it takes me a second to realize what he's saying and that it's directed at me.

I look down to find my hand is fixed. The only evidence that anything happened are the streaks of dried blood on my knuckles and fingers. Reeling, I turn around and do as I'm told. I study the bloody water as it circles the drain and disappears. It feels alarmingly symbolic.

"I can't go out there," I whisper as the water turns off, and I spin to face the drakes.

Jori offers me a clean towel, and I take it from him and start angrily drying my hands.

"They're going to think I'm Aeson's Bonded," I point out as though no one else has realized it.

Tove smiles, and all kinds of alarm bells start clanging in my head.

"I know," she chirps, her smirk spreading until her whole face is alight with glee. "They're going to shit kittens when you walk out. The circling harpies will be losing it within the hour. It's going to be great."

"But I'm not his mate," I argue.

The Seeder shrugs like that's nothing more than an insignificant detail and holds no bearing on what's happening here, but something in her eyes almost seems to contradict the action.

"They don't need to know that," she assures me. "And before you go freaking out, Frills, remember what I told you. You're a target and you need protection. This . . . " She gestures to the other Wing members and then to the room itself. "Is a good way to protect you until the king can announce what's really going on. Don't let your pride get you killed, *Syphon*."

The way my kith designation falls from her lips is both a warning and a threat. An unnecessary one at that, because I'm all too aware of exactly what's at stake here.

"If it makes you uncomfortable, you don't have to tell them you're his mate. Just don't correct them when they assume it," Jori offers, compassion warming his bronze features.

"And Aeson agreed to this?" I ask, a kaleidoscope of butterflies coming to life in my stomach as I wait for the Healer to respond.

"It was his idea," Tove assures me.

My gut lurches at her answer, and once again, instead of those words making me feel better, they throw me even more off-kilter. They do confirm my theory, however, that what happened the other day with Aeson must have been an act.

The question is, for who?

Not his Wing; they clearly know what's up, and if the commander's Wing is in the loop, then Lorn's Wing probably is too. If the performance was just for me, they wouldn't be telling me all of this, so it must have been for the Oric.

Lorn warned Tahir to keep her mouth shut, but he must have known she wouldn't. If that's true though, they'll be expecting her to blab about the whole Syphon thing and not just about the way Aeson reacted to me, and that contradicts what Tove was just saying.

Puzzlement pools through me as I try to work out all of the angles and see the game the scions are playing, but none of the pieces match up exactly right, leaving me even more bewildered.

Ogdan claps his hands and then rubs them together in eager anticipation. The sound jolts me from my haphazard thoughts and shoves me front and center back into the shit show that's about to go down. My heart speeds up and my chest tightens as the others drop their dignified, no-fucks-given, Royal Wing masks in place.

Ogdan sweeps a hand toward the door and gives me a brazen look that I swear is taunting me with *the easy way, or the hard way?*

"After you, Frills," he tells me gregariously, but all it does is make me want to deck him in the face. "Let's get this show on the road."

CHAPTER 17

Help. The word, the offering, the act itself, can be a surprisingly divisive thing. There have been times in my life where I treated the notion like a venomous threat, and others where I saw it for the lifeline it was. It took me a long time to accept that needing help wasn't a reflection of weakness or some sort of failing on my part. Knowing that you can't do everything alone, that no one is meant to, takes strength and fortitude.

I've learned many valuable lessons at the hand of someone else's support or assistance, but today isn't going to be one of those days. Maybe it's the sniping I can hear jostling back and forth in the other room, or the shit-eating grin on Tove's face, the one she keeps trying to tame only for it to creep back in place like an irritating rash that just won't go away. Or perhaps it's because I'm about to officially step back into a world I'm not prepared for and pretend to stake a claim on a dragon I have zero interest in claiming.

Fucking? Sure, why not.

Claiming? Not for all the magic in Drameric.

However, as annoying as the Seeder is, she's right. If Enslee were here, she'd be giving me the same lecture about how I can't let my pride or my aversion to The Horde screw things up. If this is my way in, if this is how I find what we need, I'll play along. Regardless of all the ways it's going to chip away at my self-respect and more than likely my sanity.

"Here we go," Chastain mumbles just as he walks through the doorway in front of me.

I fill my lungs with one last fortifying breath, and then it's my turn. My face is blank of all emotion, my shoulders square, and my bearing as regal as I can manage wearing nothing but a silk robe, a charm to hide my scars, and a hefty chip on my shoulder.

The room immediately falls silent as the members of Aeson's Wing stride out from the bathroom, and I can practically feel people straining to look past the guards to get a peek at whoever is behind them.

The sleeves of my robe drag on the ground, a train of midnight-blue silk extending several paces behind me as I step out from between the four guards and finally let the room see me. No one gasps or reels back, but I sense shock and confusion pulse through the room all the same. I stand like some statue built for worship and stare at the newcomers and their pious offerings just as intently.

Standing amidst dozens of floating racks of garments are four drakes, a kyba, a griffon shifter, and—I scent in the direction of the man to make sure I'm right—a human . . . which is a surprising addition. No one bows, but they do drop their eyes and chins for a moment in deference before their curious gazes are once again drinking me in. The sitting area of the suite has been rearranged to make room for the visitors and their wares. One plush chair is sitting front and center, and I figure that's where I'm meant to perch while they do whatever they're here to do.

No one says a word as I make myself comfortable, careful to pull part of my train over my ankle with the charm on it. As soon as I look up, two drakes step forward. They both stop suddenly and glare over at the other.

"Seniority says I go first, Seza," the drake on the left snaps, the boxy periwinkle dress she has on glimmering in the late morning light.

"Perhaps, but my client list is much longer, Bettany, which means I'm entitled to first pitch," Seza answers, the pleats layering her floor-length gown fluttering with each irritated breath.

If I had to guess, she's the one who created the outfit Tahir was wearing the other night.

Both females try to step forward again, and the racks floating behind them crash together with a clang. Instead of doing anything about the squabbling, I quickly look over the dresses they have. Not finding anything I think might work for me, I move on to the racks of clothes that belong to the other stylists and designers in hopes of spotting something practical.

It's a sea of geometric-shaped tops and bottoms, ruffles galore, glimmering fabrics that gleam and preen for attention, capes, a whole rack that looks like a garden upchucked all over it, and several more floating displays packed to the brim with even more impractical . . . dresses.

"Does anyone have pants?" I ask, and the arguing in front of me pauses. "Preferably the kind with reinforced knees or a layer of hidden armor sewn in?" I try when everyone just stares at me like I'm speaking a different language.

The human starts to step forward and then balks when both Seza's and Bettany's heads snap in his direction, their glares incinerating. Another drake takes it upon herself to maneuver in front of the human as though keeping him from sight will cause me to forget he ever existed in the first place.

"So sorry, uh . . . " The drake trails off in search of what to call me. Her blue eyes dart to the guards imploringly, but no one takes pity on her and provides her with a name or a title. "Dragoness," she finally fills in, but it rings with uncertainty when her nostrils flare and she scents me. "I've brought the latest fashions taking Four Tiers by storm. You'll be the talk of the keeps and the envy of all. If you'll just allow me to show you—"

"Any of the latest fashions include pants?" I ask, cutting the female off just as she calls forward a rack of dresses that look like they're made of strips of seaweed.

"I don't understand," Seza clucks testily.

I turn to her. "You don't know what pants are?"

Her eyes narrow infinitesimally before she gets a hold of herself. "You'll be dressing for royal functions, won't you? Public appearances? Dinners? Important announcements?" the female hedges.

I shrug, and I swear I hear one of the guards behind me snicker quietly.

"Is there a rule against pants at those kinds of things?" I inquire innocently, despite my patience starting to wear thin.

"Those kinds of things?" Seza repeats, slightly scandalized. "A rule?" she goes on, her gaze, like the other female's, searching the faces of the guards behind me for help. "Dragoness, I dress Arsenna Dacre and her kindred, the Isidores, Varuca Cesarini and the entire Cesarini line, just to name a few of the prominent dragons that trust my expert guidance. But, I promise, not one of them will hold a candle to you under my care and tutelage. Let me show you some designs I've been working on that I think will be perfect for what you *need* . . . " she coos at me as though lording a few noble names over my head will put me back in my place.

I smile sweetly at the female, and she mirrors it, taking a step closer, wrongly scenting victory.

"Seza, is it?" I ask.

An arrogant gleam enters her eyes, and she nods, aiming for demure but missing it by a mile—probably because she shoots a nasty sneer at Bettany while she's doing it.

I lean forward, the saccharine grin never leaving my face. "What I *need* are some fucking pants. Stop name-dropping like some naughty puppy that's piddling all over the carpet. I don't care who you dress or what *you* think I should wear. Do you have what I want or not?"

"I do," a silvery voice declares as the human man steps out from behind the drake that tried to block him. "Not with me, dragoness," he corrects when my eyes move to the clothing behind him. "But I can get what you're looking for."

Bettany snorts, and the obnoxious sound tugs on my last thread of restraint.

"How did you even get in here, Azo?" the female demands.

The human man glowers over at her. "I was invited, just like you."

"A mistake, I'm sure?" the griffon shifter mocks.

"Enough," I bark out, and the room goes silent.

"What's your name?" I ask the human, who seems to deflate a little.

"Azo Endebry, dragoness. I'm a representative of designer Fenox Lael."

It's clear in the way he says the name that he expects some kind of reaction from me, but whoever Fenox is, it's not ringing any bells.

"Very well. Azo, stay, the rest of you can go," I order.

"You can't be serious," both Seza and the kyba exclaim in harmony.

Several other trumpets of dismay fill the room as Ogdan and Tove step around me to escort everyone out. I'm tempted to trip Tove as she passes, but I manage to wrangle the desire and behave myself. I sit in my plush chair and pretend to be important while the guards herd the whining group and their racks. I'm pretty sure Bettany hits Ogdan with hers on purpose, earning her a warning growl from the Burner, which I'm pretty sure has the female shitting in her shiny dress.

Quickly and efficiently, the room is cleared and I return my attention to the human. His presence here is curious but ultimately none of my business, so I don't bother voicing any of the nosey questions flitting around in my head.

"How long will it take to get me what I need?" I ask the man, who looks a little surprised to still be standing here.

"Fenox can have some custom designs for you by tomorrow, maybe even the end of day, depending on what you want. She'll need to take measurements, and she'll draw up some sketches when you meet and discuss exactly what it is you'd like."

"Perfect, how soon can she be here?" I ask, feeling better already.

Azo pales and suddenly looks panicked.

Alarm shoots through me, and I turn to Ogdan, confused by the human's reaction. "What am I missing here?" I press when it's clear I've done something to upset the poor creature.

Ogdan sighs. "Fenox isn't allowed to travel to Four Tiers."

"Piss off the wrong duke?" I tease in an effort to lighten the mood and help the human stop fidgeting, but it only seems to make it worse.

"Fenox Lael is a wyvern. She can't cross into Horde territory. It's a death sentence for any wyvern that tries," Ogdan politely supplies.

Knots form in my throat, and an icy chill spills through my veins.

Why does this suddenly feel like a trap, one I didn't know I'd stepped into until now?

Yes, I grew up around wyverns, but those were trusted members of my mother's guard. Not condemning them for what happened to my parents is not the same as seeing *all* wyverns sympathetically. Most of the culprits that participated in the rebellion were caught and punished, but I guarantee there were wyverns that slipped through the cracks and slid under the radar. I have zero interest in giving any of them another opportunity to kill a Syphon who stumbles into their midst.

"If you want to work with Fenox, you'll have to go to the Wyvern Den," the Burner adds, like it's no big deal.

Well, shit. I was afraid he was going to say that.

I stare at Ogdan for a moment and then look over at the other three Wing members in the room. None of their faces give anything away, but the dread pooling in my chest has me on high alert. Didn't Ogdan say he and Jori were escorting a last-minute addition here when they were summoned? I'd wager my left tit it was this Azo guy.

Outside, I'm as calm as can be, but internally, I'm reeling and trying to figure out what to do. I was wrong about the Noctises not wanting to take me out. They just didn't want to get their hands dirty. It's probably why I still haven't met the king. Why waste your royal time when you know the problem is going to be dealt with shortly? And what better way to take care of a little Syphon problem than to let the wyverns finish what they started all those years ago?

"Okay, when can we go?" I ask evenly, refusing to let even the faintest pitch of panic seep into my tone.

They got me with this one, but I'm not going to let them know I'm on to them.

"It's still early. We can go now if you want," Tove answers, just as nonchalantly.

I swallow down my trepidation and rise from my chair with a nod.

Fuck.

I'm going to need weapons.

CHAPTER 18

A butter knife.

I'm going into battle with a fae-damned butter knife.

Two, to be exact, not that it makes me feel any better about just how fucked I am. And what's worse, I'm in a dress. One I can barely move in, which feels strategic on The Horde's part, but I couldn't insist on leaving my room in nothing but that silk robe without drawing some serious questions. I can't afford questions from the Wing members right now. I need them to think I'm oblivious, that I haven't put two and two together and tucked the answer into each one of the boots I'm wearing.

At least the boots fit and they're relatively comfy. I suppose I have that going for me, because running is probably the only way I'm going to make it out of this assassination attempt alive. The butter knives sure as fuck aren't going to cut it, quite literally, but maybe they can buy me a bit of a head start.

I'm so screwed.

"Nervous?" Farrow asks, his black eyes studying my face for a beat before dropping to where my hands are clenched in my lap.

I look down and take in the white-knuckled knot of fists I'm making and force my hands to relax.

"I don't like . . . " I hesitate for a beat, trying to figure out what to say. "Flying," I finally supply.

The lirocar we're in banks right, and I grab the seat to keep from tilting over. The interior configuration of this lirocar is different from the one I rode in before. The two captain's chairs that were in the middle of the previous airboat are noticeably missing in this one, leaving only the front and back rows of seats.

I'm currently sandwiched between Farrow and Karis, who Ogdan insisted should join us for this happy little adventure. Jori is up front in the passenger seat, and Tove, Ogdan, and Chastain are all sitting across from me, doing an admirable job of pretending like they're not plotting my imminent demise.

I'm not fooled.

Tove smirks and shakes her head. "You don't like flying? Interesting fear for a *dragon*," she gibes.

My answering smile is mocking. "Try doing it without wings. Let's see how you feel about it then."

I can feel Karis laugh next to me, but no sound actually comes out of him, which is slightly unnerving, not that there's much about the colossal drake that isn't. My entire left side is pressed against his dark brown scale armor, which would be great if he had any weapons I could try to lift. Of course, he doesn't, so I just get to sit here, uncomfortable and awkward instead.

I sigh and toss a few elbows into the sides of the drakes pressing in on me, demanding more room. Neither of them moves, but I swear I feel Karis chuckle again.

Paragon City flashes by outside the lirocar's windows, but I can't get out of my head long enough to appreciate the view. The sights are probably something to marvel over when you're not plummeting to your death. However, I'm pretty sure I'm driving to mine right now and therefore can't muster the appropriate amount of appreciation.

"Why are you all broody? I thought you'd be fine dealing with wyverns since they brainwashed—oops, I mean raised—you?"

"Tove," Ogdan admonishes.

"I'm not being broody," I defend, internally chastising my lack of awareness over what my body language and silence might be broadcasting. "And you don't know me well enough to say otherwise, so go lick a leaf."

Chastain whistles and makes a face like I've gone and done it now. He leans away from Tove, who's sitting next to him, like he's hoping to stay out of the line of fire.

"No, I'm not buying it," Tove counters, wagging a finger at me. "Something happened back at the keep with the human. You've been squirrely ever since."

"I have not been squirrely," I argue.

"Totally squirrely," Farrow interjects, an easygoing smile stretching wide across his handsome face. His red scale armor looks brighter in the light of day. His dark skin is flawless, and his black eyes glitter with a touch of delight and a dash of defiance.

I toss a glare his way, which only serves to make the teasing twinkle in his eyes brighten.

"So, what is it? Is it the wyverns? The mate thing? Or did something else happen?" Tove inquires, like she actually gives a shit.

She's good. I'll give her that.

I stare at the Seeder for a moment, studying her. She's pretty, but it's almost as though the shaved black hair and the ever present *get fucked* look in her brown eyes are an effort to downplay or diminish her allure. Anyone observing her and the others from afar would take one look at the dark green scale armor and the black vines of her dragon mark that wrap around her fingers and hands and dismiss her as a threat. Karis or Ogdan would be the obvious choices based on size and kith alone, but Tove sees entirely too much, and in my opinion, *that's* infinitely more dangerous.

I quickly sort through and dismiss a handful of things to say in response, but with the two Thrashers next to me, I need to be careful how I traverse this. I can't tell the full truth, but it needs to be enough of the truth not to flag me as a liar or spark any more of their suspicion.

I drop all pretenses and lean forward, using all of my dulled drake senses to read everyone around me just in case they try to pull something. I don't know what I could do to stop them, but I'll at least sense it coming.

Tove's relaxed but antagonistic mien falls away, and she mirrors my movement, her body suddenly primed and tense.

Good. We're taking each other seriously now.

"I want weapons," I tell the Seeder, hoping it will throw her off just enough to keep her from sniffing around anything else.

A flicker of satisfaction moves through me when surprise alights across her face.

"Why?" she asks, confused, like the thought has never crossed her mind. As a fully revealed dragon, it probably never has.

"What weapons?" Karis interjects, which throws me off because I kind of had a theory that he might be mute.

I stare at the Thrasher, his voice more melodic than it has any right to be. The sudden urge to ask him to tell me a bedtime story or to read aloud one of the dirty books Boshle, my Flight's medic, is always reading trickles into my mind. I smother the thought with a heavy helping of good sense. No wonder the Thrasher is so quiet. If the male was a chatterbox, he'd probably have a flock of groupies dogging his every step, hanging on every word and grunt.

He looks at me expectantly, like he's genuinely curious about what I'd arm myself with if given the choice. Craith would like this drake. He always said you could tell a lot about a person based on their weapon of choice.

I start ticking off a list on my fingers. "Bone blades, Zurki made, if I can get them, but anything from the Bone Isles will do. A pulse bow and two XD pistols, fourth gen, preferably, with thigh holsters. A belt of PHaSR grenades. Half a dozen batiirien spikes. A grappling gauntlet. A few fang breakers—you know, the ones that look like necklaces," I tell them, circling my throat with my pointer finger.

"Fuck the fae, are you robbing a blood bank with all that?" Farrow asks, his dark eyes wide with shock.

I shrug. "I'm game if you are."

Ogdan laughs and shakes his head. "What's the point of all that when we're with you?" he asks dismissively.

I swallow down my irritation. That was only a third of my list. I hadn't even started on any of the illegal mods I favor or the discreet weaponry I was hoping to get fabricated if I asked really nicely.

Because you might be the threat that I need a weapon for, I think to myself, but I don't say that.

"You won't always be with me," I argue instead. "And you act like this small contingent can't be overrun. I need to be able to defend myself no matter what."

Ogdan rolls his eyes, and both Chastain and Tove make annoyed little huffs.

"You're not in The Scorch anymore, Frills," Chastain counters. "All the bone blades in the world aren't going to stop a dragon that wants to get to you."

"Maybe not stop altogether," I assert, "but they would slow them down, buy me some time to come up with a plan."

"A plan to what? Die slower?" Tove argues. "Sorry, Syphon—like it or not, we're infinitely better than a bunch of weapons that can't do shit against anyone with scales. A weapon will fail you." She looks around at the others, a wicked smile slipping across her face. "We . . . well, we're foolproof."

I shake my head as prideful grunts of approval sound off all around me. I swear if they start high-fiving each other, I will throw myself out the window.

I disengage from this pointless conversation. I've known far too many people who thought they were foolproof.

They're all dead now.

The drakes tease each other back and forth, but I ignore it, my focus once again fixed outside the car's window as my mind wanders elsewhere. An older sky craft drifts closer on the right, the movement catching my attention. Out of the corner of my eye, I watch it keeping pace with the lirocar, yet it seems careful not to pull up directly next to us, as though it's trying to stay on the edge of our periphery, unnoticed.

Curious, I look back at the vehicle. I can make out a male with floppy brown hair and a face of sharp angles in the passenger seat, but the sun's glare hides the driver. I squint in an effort to discern more details about the male or the other shadows of bodies I can just make out behind him, but the sky craft suddenly veers into a far lane of traffic and slows like it's getting ready to exit.

"What are you looking at?" Farrow asks, twisting in his seat to try to see what's caught my attention.

"Nothing," I dismiss, turning back around.

Eventually our lirocar leaves the airway, and I force myself to pay attention to the path we're traveling and the buildings and landmarks around me. Mentally,

I take note of things that should be recognizable from different levels of the city and at various distances. Like a sailor uses the stars to navigate, I'll need to use buildings, sculptures, and unusual-looking plants and trees to try to find my way through the maze of this cityscape if it comes to that.

Tension once again tightens my muscles and sharpens my senses. We drift down through the various stacked blocks of the borough, and with each descending tier, the city grows darker, dirtier, and more packed with people. The carefree chatter in the lirocar draws to a halt, and it's clear I'm not the only one picking up on the distinct *proceed with caution* vibe that grows stronger as we continue to dip into Paragon City's depths.

Bright neon lights cut through the gloom of the lower tiers, advertising various businesses and entertainment establishments. The shops draped in flowers and the street markets of the city's upper levels disappear, to be replaced by packed, uninviting store stalls with windows and doors covered in a mass of crisscrossed voltage bars. Signs are posted on each threshold, singling out which Arcs they refuse to serve and warning any others what will happen if they steal or cause trouble within.

I'm all too familiar with being desolate and poor, but there's a frenzied desperation and naked ruthlessness seeping through the cracks of these lower levels. It puts me even more on edge. The airways grow unsettlingly narrow the farther in we travel, and my dragon stirs with discomfort. I don't know how the wyverns are surviving here with no access to the sky. There's not even enough room to shift or stretch their wings. Logically, I know it's designed as punishment for their part in the rebellion, but it doesn't make it feel any less wrong.

Wyverns rival dragons in size and ferocity. Few differences separate our kinds, which is why, in the past, we've often nested and prospered together. Anatomically we're different: dragons have legs, arms, and wings, whereas wyverns only possess legs and wings. We're compatible when it comes to breeding, but any offspring produced by a coupling always results in a wyvern birth, never a dragon.

However, the primary difference between us, the one that's inspired the greatest conflicts between our kinds, is that dragons have been blessed by the Source with various gifts of magic, while wyverns have not.

Head-to-head, a dragon's extra limbs offer some small advantage, but nothing that a skilled wyvern warrior couldn't overcome. But going up against the gifts of a Burner, Channeler, Thrasher, or even Render when you have nothing but scales, teeth, and speed is a death sentence nine times out of ten.

A fact that's always confused me when I've spent any amount of time thinking about the wyvern rebellion and how they targeted the Syphons. My kith was the only one with the ability to strip other dragons of their gifts. We could, in a sense, create a level playing field amongst our kinds, and yet, instead of using that ability to help advance the wyvern position, they tried to eradicate it.

Craith, Ren, Pier, and the other wyverns that raised me always said that our kith was targeted simply because my father was king and the rest of us were the top link in the chain of hierarchy, but I always felt like there was something missing in that explanation, something that would glue together all the confusing, broken, senseless shards of that day.

We could find the logic in why the wyverns and sorcai teamed up. Each had what the other lacked—the wyverns needed magic, and the sorcai needed muscle. But strategically, attacking the Syphons and not the other kiths was tantamount to attacking a dragon's head and ignoring its sharp claws, vicious tail, and formidable wings. To take on a beast and hope to win, you have to account for all of its lethal parts.

Ren always argued that the wyverns and sorcai couldn't garner enough support to take on the whole monster. They hoped that removing the head would bring down the rest of The Horde. But that theory, like so many others we survivors tossed around under the stars of a scorched sky, had so many cracks in it. Cracks that the rest of us filled with the mortar of our own theories.

Because once the dust settled and the blood was washed away, it wasn't The Dragon Horde that was brought low. After the rebellion, the wyverns were hunted almost to extinction and then banished to the deep, dark recesses of society. The sorcai covens were pruned and brought to heel. And the remaining dragon kiths not only survived with barely a scratch, but they thrived, while any thought of challenging their rule was crushed under the weight of their might and then promptly burned to ash by the new Burner king.

It made the rebellion look like a front for a larger, more sinister plan. One hatched by none other than the dragons themselves and executed perfectly. Not unlike this plan to have me eliminated by a wyvern in the Wyvern Den. I should have known this is how King Noctis was going to play it. It worked so well for him the first time, why not go for it a second time?

"We're here," Ogdan announces as the lirocar settles against a sky dock that leads into a slate-gray, windowless building that's nestled between a row of other dark, sinister-looking buildings.

"I've seen prisons nicer than this place," I observe flatly, taking in the corner shop across the way, the thin alleys between the tightly packed structures, and what looks like a lane of food stalls just down the way.

"Spoken like a true snobby dragoness," Tove taunts.

"No. Spoken like someone who doesn't agree that *all* wyverns should be punished for the actions of *some*," I snap back.

"Well, of course you don't agree," Tove coos acerbically. "You've practically been held hostage by them and fed a steady diet of excuses and *poor me* bullshit.

You can buy the *not all wyverns* claim all you want, but the rest of us know better, Frills. We were there for the investigation and the subsequent interrogations. Not every wyvern clan participated, but they knew or suspected something and didn't offer so much as a sniffle of warning. There's no coming back from that kind of fracture in trust, and you know it. Which is why you're so jumpy just being here."

Tove's smile is smug, and I fight the growing urge to jab a fist right through the center of it.

"I really don't like you," I declare in a tone dripping with caustic honey.

"I really don't care," she lobs back, and then the doors to the lirocar open and the Royal Wing starts to file out.

Karis takes point, Tove and Ogdan flank me, and Farrow brings up the rear. Chastain drifts to the periphery, his gaze sweeping and sharp as he puts himself in a support position. It's a protective configuration I know well, only it's typically Enslee at the center and me guarding her back.

Jori also takes up position somewhere behind me, but I don't lock in on where before the stone wall in front of us starts to shift and a hidden door slides open. Azo, the human from King's Keep, steps out to greet us. But it isn't the human that makes the blood drain from my face and my heart lurch. It's the wyvern next to him.

Her hair is a riot of short espresso corkscrew curls that float around her head as she draws closer. Her dress is the color of the blood that dripped down the cell walls the night I escaped the blood brokers. Her olive complexion is flawless, but it's her eyes—Ren's eyes, a unique blue-hazel hue that's burned into my very soul—that tell me I've read this situation all wrong. It wasn't King Noctis setting me up to be cut down by the wyverns.

This wyvern isn't an enemy, she's an ally . . . or at least she used to be.

She's Ren's little sister.

Relief should be flooding me at the sight of her, but I feel the exact opposite because I don't know how I'm going to face her.

How do I tell her what happened to her kindred?

How do I tell her it was all my fault?

CHAPTER 19

Her presence scoops my insides out, and devastation pings around the emptied space. Shame and uncertainty weigh down my steps, and a million inadequate apologies dance across my tongue. Fenox Lael doesn't look my way. Her blue-hazel eyes are fixed on Karis as she discreetly sizes him and the others up.

When the human mentioned the designer's name, it didn't ring with any kind of recognition. But it wouldn't—Ren always called her little sister Nixy, never Fenox. And I've never heard the last name Lael before; Renatta's surname was Sagefor. I knew Nixy lived in Paragon and that she and Ren spoke every couple of months when they could, but last I heard Nixy worked for a tailor in the goblin district. I have no idea what she's doing here.

Azo bows and Nixy drops into a deep curtsy. Her stare finally shifts to me, and the sorrow I find there is like a shot to the gut. The blow is visceral and I feel like I'm suddenly bleeding out right here in front of everyone as my worlds collide. Nixy blinks and the emotion is masked. The echo of it, however, reverberates within me, ringing like a haunting lament in the depths of my soul.

She knows.

She knows her big sister is gone.

I want to beg her forgiveness, explain what happened, and vow to avenge the incredible person we both loved, but I can't do any of that. Not here. Not in front of Aeson's drakes. This gaping wound needs to stay hidden. I won't be the reason that Fenox Lael becomes a target.

I failed Ren.

I won't fail her little sister.

Which means I can't say or do anything that might tip my hand and clue the drakes in on any kind of history or connection here.

I lift the drawbridge and slam a portcullis down on the throng of emotion attempting to storm me. Blinking all recognition from my gaze, I wait for Fenox to speak while I discreetly watch Tove for any sign that she's picked up on a tether between me and the wyvern. Thankfully, the observant drake's attention is on our surroundings and not me.

"It is an honor, dragoness. My assistant has filled me in on your requests. I've endeavored to put together a small collection that I hope will meet with your approval. If you and your companions will follow me, I can show it to you. Then we can discuss anything else you might need." With that, Fenox rises from her position of supplication and turns to lead us into the building.

The drakes move as one, a well-practiced unit with me at the center. I want to stop, to tell them I've changed my mind and then turn around and get as far away from Ren's little sister as I can. Right now, Nixy is still on the fringes of what's happening, but the minute I step into the building, that changes. She'll be right in the thick of it with me. If I say something though, if I ask to leave, it will just make the guards suspicious, and the last thing I want to do is anything that will have them looking any closer at the wyvern than they already are.

With a heavy and conflicted heart, I follow the drakes into the building, silently screaming in protest every step I take. It's brighter inside the windowless building than I anticipated. The interior is a wash of dark charcoal finishes, and it's more modern than the outside facade would lead one to believe. It's mostly empty, with the exception of a large couch shaped like an undulating snake and a low glass table that's the size of a small pond. Against the long wall of the barren room, several displays of clothing await my inspection, but I couldn't care less about anything hanging over there. All I can focus on is Fenox.

That flash of anguish I momentarily caught in her eyes haunts me. I can't imagine she's handling the loss of her sister well.

I know I'm not.

Yet here we both stand like strangers, pretending nothing's wrong. Making believe that our hearts haven't been ripped from our chests and pulverized beyond recognition.

Does she hate me?

Is she about to unravel the string of half-truths I've been knotting together to survive The Horde and insert myself here in their stronghold?

"Please have a seat, dragoness," Azo instructs me, waving a hand toward the seating area. "Let me grab you something to drink."

He scurries off before I can tell him *no, thank you.*

Aeson's guards spread to each corner of the room. Tove stays close by, nudging me toward the oddly shaped couch, and Jori must have stayed outside with the driver, because I don't see him anywhere. Fenox watches the drakes carefully as she moves to the other side of the center table, where she turns to face me. Her eyes soften as she takes me in.

"Allow me to introduce myself, dragoness. My name is Fenox Lael, and I've been designing clothing for the last forty years. I've worked closely with several high-standing members of The Horde for the last fifteen of those forty years. I could bore you with the details of what I specialize in when it comes to design and styling, but I get the impression that you're a female who knows what she wants." A knowing twinkle enters her eye.

I force myself not to react, even though my chest aches and my throat grows tight with the effort. Everything I know about Nixy is through Ren. I was occasionally there when they would talk if we were out on assignment or working out together when a call came through. But now that the female is standing in front of me, I realize we don't *truly* know each other, despite feeling that way.

"If it's all right with you, I'd love to show you what I've put together, get your feedback, and then we can go from there?"

Azo hurries into the room with a tall flute of something golden, fancy, and fizzy. He tries to hand it to me, but Tove quickly intercepts it and brings the beverage to her nose, inhaling deeply. She must not scent anything to be concerned about, because she takes a small sip and then waits.

"If you wanted your own, you could have just asked," I tell the drake.

My taunt is met with an unamused look from the Seeder, and she hands over what I suspect is champagne, with a little more force than necessary.

"I'm so sorry. I didn't even think," Azo sputters, his worried gaze darting from me to Tove and back again.

I wave off the apology. "Tove is just greedy. Don't worry about it," I reassure the flustered human.

I bite back a grin, giving myself a point in the petty game Tove and I are playing. Looking down at the drink, I swirl the golden liquid in the flute and watch the tiny bubbles grow frenzied with the movement. Alcohol like this is pricey. Ordering it anywhere down south is asking to be mugged by someone happy to relieve you of all the credits they assume you have. I'm tempted to try the delicacy, but I don't know what kind of effect it'll have on me. Probably best not to risk it.

I turn to Fenox. "Show me what you've got."

"Excellent. Right this way," she encourages.

I hand the flute back to Tove and follow Fenox, juggling concern over the fact that I didn't know that she'd inserted herself into The Horde like this. I was aware that she occasionally passed information to Ren, but I didn't know that she was actively building a network to help spy on our behalf.

It's brilliant, but why didn't Ren ever say anything to me about it? Why didn't Enslee? I know I don't usually show the same amount of interest in politics that my sister does, but I should have been in the loop of something like this. Coming off the back of the betrayal that landed me and Renatta in the hands of the Tainted, this tastes even more bitter and unpleasant.

What else haven't I been told?

The shock of seeing Nixy starts to wear off, and in its place, a barrage of questions queues up, each one more pressing than the last. I debate how I'm going to ask Fenox what the bloody fuck is going on without the drakes hearing it, but a subtle hand movement from the wyvern draws my attention. Three fingers forming the shape of a W, telling me to wait, a familiar signal that my Flight and I use all the time.

Her hands are clasped in front of her. The W of her fingers rests on top of her other hand, and as soon as she sees that I've noticed it, she adopts a more natural, relaxed position, erasing the silent communication. So, I do as I'm told and continue to keep my mouth shut.

"Azo explained that the flashier fashions of the keeps didn't appeal to you, that you were in search of more practical options. I can make whatever it is you require, but my suggestion would be to create a collection that satisfies both the practical and fashionable requirements of high society."

I snort and Fenox's benevolent gaze flickers with both amusement and reproach. It's a look I know well, one Ren wore often. Grief wraps a fist around my lungs and starts to squeeze. If Fenox notices my distracted efforts to keep a stranglehold on my emotions, she doesn't say anything. Instead, she continues on about marrying fashion with function and then starts talking animatedly about makeup looks and hairstyles.

I do my best to play my part and offer little sounds of interest and encouragement, but as we draw closer to the other side of the room, I pick up on a faint current of energy. Just as I'm about to pause to assess where this odd sensation is coming from, Ren's little sister flashes me the hand signal for *forward*.

I wonder for a fraction of a second if I'm an idiot for blindly complying, but curiosity and my love for Ren have me continuing alongside her little sister, ignoring the weird static that's starting to dance across my skin. Unexpectedly I cross a threshold, one I can't see but sure as fuck can feel. It's like walking through a collection of spiderwebs that are electrically charged.

My body tingles as the magic washes over me. The troubling sensation is quick to disappear when I make it through the undetectable barrier Fenox has erected near the display of clothing, separating it from the rest of the room.

"Don't look over at the guards or try to see the muzzler we just walked through," Fenox orders evenly. "Just keep looking at me and at the clothes. I programmed the spell to make it seem like we're talking about outfits and other asinine shit, but they can still *see* us, so don't do anything that could tip them off."

"Won't they be able to read our lips?" I ask, forcing myself to relax even though a barrage of questions are now yipping at me, begging for answers.

"No, the spell-tech accounts for that."

"Nixy, what is going on? Are you here to get me out, because as much as I would love to get the fuck away from here, and fast, I don't think this is the best way to go about it. How are they not sensing this muzzler? Ren wouldn't want you to be taking risks like this. I don't either, if that counts for anything."

I force a smile to slip across my face and gesture to a folded pile of fabric that's sitting on a floating shelf in an effort to keep up the ruse. I have no idea how this particular spell works, but hopefully this looks believable.

"Well, Ren wouldn't have a leg to stand on in that argument, because she died taking risks just like this. And no, I'm not here to get you out. If the queen is working on that plan, she hasn't included me in it. All I know is that I was contacted days ago and informed that you'd most likely been taken by The Horde. They asked me to see what information I could find on where they might be keeping you and what's going on.

"When the royal summons for a stylist came through, I figured that was our in. Azo was supposed to pitch to whoever called the meeting, wait to be dismissed, and then poke around the keep to see what he could find out. We didn't expect that the summons would be for you or that they'd take Azo right to you. What happened? How are you here? Are you okay?"

She shakes her head as she grabs several items from a rack and starts showing them to me.

"Ignore that last question, of course you're not okay."

I snort and reach out to run my fingers over the fabric she's displaying, pretending to be impressed by it. I sneak a peek over at the drakes, but none of them look even slightly concerned or suspicious of anything that's happening. In fact, they look bored as fuck, which I take as a good sign.

"Four months ago, Ren and I were taken by blood brokers . . . "

"Those same ones you kept running into on missions?" she asks, clearly having talked to Ren about it at some point.

"The very ones," I confirm. "I got out, but I didn't get far before the dragons caught up with me. I'm so sorry, Nixy, but Ren—"

Fenox raises a hand, cutting me off. She masks the motion by reaching for some kind of vest and holds it up for me.

"Don't go there, Your Highness. The queen told me what she knew, and while it wasn't much, I don't need to know any more than that. Not today. My sister died protecting someone she loved. It's how she always expected to go, and she'd have no regrets. Not one. That's more than any of us can hope for, so whatever it is you're sorry for, don't be." Her tone is sharp, her cadence determined, yet her face is serene and warm, giving nothing away.

I nod once, but the rushing rapids of grief come for me despite her understanding, or maybe because of it.

"Ren loved you fiercely," I tell her, knowing it's dangerous to tug on this thread, but it needs to be said. If I can't explain anything else, I need to at least assure her of that.

"Stop," Fenox both commands and pleads. "If you start, I'll start, and they'll know we're not talking about underwear and plaster suits."

She turns toward the displays, taking a moment to blink her welling eyes free of any moisture. I nod again and force my way through the dangerous current coursing through me, intent on keeping my mask in place from here on out.

No more slipups.

"I assume you're now my point of contact," I observe, hating that Nixy is getting even more wrapped up in this mess than she already is. Not that there's any way around it. From the looks of things, she's in deep with The Horde. I'm both grateful and concerned, with a little guilt stirred into the mix, because it feels good to know I'm not completely alone in this like I thought I was.

Fenox nods and gestures to several dresses. "Yes. That direct assignment hasn't come through, but I'm sure it will as soon as I pass along what happened today. Designing your wardrobe and dressing you is the perfect cover. I admit, I always hoped I'd be able to help. I never expected it to be like this though."

A small laugh slips out as I wander over to a stack of pants and start looking through them. "Clothing companies have been saying for ages that fashion is life or death; who knew they had it right?" I joke, and Nixy giggles, the sound loosening the tension weighing on both of us.

"How can I help?" Nixy asks, and I don't even know where to start.

"What do you know about what Ren and I were doing with our Flight, about our missions?" I ask, unsure if it's wise to bring her in, not when the Syphons are already dealing with betrayal issues within our own ranks. Enslee obviously trusts Nixy, Ren did too, but I won't pull her in any deeper if she doesn't already know what we're doing.

"You're hunting down the sorcai that cursed you. Well, their bloodline at least. Blood Crafters, right? Isn't that what they're called?"

I nod and blow out a breath. "Do you know much about the sorcai covens here? I'm looking specifically for Relacours, but I don't want to just go throwing their name around," I explain, and Nixy looks thoughtful.

"I could keep my ear out, but wyverns and sorcai aren't exactly on the best of terms. If I start asking around, it doesn't matter how discreet I am, someone is going to notice. The Magic Licensing Bureau would probably be your best bet if you're looking for records, but I don't think that's the kind of place you can hack or even break into."

I sigh. "I know, we've tried to hack it multiple times and haven't had any luck," I admit. I huff out a laugh. "Maybe I could request a tour for my mating present."

Fenox makes a choking sound. "Mating present?" she croaks, clearing her airway of shock.

"Azo didn't tell you?" I tease flatly. "I'm being held in Aeson Noctis's mating suite. Initially, I thought it was just a coincidence—I got a little Source-buzzed and mouthy, and they needed somewhere secure to interrogate me—but now I'm not so sure. The fact that they're playing dress-up with me and practically soft launching my existence has me wondering if all of this is some kind of strategic posturing."

Fenox considers what I'm saying as she pulls a measuring meter from her pocket and instructs me to spread my arms. She starts sizing me up and zipping the meter across my body. I take that opportunity to check on the drakes again. They look just as disinterested as they did before.

"If they're maneuvering you for that, it would make sense that they'd attach you to Aeson and not Lorn. Lorn's not *officially* spoken for, but there's been an understanding between the king and Duke Warrik, Jesamyn Warrik's father, for quite some time. Not to mention they wouldn't want to give you access to the throne. They'll give you a notable position where they could use you—or rather, your name—when it suits them, but not place you in a legitimate position of power."

Nixy squats down and starts measuring my legs and inseam.

"Isn't it a little soon to be maneuvering me anywhere?" I challenge.

She smiles up at me. "They move fast, Your Highness. Even if they doubt you or your story, I guarantee they've already met with the king and his advisors and plotted a way to use this development to their advantage. This is what they do. They're probably ten steps ahead of you already."

"Only ten?" I quip, but it falls flat.

"With all due respect, this isn't The Scorch. This is *Four Tiers*, and you need to catch up. If they think Aeson Noctis is the key to keeping you in line, you're in bigger trouble than you even realize. That drake is as cunning as he is vicious. If they've already got you nesting in his rookery, he'll have your wings clipped and your belly full of Noctis spawn before you know what's happening. They're trapping you, Your Highness, not playing nice, no matter what they say or how it looks."

Moths flutter through my veins, and the truth of her words clocks me right in the kisser.

"Shit," I grumble, knowing she's right.

I spent the last few days resting and recovering. It was nice not to be interrupted by anything except food. It felt considerate and respectful. I'm realizing now, however, that's not what it was at all. Of course The Horde didn't care that I was sleeping the days away; it gave them the perfect opportunity to outfox me.

I should have seen that coming, but the Noctis brothers didn't behave like I expected. To say that it threw me off is an understatement, which I'm sure was by design. Fenox is right—I need to wake the fuck up, because the last thing I need is some controlling dragon thinking he owns me.

"Technically he can't clip wings I don't have," I point out. "Or fill my belly with Noctis spawn."

"Unless they know how to reverse the curse," Nixy counters.

"That is what I'm here to find out. I just don't know where to start looking."

"Start with Aeson Noctis," Nixy proffers with a wag of her eyebrows and a wide grin. "If he wants to use you, use him right back. Males spill their souls when they're spilling their seed. Pretend like you're falling for the trap. Flirt with him, fuck him, even, and then pump him for information."

I laugh at the suggestion, but she does make a good point. As much as I'd like to never see another Noctis again, it's not like bedding one would be some insurmountable hardship. Especially if it was the commander.

Interest and curiosity diffuse through me, but I snub the sensations and focus on the plan that's starting to coalesce with Nixy's words.

"I don't have to stop with Aeson either," I muse out loud.

"Meaning what?" she asks, handing me two different tops from a rack.

"Just that Lorn could be valuable too. Aside from hunting the sorcai that cursed us, I also need to draw out the dragons that turned on my father. Orbiting both the scions is a good way to do that."

Nixy's smile grows salacious, but she shakes her head. "Dragons don't share, you know that. They'll rip you in two just for suggesting it."

I nod my head in agreement and study the flowy shirts she handed me. "I'm not actually trying to bag both, I'm just talking about leaving my options open until I know which one is more useful."

"That's a dangerous game, Your Highness, not to mention almost impossible to pull off. Their Wings talk; it won't take long for them to catch on," Nixy objects.

"Everything about this is dangerous," I remind her. "If I'm smart about it and careful, I could figure it out."

She shakes her head, not satisfied with that argument.

"If you've got a better plan, I'm all ears," I challenge, handing the tops back to Nixy—or maybe they're skirts, I can't really tell.

She looks down at them thoughtfully and then sighs. "No, but just remember you're dealing with dragons here. It doesn't take much for them to get possessive. You need to tread carefully."

She hangs the two items up and moves down to another clothing stand.

"How can I be a dragon and need a crash course in dragons? You don't have a manual lying around or anything, do you?" I ask, and Nixy laughs.

"I can give you a rundown of all the court gossip and who's wearing what for the upcoming Liberation Day celebrations, but my inside knowledge stops there."

"Fuck the fae, I forgot about the Blood Rite," I groan.

The ceremony doesn't mean much to the survivors in The Scorch. For us, it does nothing more than mark the passage of time. No one knows we exist, and therefore we get to skip the required annual trek to Paragon City, where the leaders of the Arcane and humans alike swear fealty to King Noctis and The Dragon Horde.

But in just over seven weeks, every Arcane Head of State, Alpha, Coven Leader, Chief, Premier, *and* their entourages will be arriving for the Blood Rite. Not to mention all of The Horde nobles. The blood magic involved is sacred and important, but the two-week-long celebration is a whole lot of pomp and circumstance that mostly serves as a good excuse to drink too much, party too hard, and fuck as many Arcs as your orifices can handle.

I knew it was coming, but I didn't even think about how I'd be in the thick of things or how that would impact my plans. Then again, it might create the perfect amount of chaos I need to really search and spy.

I look around at the drakes and then back to the clothes Fenox and I are standing next to. "All right, Nixy, tell me all the drama while transforming my caterpillar ass into a butterfly."

Fenox chuckles, and with a nod and a determined furrow in her brow, she starts pulling things from the racks and shelves.

"If said transformation into a butterfly could include hidden armor, plenty of places for weapons, and the ability to move without feeling like my outfit is trying to kill me, that would be great," I add, trying not to wince at some of the items she adds to the growing pile in her arms.

"Ah," Nixy exclaims. "One of those armor-winged, weapon-toting, camouflaging species of butterflies. Got it."

I smile. "Exactly. I think they're from the genus Fuck Around and Find Out."

A snort sneaks out of Fenox, and she shakes her head. Her blue-hazel eyes glitter with mirth, and I find myself feeling a flicker of hope.

"Let's get you out of that horrid dress then and see if we can give you wings," Nixy teases as she looks me up and down, one eyebrow raised in obvious judgment. "May the Source bless us with a miracle. You're going to need one to survive the Noctis brothers."

I laugh and offer her a Cheshire grin. "Wrong. They're going to need one to survive me."

CHAPTER 20

"A nice purple would look incredible with your hair, or even green if you wanted to make your eyes really pop," Azo encourages.

I spin on the platform that Nixy summoned from the ground with a touch of a button and take in my reflection in the mirrors that shimmered into place on the opposite wall.

"No, I like gray," I tell the human . . . again. "It really is my favorite color, and this is the perfect shade."

Azo sighs and, with a shake of his head, concedes his loss. Nixy's smile grows wider as she circles me, eyeing her selections and checking for anything that requires any last-minute adjusting.

"Grab that one pair of lace-up boots in the back cupboard next to the headpieces," she orders Azo.

"Ooh, the thigh highs?" he questions, a twinkle of excitement once again igniting in his gaze. "Do you want a heel or no heel?"

"No heels," I interject.

"The thick-soled ones," Nixy tells him before she starts orbiting me again.

"Enough. I'm as posh and polished as I'm going to get today," I grump, rounding on the wyvern. "You can't hold me hostage forever."

"Fine, fine, but are you sure you don't want to wear any jewelry? I really think a necklace would be per—"

"Unless it's a fang breaker, no. Now, can I get down?"

An exasperated huff slips out of Ren's little sister, and I hear several of the drakes still spread around the room stifling their laughter.

"Wait for the shoes and then you're free, and you don't need to worry about vampires here, dragoness."

"We've been telling her," Ogdan grumbles, and I lob a snarky glare his way.

"I'm going to hate myself for even asking, but do you like it? Did I accomplish what I said I would?" Nixy probes.

I turn back to my reflection and run my hands down the dove-gray corset that molds perfectly to my torso. It has a flouncy little peplum flare at my hips, and the top cups the undersides of my breasts—which are looking better than ever thanks to a bra that somehow sticks to your tits, lifting and securing them until you push a magic little button on the side to take it off.

Fenox put the corset on top of a silky, off-the-shoulder, baggy-yet-structured top that's the same shade of gray as the rest of the outfit. But my favorite part is the buttery-soft, reinforced armor pants I'm wearing that fit me like a second skin.

The outfit is exactly what Nixy said it would be—functional and fashionable. She sat me under a machine that straightened my hair until it was sleek and gleaming. Then she pressed a mask to my face that darkened my brows and lashes and made my skin look smooth and flawless before it pinkened my cheeks and deepened the color of my lips. It's not makeup but some kind of dye that only has to be applied every few weeks. I look beautiful, filthy rich, and snooty, but in a *you don't want to fuck with me* kind of way.

Nixy is a genius.

I find her blue-hazel eyes in the mirror and give her a warm, genuine smile, the kind that makes my solitary dimple appear.

"It's perfect, Fenox Lael. Thank you."

Her answering smile is bright and proud, and then she goes and makes it awkward by dropping into a deep curtsy. "Thank you for trusting me, dragoness."

It takes everything in me not to roll my eyes, but we've perfected this little song and dance over the last few hours that we've been trying on clothes, sketching designs, and making lists of everything a *proper* dragoness needs at court.

"Got them." Azo hurries over. "It took me a minute to adjust the color to the right tone of . . . *gray*," he announces, his nose crinkling with displeasure. "I don't know what it says about you that gray, of all things, is your favorite color, but a shrink would have a field day, I'm sure."

I laugh at the cheek of this human, but a low warning growl slips out of Farrow, and he narrows his gaze at the man.

"Careful, human," the Thrasher warns, and the mood in the room instantly sours.

Azo blanches and audibly swallows as he bends down to help me into the thigh-high, lace-up platform boots.

"Oooh, pockets!" I chirp, eager to draw attention away from Nixy's sassy assistant. I bend the top lip of the boot back and marvel at the built-in sheath that's hidden inside. "You get me," I coo at Nixy, and she laughs, the sound helping to lighten the simmering tension.

I get the other boot on and then hop down off the platform with a relieved sigh. This wasn't as torturous as I expected, but I'm glad to finally be dressed and done with this portion of my introduction to dragon high society. I wrap Ren's little sister up in a tight hug. She goes stiff and I instantly know I've done the wrong thing.

"Move away from the dragoness, wyvern," Tove barks, and I glower over at the female drake as I release Nixy and quickly back away from her for her own safety.

"She's been up close and personal with all my bits for hours. What the fuck is your problem?" I demand, bewildered by the sudden onslaught of aggression rolling off all the drakes.

They've each maintained their relaxed positions around the room all day, but now they look like they're ready to fight or take action, which seems like overkill for a hug.

No one says anything, not even Nixy.

My stare drops to the ground, and I shake my head.

"Sorry, I wasn't thinking," I whisper penitently, turning to Fenox.

"I'm honored to have your trust, dragoness, but you need to understand I will never have theirs," she tells me evenly, nodding at the Wing members.

My heart aches as her words float around the room, not one voice willing to dispute their validity or offer her sorrow a safe harbor. Frustration brews in my gut, but Nixy subtly shakes her head, and I'm forced to ingest my outrage and bite my tongue.

What makes me feel even shittier is that I don't have a leg to stand on when it comes to lecturing the agitated drakes about their behavior. I was just as edgy and convinced of my own demise on the ride over here. Until I saw that the wyvern I was going to be dealing with was Nixy, I was equally as untrusting and worried, which means I'm no better than them in this regard.

Shame settles in my chest. I hate what's happened between us, the chasm that exists between wyverns and dragons. With so much pain, spilled blood, and mistrust on both sides, I don't know how to fix it, or if anyone even can.

"Not huggers in Paragon City. Got it," I mumble, stepping farther away from the wyvern I'm still pretending not to know.

A heaviness lodges itself in the room.

"I'll have everything we picked out today sent up to the keep immediately, and the other designs we discussed should be ready in less than a week. I can send Azo to fit you when they're done, or you're welcome to come here if you prefer I fit you personally," Nixy tells me, her tone suddenly slightly hollow and entirely too professional.

It feels like a kick to the gut, but I know there's no getting around it. I got comfortable here, forgot my place for a little while, and just did something that could've blown our cover. I'm not exactly the epitome of warm and fuzzy; now I'm going to have to hug a few other random people just to cover our asses.

"Let me see what my schedule is like, and I'll let you know," I answer, just as stiff and formal.

"Excellent. It was a pleasure, dragoness."

Before I can think of another detached-sounding response, Ogdan steps to Azo and holds up a credit band. The human taps a few things into his own device and then presses the band to the other. A quick beep indicates that payment has been made and the transaction is complete.

No one seems to notice when I pluck the two butter knives from my old boots and slip them into the sheaths hidden inside the tops of my new footwear. The guards all converge on me, and with that, I'm herded toward the exit.

We step out into a cool, bleak-looking afternoon. The light that reaches this deck of the city has grown gloomier in the hours we've spent inside, and it takes a moment for my eyes to adjust. The sleek-looking lirocar touches down in front of us, the doors sliding open as our group approaches.

"Ugh, Chastain, I swear I'm going to sew your asshole shut!" Tove grouses, fanning the air in front of her face.

"What?" the Channeler demands, and then the smell must hit him, because his face crumples with disgust. "That wasn't me, I swear!"

Whatever it is they're grousing about reaches me, and I freeze, my head snapping up while my frantic gaze starts searching. I know that noxious smell. I've been breathing in that cloying stench for months.

The Tainted are here.

They found me.

CHAPTER 21

My gaze lands on a faintly familiar face across the street. A tall male with sharp angular features stands next to a narrow alley, his entire focus trained on me and the guards.

Disquiet whispers a warning in my ear, and foreboding wraps a heavy arm across my shoulders and pulls me closer. A rush of light wind tries to ease the olfactory assault, but I can already taste the taint on my tongue.

The male across the way lifts his arm, and the flashing lights from a nearby sign glint off the weapon he has clutched in his hand.

"Gun!" I scream in warning, diving for the drake that's closest to me.

I wrap my arms around Tove and, with surprising strength, force us both to the ground.

"What the fuck?" she grunts as our bodies kiss the pavement. She growls something else, but I can't hear it over the shouts and snarls now filling the street.

I look up to see the Tainted male making a run for it down the alleyway, but the guards around me are approaching a sky craft that I recognize from earlier and not paying attention to the fleeing man. Realization collides with fury, and I'm up and sprinting toward the alleyway after the male. He was in the car that I thought was following us on our way here, and now I know that's exactly what they were doing.

"Frills, no!" someone barks at my back, but I'm already pounding down the tight lane that's barely wide enough for me to fit down.

"That's not my fucking name," I grumble as I pick up speed.

The Tainted fuck in front of me looks back over his shoulder, his face flashing fear when he sees me barreling after him. He trips over his feet as he faces forward and tries to run faster. He stumbles but catches himself, just barely managing not to fall. I quickly close the distance between us from forty feet to twenty.

The alley we're in meets up with another street, and he darts left and then right, trying to lose me, but I'm right there with him. I don't recognize the male from anywhere other than the flyway this morning, but that means fuck all. Too many times I was out of it after being bled and tortured. I couldn't even lift my head to see who was dumping food or water in my cell, carrying me to another location, or kicking my bucket of piss and shit all over. Even if I didn't have direct contact with this asshole, he's part of the Tainted's network, which means he's a dead man. I'll hunt each and every one of them down if it's the last thing I do.

My days of running from the enemy are over.

Now they're going to run from me.

"Better move faster, motherfucker," I taunt the panicking male, leaping past the edge of a food stall and slicing through a small cluster of people queued up for an afternoon snack.

A vicious smile stretches wide across my face as the male looks back again and sees me gaining on him with every stride. He whimpers, and sweat dots his brow. His chest heaves with exertion, and I know he doesn't have much more flight in him. He'll make a stand soon and try to fight.

I pull my butter knives from my boots and get ready to use them as we squeeze down another small vein of passage that connects one run-down lane to another.

"Please," the male starts to beg. "I didn't know. I wouldn't have taken it if I knew," he beseeches, but I ignore it. My prey, my kill is only a handful of feet away now.

I reach for him, but the fucker dekes to the other side of the widening throughway and dodges my grab. I push to get even closer, and he stumbles again. This time while he's struggling to get his footing, I grab him by the back of his shirt and shove him into the opposite wall. A satisfying thud fills the alley as skin meets stone, and I have the bastard facing me with a knife to his throat before he's even done screaming from the first face-breaking hit.

"Where the fuck is Wistan?" I snarl in the male's face, pressing him into the rough rock of the building like I'm about to make him the mortar that holds it all together.

Someone drops into the alley behind me, and I whirl to address the unwelcome visitor with my other butter knife. A bright blond male rears back in surprise when I press the metal of my knife firmly against the bronze skin of his throat. He lifts his hands in silent surrender, but the gleam in his mossy-green gaze screams trouble. So does the scale armor and the insignias on his arms marking him as yet another member of the Royal Wing.

Apparently they're everywhere these days, worse than sand fleas, if you ask me.

The gloomy light of the alley makes the teal color of his scale armor lean more green than blue. A black bolt of lightning forks up the middle of his throat and chin, the dragon mark stopping just under his plump bottom lip. A lip that slowly curves up as I stand in the alley, arms out, dull knives pressed against two separate throats on each side of me.

"Who in the bloody fuck are you?" I snap at the drake.

"Is that . . . are you threatening me with table cutlery?" he asks, his already-raised eyebrows hiking even farther up his forehead. "I don't know if I'm impressed or offended. You've got quite the pair of balls on you to threaten a member of the scion's Royal Wing, let alone do it with such substandard . . . weaponry."

"Ovaries," I correct slowly so he doesn't miss a syllable. "I've got ovaries, not balls, and I guarantee they're infinitely tougher than anything dangling between your legs. Now, Stormer, answer my question, or I'll be happy to demonstrate exactly what I can do with my *substandard* weaponry."

A delighted smile stretches wider across his face before he purses his lips with faux offense. "Stormer? Come now, dragoness, that's so cold, so impersonal. Call me Herm, I insist. And feel free to press a little closer. I've never been buttered before; the sheer anticipation is doing all kinds of things for me."

He shivers with exaggerated excitement, and I roll my eyes.

"Does no one in your bloody Wing take anything seriously?" I ask with a sigh.

"Oh, we do . . . from time to time, but I promise you don't want to be on the receiving end of that seriousness. Better to stay on this side of things. Keep it light and breezy, ya know? Fewer people usually die that way. Well, with the exception of that one time in that one bar, but they started it."

I hear the distinct sound of other bodies tromping into the narrow lane behind me, but judging by the way Herm doesn't react to their presence, I gather it's probably the rest of Aeson's Wing.

"Who started it?" I ask, confused about what he's rambling on about.

"Ah, ah, ah," he admonishes. "I'll only tell you if you drop the butter knife . . . correction, knives." His playful gaze flicks to the second shitty weapon I have pressed against the other male's throat.

The runner has silent tears streaming down his face, and his wide, terrified eyes bounce back and forth between me and Herm. The front of the runner's pants suddenly grows dark and wet, and the sharp scent of urine fills the air.

Great.

"Come now, Biscuit, you've had your fun with the man. No point tormenting the poor . . . " Herm's brow furrows, and he pulls in a deep, contemplative breath. "Ah, the poor owl shifter."

"Owl shifter?" I exclaim, shocked. That can't be right. He's sorcai—all the Tainted are sorcai.

I shove my face closer to scent the other male. He squeaks in fright and tries to lean away from me, but he's still pressed against the side of the building, and there's nowhere for him to go. Earthy notes fight against the strong smell of ammonia and the metallic tang of fear. I've never met an owl shifter before, so I don't know exactly what they smell like, but what I realize is missing is the pernicious, rotten fragrance of the Tainted. This male smells nothing like them. I have no idea who he is, but he's not one of Wistan's.

I went after the wrong person.

"Why the fuck did you try to shoot us?" I demand, even more outraged than I was before.

He starts crying even harder. "My team saw the scion's guards. We were hoping to get pictures of him—they're worth quite a lot—but then we saw you with his Wing, and we got curious. We didn't know you were a dragoness, or we would have never taken pictures. We didn't realize . . . you don't smell . . . "

"Pictures?" I interrupt, completely bewildered. "You had a gun."

"No! It was just a camera. I swear, I'm a paparazzo. I don't even own a gun, just a camera. It's in my pocket, you can see for yourself!"

I look down at the male's wet pants and grimace. "Take the camera out and drop it on the ground," I order, hoping one of Aeson's Wing will take the initiative and sort the camera and its contents out so I don't have to.

"I'll delete the photos. I promise. I didn't know what you were. Please don't kill me. I have a family," he pleads as he drops a small silver device on the ground.

"Have you lost your Scorch-addled mind? What in the fucking fates were you thinking, running off like that?" Tove snarls, stomping toward me from the end of the alley, an equally disgruntled Ogdan and Farrow tight on her heels.

"Oh good, you finally caught up," I snark at the trio.

I dare a glance behind me to find Chastain, Karis, Jori, and another male in violet scale armor that I haven't met before. I think back to all the names Aeson listed off when it came to his Wing. He mentioned I'd meet Herm and Sondar when they were done with an assignment. If Herm is here next to me . . .

"Sondar?" I ask the male with long, straight, blue-black hair, equally dark eyes, and a rich russet complexion.

His pleased grin is all the answer I need.

"I see my reputation precedes me," he jokes, further cementing my hypothesis that this Wing is off-the-rails crazy and serially unserious.

"Why in all of the stars do you have butter knives?" Ogdan demands, and I throw my head back and blow out a deep, exasperated breath.

"Like I told you on the way here, I *need* weapons." I drop said weapons from both Herm and the owl shifter's throats and step away.

"No, what you need to do is stay put like you're supposed to and let us handle things," Ogdan argues, angrily pushing strands of his loose, dark red hair out of his face.

"Like I'm supposed to?" I argue, fully fed up with the shit they've been dishing out all day.

"He's got photos that need to be dealt with," Herm calls to Sondar, nodding at the owl shifter, who now looks as though he might shit his pants.

I quickly move away from him toward Tove, just in case.

"Yes, *like you're supposed to,* because we are the professionals here, not you. At what point is it going to sink in?" Tove snaps. "You could have been sprinting into a trap for all you know, running off like that. To say nothing of the fact that we're not exactly in friendly territory and you lack the vital fucking protections needed to survive any of the life-threatening things that could have happened to you here," she adds, berating me like I'm some mischievous child.

I shrug, not even a little sorry. "That smell you thought was Chastain was the Tainted. They're the ones who took me, who attacked your Wing in Lairwood. They were here. They were watching. The Horde doesn't even know they exist. What the fuck was I supposed to do, just stand there?"

The sparks of annoyance in Tove's brown eyes alight into a full-blown inferno of indignation. "If this is the kind of reckless shit you pull, no wonder you got yourself caught by blood brokers. Are you trying to get taken again? Hoping to add a few more scars to your extensive collection?"

Every ounce of humor drops from my face. "Watch it, Seeder. You have no clue who you're fucking with," I warn.

"Why don't you show me then, Syphon."

"Tove!" Ogdan barks in clear warning. "Stand down."

Tove rounds on him. "She needs to be taught a lesson before she gets one of us killed. I don't give a fuck who she is; she doesn't get to put us in harm's way like our lives mean nothing."

"I said *stand down,*" Ogdan bellows, and every drake in the alley freezes.

Tove's face goes blank. After a moment, she steps away from me and adopts a stiff position with her hands behind her back, her feet shoulder width apart, and her stare empty and fixed on the redheaded Burner in black scale armor who just issued a direct order.

I wondered what the chain of command was within the Wing. They've been good at keeping it under wraps until now. Ogdan turns to me, body stiff with tension, jaw clenched tight with fury.

"Dragoness, if it's quite all right with you, I suggest we head back to the keep."

I study the Burner, no hint of the amiable, teasing drake I've encountered up until now. My attention jumps to a dead-eyed Tove and then to Farrow, who looks equally as pissed.

"Sir, yes, sir," I grumble indignantly, pushing past the other two guards and following Ogdan back to Nixy's.

No one says a word as we pile into the waiting lirocar and promptly take off. I watch the Wyvern Den quickly fall away, wondering what happened to the owl shifter and the other Arcs that were with him in the vehicle that was following us this morning. I don't ask anyone for answers, not willing to breach the silent line that was drawn in the sand between me and the drakes back in the alley.

Tove's words ring loud in my mind. She's a bitch, but she's not completely wrong. My mistakes did cost me my freedom and Ren her life. But it wasn't my instincts or rush to action that put me or my Flight in harm's way; it was trust that fucked me over, and now I'm paying the price. The drakes can think whatever they want to think about me, but it's obvious that their impressions are being filtered through a lens of condescending misjudgment. I don't know what kind of females they're used to dealing with, but none of the ones I know need a whole contingent of guards to keep them safe.

The Horde wants me to fit in a tidy little box that they can show off and pass around for their own benefit. They've forgotten who the Syphons are, what we're capable of. But that's okay—even without my dragon, I'll be happy to remind them.

I'm a fucking Tenebrae, after all.

CHAPTER 22

The lirocar leaves the airway sooner than it should, and I look around to find that we've turned toward Thrasher Keep instead of continuing on to King's Keep. I stifle any reaction to the unexpected detour, keeping the look on my face bored and my body language relaxed.

A multitude of reasons for this deviation flicker through my mind, but thoughts of the warren of dungeons under this keep rush to the forefront of my speculations. Maybe I'm being put in the naughty corner for pissing off Aeson's Wing.

I get the impression that the drakes expect me to ask what's going on, so of course I double down on my stubbornness and decide to just roll with the punches. At least the elevators won't sneak up on me this time.

The proportions of Thrasher Keep are nothing short of astounding. The stronghold is the largest of the four keeps, and the intimidating rust-red towers look like they could be their own city. Everything about it is designed to discourage threats and intimidate visitors. It screams, *you'll have to go through me to get to the others, and you'll never go through me.*

The lirocar doesn't angle toward the ground level of the keep like I expect. It floats to the largest tower on the west end and sets down on what looks like a private dock. No one from the keep comes out to greet us, but another airboat drops next to ours, and Herm, Sondar, and Karis climb out.

Cautiously I follow Ogdan and the others inside, careful to keep my eyes on my escorts and not get distracted by the marvels around me. Keeps are big for a reason—communal spaces have to be cavernous enough to house hordes of revealed dragons—but nothing truly prepares you for the scope and grandeur of it all until you're walking through it.

Our steady steps echo off the wide walls and lofty ceilings, making our small party of eight sound like an army of hundreds. I don't see another soul outside of my party of sullen protectors, but I try not to be bothered by that as we traverse what feels like a miles-long hallway. Finally, two monumental doors appear in the distance, but I don't know if I feel better or worse with the destination now in sight.

The dark wood doors slowly open as we draw closer, but of course the massive frames of the guards in front of me block my line of sight. I'm also still pretending to be too cool to ask or to lean around the big drakes to try to get a peek of where we're headed.

I hear his voice before I see him. It instantly hooks me low in my gut and tries to tug me closer. Goose bumps sweep up my arms and across my shoulders at the sound of his rich timbre and the undercurrent of undeniable authority in it. I try to banish the reaction as quickly as it comes, but then the commander has to go and laugh, and it sends the butterflies in my stomach into a full-blown tizzy.

The Wing members in front of me finally drift apart and move to the edges of the large room. And there he is, Aeson Noctis, in all of his annoying glory. I was hoping my memories of him were exaggerated by my exhaustion and the fact that I'd just escaped a traumatizing ordeal, but nope, he's just as impressive and pretty as I remember, maybe even more so.

Fucker.

He rises from where he was sitting at a long table, and his bright blue eyes turn to find me. Several other drakes stand as I stride into the room, but my mutinous mind has no interest in them—it wants all of my focus on my make-believe mate.

"The dragon of the hour," Aeson declares evenly, and then his gaze languidly roves over me, taking in every inch of Fenox's hard work.

His perusal momentarily pauses on the skin of my exposed shoulders before slowly drifting higher to my neck. With some effort, he once again meets my hard stare, but the look now blazing in his eyes is incendiary.

"You look . . . " He pauses, almost as though he's at a loss for words, but I'm not buying it. I know what game he's playing now, and if he thinks a barrage of flowery compliments is the key to my vagina, he's in for a rude awakening.

"Hungry," I insert for him, taking in the platters and trays teeming with food, which are spread across the wide table in front of him.

Aeson chuckles, and his smile grows just shy of wicked. "I was going to say stunning, but *hungry* has the right ring to it. I too find myself suddenly famished."

A few quiet laughs move through the room at his innuendo. I have to work not to roll my eyes or glare at any of the other drakes grouped around the table. *And we're off*, I declare in my mind like some commentator reporting on a race. The commander is out of the starting gate first, but he won't claim victory that easily. Let him think he can keep me under his thumb because I'm too moon-eyed and lovesick to see what's really happening, but I've got my own tricks up my sleeve.

Aeson moves to an empty chair on his right and pulls it out. "Have a seat. I'll introduce you to everyone, and then we can eat before we get started."

I debate for a second if I should be a good girl and go sit by him, but I don't want to give in too soon and start mooning over him. That would be too obvious. I need to time my shift from *cautious and distrustful* to *falling for his shit* just right. That way, he won't see that I'm pulling the rug out from under him until he's on his ass.

"Started with what?" I ask as I cross the room to a different empty chair before pointedly pulling it out for myself and sitting in it.

The big male next to me tries to stifle his chortle as I make myself comfortable, but Aeson's smile doesn't drop from his face. He pats the back of the rejected chair once and then reclaims his seat at the head of the table before looking over at me.

"Ogdan didn't tell you?" he questions, his focus drifting from me to the redhead in the black scale armor, who's now standing at attention in the far corner.

"Your Wing isn't currently talking to me," I inform the commander before eyeing the spread of steaming dishes before me and plotting a war path of which ones I want to conquer first.

That statement lures the attention of Commander Ventis, the older female with salt-and-pepper hair, smooth skin, and light blue eyes, who's sitting on my other side. The Syphons don't have as much information about her as some of the other commanders. It's tempting to try to fill in some of the blanks our spies couldn't, but asking for her life story and then quizzing her about battle strategy is a bad move to make right now.

"And why is the scion's Wing not talking to you?" she asks.

I shrug. "They think I'm some bobble-headed princess who doesn't respect them."

"And are you?" Commander Drazyn asks from across the table, his striking bronze stare assessing.

"A bobble-headed princess? No. But they're right about me not fully respecting them," I confess.

Tove snorts and shakes her head. The other drakes around the table clock it but don't say anything. I can't tell if they're bothered by her departure from typical guard decorum or if this kind of thing is normal here. Aeson's relationship with his Wing so far has been very lax and unpretentious. I'm a little surprised to see the other drakes embrace that kind of leadership too.

"Why don't you respect them? They're Wing, Royal Wing to boot; that alone should earn some level of esteem and deference," Commander Zeir presses, leaning back in his chair so he can get a better look at me even though I'm sitting right next to him. He sets his burly hands in his lap, and I note the dragon mark on both of his forearms, a honeycomb pattern of black, gray, and skin-tone hexagons covering every exposed inch of his limbs.

I blow out an exasperated breath. I guess we're not going to eat before moving on to whatever it is we're here to do. Taking into account that I'm sitting at a table with five of The Horde's top commanders, I'm pretty sure I'm here to be interrogated. They'd probably phrase it as *answering a few questions over dinner*, but it is what it is, regardless of their attempts to make things appear more casual by opting out of wearing their scale armor.

Like I wouldn't know who they were without it.

"For starters, I don't trust them because they don't trust me," I answer, looking from Commander Zeir to Ogdan. "That, and their loyalties lie with someone else. They've been assigned to protect me, and that's all well and good, but none of them knows me well enough to do the job right, and not one of them has taken the time to figure that out. They've made a fair number of assumptions about me, probably based on conversations they've been privy to that I haven't."

I look pointedly at Aeson for a beat and then level all of my attention on Tove. Her scowl deepens.

"A protective detail is more than just babysitting. Does your Charge freeze, fight, or flee when faced with danger? Do they cry? Do they scream? What's their experience with high-pressure, volatile situations? Can they throw a punch? Handle a weapon? Do they possess any other skills that could help or hinder a life-or-death situation? Will they listen to you? The better you know your Charge, the better you can protect them. Guards who show zero interest in knowing who you are as a person are guards who aren't truly invested in your survival."

"You sound like you have some experience with that," Commander Galerus—the youngest leader out of the group—observes.

I nod and study Aeson for a moment. He and Lorn were careful not to speak to me about anything sensitive until we were in Aeson's rookery. I assume that the presence of these commanders here means they are trusted by the scion, but better to be safe than sorry.

"What do they know?" I ask the commander bluntly.

"They've been brought up to speed, and this room is secure," Aeson answers without missing a beat.

I nod and turn back to Galerus. "For my first visit to Four Tiers, my father assigned a protective detail. They were members of the Wing that watched over my brothers. The night we were attacked, those guards sought out the boys they'd been protecting for well over a decade, and they did everything they could to whisk them to safety. However, in all the madness and chaos, those guards forgot all about me. So, yes, I'd say I'm speaking from experience. Knowing your Charge, caring about them, makes you a more effective line of defense, and that's the only kind of protection anyone should ever trust."

Out of the corner of my eye, I see Ogdan's head drop a little, and the room grows quiet with introspection.

"I'm going to go ahead and eat," I announce, reaching for a bowl of what looks like cheesy potatoes and scooping a big helping onto the plate in front of me. "But don't let that deter you. Interrogate on."

Chastain and Commander Galerus both huff out a laugh, and Aeson just shakes his head as I shamelessly execute my plans to vanquish this meal. I'm sure there is some kind of etiquette that I'm breaching here, but they shouldn't have put food out if they weren't going to eat it. Especially not in front of someone who's been starved off and on for the last four months. The blood brokers gave me only meat because they thought it was better for my blood, so there's not a chance in hell that I'm letting the feast of carbs in front of me go to waste. These Horde bastards can waterboard me for all I care—as long as I get a few bites of these potatoes in me, I'd consider it a win.

"Before you arrived, we were discussing the attack that occurred during your recovery in Lairwood. Do you have any insight to offer about that?" Commander Ventis asks while plucking a few dishes from the table and serving herself.

"Nothing significant," I tell her as the other commanders all start to fill their plates. "In my experience, blood brokers usually do what they can to stay under the radar. Picking a fight with The Horde is the antithesis of their usual MO. I was as surprised that it was happening as The Horde was."

"It is unusual for blood brokers to try and take on The Horde. We agree. Perhaps this coven is different, more aggressive?" Commander Zeir muses. "The scion mentioned you called them the Tainted? What can you tell us about this new group you've encountered?"

I quickly chew the massive bite of food I just shoveled into my mouth, which is a shame because it's delicious. This conversation is really going to get in the way of savoring this meal like it deserves.

"That they're not new." I take a quick drink of water to wash everything down and note that no one felt the need to check my drink or food for poison like they did at Nixy's. "That alone should tell you a lot about how careful and calculating they are, since they're not on The Horde's radar. Initially, we also thought they were an evolution or a branch of blood brokers, but now I'm not so sure."

"And why is that?" Galerus questions, leaning forward until his elbows are on the table and his fists are tucked under his chin.

"I first heard about the Tainted on a supply run. A merchant was gossiping about a group of sorcai who'd been in the area who smelled like rotten magic. I didn't think much of it then, just made a note to keep an eye out, and that was that. But as more reports trickled in about this new coven and their stench, a pattern started to form. It just took me a while to see it."

"Rotten magic?" Commander Drazyn interrupts.

I shrug. "It's the best way I can explain it. Sometimes they can hide the smell. I've also noticed that some Arcs are more sensitive to it than others. Wyverns almost never sense it, but I could always pick out the faintest traces even in a crowd. Today, your Wing caught the scent pretty quickly, so maybe it's a drake thing," I tell Aeson, tapping my nose with a finger.

"Wait. Today? You smelled them here in Paragon City . . . today?" Aeson growls, turning from the table to face Ogdan, the demand for answers clear in the tightening of his fists and the clenching of his jaw.

"Another team is already investigating," the Burner explains. "We're pulling everything we can from the feeds in that area and canvassing the businesses and homes in the vicinity. We were unable to track the threat at the time of discovery because we were forced to pursue the Syphon instead."

Aeson's head snaps in my direction, and I feel like a kid who just got tattled on and now I'm in big trouble. I send Ogdan a blistering glare.

"Explain," the commander barks, and something in my chest begins to stir in response to the roiling fury now aimed at me.

"I recognized a male and ran him down. I thought he was one of them, but it turned out he was just paparazzi following us around in hopes of finding a story he could sell."

"You just . . . ran him down, in a wyvern borough, instead of letting your guards handle it?" Aeson presses, his tone that eerie kind of calm people use when they're really pissed.

"In my defense, things happened really fast and I took action, which is something I do when I feel threatened," I add with a pointed look at all the members of Aeson's Wing. "And they're *your* guards, not mine."

A low growl fills the room. The commanders at the table tense and look cautiously over at Aeson, the source of the reverberating displeasure now vibrating the dishes on the table.

"Don't start with me, Spare, I'm not in the mood," I snap.

So much for my plan to get all flirty and start winning him over.

Shit.

I'll have to try again tomorrow.

Frustrated, I tighten my grip on my cutlery and match Aeson's look of disapproval with one of my own. I need a lecture like he needs a butter knife through the hand. He can try to put me in my place about this, but it's going to end bloody . . . probably on both sides.

Challenge suffuses both of our gazes, and tensions slowly mount as we continue to stare at each other.

"I already explained the trust thing, so spare me the dramatics, Noctis."

One eyebrow twitches as his eyes narrow at me even more. "Dramatics?" he questions imperiously, but there's a peculiar edge to the fire in his stare that gives me pause.

Is he into this?

I lean forward in my chair, not so far that I look like I'm outright threatening the commander, but enough to flash a little extra skin.

"What else would you call all this growling and snarling, Aeson? Very unbecoming of a commander, let alone a scion, if you ask me."

Anger pulses through his clenched jaw at my taunt, but a flash of surprising heat blazes in his gaze, and it's all I can do not to gasp and point it out.

Holy shit, he is into this!

Aeson Noctis likes 'em feisty. I can do feisty. My plan to turn the tables just got way easier. I can't help the smile that pulls at my lips. I feel like I just found buried treasure, and now I need to figure out how to keep it secure without anyone else discovering it.

His scorching gaze drifts to my solitary dimple, and something alights in his eyes that I can't decipher.

"She had these," Herm announces, dousing the moment as he approaches the table and deposits both of my trusty butter knives in front of Aeson.

I jerk back, shocked and affronted.

"Hey!" I protest and then hurry to check the hidden sheaths inside the tops of my boots, which is the last place I put my makeshift weapons. My fingers find the place where the knives should be, but, sure enough, they're now empty. "How the fuck did you get those?"

The Stormer offers me a cheeky smile but doesn't answer the question as he reclaims his position on the other side of the room.

Aeson blows out a long, exasperated breath, and I'm annoyed to find his bossy asshole mask firmly back in place. Commander Galerus eyes the flatware and promptly covers his mouth with his hand, I'm pretty sure to hide the grin that's sneaking across his face.

"Why did you have these?" Aeson asks, lifting one of the dull knives and inspecting it as though he suspects it might transform into something more akin to an actual weapon if he stares at it hard enough.

"Are you really not getting the whole 'I don't trust *any* of you' thing? Because there are only so many ways I can say it."

I take a bite of something that looks like a vegetable and pause because it's unexpectedly sweet. I quickly sample another mouthful and bite back a groan of approval. I may not trust The Horde, but damn, whoever is in the kitchen knows what they're doing.

"And *this* is the answer?" Aeson challenges, holding up the butter knife so the rest of the table can properly see it. "What can you even do with this?"

"Plenty," I tease and then throw in a saucy little wink for good measure.

"I, for one, wouldn't mind seeing that," Commander Galerus murmurs as he smooths a hand over his man bun.

Aeson snaps his glare toward the other male, and Galerus's grin dies a quick death. I try not to laugh when Aeson inhales deep and slow, looking around the room like he needs something to ground himself so he doesn't rip the other male's head off and spew fire down his throat.

Dragons really are so damn possessive.

"We will address this and the guard issue later," Aeson grumbles after a long, agitated moment. He drops the butter knife back onto the table, and an insulting ping rings out instead of the hearty thunk a good knife would make.

I really need some proper weapons.

Despite that, I'm still tempted to grab the knife currently resting at the side of my plate and shove it in my boot. Embarrassing as it is, it's still technically better than nothing. The thought that sticky-fingers Herm will probably just magic it away again is the only thing that stills my hand. Well, that and a girl can only get caught with butter knives so many times before it starts to affect her reputation.

"What do these Tainted—as you call them—smell like?" Ventis asks, redirecting everyone's attention back to the important subject at hand.

I wait for a beat for someone from Aeson's Wing to answer, but when I look up, I realize the female commander is addressing me specifically.

"Um, like a dead body that's been festering in the heat of the deadlands for days. It's like cooked meat that's gone bad, but there's a distinct hint of that peppery magic smell that a sorcai cast has."

"Are you sure they're sorcai?" she counters.

"Yes. I've seen them wield just like the sorcai do. They look the same, their magic smells the same, they use the same methodology to cast and manipulate magic. If it walks like a duck and quacks like a duck, it's probably a duck, even if it smells like rotten foie gras," I joke.

Nobody laughs.

"You mentioned you found a pattern to their movements?" Drazyn inquires. "What was it?"

I pull in a deep breath and quickly weigh the pros and cons of telling these commanders the truth. Earlier today, I probably wouldn't have, but earlier today, I wasn't confident I was right. The Tainted showing up outside Nixy's, however, confirmed it.

"Me," I answer simply. "I think they're hunting me."

Aeson stiffens and each of the other commanders seems to sit up a little straighter, their polite demeanors instantly growing more serious.

"And before you ask, I don't know exactly why. I didn't even start piecing it all together until after Lairwood, but today cemented it. For some reason, the Tainted really want my blood. And, from the look of things, they aren't afraid to take on The Horde to get it."

CHAPTER 23

Aeson growls in warning. Menace vibrates in his tone, and determination and wrath are etched in his features. His dragon mark seems to ripple, and what's strange is that I swear I can feel the movement across my own throat.

"They can't have you," he rumbles dangerously.

"Great," I snark, rubbing my neck. "I'll be sure to let the Tainted know that the next time I see them. No doubt they'll apologize profusely and immediately leave the city, never to be seen again. My hero!"

Aeson's glower is scorching, but now that I know he likes it when I go toe to toe with him, all it does is make me want to rile him up even more, see how far I can bend him before he snaps.

"Good to see that mouth is as tart as ever," he mutters dryly, but I catch the spark of desire that flickers across his face as his eyes dart down to my lips before he quickly looks away.

"Did you just call me a tart, Spare?" I gasp dramatically, tilting away from him as though I just can't believe my ears. "Don't make me challenge you to a duel to restore my honor, Commander."

Aeson opens his mouth to argue, but Commander Drazyn interrupts.

Cock block.

"We've strayed very far from the purpose of this meeting," he points out, but his efforts to rein in the conversation are spoiled by the chuckle Commander Zeir lets loose when I flip Aeson off.

Abruptly, a loud knock fills the room. All eyes swing to the double doors as Gatlin moves to answer it. A male in bright red scale armor enters and then bows deeply.

"Scion, the initiates await your Call to Arms."

The drake doesn't wait for a response before he straightens and leaves. Gatlin shuts the doors behind the unexpected visitor, and I look around the room, trying to figure out what's going on.

Call to Arms?

Are we at war?

Aeson stares at me, his gaze suddenly intense, and a tremor of awareness creeps up my spine and unfurls in my chest. He leans closer, and I realize that move is just as effective on me as it was on him earlier.

He's in fitted black clothing that I didn't take time to appreciate when I first walked in and needed to get the lay of the land. His top is some kind of supple leather, probably made from a rare animal with a price tag higher than I'm capable of counting to. The arms are a different fabric that molds to every muscle like it's been poured on. There's a hood that looks like it would cover his neck if he pulled it up, and I wonder if it's been designed that way to hide his dragon mark and face when he needs to.

It makes me think of the owl paparazzo from earlier and how he was following Aeson's Wing members on the off chance they might see him. It's hard for me to picture someone like him ever needing to hide, but I never thought about how hard it would be to just exist when everyone knows who you are and probably wants something from you.

I've lived a life of anonymity and inconspicuousness. I've clutched my secrets to my chest and, until now, have never been forced to reveal them. I can't imagine what it's like to live on the other side of that coin with everyone knowing everything there is to know about you, or thinking they do anyway.

He dips his chin and sort of looks at me through his lashes, like he's preparing to tell me something of vital importance. My nerves start to quaver as he takes his time to speak. Did something happen? Did The Horde find the others? Is that who they're going to war against?

"We're going to protect you," he finally tells me, and my gut sours even more, because what in the Blood Rite does *that* mean?

"Protect me?" I ask, and he nods solemnly. "From what exactly?"

His brow furrows as though he thought the answer was obvious. "From everything. From these Tainted, whoever they are. The blood brokers. From the dragons who betrayed your kith."

Relief swarms me, and the wasps in my stomach instantly calm. Ens and the others are safe. He's not threatening me.

"I know you don't believe that, that you don't trust us yet," he continues, "but we will protect you. *I* will protect you, Ever. No matter what."

Damn. The sound of my name on his lips is a potent shot I'm utterly unprepared for. Now I'm the one staring at his mouth, wondering if I would taste as good there as I sound. His fingers twitch, like he's suppressing the urge to reach across the table and touch me, and I consider what I would do if he gave in to the impulse instead of fighting it.

Confusion permeates my sudden fervor, because this isn't part of the plan. Yes, I need to make him think I'm interested, that I'm falling for him, but I'm not supposed to actually feel any of those things. Somehow his presence is poking holes in my good sense, and I don't know whose game we're playing here. I'm setting the terms and positioning the pieces, but somehow we're playing on his board and he's controlling the moves.

Before I can even attempt to wrangle my reaction and think of something to say, Aeson stands and then strides over to the far wall. The wall retracts at the commander's approach and reveals what looks like a viewing box with several rows of descending seats and a large arena beyond.

Without a word, the commanders around me get up from the table and follow him. I watch them go, slightly unnerved, but eventually my curiosity edges out my apprehension, and I trail after them.

Aeson's Wing moves with me, but I don't bother asking any of them for answers. If anyone wanted me to be in the loop of what's going on, they would have just told me. Besides, this tracks for The Horde; why be straightforward when you can be flashy?

The other commanders take a seat, but Aeson waits at the back of the box. His presence there feels like an invitation, and I let that thread of instinct tug me over to him. As I get closer, I'm able to see what appears to be a large training area below. Unease stirs in my center when I draw even with Aeson and take in the drakes all gathered in the center of the arena.

Rows and rows of them, standing in sharp formation, hands at their sides, feet together, eyes forward, and faces blank of all emotion. There must be fifty of them, mostly males, but a few females are sprinkled in too. They're all wearing matching gear for forms: loose black pants and fitted tank tops. Dragon marks of all kinds wrap around limbs, peek out from under clothing, and decorate several shaved heads.

"Fledglings?" I ask Aeson as my eyes flit between the rows of individual soldiers.

"Flight Leaders," he corrects. "Hoping to move up the ranks into a Wing. We put a call out a few days ago. They've answered it."

Understanding washes over me, clearing away any lingering residue of doubt. A Call to Arms. This is what he meant. It's an invitation.

"Are you filling ranks or forming a new Wing?"

My trepidation simmers to a tepid caution. I've heard about this kind of thing. Craith used to tell stories about the trials, contests, and sparring involved in advancing through the ranks of The Horde. He never referred to it as a Call to Arms, or knew much about dragon Wings, as wyverns were never allowed to be a part of them, but I'm instantly intrigued by whatever is happening.

"We're forming a new Wing," Aeson replies, his hawklike stare keen as he surveys the turnout.

"Oh? Whose?" I ask politely, brushing my arm against his as I rise up on my tiptoes and pretend like I'm trying to get a better look at what's happening down below.

He turns to me, and there's an unexpected spark of satisfaction flickering across his face. "Yours," he declares matter-of-factly, and then he glides down the stairs to the front of the box, and every head in the arena snaps up in perfect unison to greet him.

A ripple of fervent anticipation eddies through the waiting Flight Leaders, and my stomach drops.

Well, shit.

I know he said we'd address the whole Wing issue later, but I didn't think he meant this. My irritated stare flickers over to Tove. Why do I once again feel like I've been set up? Did his Wing plant the owl shifter? Did they purposefully set off this whole chain reaction of trust issues just so I'd end up exactly where Aeson wants me?

Or is this all the commander's doing? Enamor me with vows of protection and then dangle safety and trust like they're pretty little baubles that are mine for the taking as long as they're wrapped in a Wing-shaped package.

I force myself to inhale slowly and then exhale even slower. Nixy warned me. She said they moved fast. I knew they were cunning, but trying to anticipate all the ways they could be trapping me is going to make my head explode.

Now, if I can just get out of this Wing nonsense. The last thing I need is any more of Aeson's spies buzzing around me, which is exactly what will happen if I don't play this right. I need to counter his move, but how? And if I can't, how do I use this to my advantage?

"Over the next five days, you have a chance to prove yourself," Aeson declares, his voice booming through the arena. "It will not be easy. It will take everything you have and still demand more. Many of you will fail. And even if you succeed, you still have to be chosen for trial. This Call to Arms is a royal one. As always, the blood oath is to the death."

A cheer goes up from the formation of drakes as though they're celebrating the possibility of their impending death. Crazy fucking dragons. I wasn't sold on the whole Wing idea, but I'm sure as shit not up for anything involving blood oaths and death decrees.

"Now . . . " Aeson bellows, a tinge of excitement echoing through the reverberation. "Show us what you've got. Show us what it means to be Horde! Begin!"

A roar of approval crashes through the arena, and I feel the ground under my feet tremble from the force of it. Goose bumps pebble my skin from the raw power, and I feel my own call to action pumping through my veins.

Aeson turns around and looks directly up at me. A cacophony of noise reaches our viewing box as instructors below begin to assign groups of drakes to run the various courses that have been set up around the arena. Several vid screens have materialized in front of the commanders. Some of them show live feeds of what's happening on the ground, and others have still shots of the Flight Leaders who are participating, with their details and stats listed out. It would be an impressive setup if I had any interest in picking a winning team, which I don't.

I can't let this happen.

I have a Flight at home I'm responsible for, my own people to protect, and even though Aeson doesn't know any of that, the way he's trying to back me into a corner with this whole thing isn't going to work for me.

I glare down at Aeson and then at the other commanders, who I realize are also now staring at me. I don't even acknowledge Aeson's Wing members, because fuck everyone at this point.

"No," I assert, holding up my finger in that angry-mom way that Saba uses on her kids. It always makes those vicious little wyverns listen; maybe it can work for me too.

"No to what?" Aeson asks, confused.

"No to all of it," I declare, and then I turn and calmly walk away.

I have zero clue where I'm going, but they can run their little obstacle courses and play their Wing games all they want. I'm not going to sit here and make nice while they tie their puppet strings to me and try to force me to dance for them.

I don't dance for anyone.

"Claws," Aeson shouts, but I ignore him.

I make it to the table in the other room before I sense someone reaching for me. I duck to avoid the grab, and swipe a familiar butter knife from the table. Like the trained grappler he is, Aeson presses his advantage, trying to wrap me up in his massive arms and cage me in against his body. That sort of thing worked on me back in Lairwood, but I've had time to rest and recover since then.

I spin out of his grasp and do my best to kick his knee in. He jumps back, keeping the thick sole of my boot from cracking his patella like an egg. Ogdan approaches me from the side, so I grab a plate of food off the table and chuck it at him. He leans out of the way but then looks up at me with disgust when something from the plate splashes on his pristine onyx scale armor.

"That was uncalled for, lass," he scolds, but I'm not distracted and turn to keep Sondar and Herm in my sights as they try to slink closer.

"Back off," Aeson barks at his Wing, and instantly everyone gives us distance.

"Such good boys," I taunt the guards, purposefully ignoring Tove, figuring it'll irritate her more than any name-calling would.

"Stop taunting my Wing, Claws," Aeson censures.

"Stop trying to corner me," I counter, moving away from him as he advances.

"Is there a particular reason why you've armed yourself with a butter knife again?" he asks, stalking forward until we've done half a circuit around the table.

I shrug. "I keep warning you assholes not to touch me, and you keep trying to touch me."

Aeson chuckles, and my butterflies decide to scramble the jets and fly formations in my stomach.

"So what's the plan, Claws? You know . . . when you've made your way through the cutlery and fine china, how are you going to best all of us then?"

I quickly glance around the room, assessing my options. "The chairs look pretty sturdy, bet you I could do some damage with them."

His smile grows even wider. "Why are you even mad? The Call to Arms just started," he asks innocently, like he doesn't know exactly what he's doing.

"I don't want a Wing, Aeson," I tell him curtly.

"And why is that?" he asks, taking a step closer and pushing me another step back.

"For starters, I don't need one."

"Wrong," he interjects. "Every prominent dragon receives a Wing. The king. His advisors. Members of the royal family. The nobles. We all have protection, it's necessary."

We take another half turn around the table.

"It's not *necessary*. I've survived just fine without a Wing," I point out, barely managing not to cringe at the weak argument. But it's not like I can just tell him I know he's putting on a convincing show of concern all so he can handpick an expert team of babysitters for me.

Aeson gives me a judgmental look, the kind that taunts *you can do better than that.*

Maybe if I were as skilled at deception and strategy as he is, I could.

"What is this?" I whisper-shout, gesturing to the spectators' box. "Tove said making people think I was your mate for a little while would protect me. That I should play along, but it's temporary . . . *That* doesn't look temporary." I wave a hand at the arena and plaster on my best doe-eyed, poor-me look.

Aeson's smile immediately turns into a scowl, and he looks over at Tove, who's shooting poisoned darts at me with her eyes. Pretty sure she's never going to *help me out* again, not that we were exactly frolicking toward bestieship before this.

"I just got here. I'm not Horde. I'm not part of the royal family. And we're not actually mates. Why do I have to choose a Wing now?"

We've almost circled the table for a third time, and it feels like some fucked-up game of chase. It's pointless, and I don't want to keep playing, yet stopping feels like giving in, and when it comes to dragons, if you give an inch, they'll take *everything.*

"This has nothing to do with me and you and everything to do with your safety . . . "

I open my mouth to argue that there is no him and me, but he cuts me off.

"You are Ever Tenebrae, daughter of King Merik Tenebrae. As the last Syphon, you are part of a royal kindred. Revealed or not, you are a dragon, which means you are part of The Horde. You need to be protected," he tells me earnestly, his bright blue eyes fervent and his face resolute. "You're one of us, Claws—stop fighting it."

My heart lurches and rolls like it's trying to avoid the points he's making. He takes three strides closer this time, like he's hoping I'll finally allow myself to be caught, but once again I dance away.

"Do you even know how a Wing works?" he asks when I load another argument on my tongue and prepare to fire. "Members of a Wing are only beholden to their Heart," he continues before I can say anything. "That's what we call the dragon they vow to protect. You were right when you said that my Wing had divided loyalties. They will do what their Heart orders, but ultimately, if we're both in danger, their vow of protection to me would overrule any order to protect you. There's a lot of nuance to the relationship that's hard to explain, but when you take a Wing, the only person they're loyal to after their oath is you. Not even the king can supersede that."

I throw up my hands in exasperation. "Why the fuck would a bunch of strangers want to make me their Heart? They don't know me, and I don't know them. That doesn't engender trust on either side. It makes no sense."

Out of nowhere, he leaps for me. I yelp with surprise, but I don't react fast enough and instead of twisting out of range, I somehow make it easier for Aeson to pin me against the wall. He presses closer, his arms caging me in, and I impotently press the tip of my dull butter knife under his chin.

"That's why there's a Call to Arms. That's just the beginning of how a Wing is formed. Each day for five days, the selection pool will narrow. On the last day, you'll choose a select number of guards that you think will work best for you. After that, there's a trial period where you'll get to know them and they'll get to know you. Once that probationary time is over, the final members of your Wing take their oaths, and everything is solidified in blood."

I consider his words carefully, churning them around in my mind as I look for loopholes and traps, but he's just so damn close it makes it hard to think straight. My pulse is loud and insistent in my ears, my chest is tight and heavy, and my lungs no longer seem interested in oxygen unless it's laced with him.

"What's to keep them from betraying me, from learning my secrets and vulnerabilities and then quitting after the trial and selling me out to someone else?" I ask softly.

The smile he gives me feels like both a taunt and a promise. He surrounds me, pressing closer and completely overwhelming my senses. I snap into focus and remind myself that I can't let Aeson Noctis beguile away my control. I need to steer this in a way that works for me.

Executing phase one of my plan, I let myself relax against him. Just enough to make him wonder if I'm softening toward him and subconsciously giving in. To play on the fight he also craves, I press my butter knife even harder against his skin.

To my surprise, I actually nick him. I didn't know the buttery little bastard had it in him. I'd almost feel proud if I didn't now have to watch a lone drop of blood slip down the muscles of Aeson's throat.

Why does it smell so good?

Aeson reaches over and plucks the flatware from my hand. I don't even put up a fight. We both know it's done all the damage he's going to allow. He drops his head a little, his weighted gaze roving over my face and pausing on the spot on my cheek where my dimple is currently hiding.

"Once your final trial starts, any drake that isn't chosen to become a member of your Wing is put to death," he explains in a tone of voice made for whispering dirty things instead of discussing the finer points of killing off Wing applicants. "From the moment they're selected by you for that final trial, they know that they either earn a place by their Heart's side or forfeit their life. And it's not just one-sided. If you as a Heart prove unworthy, if your guards would rather die than swear an oath to you, that's its own kind of death sentence. You would be left unprotected, and in our world, no one survives alone for long."

I shake my head and at the same time run the back of my fingers lightly over his stomach, feigning absentmindedness, like I'm too lost in thought to realize what I'm doing. "I don't think I'm ready for that kind of commitment, Aeson. It's not you, it's me. I'm just not in the right place in life, you know, for a death oath."

A few muffled titters sound off from behind the commander, and I'm reminded that we have an audience.

In a deft move, I slip out between Aeson and the wall and put distance between us. A low growl rolls out of him as he turns and tracks me again.

Another drop of blood slips down his neck, painting a little line across one of the flames of his dragon mark. The unexpected wound only coaxes out a few drops, but in a world built on blood, it feels like a monumental waste. There are people out in Drameric that would kill for the minuscule amount carving a slow path down his throat, and yet he makes no move to stanch it.

He takes a step toward me, and something in his body language as he moves has me instinctively dropping into a defensive stance. He pauses and studies me for a moment. After a beat, he nods to himself like he's come to some secretive conclusion.

"I'll fight you for it," he offers, and it takes a second for my brain to catch up with what he's saying.

"Fight me for what?"

"For your Wing. You insist you don't need protection, that you're somehow the exception to the rule, so prove it. If you win, no Wing. If I win, you give at least ten drakes a final trial."

I go still, his offer floating tenuously in the air between us. Ten drakes is a lot, but if I win . . . I study him, sizing him up, weighing the odds that I could actually come out on top. If I had more time to train, I might actually have a shot. That, or if I blindfolded him and tied his hands behind his back, I'd probably need to bind his feet while I'm at it, maybe a gag too . . . but I doubt I could get him on board for that.

"Four drakes," I parry warily.

"Eight."

"Six," I rebut.

"Six," he agrees . . . a little too quickly.

I want to argue, but technically I just got what I wanted. Besides, all I need to do is win and I can have *zero* Wing members.

"No affinities, you can't call your scale armor, and I get to choose three weapons," I haggle. It's not blindfolded with bound hands and feet, but it's better than nothing.

His answering smile is sly. "No affinities, I won't call my scale armor, and I'll do you one better than weapons—we'll use a haptic simulator. *That* will make us as evenly matched as we can get."

I scowl at him, not sure if I'm irritated or impressed with the way he just baited me. I should probably say no—he looks a little too eager for me to say yes—and yet I can't help but wonder how I would fare against him. I got a little taste just now, and even though I know it's dangerous to be gluttonous about it, I want more. And not this cat-and-mouse shit that we've been doing here. I want to see what I can really do against a dragon.

It's risky, especially if we're using tech I've never even heard of, but that's never been a problem for me before. I do some of my best work when I'm up against the wall.

My smile is slow, but the gleam in my gaze is undeniably eager. My heart speeds up, and I can already feel adrenaline pumping through my veins just begging for release.

"All right, Spare. You've got yourself a deal."

CHAPTER 24

"Whoa," I marvel as I follow the others into a room that could fit the entire Syphons' camp back in The Scorch at least five times over. "What is that?"

Aeson's grin is cocky as he approaches the massive glass enclosure sitting dead center in the middle of the sprawling chamber. "That is our fully integrated bio-haptic training simulator."

"The little one anyway," Commander Ventis announces from behind us.

"Little?" I question with a raised brow.

"We have a bigger version in the south range that we use for flight combat training," she tells me with a small, dismissive shrug.

"Damn, how big is that one?" I ask with an impressed whistle.

"Big," she answers simply.

Aeson's Wing files in around us, some of them heading toward the bleacher benches on one side of the training facility, while others take up positions around the room to watch and guard from. My wonder-struck gaze drifts to rows of sleek, modern conditioning equipment, and when I look up, I notice a few observation boxes above.

My thoughts flash to the ragged, piecemeal facility we have back home and all the hours I've spent in it, training, bleeding, pushing myself. I've probably spent more time there than I have anywhere else, and I have the sudden urge to stamp my sweat and hard work all over this place and claim it for my own.

Dragons are covetous creatures. We collect, hoard, and squirrel away anything and everything that we find valuable. I don't typically have to combat the innate drive to keep and claim since I haven't revealed, but when the need to take and own hits, it takes no prisoners, and this place and everything in it calls to me. A few months training in a facility like this and I'd be back to the condition I was in before the Tainted took me.

"You're drooling," Aeson whispers in my ear, his sudden closeness jolting me out of my thoughts.

He tugs lightly at the end of the ponytail I just haphazardly threw up, tilting my head back until I'm looking up at him.

"If this place is doing it for you, Claws, wait until you see my private gym."

His smile is impish and he releases my ponytail and taps his finger under my chin to close my mouth. I didn't even realize it had dropped open.

I glower over at him, annoyed that I let myself be dazzled so easily. "Careful, Spare, or I'll think you like me," I taunt, needing space between us but not wanting to step back and make him think I'm retreating.

"Careful, Claws, or I just might."

The asshole chuckles as he walks away to join Sondar and Farrow, and I discreetly wipe at my mouth, just to be sure nothing is there.

He's good. I'll give him that. I could almost believe he means it, if I didn't know what was at stake.

The weight of someone's gaze is heavy on my shoulders, and I look around to find Commander Ventis watching me intently.

"So how does this work?" I ask her, ignoring the prickle of warning at the back of my neck and instead studying the simulator in front of me.

"The system will take a few scans, and then it will run you through a series of maneuvers and drills to gauge things like your range of motion, the force of your hits and kicks, your bite PSI, things like that . . . "

"Bite PSI?" I question, taken aback. "Is that . . . a thing?"

One dark eyebrow twitches at my question, and I can feel the judgment radiating off the micro-movement. "We like to train for all actualities, which, for dragons, includes biting. However, we can list that as a disqualifier for your match if it makes you . . . uncomfortable."

I watch the female warily as she confidently approaches the solid wall of the simulator. A seam appears, and then a doorway suddenly materializes, granting entry.

I don't know why Ventis volunteered to help when Aeson told the others where we were going and what we were doing, but I don't get the impression she's my biggest fan. She's not entirely prickly, but something about me is clearly bothering her, and I wonder if she'll have the guts to outright tell me what it is or if she'll continue to stew.

"Sure, no biting," I agree distractedly as I follow her into the transparent enclosure.

Aeson and Sondar are already on the other side of the big cube, and a ribbon of curiosity about the scion and biting starts to wrap itself around my thoughts as I watch him. Quickly, I slam the door and then scurry away from that unwelcome stream of consciousness.

Ventis wanders to the corner closest to us and taps a circle on the floor with her foot. Unexpectedly, a faint mechanical hum fills the air, and a control tower rises from the ground. She swipes her hand over the top of the rising pillar, making a keyboard and screen light up.

"Once we've established some baselines for you, I'll place a few tactors on your body that will create a bio shield that controls the sensory feedback from not only your opponent, but the simulated environment as well," Ventis continues to explain.

Curious, I reach out to touch the wall closest to me. Surprise filters through my bewilderment when I find it isn't glass like I thought it was. It's not even hard like a wall should be. There's a give to the density of the clear panels, like they're designed to absorb and distribute the force of a direct hit.

Fascinating.

"How does the simulator even the playing field between opponents?" I ask absently while I circle the controls Ventis is keying things into.

"It doesn't make two opponents equal per se," Ventis counters. "Your skill level and experience are still your own. All the simulator does is regulate the force used against one another and help mitigate any damage. The tactors will still mimic the appropriate pain drives and trigger other physical responses, there just won't be any actual damage done to your body. I suppose the *even playing field* is that you won't die. Which is more than could be said if this were real."

I roll my eyes at her dig, not letting it get to me. I'm harder to kill than she realizes; the last week alone has proven that.

"In other words, my opponent can still hit like a tank, but the pain will all be in my head?" I hedge.

Ventis considers my question for a beat and then nods. "More or less. Now, stand on the X and we'll begin . . . please." She tacks the last part on like it's an afterthought, and I fight the urge to blow out an exasperated breath.

Nope, she's definitely not on Team Ever.

I hesitate, looking around for a locker room. "Do I need to change into something else?"

"Do you have anything to change into?" she queries, tapping away at the console in front of her but offering no help beyond that.

I look over to see if Aeson is still in his nice clothes and find him punching a battle dummy that's risen from the ground. Different sections of the dummy's body light up, and Aeson aims a hit or a kick there based on the monotone instructions that seem to be coming from the dummy itself. That must be how the simulator determines the base level of force we'll be using when we fight.

Aeson hasn't changed into anything more fitting for sparring, but I note his clothes don't seem to be restricting his movements in any way. The same cannot be said of mine. Then a thought occurs to me, and I look down at my fussy outfit with a mischievous smile.

Finding the clasp at the center of my corset, I unhook it. The stays automatically disengage and I pull the contraption off. I decide to keep my pants on, figuring the patches of armor Nixy said were sewn in will be helpful. Then I remove my silky, off-the-shoulder top and start to unlace my boots.

Back at Nixy's, I gave my strapless bra the jump test, but I do it again now, twisting and darting around just to be sure everything stays where it's supposed to. Although, if this fight figuratively goes tits up, I'm not above using a wardrobe malfunction in my favor.

"What are you doing?" Aeson demands, suddenly behind me when I turn around from tossing my discarded clothes out of the cube.

I barely manage to avoid slamming into him while also tamping down on a surprised gasp at his popping up out of nowhere. He moves very quietly for someone the size of a mountain.

"Getting ready to be scanned. What are you doing?" I ask innocently, stepping around him to go stand where Ventis indicates.

He hovers over me as I move, his big frame working to block me from the view of anyone else. His gaze is a sweeping threat as he looks around to ensure no one is watching.

"Why are you naked?" he demands, his hands fluttering at his sides as though he's debating whether to use them to cover me up. His hard eyes slip slowly down my body, and I feel it like a warm caress against my skin. Heat settles low in my core, and when Aeson looks back up, I find the same heat banked in his gaze.

Leaning a little closer, I bark out a sultry laugh. "I'm hardly naked, Aeson. I can get naked if you need to see the difference though."

A low, spine-tingling growl vibrates out of him, sounding simultaneously like a warning not to dare and an invitation to take this conversation elsewhere. I suppress a smile.

"Why aren't you wearing a shirt?" he grumbles, pressing even closer to me until I feel his breath tickle down my cheek and sweep across my neck. A needy shiver rolls down my spine, and goose bumps scatter across my body.

I look up at him with a demure bat of my lashes and a playful tilt to my lips. "Because I can't move in my clothes the way I need to. What's the matter, Spare? Distracted by a little skin?"

His voice drops low enough to make me shiver. "Is that what you're doing, Claws? Distracting me?"

Pressing up on my tiptoes, I skim my chest lightly against his, just enough that he can feel a hint of my hard nipples through my bra. I drop my voice to a whisper, and he leans down, hungry to capture every word. "No, I simply don't want anything getting in the way of kicking your ass."

At my words, the black of his pupils overtakes the bright blue of his irises. With a satisfied smirk, I drop down and step back. Before he can say or do anything, a small drone separates from the console Ventis is standing at and flies toward us, stopping a few feet away where it hovers about chest high. Aeson is forced to back up to give the little machine room, and a bright beam of green light suddenly shoots out and starts sweeping up and down my body as the drone slowly rotates around me. When it finishes its circuit, the little floating ball zips away and nestles itself back into the console to upload its data.

"Fine," Aeson snaps. "Two can play this game."

With that promising declaration, he drags a finger down the side of his shirt. The movement must activate a hidden zipper, or maybe he uses a claw to slice right through the seam; either way, there's now a split in the fabric where there wasn't one before. He removes his shirt and then kicks off his boots so we're both in matching stages of undress.

Instantly, his dragon mark draws my eye, and I'm tempted to step closer and really study it. I stop myself, figuring there will be plenty of time to look when we're beating the shit out of each other. Aeson puffs up a little as I take him in, and I shake my head at his arrogance. Not that I can really fault him for it—if I had muscles on muscles like that, I'd never put clothes on.

"That's an interesting battle strategy, lass," Ogdan lilts, his gray eyes bright with mischief as he approaches.

I sigh.

"Not a very original one though," Tove gibes as she joins the party.

"I like it better when you're both giving me the silent treatment," I declare flatly. "And it's not a strategy," I lie. "I don't carry around a change of clothes on the off chance someone wants to fight me. And no dragon means no scale armor either, dang it." I snap my fingers and make an exaggerated pouty face.

"At the rate you're pissing people off, maybe you *should* start carrying around fighting gear," Tove counters.

"Scion," Ogdan calls, interrupting my caustic retort and nodding in the direction of the entryway. Three concerned-looking drakes I've never seen before are standing over by the room's vestibule.

Aeson nods, his features darkening slightly with concern, and then he walks away without another word, Ogdan and Tove right on his heels. I try to eavesdrop on what's going on with the visitors, but Ventis calls up my own battle dummy from the ground and runs me through a series of drills to establish my baseline for the simulator. By the time I'm done, Aeson is back on his side of the cube, and Sondar is putting what looks like tiny neon-green stickers on the commander's temples, shoulders, wrists, and ankles.

Ventis steps into my line of sight, a case in her hand with bright green stickers no bigger than my pinky nail. These must be the tactors. Without asking or telling me what she's doing, she places a sticker on each of my temples, shoulders, wrists, ankles, and one on my chest.

"Are you going to tell me what I've done to offend you, or should I keep pretending that you're not looking at me like I'm a puddle of piss you just stepped in?" I ask the female evenly as she works.

She doesn't immediately respond, but her scowl cuts so deeply into her features, I'd be surprised if it doesn't leave permanent marks. She pulls in a measured breath as though readying herself for something.

I do the same, only more discreetly. Just when the silence starts to skirt uncomfortable, she finally looks me in the eye.

"Who is your mother?" she asks me point-blank, a hard edge in her ice-blue eyes.

I study her for a moment, wondering where she's going with this. It's not odd that she's curious, but something in the way Ventis is asking makes me think this isn't about curiosity—this feels like it's about condemnation.

"Does it matter?" I counter, examining her reaction to my purposeful evasion.

"It does," she responds simply, giving me nothing more than that.

I narrow my gaze at her. "Why?"

She considers me carefully. And she must see the obstinacy set in my features, communicating that if she wants me to answer her questions, she better be willing to answer mine.

"Because I grew up with Paloma—Queen Tenebrae," she quickly corrects. "We were very close. And I'd like to know who the king betrayed his mate for."

I keep my face blank, my body still, as defensiveness washes over me. A dogged determination glints in her gaze when I don't fulfill my end of the unspoken bargain and answer her question now that she's answered mine.

She shakes her head and her stare grows distant. "When the scion informed me of who you were, I thought I could remain impartial, professional, but you look like him—like your father. I wasn't prepared for how that would make me feel. I'm trying not to, but all I see when I look at you is the way he betrayed one of my dearest friends, and . . . " She trails off, her face forlorn and her words haunted.

I nod, my exhale tired as her words fall heavily between us. She's hurt and heartbroken, and I'm the only one left to aim it at. It's unfair and frustrating, and yet, as much as I want to hold her wrongful estimations against her, there's something in the loss shrouding her that quiets my hurt and calms my indignation.

I've been there, wounded and suffering and needing someone to blame. I understand the need to try to make sense of something nonsensical.

"I met the queen," I tell the commander placidly, willing to extend a little grace and empathy despite her resistance to offer me the same. "She gave me this oval-shaped, dark brown candy that her sons loved, and I instantly shoved the whole thing in my mouth. It. Was. Awful. To this day, I can't remember what it was called, but I will never forget the taste."

I scrunch my face in disgust and fight off a shiver of revulsion at the dusty memory before continuing.

"I quietly panicked because I did not want this candy in my mouth anymore, let alone have to eat it, but what else could I do? I didn't want to offend the queen or her sons—who apparently had horrible taste in treats. But she must have seen the dilemma written all over my little face, because she held the bottom hem of her dress up to my mouth and told me it was okay to spit it out if I didn't like it. So I did. I spit this glob of nastiness right into the middle of her beautiful dress, and she didn't even bat an eye."

A sad smile slips across my face, and my throat grows tight as I recall the softness in the queen's voice and the kindness in her face as she took my hand and gave it a comforting little squeeze.

"I was so nervous, so worried about upsetting her, about ruining her pretty clothes, I started to cry. And then she wrapped me up in a firm hug and let me. She wiped my tears with the clean part of her skirts, and she asked me all about the things I liked to do and eat, about my favorite games and subjects. When I was finally done feeling emotional, she held my hand and said, 'Ducky, let's go find you the treat you deserve,' and we raced to the kitchens and told the chef all about my favorite tart . . . and then we made it. The queen rolled out pastry dough and helped hand-whisk custard because *I* told her that's how the cook did it back home."

My fond smile dims with sorrow, and I notice Commander Ventis lifting a hand to her mouth to hide the tremor of grief there. I take a moment to lock my own sadness down so I can continue.

"I think your loyalty to the queen's memory is admirable. I was only six when we met, but even then, it was obvious she was the kind of dragoness who merited it. If anyone felt betrayed by my existence, it wasn't her. She was kind, and she was loving, and she didn't deserve to die the way she did."

I pause, a flash of blood suddenly marring my vision as screams fill my head, echoes of Queen Tenebrae's horror when her begging and pleading for the lives of her sons fell on cruel and heartlessly deaf ears.

My chest aches, it fights my demand for air, but I force myself to breathe in quickly through my nose and then slowly release it out of my mouth. I do it three more times until I'm once again back inside the simulator, looking into the solemn gaze of Narine Ventis, First Commander of The Horde's Air Fleet.

She watches my momentary struggle but doesn't say a word. I clear my throat and fist my hands to cover the unwelcome quake in them as the flash of memory fades as quickly as it came.

Resolve and perseverance harden in my features, and I level Commander Ventis with a fortified gaze that dismisses the pity now floating in her own.

"I don't deserve your condemnation," I point out. "Whatever you may think about my father, I didn't ask to be born. I didn't ask to survive. And I didn't ask to be here."

Silence filters in between us, and we both let it linger. Her light blue gaze roams over my face, and then she surprises me with a firm nod, a simple, unadorned gesture of acceptance and understanding. She backs up a few paces, and half of a grief-stricken grin slips across her face.

"Gulappe," she offers.

Confusion settles across my face.

"The sweet her boys loved," she tells me. "It was called gulappe. It was made out of fermented molasses and very much an acquired taste."

I shake my head, a small laugh sneaking out. "See, even the name sounds gross."

Commander Ventis chuckles, but I can clearly hear the loss and heartache in the gentle sound. She turns to leave, and I wonder if I just made things better or worse, or maybe changed nothing at all. I knew there would be drakes who didn't understand the choices my father and the other Syphons made, but I always thought their judgment or resentments would be reserved for them, not me.

"He likes to talk while he fights," Ventis calls over her shoulder. "Commander Noctis. It lets him set the pace and distract his opponent while he sizes them up. Don't let him set the pace, Ducky."

And with that, Commander Ventis calmly walks out of the simulator and then leaves the room altogether.

"What was that about?" Aeson asks as he strides over, his questioning gaze bouncing from me to the now-empty doorway.

"Nothing to worry your pretty little head about, Spare," I tease, shaking away my lingering emotions and getting my head back in the game. "Now, are we here to have a tea party or fight? Let's do this."

CHAPTER 25

Sondar claps his hands once, and the loud sound reverberates off the clear walls of the simulator. "Okay, what are we fighting until? First blood? Knockout?"

"Submission," Aeson interjects, not missing a beat, his arrogant grin grating as he turns it on me.

I cross my arms over my chest. "Good luck with that," I mumble, but don't outright object.

"Hard limits?" Sondar inquires.

"Biting, hair pulling, and eye gouging," I briskly list off.

The male nods, tucking a long lock of blue-black hair behind one ear as he keys things into a band on his wrist. He turns to Aeson. "Scion?"

"Her hard limits are fine. I don't have any to add. I, for one, like a dirty fight." He glances pointedly over at me, but there's no playful air or hint of teasing; he looks determined and formidable.

I work not to react, mostly to the annoying heat that starts to pool low in my belly at his words. Something in his tone gives me pause. It's not the innuendo or even the taunting intonation, it's the declaration ringing through the statement. It's as though he's letting me know that he's willing to do anything and everything to win, and I don't think he's referring to just this fight.

Is he on to me?

Does he know I'm on to him?

"Weapons?" Sondar asks, like he's reading off a doomsday checklist.

"None," Aeson declares, a challenging glint in his eyes.

I shrug, feigning indifference. Inside, however, I'm spinning with concern. I was really hoping for a bow staff or maybe a missile launcher to help me go up against the scion's strength and size. Looks like speed and smarts are going to have to cut it.

Evenly matched, my ass.

"Any opinions about location, or should I let the simulator randomly choose?" Sondar queries, his dark gaze fixed on the wristband as he continues to program the parameters of this fight into the sim's systems.

An idea occurs to me, and I pounce on it. "I have an opinion," I declare, and both males turn to me with a questioning brow.

I don't say anything more, and Sondar strides over, offering me his arm so I can access the keypad and screen on his device. Selecting the search window, I type in my selection. Excitement trills through me when I find exactly what I'm looking for. My smile is wide and satisfied as I load the environment into the system, and Sondar steps back. He looks down at what I chose and chuckles, shaking his head.

"Good one, Frills," Sondar accedes, and my smile instantly dies.

"Ever. My name is Ever. Why is that so hard for all of you?" I grump, already knowing it's a lost cause.

"I don't know. Why don't you call me 'Spare' again while I think about it," Aeson retorts, looking just as put out as I feel.

A snort of a laugh escapes me.

Touché.

"All right. I just need to administer the eye drops, and you two can get on with your . . . uh . . . whatever the fuck this is," Sondar teases, and laughter erupts from Aeson's Wing over in the spectator seats at the end of the room.

"What are those for?" I ask as Sondar holds a dropper over one of Aeson's eyes and then the other.

"These connect you with the simulator's virtual environment. When the program is over, the tech deactivates and your body flushes it out in a day or so."

Ignoring the tinge of disquiet that hums through me, I nod and tip my head back so he can drop the tech in my eyes. I've come this far—it's all or nothing at this point.

The drops are cold and somewhat shocking. I blink the slight sting away, my vision hazy but quickly clearing. Not sure what to expect, I look around, but I only see the same diaphanous walls of the simulator and the training room beyond. Then I blink again and I'm standing in the torrid sun, surrounded by the endless black sand dunes of The Scorch.

Home sweet home.

I close my eyes and tilt my head back, feeling the full wrath of a sun I know isn't really there. I pull in deep lungfuls of clean, arid air and detect the subtlest notes of petrichor in the blistering breeze. It must have rained not too long ago.

The sensory feedback of this simulation is like nothing I've ever experienced before. Of course, I knew tech like this existed in theory, but experiencing it is a whole other matter. Part of me is tempted to start walking, to try to get home. I know it's impossible, that I'm not really in the deadlands, but it feels so real, smells and looks real, and my heart aches for it all the same.

A deep and profound loneliness all at once consumes me, and I wonder if this will be the closest I'll ever get to The Scorch again. Will *home* only be within reach through tech-altered senses—never in truth?

An electric buzzing suddenly skitters across my skin, and my eyes snap open to find a thin, barely there, translucent coating covering my entire body. This must be the bio shield Ventis mentioned earlier.

I look over to see Aeson has the same subtle glimmer of tech surrounding him, and he's shifting his weight from foot to foot in obvious discomfort.

Looks like the sand is too hot for the scion's delicate feet.

Good.

"Take your positions," Sondar shouts, pointing to two white circles in the sand about thirty feet apart.

My pulse instantly picks up with excitement, and nerves prod at the sleeping butterflies in my stomach, waking them up until my insides feel like a quivering, flapping mess.

I can do this.

I can beat him.

Easily, I stride over to my mark and then turn and watch Aeson as he struggles not to sink into the sand with every step he takes. I wave away the satisfaction that blooms in my chest with his efforts. There's no point getting ahead of myself. I have no doubt a little heat and sand aren't going to keep him down for nearly as long as I'd like.

"The chime will indicate you can begin. Remember, no biting, no hair pulling, no eye gouging, or you'll be disqualified. Otherwise, the first to submit loses," Sondar declares, but he's nothing more than a disembodied voice floating amidst a sea of black sand.

"You can tap out anytime," Aeson calls to me as he finally makes it to his mark.

"Eat sand," I croon back with a wide, dimple-flashing smile.

Adrenaline floods me, and I slow my breathing in an effort to calm the steady thundering of my pulse. A bead of sweat slips down my temple, and more starts to pool in the hollows of my collarbone. I picture Craith or Iker across from me instead of the dragon scion. Imagine the way they'd taunt and circle me in the training pit back home.

A sharp note peals through the hot, undulating air, and I tense. My focus narrows on the only thing that now matters: destroying Aeson Noctis.

He stands on his mark, eyes sharp and eager, as he studies me. "Ready to show me what you've got, Claws?" he asks, his smirk taunting.

He says something else, but I tune him out, taking Ventis's advice and setting the pace. I start walking toward the commander, my speed picking up with every stride until I'm all-out sprinting. Surprise flares in Aeson's eyes, and his jaw tightens as he watches me come for him. He quickly adopts a strong defensive position, his knees bent and his hands ready at his side.

Less than ten feet away, I start to get low as I sprint across the sand. He matches my positioning, using his fighting prowess to read my body language, which is telling him I'm coming in for a hard body tackle. When I'm almost on him, we both dive at each other. Only I don't go low like Aeson's expecting; I aim high and clear him altogether.

I soar over him, weightless and floating for a fraction of a second before sand explodes all around us as the scion tackles nothing and drops hard to the ground. He recovers quickly, rolling back onto his feet just as I touch down behind him, but I'm already running deeper toward a large hill of sand where it'll be harder for his big, heavy frame to maneuver and easier for me to start tiring him out.

A deep, threatening rumble vibrates across the desert floor behind me, and I feel Aeson's growl roll through me as clearly as I hear it bouncing off the hillside of dunes in front of us.

"You can't run forever," Aeson warns, his voice like rolling thunder.

I sense him giving chase behind me, but I don't waste time turning to look. All my focus is on gaining ground. But as I run, something uncurls in my depths, responding to the resounding growl of the predator behind me.

I just start to make it up the gritty slope I was aiming for when I feel him at my back. Without a second of hesitation, I dive forward. Massive arms wrap around my thighs, throwing off my center of gravity, but I manage to get the handfuls of sand I was aiming for. I twist, as Aeson tries to pull me closer, and toss the sand in his face, aiming for his airways.

He ducks his head to try to avoid the onslaught, loosening his grip enough that I'm able to scramble away from him.

"How's that for dirty, asshole?" I snap, flipping back onto my feet and aiming a kick at his head.

I connect with his shoulder when he quickly drops back to protect his face and skull. He grabs for my leg, but I retract it too fast. With an unexpected burst of speed, he dives for me with a snarl.

Shit.

Throwing myself to the side, I coil, midair, and just barely avoid his massive reach. I land, and somehow he's already there trying to swipe my legs out from under me. I jump to avoid it, but he clips one foot and I go down. Pain blooms in my shoulder and side as I crash to the ground. Sand plumes around us as we slide through the onyx grains. I try to angle myself to get in a few hits, but he covers me too quickly with his massive body and starts to work to pin me.

"You're good, and fast, but you'll have to do better than that, Claws."

I land two succinct elbows to his ribs, and he grunts in response, even though I'm pretty sure it hurts me more than it hurts him.

"Are you made of fucking stone?" I croak as he presses his full weight onto me and tries to pin me in the sand.

But this is my terrain, not his, and I simply sink and squirm, the loose ground not giving him the purchase he needs to properly hold me in place. I wiggle out from under him enough to aim a knee for his nose, but he swiftly lifts a hand and stops me. I throw more sand in his face, and he roars at me when I manage to kick free and start scrambling away from him like some slippery desert crab.

"That's getting old," he grumbles, spitting sand out of his mouth, and then he really starts moving, almost like he was in first gear before and now he's warmed up and ready to go.

Fuck, fuck, fuck!

I spend the next sixty seconds of my life dodging and weaving his brutal strikes with only millimeters of space to spare and nothing but panic and instinct pumping in my veins.

Suddenly, Aeson loses his footing when he steps into sand that's looser and deeper on this part of the dune, and I'm on him, capitalizing on his mistake with a crisp roundhouse that connects right with his jaw.

The crack of unforgiving bone on bone vibrates up my leg, and his head forcefully snaps to the side. I follow through with another kick to his inner thigh and then move in for the kill, but he uses my own dirty trick of sand to the face to force me back.

I blink granules from my lashes and spit more out of my mouth. I'm breathing heavily as I regroup, assessing my options as Aeson drags a thumb across his lips like he expects it to be bleeding. It's not. His bio shield has done exactly what it's designed to and kept him from sustaining any actual damage.

I smile over at him as he cracks his neck and takes me in.

"You can tap out anytime," I taunt.

The tip of Aeson's tongue darts out to test the corner of his lip where his pain receptors are telling him he's injured, and then he aims a dangerous smile my way.

My stomach flops around like a beached fish, and I don't know if I'm excited or worried about the renewed gleam in his eye.

"I don't tap out . . . ever," he informs me, rising to his full, towering height. Sand sticks to his sweaty chest and throat and pours down the rest of his muscled body in tiny streams.

"Neither do I," I snarl, and then I leap for him.

He catches me, but my hits are swift and packed with power. I'm out for fucking blood, done with playing, done with being underestimated, done with holding back. He aims body shots at my torso as I hammer blows to his head. I feel my bones break under the onslaught, but I know it's not real. I know it's just a mind fuck.

I'm feral and relentless in my attack, raining down blow after blow. Aeson slams us into the sand, fracturing my momentum and momentarily knocking the air out of me. But I've been held down and tortured by the Tainted for months. Pain and empty lungs aren't going to override my bloodlust.

Aeson wraps a hand around my throat and bellows in my face, deep and long and menacing. I feel the dominance reverberate through me, the claim, the demand to submit. So I open my mouth and roar right back, because fuck that and fuck him.

Out of nowhere, something visceral, something primal, weaves its way around me, sinking into my depths and latching on. It tugs and coaxes, and then . . . my dragon stirs.

My other side slinks just under my skin, stretching and keening for a way out. A buzz of power fills my limbs and hums in my head. Unmistakable desire floods my system and then Aeson's lips are suddenly on mine. Shock and confusion fire through my synapses, but his mouth moves, demanding access, demanding everything, and abruptly I'm lost to a wave of lust and need that wholly consumes my entire being.

I open for him, meeting his tongue with my own, claiming dominion over his full lips and drinking him down. His hand tightens possessively around my throat, and I moan my approval into his mouth. His tongue strokes and taunts, his lips conquer and imbibe.

He rolls his hips into me, and I spread my legs, needing every inch of him closer. The gritty sand on our skin abrades and scrapes as we press against one another, demanding more. My dragon rides the tide of desire, stoking my hunger and heating my blood until it's molten and searing.

A deep purr rumbles out of Aeson's chest, and his kiss grows rougher, more dominant. His other hand grabs my ass, pulling me tighter against him as he grinds his hard length against me. I nip his bottom lip, my own need for dominance demanding I give as good as I'm getting.

He hisses, but the enthused purr that slips out of him has even more fervor pooling between my thighs.

Out of nowhere, a grating tone rings out and a monotone voice declares, "Simulation over."

The sand underneath us disappears, and the hot sun above us is replaced by bright lights. My back is pressed against a cold, hard floor, and mystification has me pushing Aeson away and sitting up.

"What the fuck is going on?" I demand, looking around and instantly remembering where we are and what we're supposed to be doing.

Aeson's Wing is positioned directly outside of the simulator, their expressions blank but their body language tense.

"Why the fuck did you pull us out?" Aeson snarls at Sondar, and indignation and chagrin heat my cheeks and drip down my throat.

Holy fuck, I was just grinding and kissing Aeson in front of all of them.

"I didn't pull you out. Ever disqualified herself," Sondar rushes to defend.

My head snaps in the direction of the guard. "What? No I didn't. We were . . . " I pause, gesturing between me and Aeson.

My face suddenly feels like it's on fire, and I try to scoot back from Aeson. He immediately growls his objection to any more space between us.

"And then it just stopped," I finish.

Sondar suddenly looks as though he'd rather be anywhere but here, and his eyes flit around the room like he doesn't know where to let them rest. "It says you breached a hard limit. You were disqualified when you . . . uh . . . bit the commander."

I open my mouth to argue, and then it hits me. I nipped him. It was the sensual kind, but . . . I pinch the bridge of my nose and blow out a frustrated breath.

Fuck.

I push Aeson away and quickly get to my feet. He rises with me, looking just as frustrated and not nearly as embarrassed as I feel. He takes a step closer, but I skitter back, needing space.

Irritation and anger froth through my veins, but I don't know if I'm pissed at Aeson or at myself.

What the fuck was I thinking?

"Look at me," Aeson commands. It's gentle, not forceful, and somehow that makes everything worse. "Ever?" he presses, but I shake my head.

My stare is fixed on my hands, and I search for any sign of my dragon, but just like every other time when I need it, it's nowhere to be found. A hollow ache starts in my chest, and the driving need to get far away from this place and Aeson Noctis is suddenly overwhelming.

I move toward the wall of the simulator, and thankfully, a door appears, letting me out. Aeson is tight on my heels, his presence silently demanding, but he doesn't say anything as I pull the tactors off and then grab my clothes from the ground.

Stupid, stupid fucking move, Ever, I chastise internally as I pull my shirt back on.

Be attracted to him, fine. Kiss him, sure, why the fuck not. But don't lose control. Don't lose sight of what you're here to do. And don't lose on a technicality that you fucking imposed.

I wrap my corset around my torso and refasten the top clasp, which activates the others and pulls everything tight until it's once again hugging every curve. I shove one leg into a boot and start lacing it up.

Frustration and disappointment curdle in my gut as I pull on my other boot. He warned me he played dirty; I should have listened. I should have known he'd try to beat me at my own game.

"Well." I clear my throat, pulling my hair down and running my fingers through it until it's somewhat tame. "Looks like you win, Commander."

I finally look up at him and instantly regret it. He looks angry, wholly unrepentant, and devastatingly beautiful. "Not yet, not completely, but I will."

With that, Aeson walks away.

I watch him go, wondering exactly what that's supposed to mean, and worrying that I already know.

CHAPTER 26

A loud roar shakes the ground under my feet and vibrates through the stone bench I'm sitting on. A shadow flickers over me, the gloom devouring my perch one second and disappearing the next as a mighty, acidic-orange dragon streaks by overhead. I watch the majestic beast catch a current in the direction of Talon's Reach, and then I turn around and observe the next initiate preparing for their run.

"Burner. Ash dragon," Herm calls out from where he's standing behind me next to a large arch covered in stunning magenta flowers.

"Nah, I think he's a Channeler. Mist dragon maybe," Blay counters, his purple scale armor only a few shades darker than the blossoms surrounding him.

I ignore the banter, just like I've been ignoring it all morning, and watch as a new male prepares for his turn to showcase how quickly he can shift from his drake form into his dragon. I've watched a few of the other Call to Arms events this morning, but when it comes to choosing future Wing members, this one makes the most sense to me. I know better than anyone how important it is to shift, and how fucked you are when you can't.

As a bonus, the competition is helping to keep Jori, Herm, and Blay occupied with betting and commenting on the initiates' shifts, which means no one is asking any questions—or giving me any shit—about what happened with Aeson yesterday. Which is good, because I still don't know what to make of any of it, and I've decided the best way to move forward is just to pretend like it never happened.

I've found a little garden alcove on the Render Tier that has a perfect view of the runways on Thrasher Tier, where the Call to Arms is taking place. Down below, the drake waiting for his turn to shift gets the nod from the instructor that it's go time. He pulls in a few readying breaths, and then he takes off with a surprising burst of speed and sprints down the runway that's been commandeered for this trial. There is a pair of yellow flags located about halfway down the strip that marks when the drake is clear to reveal his dragon.

The male crosses those flags and promptly leaps into the air. I hold my breath, waiting to see what kind of dragon he'll shift into, but his reveal doesn't immediately take over like it did with the others. The initiate catches good air for a moment, but when he doesn't sprout wings, claws, and scales, gravity has no choice but to humble him.

"Oooh," Jori groans as the drake crashes back down to the ground, hard.

I wince, and the initiate rolls twice, dirt swirling around him in an explosion of limbs, dust, and failure. Just when he's about to skid to a stop, his shift finally kicks in. Scales overtake skin, spikes replace hair, and wings rip free from the male's back. His size quadruples and then quadruples again until the drake is gone and the dragon is revealed.

The blue-gray beast bellows an unmistakably irritated snarl and then surges from the ground with several flaps of his powerful wings. The wind kicks up as the massive creature stretches for the sky. He circles the training field once and then heads in the same direction as the orange dragon and all the others that came before them.

"Well, he got up there eventually. If he scores well for the rest of the tests, this might not boot him out of the running," Blay observes, and Herm and Jori grunt their agreement.

"We all had our own issues with performance anxiety back in our day," Jori points out thoughtfully.

I bite back a snicker.

"The minute you know your Call to Arms is royal, there's a lot more pressure on everything and way more eyes watching every move you make," he adds as he watches the blue-gray dragon weave through the sky.

"True," Blay agrees. "I had trouble getting up and off a deck during mine. They gave us these huge loads we were supposed to shoot off midflight, and I really struggled."

This time, I can't hold back my giggle. All three of them turn their puzzled gazes on me.

"Are you three even talking about Wing trials anymore, or is that code for something I really don't want to know about?"

My smile is wide as I tease the guards, but their faces remain perplexed, like they have no clue as to why I'm tittering away over here. It makes me laugh even harder.

Admittedly, I might be a little slaphappy. I haven't been sleeping well, and the last few nights were no exception. I sigh and run a hand down my face as my laughter fades and slowly drops away. The amusement is a welcome reprieve from the melancholy that was starting to seep past my serrated edges. I should have known it was a bad idea to sit here for as long as I have, watching drake after drake do the one thing I wish I could but can't. Reveal.

I probably should have saved myself the mind fuck and left a while ago—what started out as fun and informative has quickly morphed into something torturous and crushing—but there's something undeniably magical about being around dragons. I've seen them as the enemy, as something to be feared, as the architects of my impending death. But sitting here, watching them like this, it pulls back the curtain on something I've never truly appreciated until now.

Dragons are incredible.

Massive and fearsome. Stunning and lithe.

They're everything I'm fighting to have and everything I mourn.

Every day I spend here in Four Tiers opens my eyes to what I've been missing, for no other reason than I haven't taken the time to see it. My focus has been fixed for so long on surviving and trying to break this bloody curse that it's given me blinders to everything else. But broken or not, I am a dragon inside, and I'm starting to see and understand what that means.

Another dragon whips past us, and just like with all the others, I turn my head toward the sky, close my eyes, and wait to see if my dragon will react to the other's presence. I search my depths for the shattered pieces of what I am, hoping against hope that they'll magically awaken and I can be one step closer to being whole . . . but nothing happens.

My eyes flash open and I exhale an annoyed breath. I wanted to see if all of the roaring, trumpeting, and revealing might have an effect on me. If it might call to my dormant other half the way Aeson's been able to since I got here. It was worth exploring, but so far, there's been nary a stir or a peep of anything in me other than frustration and a growing headache. A fact that's really killing my theory that my reactions could be a proximity-to-dragons thing and not specifically an Aeson thing.

Unfortunately, it seems like that fucker is special. I just wish I knew how and why.

"Scion Noctis approaching," someone declares loudly, like an ancient herald demanding everyone rise to pay respects to the incoming royal.

"Think of the devil and he shall appear," I mumble peevishly, ignoring the flutter that starts in my stomach.

I don't turn around to greet the commander, still not quite ready to see or speak to him after what happened the day before. I'm not even sure what to say. It's just my luck that the only instincts that seem to be waking up from their long, cursed sleep are the insatiable horny dragon ones and not the big, scary, scaled kind.

Part of me is tempted to call Aeson out for setting me up, for wanting to use me. And another part of me is tempted to let him . . . to see if riding his cock will release my dragon.

I snort out a laugh.

What if the key to breaking the curse isn't based on blood and bloodlines like we thought? Maybe the solution is of the fairy-tale variety—only it isn't true love's kiss that sets us free, it's dragon dick.

I shake my head at myself. I really need some sleep. At least one night free of any nightmares or jolting awake in a panic until I realize that I'm not in a cell anymore. Maybe then I'd be able to get my head on straight and stop thinking about Aeson . . . and his lips, his voice, that possessive way he looks at me, his body . . .

"My brother will be glad to hear that you're taking the selection of your Wing so seriously."

I jolt in surprise and turn to find Lorn Noctis standing over my shoulder. My lurid thoughts hastily skitter away at the sight of the heir, and I bat at the irritating buzz of disappointment that tries to dive-bomb me.

"He was worried you'd still be difficult even though you lost your . . . little agreement," Lorn continues, and I fight the urge to roll my eyes.

"Me, difficult?" I chirp. "That doesn't sound right at all."

Lorn tilts his head like he's conceding to my point, but his grin is cheeky. "You've certainly been quiet since you got here. I expected at least one escape attempt by now."

I don't bristle at the implication that he's had eyes on me. I knew I was being watched—hence the being quiet—but it's still vexing as fuck that he's so comfortable with brazenly pointing it out. What's worse is that I can't tell if he's simply being factual or reminding me not to step out of line.

I wave off his comment. "I considered it, but then the royal chef introduced me to her boysenberry cheesecake, and I decided it might be worth sticking around for a bit."

Lorn chuckles. "That's Aeson's favorite dessert too," he tells me, and I like *that* even less than the reminder that I'm always being watched.

"I never said it was my favorite; I just said it was worth delaying my plans for a day or two," I correct while casually examining my nail beds.

Lorn's eyes glitter with amusement, but it's not the same kind of gleam that tells me he's into this kind of back-and-forth. It's the look of a predator that thinks it's diverting to watch its prey put up a fight. The cat is happy to let the mouse struggle. It might even let it go a few times for the entertainment of watching the mouse frantically try to scurry away before being caught again. But eventually the cat's going to get bored and bite the little mouse's head off, and that will be that. I wonder when Lorn will flash his teeth at me?

"I'll have the cooks send up their almond tart next, or maybe their chocolate fudge cake. See if we can convince you to give us a few more weeks of your time,"

Lorn teases, moving to the end of the bench I'm sitting on, but he doesn't sit down.

I think he likes the height advantage it gives him, not that I'm any closer to bridging the gap even when I'm standing. Both Noctis brothers are huge.

"Not a lot of cheesecake down in The Scorch?" Lorn asks evenly, like it's a throwaway question meant to keep the conversation going and nothing more.

I know better.

"Not a lot of cake or indulgences of any kind, outside of the brothels," I answer, content to stick to inane subjects instead of broaching any of the more important topics I'm sure he's here to press me about.

"What do you get, then? Food-wise, not in the brothels," he clarifies with a smirk.

"Snake meat and dune boar," I answer, not missing the desert cuisine even a little.

I'm careful to select two things that won't point to a specific region or help Lorn glean any other details about where exactly I grew up. I know The Horde is actively searching The Scorch for wyverns and anything else they can find. Last I heard, they were still coming up empty, and I'd like to keep it that way.

Lorn winces. "Sounds . . . gamey."

I huff out a hollow laugh. "Accurate description."

My thoughts wander to our makeshift settlement, and I can't help wondering how everyone is. If they miss me. If Enslee even told them I'm alive or if she's keeping a lid on it while she tries to flush out our traitor.

We certainly didn't have much growing up. A fact that shouldn't be true for any dragons living in Drameric. Not when our blood carries the most potent concentration of magic and therefore has the highest exchange rate on the market. But there's a death sentence in every drop of Syphon blood, and we never risked using it. We did trade sorcai blood after our hunts, when we were in desperate need of credits, but even then, we were as careful and circumspect as possible.

Something dawns on me, and my thoughts turn dark. From the moment I pieced together that our run-ins with the Tainted weren't random like we thought, I've been trying to figure out how we ended up on their radar in the first place. I figured we caught their eye somehow and that's when the hunt began. However, now I think one of the intermediaries we used to procure credits in exchange for blood must have tipped them off. A couple were very focused on us and what we were. We offered our usual cover, which seemed to satisfy them, but now I wonder. If I'm right and our cover was somehow blown, it means the Syphons have more snakes in our nest than we thought.

Our attention has been trained mostly on The Horde. As far as we were concerned, dragons were our biggest threat. And while that still may be true, that myopic focus has kept us from spotting the other real dangers skulking in the shadows.

Shit.

I need to talk to Enslee. I need to warn her. We could have been followed, or watched, and we didn't even realize it.

Irritation and worry overtake my thoughts. Maybe I can get Lorn to give me a com. I look over at the heir and consider my options. He'd probably be the better brother to approach about it. His countenance leans more calculating and less controlling than Aeson's. Lorn, of course, would carefully monitor every call I made, but maybe Nixy could help me hack a secure line.

It would be risky, but the sudden ache to speak to my sister, to hear her voice and know that she's okay, has me willing to chance it.

"Why are you looking at me like that?" Lorn asks, his cool blue eyes intently studying my face.

I realize with a start that I've been staring at him like some weirdo as I work through a possible plan. Heat suffuses my cheeks. Immediately, I phase out of creeper mode and drop my gaze.

"I was just wondering when you're going to tell me why you're here?" I lie, internally patting myself on the back for a quick recovery.

"That answer was dishonest, Scion," a large male announces out of nowhere.

I launch a glare in the direction of the Thrasher I forgot was even there. Lorn's guards are quieter and more adept at blending in with the scenery than Aeson's. The male's beard and ponytail are the exact same dark brown color as his scale armor, but his eyes are a rich swirl of green and gold. The unusual hue stares me down, daring me to deny the lie he just caught me in.

Dick.

Lorn turns to me expectantly with a raised eyebrow and a smirk. I keep my eyes trained on the Thrasher, unwilling to confirm or deny anything.

"What's your name?" I ask the giant lie-detector pain-in-my-ass.

"Selik," he tells me, an annoying gleam in his pretty, swirling eyes.

"I forgot that you haven't met everyone," Lorn murmurs apologetically. "This is Onalar and Lyndry," he introduces, waving in the direction of a green-armored Channeler and a Burner brandishing bright orange scale armor.

I exchange nods with Lorn's Wing members and then turn back to the scion. "Really though, what do you want, Heir?"

Lorn laughs and presses a hand to his chest. "You wound me, Princess. Can't I catch up with a friend, see how she's doing?"

"We're not friends."

"But we could be," he counters, not missing a beat.

I study his face, his body language, the teasing glint in his light blue eyes. He's abandoned the crisp white suit and cape I last saw him in for a more relaxed, black-and-white fitted jacket and matching pants. It almost looks like he's wearing fancy moto gear, but the neck of the jacket wraps halfway up his throat, and there's a panel in the back that resembles outdated tuxedo tails. I'm sure it's the height of men's fashion here in Paragon City, but it looks entirely too fussy for me to truly appreciate, even if it does highlight every chiseled inch of Lorn's gargantuan frame.

My eyes flick dismissively from the heir back to the event below us. "I'll pass, but thanks for the offer."

Lorn chuckles, not at all deterred by my rejection. He follows my gaze and turns to watch a drake run full tilt down the runway below before shifting into a lean chartreuse dragon. A weighted silence slips between us. One that breaks when Lorn finally turns back to me, his powder-blue eyes filled to the brim with calm confidence.

"I have something I want to show you." A lock of white hair dares to drift down over his forehead, and he brushes it back, his eyes set intently on me.

"What is it?" I ask, suddenly anxious.

"Let's let it be a surprise."

I roll my eyes so hard it's a wonder they don't fall out of my head. "Not a chance. I hate surprises."

"I thought you were pretending to not be difficult?" he points out, a spark of mischief alighting in his gaze as he holds a hand out to me like he fully expects for me to take it.

"You don't know me well enough to surprise me with anything I'd like," I tell him, ignoring his outstretched hand until he drops it back by his side. "And even if you did . . . the surprise would be ruined by the fact that I don't like surprises."

Suddenly uncomfortable with the way Lorn is towering over me, I stand up. Which might have been a better move in theory than execution, because now I'm practically pressed up against his chest, and his three Wing members all take a cautious step in our direction.

Perfect, Ever. Rub your tits on him and freak out his guards.

Way to think this through.

Lorn holds up a hand to his Wing at the same time we both move away from each other. My face is on fire with embarrassment. I keep my eyes trained on the ground and straighten my outfit while I try to calm my chagrin. My hands are clammy as I run them down the inky fabric of my nice pants to smooth any creases. The trousers fit tight on my calves, loose around my thighs, and sit low on my hips. Nixy told me to pair them with a long-sleeve top that bares my stomach and wraps around my chest and neck with various strips and straps that I managed to get tangled up in until Tove came grumbling to my rescue.

I've felt perfectly comfortable in the outfit all day, but suddenly I feel underdressed and unprepared to deal with the Burner heir and whatever it is that he wants.

Lorn clears his throat, and I swear the faintest touch of a blush sits just at the top of the collar of his shirt.

"Okay, we've established that you don't like surprises. How do you feel about gifts?" he asks randomly, and it's just off the wall enough for me to forget about the awkward tension and look up at him.

"Gifts?" I ask, confused. "Why does that matter?"

"You said I don't know you well enough to know the things you like. I'm trying to fix that," he argues.

I stare at him for a second, trying to see what angle he's playing now, but his face and body language give nothing away. "Well . . . don't."

He barks out a laugh at the stiff admonishment. "Don't get to know you? Why not?"

"I'm not that interesting," I counter dismissively.

Lorn's grin is impish. "I disagree, I find you very interesting."

"Well . . . don't do that either," I warn, turning to walk out of the alcove and away from whatever is happening here.

Is he flirting? Does he think I'm flirting? I'm not, but maybe I should be, like I planned. Except I don't know how effective that plan is anymore, not when I'm constantly scrambling to catch up with the Noctis brothers. Even when I think I get ahead of them, they quickly knock me on my ass and show me I was never even close.

I pick up the pace, eager to flee. I don't like feeling as though I'm ten steps behind them; I need to regroup and think. Of course, I don't get a minute to recalibrate, because Lorn jogs to catch up with me, his long legs eating up the distance much faster than I can create it.

"If you're trying to dissuade me from finding out more about you, this isn't the way to do it," Lorn declares as he draws even with me.

"Then what will?" I snap, walking faster.

He shakes his head and surveys me as he keeps pace. "What are you running from?"

I scoff. "You. I thought that was obvious."

"Ever, I'm serious," Lorn declares, reaching for my arm and pulling me to a stop.

I let him, because I'm supposed to be figuring out how to get closer to Lorn, not dodging him, but it's so much easier said than done. I feel like my hackles automatically go up whenever there's a Noctis nearby. My finely tuned survivor instincts tell me to bolt far away and fast, but the answers I'm looking for require connection and closeness, two things that don't exactly come naturally to me.

"Fine," I huff after a beat, knowing I need to drop my guard at least a little—or appear to anyway. "What do you want to know?"

Lorn studies my face, his eyes flicking between mine. I'm not sure what he finds in my gaze, but whatever it is, it has the tension bleeding out of his shoulders.

"Nothing too crazy, just all of your deepest, darkest secrets," he tells me casually.

I snort out an indignant laugh. "Oh, is that all?"

"That, and I'd like to circle back to the gift question."

Another dragon goes soaring by us overhead. The flap of its wings stirs the sweet scent of the flowers all around us.

"Well, you already know *what* I am and *who* I am. It doesn't get much deeper or darker when it comes to me. The way I see it, if we're trading secrets, you've got some catching up to do."

"Fair," he concedes with a smile that's simultaneously inviting and disconcerting. "Is there a reason you won't tell me what kind of gifts you like? You seem dead set on not answering."

"Why do I need gifts?" I ask, irritation whirring around me like a cloud of cactus gnats.

I have no idea why this line of questioning makes me so uncomfortable, but it does, and for some reason, he's not going to let it go.

Lorn looks at me like I just asked the silliest question he's ever heard. "Everyone needs gifts . . . and before you give me a master class in stubbornness, I'm asking specifically because tomorrow you'll take your official place amongst The Horde. It's tradition for your family and friends to give you presents to celebrate your Naming Day. I want to know what you like. I want to know you well enough to pick out something you'd be happy to get, instead of giving you something you have to pretend you like because you don't want to hurt anyone's feelings."

"I'm not that nice," I snort.

Lorn's grin spreads wider across his face. "Still, I want to know, and I'm not going to shut up about it until you tell me. I'll hound you if I have to, cancel all of my meetings and appointments just so I can breathe down your neck and ask over and over again what you want for your Naming Day."

Agitation warms my blood, but I can tell he means business. He'll do exactly what he's threatening to in order to get his way. It will be a clash of stubborn titans. I almost want to test him, see which one of us would come out on top, but I don't have time for this shit. Not to mention, the last thing I need is another scion all up in my business 24/7. One is bad enough.

Lorn's determined gaze softens a little, and he reaches up to capture a strand of my hair between his fingers. I freeze, my eyes darting to his touch. And just like in the rookery the other night—when I realized it was his lap I was sitting in after my freak-out and not Aeson's—I'm confused by why he's touching me and unsure how I feel about it.

"I know this can't be easy," he tells me gently. "It should be your family giving you presents and getting you ready for what's to come. I'm sorry they're not here to help you, the way you deserve."

The word *family* bounces around the hollows of my chest. The last time I was in Four Tiers, my father intended to Name and Claim me in front of The Horde. Now it will be Lorn's father, King Noctis, announcing my existence. It's a fucked-up full-circle moment I hadn't thought about until now.

But he's right, and fuck, does it hurt.

You'd think time would dull the sharp edges of grief, but it doesn't. Somehow it stays razor-sharp and ready to slice you open when you least expect it. And you will never heal, because you will never stop bleeding.

Loss is the price you pay for love. But as grief carves me open once again, I can't decide if it's worth it.

A forlorn exhale cascades out of me, but then an idea occurs. The flicker of thought presses my demons back, and a spark of satisfaction winks to life as I settle on an answer that will let me kill two birds with one stone—or rather, a perfectly balanced dagger, if someone is nice enough to gift me one.

A wry smile spans my lips. Delight rises through my features and morphs into a clever twinkle that permeates my gaze.

"Weapons," I finally answer. "I like high-grade weapons."

Lorn stops walking and just stares at me for a second. He looks shocked and confused, and I spot a little concern threading through the other emotions too. Unexpectedly, he barks out a laugh. It's not the measured snicker with a touch of arrogance that he's already directed at me a few times, but a deep, genuine expression of stunned delight.

"I should have known," he guffaws, shaking his head. "I thought maybe a necklace or something more sentimental, but . . . weapons . . . "

His laughter rings all around us. It rebounds off the shrubs at my back and nudges me forward, like it wants me to get in on the fun too. I side-eye the scion, but the longer he cackles, the more catching it is, and I feel the corners of my lips tilting up in response.

An air gondola glides by, its abrupt presence diffusing the moment and drawing my attention. The airboat lands in a nearby clearing, and Lorn wipes a few laugh-tears from his eyes and then gestures in the direction of the aircraft.

"Let's go, Princess, your chariot awaits."

"Go where?" I instantly demand, but he doesn't answer as he starts to trudge off in the direction of the gondola. "I thought we established that I don't like surprises," I shout after him.

"The sooner you get on, the sooner we'll get to where we're going, and then it won't be a surprise anymore," he yells back, as though that somehow makes this all better.

I sigh and fight the urge to argue. I've learned my lesson when it comes to underestimating the Noctis brothers. Lorn is going to get what he wants. But that's okay, I'll save my fight for when it really matters. Because I too excel at getting what I want . . . one way or another.

CHAPTER 27

The air gondola zips toward the back side of Four Tiers. It groans in protest as it starts to slow, noisily complaining over its stuffed confines. We've crammed eight people onto a floating platform designed to fit six, and seven of those eight bodies happen to be the size of a keep tower, which isn't helping things at all.

I think it's safe to say that one of Lorn and Aeson's prerequisites for their Wing members was that they either had to be the size of a barge or look as though they singlehandedly consumed their entire Training Flight. I suppose the *go big or go home* stipulation makes sense when you consider the bulk of the scions. Surrounding yourself with a Wing that's much smaller than you is just asking for other dragons to constantly challenge the Wing's abilities and the Heart's authority. When it comes to dragons, size most definitely matters.

Any dragoness would agree.

The gondola lists to the left slightly as Onalar—Lorn's hulking Channeler—tries to force Herm and Jori to give him more room. It's a futile effort. There's none to give. But if the big ice dragon doesn't stop griping and making this thing wobble, I swear I'm going to shove him off of it.

The view of the Talon's Reach mountain range is stunning from this height, but I have to force my hands to loosen from tight fists to tense fists as the peaks draw closer. I must say I'm not the biggest fan of the fact that we're more or less riding on an overgrown hoverboard above the manicured keep tiers, one that tips and pitches with every squirm and wriggle. It's not exactly reassuring that, aside from the platform we're standing on, there's only a thin, translucent casing that protects us from the unpredictable winds of Talon's Reach or the sharp cliffs and rocks we're speeding toward.

My stomach churns with apprehension, and beads of cold sweat dot the back of my neck. I keep telling myself that if we go down, all of these gargantuan drakes will break my fall, but the truth is they would shift and survive just fine. My broken ass would be the only one riding this thing into the rocks.

One of the waterfalls that trails down the back of King's Keep comes into view, and the roar of rushing water drowns out the grunts and grumbles of the squished drakes caging me in. The air gondola drops and the falls' mist reaches up to greet us, kissing the clear barrier and leaving tiny droplets of water as we skirt closer to the torrent.

"I used to play here a lot when I was young. I'd come here with your brother Novak, and we'd spend hours exploring and running around," Lorn tells me unexpectedly. "It was one of his favorite places."

I follow the scion's fixed stare to the dark, slippery-looking rocks that flank the base of the waterfall. Echoes of children's laughter suddenly ring in my ears, and a phantom image plays across my vision of my brothers heckling one another as they leap from one slick stone to another, daring me and Enslee to keep up. All too quickly the memory fades into vapor and disappears among the swirling mist.

"I know," I answer after a beat, swallowing past the ache now rippling through my chest. "It was the first place Novak wanted to show us when we got here."

"Us?" Lorn asks, tearing his bright blue eyes from the falls and turning them on me.

"Me and my mother," I supply promptly.

Lorn nods, but his gaze is thoughtful as it roams over my face before drifting back to the powerful rushing water and the treacherous stones below.

I refuse to let my heart beat any faster than it already is, and I deny access to the flush that wants to crawl up my throat and redden my cheeks. Hastily, I banish the flicker of fear trying to roost in my relief, because, yes, I just fucked up—and it could have been very bad—but I recovered. It's okay. No one knows . . . or they won't if I can keep my tells in check.

My eyes want to stray to Selik, Lorn's Thrasher, who thankfully is standing on the far end of the air gondola, but I force my gaze to the falling water. Worry tries to spur me into testing the air for any taint of dishonesty, but I don't dare move or do anything else that might tip my hand or push my luck. As far as I can tell from my strained periphery, Selik isn't giving Lorn any signals demarcating my lie. Neither is the scion looking over at his Wing member as though he's trying to confirm any suspicions. They both look exactly like they did before my mouth got away from my brain.

The floating platform we're on winds toward the side of the breathtaking waterfall. For a second, it almost looks as though it's aiming for the water, but then I see that there's a stony alcove just behind the deluge thundering down from high above. The gondola floats smoothly into the dark space, only it's not an alcove at all, but an entrance to some secret location hidden behind the cascading rush of water.

Shadows swallow us whole, and for a moment, I can't see my own hand in front of my face. All I can hear is the muted rumble of thousands of gallons of water pummeling the mountain all around us, and then the sound starts to fade as we drift deeper into the darkness.

A faint, rosy glow blooms in the distance like some ancient lighthouse of old. The light grows brighter and bigger, dancing across the glittering black stone walls encasing our path and revealing a calm stream of water slipping through the crags far below.

All at once, our gondola abandons the dark, and bright, florid light illuminates everything around us. A stunning cavern comes into view, and my eyes don't seem to know where to flit first.

I've long lived in a world of magic, but I can count on one hand the amount of times it's felt *magical*. This just might make the list.

The walls of the large space sparkle as though made of black diamonds. There's a crystal chandelier dripping from the expansive ceiling, crafted to mimic the appearance of eddying water. A single golden tree glimmers in the center of the sprawling grotto, with two half-moon-shaped sofas framing each side of the large, braided trunk. This place feels ancient and reeks of power, and I have no idea what it could be.

"Where are we?" I ask, but my attention catches on a tall, lean male with a bald head and an ocher complexion. He stands behind what appears to be a reception desk, in an expertly tailored mauve suit that's a touch darker than the rosy light filling this cavern.

"This is the royal treasury," Lorn announces, pride coursing through his tone.

Utterly dumbfounded by that answer, I spin to look at him. "Treasury? Why would we visit a treasury?"

My mouth suddenly feels as arid as the deadlands, and my thoughts flit to the conversation we just had about gifts and my Naming Day. The fact that I'm standing here and not in the middle of an armory probably means I'm not going to be getting what I asked for. But if he expects me to get giddy over a necklace or something equally as useless, things are about to get really fucking awkward.

"When your father was killed and there was no surviving kindred or kith, his Crush was automatically left to the next king. My father has never touched it, other than to add pieces of King Tenebrae's trove when it was cleared from his towers in the keep. The king has ordered that it all be given back to you. Consider it his gift to you for your Naming Day. I brought you here so you can claim it and take your first official steps into the arms of The Horde." Lorn's voice grows soft and regretful. "Where you were always meant to be."

I stare blankly at the heir, unsure how to process everything he just said. Disbelief and astonishment start to circle one another in my chest. My heart is entirely too heavy, but my head feels alarmingly light.

I've spent an innumerable number of hours wondering what it would be like to reclaim everything that was taken from me, from my sister, from the other Syphons. Some days it was the only thing that dug me out of the trenches of agonizing loss. That possibility of one day righting the wrongs has fueled me for a very long time. But in all those hours and days spent pondering and plotting, I never once thought that King Noctis and his heirs would simply hand it over for no other reason than it's the honorable thing to do.

Dragons don't part well from their treasure, and yet here they are, doing just that.

But why?

"Don't give me that look, Princess," Lorn censures lightly.

"What look?"

Lorn shakes his head, but the smile he offers is rakish. "Like you're waiting for a trap to spring."

I stare at him blankly. "Well, that's going to be hard, because that's *exactly* what I'm waiting for."

Lorn chuckles, but it's not as carefree as it was before, and for some reason, that bothers me. The air gondola docks and the others begin to file off, but Lorn and I continue to watch each other, a silent battle of wills taking place.

"I have never met anyone so determined to misinterpret and misunderstand everything around them," he observes, and he sounds somehow both impressed and bothered.

"You should get out more, then," I quip.

Lorn runs his fingers through his snow-white hair and watches me with a challenging glint in his gaze. The movement does nothing to muss the neat coif. Every strand of hair falls perfectly back into place when he drops his hand, and I stare at his locks, offended by their easy surrender.

"Why do you refuse to see kindness for exactly what it is?" he lobs at me, inching closer despite the platform clearing of Wing members and leaving us with plenty of space to separate.

I laugh, but it's absent of flowers and full of thorns. "Because kindness is nothing more than a pretty bow around a pretty box. Foolish people assume there's something beautiful or valuable inside the lovely packaging. Survivors know otherwise."

Lorn studies my face like he's hoping to find a way to unravel my glower. "What's inside, then?"

"Self-interest," I reply evenly. "On the least harmful side of the spectrum, people do good things because it makes *them* feel good. Then there are those who know that pretty packaging creates a path of least resistance to what they want. Regardless of where on the spectrum it stands, things like kindness and generosity are about the giv*er*, not the giv*ing*."

Lorn scoffs. "That's an incredibly sad and jaded way to go through life, Princess. Kindness and compassion aren't just pretty packaging, they're the gift. Not every benevolent act hides a venomous viper in its depths."

I shrug and step back to put distance between us. "I have plenty of fang marks that prove otherwise, Heir."

Lorn's eyes narrow with affront. "Not from me."

Jori steps off the gondola and it sways slightly. I push my hands out to help keep my balance as I ride the wave of movement. Thankfully, it settles quickly, and I turn to follow the others.

"I've only been here a week, Scion. There's still plenty of time for you to sink your fangs in me," I call over my shoulder as I step off the floating platform.

Relief filters through me when I'm once again back on solid ground. I don't do anything embarrassing like lean down and kiss it, but it's tempting. Air gondolas are not for me.

My mind buzzes with wonder as I make my way deeper into the cavern. I step under the gilt canopy of branches, and the golden leaves high above flutter almost as though they're saying hello. Stunned, I stop midstep and stare at the lofty branches. My eyes trace the limbs of the tree down to the thick, braided trunk, and awe builds with each inch I survey. It isn't a flashy, golden sculpture like I thought it was—it's a real, living, flourishing gold tree.

My first instinct is to pluck a few leaves off and shove them into my shirt for later. I look around to see if anyone is watching me, which is stupid because everyone is watching me. Herm smiles like he knows exactly where my mind just went, but I ignore him and try to look like someone who isn't currently casing the royal treasury.

Technically, if I'm really here to claim my kith's Crush, my stealing days are far behind me. But, worst-case scenario, if my suspicions prove to be right and all of this is too good to be true, I'll have to snap off a branch on my way out.

I skirt the tree trunk, mostly to put some distance between me and temptation, and take in everything else. Soft, rosy light from the rippling chandelier dances on the ground as I walk, and for some reason, I want to roll around on the lush sofa like it's catnip and I'm some back-alley stray that has no choice but to give in.

I wonder if they'd let me steal these and put them in my room? They'd make excellent additions to my trove.

I pause at that thought. One, because I don't have a trove—and when have I ever given two shits about furniture, let alone wanted to claim a couch? And two, the room in Aeson's rookery is *not* mine, it's his. I just stay in it temporarily for the time being.

"My Scion, what an honor it is to see you. How may I be of service today?" the male in the pink suit gushes as Lorn approaches the reception desk with graceful, long strides.

"Thank you, Linden, I hope you and the roots are well," Lorn greets, and the male dips his head, communicating both pleasure and confirmation that he and the roots are doing amazing.

Whatever that bloody means.

"By authority of King Noctis, I need to cede the Tenebrae Crush," Lorn declares, sounding all official and princely. He steps to the side and gestures in my direction.

Linden's professional mien is on point, because he doesn't even bat a lash or twitch a muscle in surprise or question. He simply bows slightly and offers a subservient smile before he raises his hands and begins typing on a keyboard that flashes into existence below his fast-moving fingers. Then, out of nowhere, a translucent, glowing leaf materializes in front of one eye like a bespoke view screen.

What captures my full and undivided attention though is that the data Linden is entering on his keyboard starts to scroll across the exposed parts of his ocher skin in flashes of bright molten gold. A language of symbols I don't recognize streams across his face, wrapping around his forehead and cheeks before slipping past his bald head. Other lines of information snake across his throat and hands, disappearing under the fabric of his rosy jacket and shirt.

Completely mesmerized by the strange occurrence, I drift closer to the reception desk and to Linden, my eyes tracking the glowing movement of symbols across the male's smooth skin.

"Please don't disrupt the current," Linden declares, his focus moving from the glowing leaf screen over one eye to me before his stare drops pointedly to the ground.

I follow his gaze and gasp when I find more golden symbols slinking linearly across the ground toward the massive, gilded trunk of the tree. I watch the unfamiliar cyphers move like a line of hardworking ants that just found an abandoned picnic to raid. I hop back to keep from stepping in the middle of one of the currents streaming from Linden into the tree itself like the two are linked.

My eyes snap up to Lorn, questions teeming in my wide stare. His broad smile is painted with thick strokes of self-satisfaction as he watches me take it all in. The branches above me shiver and then shift. I flinch and look up just as a sturdy, forked limb drops down. One arm of the bough stretches toward me, and the other reaches for the scion.

"Please place a hand in the center of the foliage," Linden instructs mechanically.

I freeze, caution edging my stare as I examine the singular plate-size, four-pronged leaf in front of me. Lorn places his palm in the center of his leaf, and after a long pause, I hesitantly move to do the same with mine.

It's surprisingly warm and much softer to the touch than I anticipated. Despite knowing that this isn't a solid-gold tree, I still expected it to feel like metal. It smells surprisingly floral and sweet while still carrying an earthen undertone, like mineral-rich soil. The delicate veins on the leaf are raised and fuzzy. They tickle my palm as they seem to map every line and crevice of my hand, almost like they're a biometric scanner of some sort.

Linden announces that we can remove our hands, but when I do, shock rings through me. There's a bloody handprint stamped onto the leaf.

"Hey," I exclaim, indignation ringing in the solitary word. "How did it steal my blood?"

I reach for the gilt thief, intent on reclaiming what I didn't know I was offering, but the forked branch shoots up into the canopy, pilfering my print and hiding it within what must be hundreds of other branches and their gilded quilt of leaves.

"The transfer is complete. Would you like to access your Crush now, Dragoness . . . " Linden trails off, his eyes searching the small vid screen still sitting in front of one eye. "Tenebrae." His cadence stalls as he reads the name.

Shock spills across his face, and his mouth drops open as though his jaw is laden with so much awe and wonder he can't keep it closed. With a hasty wave of his hand, the glowing leaf-shaped screen disappears from his eye, and he surveys me, utterly thunderstruck.

"Is it possible?" he whispers. "The roots know, so it must be," he continues, answering his own query.

The tree shimmies as though offended at being questioned, and I deftly slip into a defensive position in case any more blood-stealing limbs want to have a go.

"My apologies. Scioness Tenebrae, would you like to access your Crush now?" Linden repeats.

I chance a glance over at the male to find he's once again wearing an indifferent professional mask. I can't tell if he was apologizing to me or the tree, but I suppose it doesn't really matter.

"Uh . . . sure," I answer, sounding anything but sure.

This feels wrong. Not that the Crush is now mine, but that Enslee and the other Syphons aren't here to explore it with me. The money, the treasures, the priceless collections of who knows what, they don't just belong to me. They belong to all of the Syphons. I should wait for them, but I can't say that. And I can tell by the expectant look on Lorn's face that trying to get out of this right now would invite questions I can't answer, especially not with a Thrasher here searching every word for lies.

Linden watches me like he's waiting for me to give him some sign that I'm good and ready for whatever is about to happen. The only problem is I'm not ready, not in the slightest.

What if there's a portrait of my dad—or worse, my brothers—staring me in the face? Lorn said they added things to the Crush from my father's tower, so does that mean the furniture from his rooms is down there? Would they have wiped the blood off or left it?

My breaths come quicker, and my heartbeats pick up, like the two are trying to race each other. All at once, I recognize the telltale signs of a freak-out, and I quickly work to shut it down. Clearing my mind of all the triggering things that may or may not exist in this Crush, I focus instead on my breathing, on the fact that I'm standing in a magical cavern with a gold tree and a man who I'm pretty sure is a walking, talking root from that tree.

I'm safe.

I'm protected.

I can do this . . . even if it hurts.

I inhale slowly through my nose and then blow it out of my mouth in an effort to center myself. I do it over and over again until it feels like it's working.

Before I can change my mind or start panicking again, I give Linden a nod. His eyes are gentle and his smile is understanding as his fingers start flying across his reappearing keyboard.

A deep rumble ripples through the stone all around me, and I turn to search for the source, but it sounds as though it's coming from the mountain itself.

Flashes of my father's face, my mother's, my brothers, the queen, what they looked like dead, blow after blow land like a sucker punch to the gut. I take the hits and wade through the pain, knowing there's no avoiding it, not anymore. I've run from all of this. I've hidden from it. I've used it to fuel my retribution and to keep me moving forward. But now comes the hardest part, the part I've avoided at all costs. I need to start facing it . . . and I need to start now.

CHAPTER 28

The rumbling of the mountain grows louder, but when I look around, no one seems particularly bothered about that. Instead, everyone's concerned stare is trained on me as I struggle to keep my shit together. As annoying as it is to have an audience, I've always worked better under pressure, and it helps to ground me in an unexpected and welcome way.

"The roots are rotating the vaults, the entryway will automatically open when yours has been accessed," Linden tells me.

I can't tell if he's trying to give me something else to focus on or if he thinks I'm freaking out about the noise and he's explaining what it is in hopes that I'll calm down.

I look over at the tree and notice a subtle tremor is moving through the trunk and subsequent limbs.

Linden's words make me picture a giant lazy Susan of treasure spinning under our feet. I have no idea if that's how the *roots rotate the vaults*, but it's the visual I'm going with. The rumbling morphs into a low, bone-vibrating groan before it suddenly stops.

In three strides, Lorn is suddenly next to me, and then his Wing and Aeson's both move into position around us. Herm, Jori, and Blay stand on my side, and Lorn's Wing guards his. Out of nowhere, light filters through the seams of the braided tree trunk. It grows brighter to the point of almost being blinding, while the woven gold of the trunk slowly loosens until a large, arched entryway appears.

My eyes search the opening in the tree for anything that resembles a Crush, but all I see is the same glittering black stone that the rest of this cavern is made out of. Lorn's hand presses against the small of my back. I flinch at the unexpected contact, barely managing not to pull away or deck him.

"We have to step in," he tells me, gesturing with his other hand at the empty entryway.

"Oh, right," I chirp, and then I hesitantly step forward.

Lorn's hand doesn't leave my back, and I end up having to press closer to him as everyone steps inside the golden opening. Immediately the braided seams start to close back together, and all too quickly the trunk seals itself up, completely trapping us inside.

Small spaces have never been an issue for me, but as the seconds tick by and nothing happens, I can feel the cold touch of claustrophobia as it starts to slink closer and closer. Lorn's palm starts to grow warmer where it's pressed against the skin of my back. The pounding of my pulse grows to a crescendo in my ears until it's all I can hear. Heat sparks in my cheeks, and I don't know what to make of the scion's touch. Is he trying to comfort me, or is this motivated by something else?

I should step closer to him. I should encourage this, just like I planned. But all of a sudden, my feet are leaden, and a heavy boulder has decided to take up residence in my chest. The overwhelming urge to slap Lorn's hand away and put as much distance between us as I can starts to peck at my limbs. The longer I ignore the urge, the more it digs under my skin like an infestation of skittering insects.

It's completely counterintuitive to what I've planned and the opposite of what I need to be doing. If he has been flirting with me, if he's acting on attraction, then I should be trying to hook him closer to get what I need. And yet, I'm on the verge of giving in to the driving force demanding that I push him away from me. Then again, maybe this has nothing to do with attraction and everything to do with the Noctises trying to throw me off. Maybe this is meant to unsettle me and nothing more.

The floor beneath us suddenly lurches, yanking me from my frenzied thoughts, and then we slowly start to drop. A ticking sound fills the tree trunk as we descend, and the stone platform that we're standing on rotates until we're all facing the other side of the tree.

An exit starts to form in the trunk, or maybe this is an entrance too, because it grants access to a new gleaming room. I wasn't sure what to expect—a cave with mounds of treasure was high on my list—but I'm surprised to find a large expanse of walls covered in drawers and doors. Every surface is made from some kind of metal that has a patina to it that's not quite bronze or gold but something unique and in between.

It reminds me of a feed I saw once on a vid screen in the human district. I think they called them safety cubes or something along those lines. Big treasure hoarders, or *banks*, as they call them, let special humans store their valuables in these kinds of cubes. The cavernous space in front of me looks similar, only the drawers and doors here are bigger and seem to cover every surface.

In awe, I step out of the tree trunk into the chamber. Only Lorn moves to follow me, his Wing and Aeson's staying within the open trunk. The tech I can sense here is top-of-the-line, and the room itself is massive. A bright purple light flashes across the ground, and I freeze. My eyes drop to my feet, and I see a list of data scroll by quickly with different dates attached to names. I recognize a few of the names as precious metals.

Huh. Weird.

There's a seam in the ground and I step over it, only for a new list to light up in purple next to my foot. This one appears to be a list of gems, rare and common, again with dates attached to the designations.

"There are vaults built into the ground too. If you want to call them up or access their contents, tell the roots what you want and they'll obey," Lorn tells me, pointing to the different sections that make up the entirety of the floor and then to the drawers and doors on all of the walls.

Astonished, I suck in a sharp breath and quickly stride over to a row of drawers. A new list, alight in bright purple, scrolls across the drawer front. It contains rings of some sort, and it tells me not only who they belonged to, but the gems and metals used to make them and their sizes.

"If you press your finger to the upper right-hand corner of any of the vaults, it will tell you the current monetary value of its contents," Lorn instructs.

I test the drawer of rings and press the pad of my finger to the corner, and the list of contents disappears and a string of numbers takes its place. They keep ticking by until the digits look more like an international com number and not what a single drawer of rings should be worth.

"Fuck the fae," I whisper, aghast as I spin to take in the whole vault.

I'm tempted to pull open every drawer and door. I want to inspect each item, take note of what my father and kindred contributed. Suddenly I need to know which items they valued enough to add to their Crush, and I'm desperate to discover the treasures that called to their dragons. But as quickly as the overwhelming desire comes, I shove it away even faster.

This Crush isn't mine alone. I have no right to touch anything until all the Syphons are here and can decide what to do. We lost everything together. We'll reclaim it all the exact same way.

I allow myself one more spin to take it all in. My stunned gaze lands on Lorn, and I shake my head in utter disbelief at the magnitude of it all. A wide smile blooms across the scion's face, and a deep, resounding chuckle fills the vault.

"I guess the days of caves filled with piles of gold, jewels, and the skeletons of humans who tried to steal from a dragon are long gone," I note, completely gobsmacked but doing my best to rein it in.

Lorn's chuckle blooms into a laugh. I notice that no purple lists light up at his feet when he moves and realize that effect must only be keyed to me.

"Yes, Princess," Lorn teases. "*Those days* are very far behind us. That lore only exists in fairy tales now."

"Fairy tales and in the daydreams of broken little Syphons," I mumble to myself.

Carefully, I walk around, noting what lights up on the floor and the walls as I go. There are a lot of things I would expect to find down here—jewels, crowns and tiaras, centuries-old coin collections, pottery, art. But there are vaults for things that surprise me too—ancient documents, digital photo albums of ancestors long forgotten, clothes, books.

I have to stop myself from reaching for the archives of photos. It's funny, because I was terrified I might find exactly that down here. But now that the images are at my fingertips, all I want to do is see my kindred's faces again. I want to replace the last memories I have of their shattered bodies with new images of them laughing and . . . living.

I stare at the drawer longingly, torn and conflicted, and then I force myself to walk away. I will look, I'll scour their archives and soak up everything I can about everyone I've lost, but not today. Today I need to focus on anything that might help me, anything that might point to answers about who might have planned the attack or how we were cursed.

It's a long shot that anything useful might be down here, but I'd be an idiot not to look. Treasure looks different to every dragon. Some desire gold, others covet jewels or lands, and then there are those that deal in secrets and see the value in gossip. If I'm lucky, I might find a vault filled with classified information or maybe even royal secrets.

I move to a vault storing thousands of books and start scanning the titles in case anything helpful stands out.

Lorn clears his throat and moves closer. His Wing and Aeson's are still standing under the golden arch of the tree trunk, watching and waiting.

"You mentioned that I owe you a few secrets. This feels like an appropriate place to pay up," Lorn declares, apprehension dimming his half smile.

That unexpected emotion from him gives me pause. He rubs the back of his neck, a nervous tell that puts me even more on guard, because Lorn Noctis isn't the type to be nervous . . . ever.

I don't trust it.

My focus shifts from the vault to the heir, and I wait for whatever bomb he's about to drop, or maybe it will be less bomb and more knife in the back.

I guess we'll see.

He surveys my face, and the debate happening in his pretty blue eyes is obvious. My mind picks up a baton of paranoia and runs with it, forcing me to think through a thousand different disastrous possibilities for what he's about to say.

"I knew about you," he tells me, his handsome face a mix of trepidation and shame.

My mind stalls and my heart stumbles. Of all the things that could have slipped out of his mouth, *that* confession was not one I was ready for or one I could have ever seen coming.

Every muscle in my body goes tense, and I blank my face of all emotion. I stand against the wall of my kith's Crush like a speechless statue while a riot of emotions rampages through me.

"I don't understand," I tell him guardedly when I can finally find my voice.

"Your father came and got Novak and Ronin one day when Aeson and I were playing with them. We didn't see them for a few days after that, which was odd. We played every day and had tutoring sessions together, but they missed those too. When we saw them again, it was clear something had happened, but Aes and I didn't know what, and they wouldn't tell us, no matter how much we pressed."

Lorn blows out a deep breath and looks around like he's in search of an anchor as he continues.

"We dropped it, but a couple weeks later, Novak told me he had a secret. We shared everything, told each other everything, and I think it was killing him that I didn't know. Especially when he was so excited about it."

My eyes flick back and forth between Lorn's, like I can somehow ferret the rest of the story from his gaze alone. My throat grows tight, and the fluttering in my stomach grows sharper, threatening to start stinging me at the sorrow I find cloaked in his features.

"Novak ran me through drills and all kinds of challenges our thirteen-year-old minds could come up with to prove I was worthy of his secret, that it would be safe with me." Lorn smiles, and a hollow chuckle sneaks out of him, but his gaze is faraway and steeped in the past.

There's a sadness in his eyes, the kind that always tints the memory of a lost loved one. An ache ripples through my own memories of my brother, because Lorn knew him better than I did. They'd been best friends practically since birth. I had days with Novak. In comparison, Lorn had a lifetime of memories with him.

"I was sworn to the highest degree of secrecy, and then your brother told me that he was going to have sisters. His dad had sat him, Ronin, and Brooks down and told them all about it. King Tenebrae told them that they couldn't tell anyone else, not for a couple of months. Not until after his sisters arrived and he met them, and their dad could make sure they were safe."

Emotion wells in my eyes, but my heart hits every rib as it drops from my chest into my stomach. Panic floods the now-empty cavern, but I force my brow to furrow and for confusion to seep into my gaze as Lorn Noctis says *sisters* for a second time.

"He didn't tell me anything else, probably because he didn't know anything else, but we talked about little sisters and wondered what it would be like to have them. I wasn't much help, as I'd only had a little brother, just like Novak. But we knew girl dragons were precious, and we were excited to discover all the reasons why when the secret sisters arrived. Then we played games and went to classes, and life marched on.

"When Novak died, the secret was buried under shock and grief. It surfaced in my memories a long time later, but by then, I assumed that the queen was probably pregnant and that's why King Tenebrae had told Novak and your brothers about sisters. I didn't think anything of it, really, until I met you . . . "

Lorn closes the distance between us in three strides, and I fight the urge to flee. His sad eyes rove over my face, and he lifts a hand and wipes a lone tear that trails down my cheek.

"I'm so sorry, Ever," he whispers, the words raw and sharp. "I didn't understand what Novak was telling me, that you existed. I should have looked into it, asked questions, or tried to confirm something, anything. I made assumptions and it meant you were out there in our world alone, that you learned to hate us, that you were . . . hurt."

Lorn's face collapses in pain, and I feel it wedge under my sternum and go for my heart. He reaches for me, wrapping his big arms around my body, and I let him, because all of a sudden it feels like he might be the only thing holding me together.

Maybe if he'd told me somewhere else, or if I wasn't already so raw and teetering between grief and loss. Maybe then I could have reacted differently, could have kept myself together, but his truth is a hammer to my already-weakened defenses.

We stand there, his cheek resting on the top of my head, as sorrow twines its way around us, holding us both in an exacting grasp neither of us will ever escape from. His genuine sorrow pulses off of him in waves, and for some inexplicable reason, I feel the need to comfort him.

Maybe it's because this is real. For the first time in all my interactions with the scion, I don't question whether this is a play or some kind of trick. His guilt is palpable, and unwarranted, and I feel it heavy in the air all around us.

"It's okay," I offer, and I'm surprised to find that I mean it. "You were a kid. How could you know?"

"I should have. He gave me all the pieces, but instead of fitting them together, I dismissed them," he argues, and I smooth my hands down his back as I press my cheek against his warm chest.

I don't hold it against Lorn, but a small part of me wonders what would have happened if he'd come looking for us. If he'd realized what the secret meant and searched. As much as I'd like to imagine that things could have been better for me and the other Syphons, the reality is that we'd all probably be dead. With no way to reveal and protect ourselves, whoever hunted our kith and kindred would have come for us too.

For the second time since I was discovered by The Horde, I wonder if we've gotten the Noctises all wrong. I've been on the defensive since I arrived, but what if they were just as wounded and fractured by everything that happened as we were? Surprisingly, I find myself willing to pull at those threads and see how they unravel, but another part of me worries what I might find in the end. Because as much as I want to hate the scions, they're making it much harder than it should be. But I don't know if my bruised and battered soul can withstand the damage it would take if I started to believe them, only to find out that they were playing me all along.

I wish I knew if my fear was unfounded or justified. This kind of trepidation could be a warning from my intuition, but it could just as easily be a result of prejudice and fear.

My stomach twists uneasily.

"But here's the thing," Lorn goes on, his tone now edged with determination.

He leans back and looks down at me, his eyes bright and intense. I go still, and unease percolates in my gut. He tucks my hair behind my ear, and I'm too frozen to untuck it even though I hate how it feels.

"Novak said *sisters*," he tells me deliberately, evenly, giving me time to process each syllable like it's the most important combination of words I'll ever hear out of his mouth. "I don't think Novak made a mistake, Ever. I think your father told him sisters—plural, not singular—for a reason."

Shit. Shit. Shit.

I was really hoping he wasn't going to focus on that despite the fact that he keeps bloody repeating it. I beg my vitals to stay calm and collected even though I feel the exact opposite. I force myself not to look over at the tree trunk to see if Selik is listening in. I know he is, with everyone watching us like hawks.

Fuck the fae, and fuck too-observant scions and their Wing.

Measuredly, I shake my head, but I keep my eyes trained on Lorn's as feigned bewilderment washes over my face.

"But he had to have misunderstood, Lorn. There's only me here," I counter, careful not to sound too defensive or worried by his revelation. "Or maybe he hoped there would be more but it didn't happen before my father was killed. That was the goal of this whole breeding situation in the first place. It would make sense for him to want that."

Lorn looks as though he's considering the possibility, and I use it as an opportunity to pull out of his grasp and put some much-needed distance between us. I pretend to think and pace while I do, as though his speculations are worth considering, when really I'm trying to figure out how to steer him away from all of this without giving myself away.

My gaze catches on a large door and the purple list that lights up as I wander by. Absently I scan the list as I wait to see if Lorn will take my bait. The word *mirrors* flashes across the vault door, and something about it plucks at long-forgotten, stale, and dusty thoughts. The list disappears as I continue pacing, popping back up when I make another round.

"Maybe," Lorn mumbles. "But what if he wasn't just hoping for it? What if there *were* more children?" he asks, and I don't like the dogged undercurrent thrumming through the question.

Dammit. He's not going to let this go.

"Hear me out," he implores when I open my mouth to try to redirect him again. "If the king implemented this *breeding program* and he had you, he could have had others that only *he* would have known about. What if there are more Syphons out there? Other dragons hiding just like you were because of what happened?"

He closes the distance between us, and I stop pacing to look up at him.

"What if you really do have a sister out there, but the other Tenebrae daughter wasn't brought to Four Tiers like you were? What if she's waiting for us to find her, Ever?"

I jerk back, his words snapping at my face like half-starved dogs. Lorn reaches out to steady me, and hope flashes in his ice-blue eyes.

"I failed you, failed to see what Novak told me for what it was. I don't want to do that again," Lorn whispers, an ache in his voice that echoes through me.

It stalls the argument I'm readying to launch and makes me take a second to really hear him. I sift through everything he just told me and focus on his sorrow, on his apology for not understanding the magnitude of the secret Novak shared.

Lorn pulls me closer, and something dawns on me. This is my hook. I was looking for an *in* with the scion, a way to connect and build trust so I can find what I need. This is my *in*. I don't need to flirt or pretend to care about him and his friendship. I need to help him rescue the damsel in distress. I need to help him find the other sister, even if she doesn't exist—at least not in the way he's thinking, but he doesn't need to know that.

I don't need to steer him away from this train of thought. I just need to direct him as far as I can from where the real Syphons are—where Enslee is—and this is the perfect way to do that.

I stare up at Lorn and I let a little hope leak into my eyes. "Do you really think it's possible?" I whisper as though afraid to believe.

"I do," he quickly answers. "And I think we could find her."

"Okay," I answer after a long, drawn-out moment where I pretend to carefully consider what he's saying. "I don't know if you're right, but if there's even the smallest possibility that there might be more Syphons out there, I want to help them."

Lorn's smile is resplendent, and the optimism suddenly wafting off of him is unmistakable. For a moment, I almost feel bad, and then it hits me.

Mirrors.

I know why that word caught my attention. Even better, it's exactly what I've been looking for.

"What's wrong?" Lorn asks when I pull away from him.

"Nothing, I just saw something that made me think of my dad. I'd forgotten all about it until right this second." I stride over to the door and pause in front of it. "Open the mirror vault," I call out into the room, feeling like an idiot, but Lorn said the roots would listen if I bossed them around.

The glowing list on the door instantly disappears. There's a quiet whoosh that moves behind the wall, and then the distinct snick of an opening lock comes from the door itself. I back up as it swings open to reveal an antechamber filled with mirrors.

All different sizes and shapes greet me. Some gleam in the light, looking new and pristine, while others appear ancient and fragile. Every inch of every wall is covered in hanging mirrors, and I spot a rack that holds the ones made to lean and not hang. They're framed in gold and jewels, wood, and tarnished metal. Some don't have frames at all, just raw edges that look worn down by time.

"I forgot he collected these," Lorn declares almost reverently. "My father has quite a few of your father's collection still hanging in the royal offices and rookeries. He couldn't bring himself to take them down."

I hold my breath as I enter the vault, and a sea of reflections suddenly surrounds me. I stare at the repeating patterns of flame-colored hair, jade-green eyes, and smooth alabaster skin—thanks to the charmed anklet I'm wearing.

"Treasure looks different to every dragon," I whisper to myself as I take the mirrors in. "I asked my father why he liked them so much when he was showing me around his office. There was a whole wall of different shapes and frames. Some of the reflections were shiny and bright, and others were worn and warped, but he cherished each one," I tell Lorn longingly as I let the memory painfully rise to the surface.

My pace is measured and calm as I walk deeper into the antechamber, and I carefully and discreetly begin searching the glass surfaces for a symbol, one my father told me and Enslee about. A crest he discovered that will turn a simple mirror into so much more.

"He always hung the mirrors in a room so he could see Four Tiers and Paragon City in their reflection. Did you know that?" I turn and ask Lorn, who's respectfully still standing outside in the main part of the vault.

Lorn shakes his head.

"He told me it was so he could always see a reflection of what he was fighting for and the people who would suffer if he wasn't the best king he could possibly be every second of every day."

I run a finger over the intricate details of a pretty floral frame, but then I move on because it isn't what I'm looking for.

"He spent every second of every day worrying about The Horde and the people of Drameric. He did everything he could to be the best possible leader for everyone . . . and they killed him."

Emotion pricks my eyes and I try to blink it back.

"They killed his babies right in front of him. Then his mate." My voice cracks and a tear escapes and flees down my cheek. "And then they ripped him apart, like they hadn't already shattered him, tortured him, destroyed everything good he ever did or tried to be. He wanted the best for his people. The best for Drameric. And that's how they repaid his efforts."

I shake my head, rage and sorrow swirling and churning until all that's left in me is the weapon that will make them pay for what they did. I stare into the span of my light green eyes, each of them the very shape and exact color of my father's eyes. I let myself pretend for a moment that he's here, looking back at me, guiding me to find what I need.

And then, just like that, I see it.

A crest, no bigger than a thumbprint, etched into a mirror that takes up a third of the back wall. It's not the cure to the Syphon curse, but it might very well be the key to finding it.

I drift toward the sizable rectangular mirror with an intricate bronze frame. With each step, my reflection grows larger and crisper. I don't recall ever seeing this mirror when my father was showing us his collection in the keep, but I'm drawn to it like the beacon of hope that it is.

"Can I have this?" I ask reverently, turning to look at Lorn.

He offers me a sad smile, his countenance somber and reverential. "You can have anything you want, Ever. All of it is yours now."

I stare at the scion, his words settling in my cracks and turning to cement.

All of it is yours now echoes in my depths.

Not yet, but it will be.

I give Lorn a grateful nod and turn back to the mirror. My thoughts are frantic with plans I'm eager to execute, but on the outside, a dangerous calm has washed over me. For the first time since I was taken by The Horde, I see a path, a way to find what we need.

I'm going to break this curse on the Syphons. I feel it in my sorcai-cursed blood. I'm going to fix what never should have been broken. And then I'm going to hunt down everyone who had a part in it and teach them the true meaning of pain.

I nod and my reflection nods back at me. "I think I'll hang it in my room," I tell Lorn absently as I study my hardened features in the mirror. "Maybe it will keep the bastards that killed my father from sneaking up on me too."

CHAPTER 29

My thoughts are a frenetic tangle of anticipation, simmering anger, relief, and tempered determination. Plans and strategies jostle for prominence in my mind as I'm distractedly led through the white stone halls of King's Keep. Small groups gather in the large chambers we traverse, while others rush around, busy with final preparations for tomorrow's Naming. There's a noticeable increase in guards standing sentinel in passageways and manning various entrances. Security has most definitely been heightened, but that's to be expected with the influx of dragons to Four Tiers.

Traffic around the keeps has more than tripled, and there's an eager buzz in the air that wasn't there before. I ignore it all because I have no idea what to make of any of it. Tomorrow at my Naming, I will finally come face-to-face with King Noctis. He hasn't sought me out the entire time I've been here. He's made no attempts on my life. I haven't been interrogated—not the way I thought I would be anyway. In fact, my time here in Four Tiers has been the opposite of unwelcoming.

At first, I thought maybe he was trying to lull me into a false sense of security, but the king could have gotten rid of me a million different ways by now, and he hasn't. Which means he wants me here, but why? It's all so fucking confusing.

I brush my thoughts to the side, knowing no amount of harping on them is going to help me figure out what the hell is going on. I have no idea whose Naming The Horde thinks they're gathering for tomorrow, and while I should spend some time worrying about that, it feels like tomorrow's problem. Tonight, I have more pressing things to focus on.

A few lingering stares track me, Jori, Blay, and Herm as we navigate the keep, but no one stops us or voices the curiosity I see lighting their gazes as we make our way toward the royal towers. I've been quiet since we left the treasury. Thankfully, my guards for the day haven't said anything or pushed to fill the silence. I know they heard what Lorn and I were talking about in the vault, and I think they're doing their best to give me some space after the emotional exchange.

To be fair, I am stewing, but not for the reasons they probably think. Despite what happened down in the vaults of the Syphon Crush, I'm not currently locked in the ache and agony of the past. Instead, I'm doggedly plotting my future. The one that just got infinitely brighter with the discovery of the Vitric Port—or Syphon Glass as my father liked to call the magic mirrors.

The one I found is being delivered in a few hours, and when it does, I'll be one step closer to turning my abstract conceptualizations about finding the cure for the Syphon curse into reality. What was only a notion before, a plan to take advantage of my current position here in Four Tiers and look for what the other Syphons and I have been hunting for decades, is now a real possibility. That is, if I can stay focused and cautious enough to not get caught. Something that might be easier said than done, because I only know the basics about how a Vitric Port works.

My father told me and Enslee about the magic mirrors and what they can do when we visited King's Keep. Not much longer after learning about the mirrors, I used one for the first time. It's how my sister and I escaped the night our kindred and kith were slaughtered. I've never seen a Port since and haven't given their existence much thought. Probably because I never imagined a scenario where I would be back in King's Keep and in a position to use the Syphon Glass again, but here I am.

Now, if only I can remember exactly how they work. It should be as easy as dipping back into my memories, but the problem is I've spent the last sixty-two years doing everything I could to *not* do that. My mind isn't a safe place. Too many things locked up in my head are shrouded in agonizing loss and trimmed with crippling fear.

Over the years, I've tried to separate out which thoughts, smells, and recollections are safe to explore. But trauma is corrosive. It eats away and corrupts everything it touches, turning even the most innocent memories into live grenades. I can reach for something from The Wells when I was little—somewhere untouched by death and destruction—but if I hold on for too long, if I spend too much time there, my happy recollections detonate into a horrible explosion of blood, screams, death, and silence. It's how it always ends and always will, no matter what I do or how I try to get around it.

I can't think of my mother's smile or the way her gray eyes would sparkle when she looked at me without then seeing the fear and heartbreak on her face when she was surrounded and she knew there was no way out. Every thought of my father, of the way he lit up the day Enslee and I walked out of the gate in Four Tiers and into his arms, is tarnished by the way he was torn apart in the end. And my brothers . . .

I shut my thoughts down. Blank my mind. Refuse to wander any deeper than I already have, which is a problem, because I need to go back there. I need to remember exactly what we did to get out, and it's going to fucking suck.

My mind drifts back to Enslee and the warning message I need to get to her. Maybe I can slip something to Nixy tomorrow when she's getting me ready for my big Naming debut.

The elevator ride up to Aeson's rookery is short. My ears pop as the doors slide open, a result of our drastic change in altitude. Jori, Blay, and Herm surround me as we exit the car and head down the now-familiar wide hall. Bio scanners do a quick sweep of each of us as we approach the commander's expansive quarters. Locks disengage on the thick, heavy, sealed door before it swings open, granting us entry.

"Welcome home, Ever Noctis and Royal Wing," a robotic feminine voice greets as we cross the threshold into the rookery.

"What the fuck?" I ask no one in particular as astonishment lassos my limbs and I trip over my feet. Quickly I regain my balance and eye the open armored door with disdain. Every other time I've been scanned for access to Aeson's rookery, I was greeted as "Authorized Visitor," not *Ever fucking Noctis.*

Blay is wearing an annoying grin when he looks back at me. "Tove was doing systems checks in preparation for tomorrow. Looks like she made some updates."

A wave of irritation laps against my shock, and I let loose a few choice expletives as I squash a tendril of approval that tries to spread through me. Point to Tove in our running tally of petty moves against one another.

Bitch.

I'm going to need to up my game.

Laughter bounces out of the open doorway. My head snaps in that direction, and I find none other than the aggravating Seeder herself, bent over at the waist and grabbing her side.

"Your face," Tove chortles, her features bathed in glee. "You should have seen your face!"

Her guffaws set off a round of titters all around me, but I manage to stay stoic against the rising tide of their gaiety.

"Keep it up and see what happens to *your* face," I grumble, but it lacks any real bite as Tove backs up so we can enter the rookery.

She cheerfully sighs and rubs at a stitch in her side. Her hand is covered in the black vines of her dragon mark, and her brown eyes twinkle as she wipes laugh-tears from her cheeks. I notice her countenance is missing the usual vitriolic intensity I'm so used to seeing when it comes to Tove, but I refuse to appreciate the change since it's at my expense. It does, however, make the chagrin of her well-executed prank sting a little less—but barely.

"I was going to change it back later today, but I think I'll keep it," Tove taunts. "You know, for your protection."

The small amount of amusement swirling within my aggravation instantly sours at the jab. My glower is caustic, but it only encourages her delight. I want to wipe the smug look off her face, but I'm no stranger to a good prank. It's better to focus my energy on future retaliation.

And boy, am I going to retaliate.

"I'll be sure to update my stationery posthaste," I deadpan. "Maybe get it tattooed across my ass." I stroke my chin contemplatively. "I think I'll make you call me Mommy when Aeson and I finally make it official. Oooh, or Bestie. Maybe My Goddess—that has a nice ring to it."

Herm's chuckle helps to clear some of the satisfaction from Tove's face. I blow a saucy kiss his way, and he pretends to pluck it from the air and tuck it into a pocket his scale armor doesn't have.

"Ooh, I'm telling the commander," Jori teases from behind me, and I roll my eyes at the schoolyard taunt.

We amble into the great room located in the center of Aeson's rookery. It has a dining area off to my left that comfortably seats thirty, a lounge space made up of several sofas and half a dozen chairs, and a handful of emulators toward the back wall. Apparently, they can turn into any kind of gaming table in existence—or at least that's what Chastain said when he showed me around on my first day here.

The walls and floor of the rookery are the same white carved dragon stone as the rest of the keep, but Aeson's tower is surprisingly warm and inviting thanks to the soft, colorful carpets, the art adorning the walls, and the other decorative accents expertly peppered throughout. Not that I've spent much time in this space. I usually try to avoid it because it's where everyone congregates during their off time, and I'm not here to make friends.

The thick door behind us shuts and rearms itself automatically. King Noctis has made quite a few updates to the security systems protecting King's Keep since my kith and kindred were slaughtered within its walls. I can't help but wonder how long it would take a group of very motivated dragons and sorcai to break through the armored barriers and lethal systems now in place.

I'm sure it's not impossible. Nothing ever is. Where there's a will, there's a way. I have the annihilated bloodline to prove it.

My guards for the day instantly relax now that we're secure within the walls of the rookery. They start teasing each other and discussing some kind of status update, but I ignore it and head in the direction of Aeson's room and my temporary prison cell, aka his mating suite. But before I can make it more than a few steps away, Ogdan appears in the entryway on the west side of the tower, the side that houses the Wing's suites. He must have gotten a notification that we're back, because the big Burner heads right for us.

"Frills, before you can run off and hide for the night, we need to go over the plan for your Naming," Ogdan declares, foiling my attempted escape.

"Hide? I don't hide," I object, despite knowing damn well that's exactly what I was hoping to do until my delivery arrived.

"We all know you're hiding, Biscuit. Being surrounded by this level of excellence and sex appeal can be intimidating—we get it—but fear not, we're a friendly lot," Herm gibes as he gestures around the room.

My scoff is chock-full of derision. "I take back my air kiss, Hermie. There'll be no more air kisses for you."

Herm's arrogant amusement instantly shifts to affront. At first I think it's because of the new nickname I just lobbed at him, but then he presses a hand protectively over the nonexistent pocket where he deposited my nonexistent kiss.

"You can't do that, Biscuit," he petulantly argues. "This is mine fair and square!"

"Maybe it's not *us* she's hiding from, but a certain commander," Jori sing-songs with a wag of his eyebrows as he passes me.

My face is a mask of shocked incredulity as I look over at the normally amiable and quiet Healer. "You're supposed to be the nice one," I remind him since he seems to have forgotten.

"Nah, that's Karis," Jori dismisses with a laugh while making a beeline toward one of the wall synthesizers to get a drink started. Something hot, judging by the cup with a handle that begins to print as the Healer with the ash-brown hair and hazel eyes turns back to me. "Want something?" he asks.

I wave Jori off and focus on Ogdan, who's shaking his head at all of us while moving toward the lounge area. He brushes his burgundy hair back from his face, and I notice he's not wearing scale armor. I've never seen him in normal clothes before, and it throws me for some reason. He probably had the morning off—I know the Wing rotates their schedules—but I study the loose emerald-green pants and short-sleeve top he's wearing like I've never seen anything like it before.

Herm herds me closer to the sofas, and I perch on an ottoman directly across from Ogdan. Herm settles on the arm of a couch, and Blay leans against a wall by the west entryway. His body language is casual, just like the other two, but all of their gazes are alert and rimmed with a wariness that instantly puts me on edge.

"Have you spoken to your stylist about preparations for tomorrow?" Ogdan asks randomly.

It takes me a second to wrap my mind around the unexpected question. I examine it for a moment, looking for the trap or hidden meaning, but when I don't immediately see anything, I answer.

"I have no way to contact her, so . . . no, I haven't."

Ogdan nods and starts tapping something into the cuff on his forearm. "I believe the scion is already taking care of the com issue. It should arrive around the same time as your delivery from the treasury. I'll have Miss Lael reach out," he tells me secretarially.

I nod cautiously, still unsure where Ogdan is going with this, but a small rush of relief slips through my apprehension. I work to school my features, careful not to let anything slip, but Ogdan's unknowingly helping me, and I could really use the assist. I was going to try to slip something to Nixy tomorrow, but if she's going to call me today, I can work with that.

I keep my breathing even and my body still despite the urge to get up and start pacing so I can work out some kind of code or way to clue Nixy in without using visuals or outright saying anything. I have no doubt whatever com they give me will be closely monitored and scrutinized. But if the com's going to get here around the same time as the mirror, I have a few hours yet to come up with something.

"Tomorrow, Karis and Farrow will be your security team leads," Ogdan continues, his gray eyes jumping from the screen on his forearm to me. "We've been making do so far, but with the security risks, we're bringing in extra help. The Horde commanders have decided to give the current top ten ranking initiates in your Call to Arms an opportunity for some hands-on experience, meaning they will make up the remainder of your security detail for the night."

Ogdan's announcement has me sitting up straighter and my focus sharpening. "They're going to assign unvetted strangers to watch over me while The Horde finds out who and what I am for the first time?" I ask, aiming for calm and collected but missing by a mile.

My hands fist the fabric of the ottoman I'm sitting on, but as soon as I realize I'm doing it, I force myself to stop.

Ogdan waves me off dismissively. "All of us were strangers not so long ago. It'll be fine."

Fine?

It'll be fine?

All the ways it will *not* be fine quickly flash through my mind. Instantly I zero in on the mention of the commanders who made this decision. Was it the same ones I met at that lunch with Aeson, or was it one of the others I know about but haven't officially met? I guess it doesn't really matter who came up with this bullshit decision. What matters is why they'd want to give a bunch of unvetted strangers access to me at all. Suspicion burrows through me.

I open my mouth to argue that this is ridiculous, that it doesn't make sense, but then I close it. Ogdan isn't asking me how I feel about this plan, he's *telling* me.

He doesn't care what I think.

None of them do.

I blow out a breath and force the tension from my shoulders. I already knew there could be an issue with my future Wing. Mostly because there's no way to know ahead of time if they're pro- or anti-Syphon. I figured the whole death-vow thing would help me navigate that, but I won't have that layer of protection tomorrow, and that feels intentional.

"Look at it as an opportunity to get to know the initiates and how they work," Ogdan encourages, but it comes across as high-handed and dismissive. "Six of the ten probies assigned to this detail will be part of your future Wing. They're all trained, capable, and dedicated. Farrow and Karis will be there as backup if needed, but there shouldn't be an issue."

Jori sips his drink, the slurping sound loud in the quiet that blankets the room while I stare at the two Wing members across from me. Ogdan shifts his weight as he watches me, like my silence is making him uncomfortable.

I'm okay with that.

"It's not that we don't *want* to look after you, Biscuit," Herm interjects after a beat. "We're just ensuring that both you and the commander have adequate coverage."

I just started entertaining that insecurity in my mind, so I must not have my face and body language on lockdown like I thought. Not if the Stormer is reading me that easily.

"Sure," I tell him in the same dismissive tone Ogdan just used. I even use the same glib gesture to wave away the adept observation, pretending it missed the mark despite the way it's currently lodged between my ribs and making my chest ache.

I know it's stupid. I'm no worse off than I was before. But I can't help feeling like I'm six years old again, watching guards carry my brothers off to safety while Enslee and I are left behind and vulnerable.

Once again, I'm reminded that I'm not one of *them*. I'm not Horde. They can pretend otherwise, but at the end of the day, they keep showing me that they don't consider me an equal. I'm not entitled to any answers or even a say in my own life.

I'm a pawn.

Nothing more.

I'll shove that assumption down their throats soon enough, but it won't be tonight. Tomorrow will either go off without a hitch or, more than likely, someone will try to kill me. I wonder how many of my new guards will piss their pants when that happens. Or will they be the ones planning the attempted murder?

They're in for a rude awakening though. Death and I have an unspoken agreement. We like to flirt and toy with one another, but we keep it cutesy and never go *all the way*.

I rise from my chair, and both Herm and Ogdan mirror me like they're adhering to some old-fashioned sense of decorum. Herm looks skeptical, and unease settles in Ogdan's features, but I quickly decide it's not my problem.

"It's been a long day. Is there anything else?" I ask stiffly, but I don't wait for an answer before I peel away in the direction of my dragon-stone cage.

Blay straightens from where he was leaning as I approach, and then the sound of the locks disengaging on the armored door fills the room just before the thick tungsten barrier suddenly swings open.

A flat feminine voice intones, "Welcome home, Commander Noctis, Royal Wing, and Authorized Visitor."

I turn to see Chastain and Sondar striding confidently into the great room. Their Heart, Aeson, is centered in the cluster of guards with Farrow and Karis bringing up the rear, but it's the commander's *Authorized Visitor* that draws my eye.

Statuesque and stunning, the female has a shrewd gaze that's a mesmerizing shade of periwinkle, flawlessly smooth bronze hair, perfect pink lips, and a bodysuit that I'm pretty sure was painted on. I have no idea who she is, but something about her instinctively sets me on edge. I can't immediately put my finger on what it is, though I try. I can sense it on the tip of my tongue, the answer teasing the periphery of my thoughts. I try to catch it, to examine it, but I can't seem to get a grasp on what's setting me off.

And then her scent hits me.

Sharp and electric with notes of fresh-tilled soil and an undercurrent of sun-dried animal pelt—deer, I think, or maybe it's elk.

She's sorcai.

And from the smell of it, she's armed with active spells.

Warning zips up my spine and blares in my head. A curtain of red drops over my gaze, and a menacing growl rattles my chest.

She's dangerous.

She shouldn't be here.

But that's okay. I'll fix the commander's mistake. I'll rip her impudent little heart right out of her traitorous fucking body.

CHAPTER 30

The lie of a friendly smile on the sorcai bitch's face instantly drops when our eyes meet.

Alarm fills her periwinkle stare at the same time my lips peel back in a snarl, and I spring for her. Startled shouts and frenzied warnings sound off around me, but I shut all of that out, focusing only on neutralizing the immediate threat.

A roar fills the room, but whether it's mine or someone else's, I can't say for sure. My dragon surges under my skin. It batters impotently against the bars forever caging it in, begging me to move faster, to kill quicker.

I obey.

Terror flashes across the sorcai's face. She tries to stagger back, to get away from me, but Karis's big body blocks her escape. A scream builds in her throat. She fumbles for something at her waist, but she's too late, too slow.

I reach for my prey, delight detonating through me when I'm almost on her. The blood in this sorcai's veins doesn't sing like the ones I've been hunting all these years, but she'll die all the same. She forfeited her life the second she dared to step into *my* lair.

A wall of black scale armor and muscle steps into my way. Strong arms catch me midleap, and then my trajectory is altered as someone bodily carries me away from my target. I bellow my frustration and work to break free, but it's just more noise joining the cacophony of chaos already crescendoing all around me.

"Get her out!" someone booms.

"Chastain, clear the scent!" someone else commands.

I don't track who is screaming what, because I'm being robbed of my kill, and I'm fucking pissed. All I see is red. All I feel is a driving need to destroy, to protect. Flashes of memory ricochet off my rage, showing me another time sorcai stormed the royal tower I was in and everyone died. A keening snarl spills from my lips, and then suddenly everything around me goes dark.

Shock and bewilderment stall the desperate drive to end the sorcai and erase all evidence of her existence from the lair.

Did they knock me out?

No. I can still feel and hear.

My breaths are loud and harsh against the sudden onset of silence. A warm, viselike body wraps around mine as it carries me deeper into the darkness. I stop struggling against the band of muscles caging me in, and the call for vengeance begins to quiet in my mind. The scent of sorcai and spells slips away to be replaced by something deeper, something masculine and soothing with a hint of char.

"Shhhh," a deep voice comforts as a frustrated whimper slips out of me.

I feel off-kilter, untethered, but I have no idea why.

Soft lips press against the juncture where my neck meets my shoulder. I fight against the touch, rallying an internal war cry to kill the sorcai, but there's no escaping this hold on me. My arms are pinned to my sides. My back is flush with an unyielding muscular chest, and I'm pretty sure my useless wiggling is only turning Aeson on.

I know that's who has me. I want to be annoyed about it, but suddenly all I feel is . . . spent. After another surge of *fuck you, let me go* proves pointless, I finally give up. A growl that feels and sounds like rolling thunder vibrates through my back. Aeson's approval of my submission has me clenching my teeth and wanting to remobilize, but the will to fight is hemorrhaging against his warm body and rumbling assent.

"That's better," Aeson murmurs, his lips skimming the shell of my ear. "Breathe me in. Feel me. You're safe. It's just us. No one else is here."

Every rich and resonant syllable douses my blazing anger until I'm left guttering and confused. Each second swallowed up by the dark and trapped in the arms of Aeson Noctis has my head clearing of fury and fog, and soon I'm questioning what the hell just happened. I try to make sense of my reaction, but I can't.

Sorcai aren't my favorite people by any means, but their presence doesn't usually trigger . . . *that.* The female wasn't Tainted. She didn't smell like a blood broker or belong to the Relacour line. There was no reason for my violent reaction, and yet I can still feel the faint call for death thrumming in my blood while my dragon paces back and forth in the center of my chest.

Tension dissolves into defeat as I continue to breathe Aeson in. My lungs fill with him, and it has me melting like I'm nothing more than a pillar of ice that's trying to withstand the radiant attention of the sun. But what chance does an icicle have against a flame?

Aeson's hold loosens ever so slightly, and I allow myself this one moment of weakness. He can't see me. I can't see him. I can take a second and just . . . be.

My head rests back against his chest, and I close my eyes.

"She was here to look at your anklet," Aeson tells me, the tip of his nose tracing the line of my jaw. "I know you like wearing it, and I didn't want the magic to run out before you were ready. I thought you would be more comfortable doing it here because you'd have to take the charm off for her to examine it. I was wrong. It won't happen again. No more visitors until you say otherwise."

My eyes flash open and I try to look up at him. I can just barely make out the scruff on his jaw and the border of his full lips. His apology surprises me, but I'm more taken aback by the satisfaction that hums through me at his declaration. Why do I care if he has visitors?

I shouldn't.

I don't.

And yet Aeson's capitulation undeniably soothes something frayed and jagged in my chest.

My dragon finally calms.

Aeson's mouth ghosts over my shoulder and up the side of my throat. Need heats my blood and burns away the last of my bloodlust. Desire pools between my thighs, and I clench them. Aeson's chest expands, the hard muscles of his pecs pressing against my back as he scents me. Another roll of approving thunder slips out of him and vibrates into me while he splays a hand across my stomach and presses my ass more firmly against his hard length.

I bite back a moan, but I'm not fast enough to trap the gasp that escapes when Aeson nips the lobe of my ear. I'm playing with fire, in more ways than one. I should move away from the commander, demand distance. But the thought of doing any of that right now feels wrong, and I'm so fucking tired of feeling wrong.

With each slow blink, my eyes start to adjust to pitch-black shadows surrounding us. I can just make out gloomy shapes that look like couches and one on the opposite side of the space that I'm pretty sure is a bed.

"Where are we?" I ask, puzzled.

"My room," Aeson answers evenly, his breath once again teasing my ear.

Every cell in my body suddenly comes alive. I'm all at once glaringly aware of the way Aeson's massive arms cradle me. The press of his large palm against my stomach is suddenly at the forefront of my focus. The scrape of his five o'clock shadow against my temple feels perfectly indecent, and the pitch of his resonant voice is quickly becoming something I'd like to add to my favorite playlist and listen to on repeat.

He's holding me like my weight doesn't even faze him, subduing me with nothing more than his presence, and it's so good . . . and so, *so* bad.

"Lights to one hundred percent," I call out, needing a shock to my senses to help snap me out of whatever spell Aeson has me under.

Did that sorcai bitch get a shot off and I didn't realize? Something to make me all docile and bewildered?

Unsurprisingly, Aeson's room doesn't obey. I can feel the amused smile that stretches across the commander's face, but my attention is drawn to the way his thumb is arcing across the bare skin of my torso and stopping just under the bottom hem of my top—which is way too close, and not nearly close enough, to the bottom swell of my breasts.

"Lights at fifty percent," Aeson orders, and instantly incandescence chases away the dark's inky claim.

Once again, I'm both annoyed and pleased by Aeson's assent to my wishes. I wanted light and now there's light. I wanted to shank his guest and now no more guests. It's what I'm asking for, but why the fuck is he giving in to me?

"If I put you down, are you going to attack anyone else?" he asks me, and there's no missing the inflection of amusement in his question.

"Maybe. Maybe not. It's hard to say," I grump while trying to cross my arms over my chest. Unfortunately, his arm is still banded around me—and therefore in the way—so I'm forced to leave mine hanging at my sides while my feet dangle above the ground.

I look like an idiot.

Why did I want the lights on again? Oh right, illumination makes me less inclined to hump the scion.

"I'm fine," I huff. "Unless any more sorcai or wyverns come storming in here. She must have triggered a flashback or something," I tell the commander dismissively, even though that's not totally accurate. I did see flashes of the night of the rebellion, but that was after I was already triggered by something else. I still have no idea what though.

"A flashback. Sure. That must have been it," Aeson agrees, except something in his tone makes me think he doesn't actually believe that's true.

He sets me on my feet, and I sense a split second of hesitation before he steps back. Deliberately and slowly, he lets his hands slide off my body as he moves farther away. I shoot a glare at him over my shoulder and ignore the way my blood heats at the sensual contact. His nostrils flare, scenting me, and his smile is wicked and unapologetic as he finally puts a few feet of distance between us.

"It was a flashback," I argue, more to put some emotional distance between us as well as physical space.

"Sure," he agrees again, but it's placating and ambivalent.

"What does that mean?" I demand, both annoyed and curious.

Aeson's smile widens even more, and I instantly question if I want to hear whatever he's about to say.

"It's nothing, Claws. It's perfectly normal for dragons to feel territorial in these kinds of situations. You didn't do anything wrong."

My brow furrows.

"These kinds of situations?" I repeat slowly.

He steps closer to me, and I have to crane my neck to maintain eye contact. Damn, he's big.

"Yes, Claws, *these* kinds of situations," he reaffirms, lifting his hand and running the back of his fingers lightly across my cheek.

I startle as his meaning hits me.

"Wait," I demand as I back away from him. "You think I went after that sorcai because I was feeling territorial over . . . you?"

The humor drops from Aeson's face. "I don't think, Claws, I know. I've seen territorial displays before. You would have too if you were raised around other dragons. That's exactly what happened."

I flinch at his statement about growing up with other dragons but quickly shake it off. "I'm sure you've had your fair share of girls fighting over you, but your overinflated ego is misleading you if you think that's what was happening out there." I gesture in the direction of the great room.

Aeson's snort is incredulous, and he folds his arms over his chest, mirroring my stubborn stance. "I don't need you to admit it, Claws. I know what I saw. So do the others."

His mention of his Wing pisses me off even more, and an irritated growl crawls up my throat as I stride in the direction of the door that connects our rooms. This pointless conversation is over.

"Arrogant, presumptuous asshole," I grumble to myself as I go.

Why the fuck would I feel territorial over Aeson Noctis? I'd like nothing more than to get as far from The Horde as I can. Yeah, I kissed him, but it was just a kiss. A moment of weakness, nothing more. I hate The Horde. I hate *him*, his father, his older brother, and anyone else that benefited from the slaughter and suffering of my people. Does he not remember that they brought me here against my will? I'm sure as shit not fighting to stay, let alone getting all growly over his big Burner ass.

I'm halfway to the door when a large hand wraps around my arm and spins me back in the direction I'm trying to escape. I move to break Aeson's hold, but the fucking dragon has speed and strength on me, and he gets ahold of both of my wrists. I try every move I know to reclaim my limbs, but every headbutt, kick, twist, hit, and body check fails me.

I clench my jaw and level Aeson with a murderous stare that doesn't faze him in the slightest. It's crystal clear the only way he's going to let go is if he wants to. That, or if I shoot him with a pulse bow, but since I'm fresh out of those, it looks like I'll be gnawing my arm off just to make a fucking point.

He steps into me and I back up until I hit a wall.

"You need proof, Claws? Fine, I'm happy to supply it," he growls, and try as I might, it affects me.

I *hate* that it affects me.

He leans down until his eyes are level with mine and there's no escaping his gaze or the intensity filling it.

"Was it her presence or her scent that set you off?" he asks, watching me, surveying me, his blue eyes blazing brighter with the question. "My guess is scent. That's usually the one we're more sensitive to at first. Did you see red, Claws? Imagine a hundred ways to kill her in the blink of an eye? Did your body move before you even told it to?"

He nuzzles the tip of his nose against mine, and I don't know if I want to snarl at him to back off or claim his mouth to shut him up.

"What calmed you, my Syphon? Was it the loss of your sight, the change of scenery, or was it me? My touch? My scent? My hard dick pressing against your perfect ass? If I reached my hand inside your pants right now, would you be wet for me, Claws? Are you dripping for me? What kind of sounds will you make when I play with this pussy? Should we find out?"

Fuck me. I think we're about to.

Desire fries my synapses, and longing anchors me to the way Aeson guides my hand down over my pants. He molds his fingers over mine until we're both cupping between my thighs. My breaths are quick and needy. My nipples are hard, my breasts heavy, and my skin is entirely too sensitive for the way his breath is dancing down my neck and quivering across my collarbone. He grinds our palms against my clit while his words edge me closer to a truth I don't want to acknowledge.

A soft moan escapes me, and Aeson's knowing smile grows in response.

"Mmmm, just like that," he whispers lewdly as he presses his forehead against mine. "Get nice and ready for me. Then I'll lick you clean before I fuck the stubborn denial out of you."

My hand presses harder, and the pace of the rhythmic circles against my clit starts to pick up. I pretend it's his doing, but it might be mine. This is a really bad idea, but just like our kiss before, it feels entirely too good to stop. I've been nothing but tense and on edge since I was brought here, and the idea of unraveling, even for just a second, is too tempting to walk away from.

If I can just take a small break, breathe for a little while without feeling like I'm being crushed by all the fear, anger, and pressure, then I can pick it all back up and carry on.

"Fuck," I whimper as my climax starts to build.

"There it is, my Syphon," Aeson purrs. "Break open for me, beautiful. I want to see your surrender dripping down your thighs."

My head falls back and I ride the ascending tide of our combined touch and his filthy words. Out of nowhere, a hard knock pounds through the room. The sound startles me out of my chase for release, and my head snaps in the direction of the door. Aeson's snarl is baleful and dangerous. And it almost tips me over the edge, but then his hand stops between my thighs, and the orgasm I was eager for flutters away.

"What?" Aeson snaps, lifting his head from mine and shooting daggers in the direction of the door and whoever's daring to interrupt us.

"Your meeting with the Council starts in ten minutes," Karis announces tentatively.

Looks like the big man drew the short straw.

Aeson's frustrated sigh brushes across my fevered skin, and he puts a few inches of space between us. It's exactly what I need to come to my senses. I breathe air that isn't saturated with only his scent, and it helps me realize how fucking stupid I'm being right now.

Before he can change his mind and erase the distance he just put between us, I slide out from where Aeson has me pinned against the wall. He lets me. And something inside of me is both relieved and disappointed by that. I'm quick to kick the latter part of that thought in the face and focus on straightening my clothes and collecting myself.

I can feel Aeson's eyes on me, but I don't dare meet them.

That was close.

Too fucking close.

Flustered and all at once pissed at myself, at my traitorous body, and at the scion, I spin to leave. I need to get out of here and as far away from Aeson Noctis as I can get. But something sparkly suddenly catches my eye, and my steps slow despite myself. The wall we were up against isn't a wall. Well, it was when I was next to it before, but it must have some kind of cloaking tech on it, because now it's a glass-encased cabinet filled with shelves and . . . treasure.

Holy shit, this must be Aeson's trove.

Immediately I tell myself to look away. A dragon's trove is not something to fuck with, but I can't pull my stare from what's sitting front and center in the middle of all the shelves. And then I can't stop my steps as they carry me closer.

I've never seen anything like it. It's some kind of jeweled flower, but the breathtaking bloom looks as though it was plucked from the deepest reaches of space itself. Glimmering, crystalized stars speckle the delicate surface of the petals, and the stamen in the middle can only be described as a small bouquet of gossamer galaxies.

"It's a constellation lily," Aeson tells me, and I freeze and hold my breath as he draws closer. "It was my grandmother's. The pride of her trove. I would stare at it for hours every time we'd visit her when I was young. Surprisingly, she always let me, even though she wasn't otherwise prone to those kinds of soft indulgences."

I dart a glance toward Aeson, but he doesn't look protective or offended by the covetous way I'm staring at something he, no doubt, considers precious.

"No one was more shocked than I was when she gifted it to me the day I moved into my own tower and officially started my own trove. I was speechless. I'd never felt so excited and so worried that any second, she would tell me she made a mistake and take it back. But she set it in my hands and then told me that every dragon deserved to fill their life with treasures that they'll cherish, revere, and protect. She brushed my hair out of my face and cupped my cheek and said that one day I would discover something infinitely more precious than this breathtaking flower. And when that day came, only then would I start to understand just how much she loved me, because seeing me admire and appreciate her beloved constellation lily brought her more joy and contentment than the flower itself ever did."

I can't help the small smile that slips across my face. I never met the Noctis matriarch, but her stout and ferocious personality was legendary even out in The Scorch.

"She died shortly after my mother did," Aeson tells me, his voice growing soft and sad.

I remember hearing about the queen and how she died trying to bring a third son into the world. The baby didn't make it either. Back then, the information was nothing more than a fact added to files about the Noctis monarchy. But standing here now, with Aeson so close I can feel his heat and sorrow, it adds an element of reality to it all. Suddenly what the commander went through and the grief he feels isn't just intel, it's a piece of his story, a part of who he is. And for the first time since I heard about what happened, I feel for what he lost.

There is a finite number of people in each of our lives who truly love us. That love warms us against the frigid toll life can take. It's a light that guides us and fortifies us, and losing it leaves us dimmer, leaves our lives darker.

I lost myself in the black abyss for a while. But like the petals of the constellation lily, pinpricks of light have speckled their way through my darkness. My sister. The other Syphons. The wyverns that helped protect and raise all of us.

I study the commander's reflection in the pane of glass in front of me. His stare is sorrowful and fixed on the beautiful flower that caught my eye. He looks up and our gazes meet in the glass. We stare at one another, and for a flicker of a second, it feels like . . . everything.

"I'm sorry," I offer, but I don't know exactly what I'm apologizing for.

Am I sorry for his loss? His sadness? Mine? For this fucked-up game we're playing? Or for what I'm really here to do?

A wistful smile tips the corners of his mouth up. "Don't be. After her rare declaration of love, she cuffed me on the back of the head and told me not to break it or else."

A small laugh sneaks out of me, and I straighten, pulling my gaze from the display case and stepping back. Aeson waves and once again the glass shelves and the glimmering collections they hold disappear behind the facade of a dragon-stone wall.

I haven't seen this kind of tech before. The wall feels solid. I knock on it, and it doesn't even sound hollow. There isn't the slightest hint that anything else could exist here aside from carved stone.

I don't know if trove tech like this existed back in my father's day. Maybe it didn't, or maybe my father was just old-school. Older beings can be like that, distrustful or resistant to change. My father had a spelled armoire for his trove, and thank fuck for that, or Enslee and I wouldn't have had anywhere to hide the night our world ended.

"I have to go," Aeson tells me after another drawn-out moment where our thoughts wander to different times and places.

I clear my throat, giving him a nod, and then I once again move for the door that separates our rooms. I realize as I go that Aeson's space is a mirror of mine. Bed fixed against the same wall, same sitting area and large archways leading outside. His space is more masculine, darker woods, more leather, bulkier furniture built to be comfortable for someone of his massive stature.

"This isn't over, Claws. It's to be continued," Aeson calls to my back as I twist the knob and open the door that separates our spaces. A door that, until now, has always remained closed.

I try not to read into that while I step from his room into mine.

"I'll see you tomorrow at your Naming," he tells me, the promise and warning in that statement dangling on a tantalizing string.

I escape without a word in response or a look over my shoulder. I close the door behind me and press my forehead against the dragons carved into it and sigh.

What the fuck was that? I demand, but of course, no answer is forthcoming.

Aeson and I can never be anything but enemies. He may not know that yet, but it's only a matter of time. Yes, he burns bright and hot, and the cold, dark parts of my broken soul crave that heat, but it could never work. A moth will never survive its love for fire. Ice will always bow to the sun. And I can never be Aeson Noctis's mate, not when I'm here to become his reckoning.

CHAPTER 31

The sky is a bloody battlefield of red. It's as though the day is fighting off the night, and their fury has left dusk covered in gashes of scarlet and ruby, rust and vermillion. The last of the day's light stretches as far as it can reach, but night's oppressive claim proves too powerful. It smothers twilight's desperate glow, stealing the last of its hope until tomorrow, when the battle begins once again.

My spot on the railless balcony attached to my room is the perfect place to watch the day die. I sit peacefully and observe the bloody struggle as the lights of Paragon City wink and flare their encouragement. The display feels fitting for what's to come.

The com ring on my finger pings unexpectedly, and the sound jolts me from my macabre thoughts. I'd almost forgotten I'd put it on. The silver band is thin and has little flowers carved into it. A flat black oval sits at the top of the ring where the tech is housed. It's fancy and dainty and does a bunch of stuff I can't be bothered to figure out, but I expect nothing less from Lorn. Only the best of the best for the princes' pet.

The ring arrived at the same time as the mirror, but I've been so wrapped up in figuring out the Syphon Glass that I became distracted.

I sit up and brush my hair out of my face, schooling my features so I look bored and too rich to care about anything. I need to be very careful how I go about this and be sure not to do anything that might tip off whoever I'm certain will be monitoring this call.

I answer the incoming feed, and Nixy's face pops up, floating above the flat black oval on the top of the ring.

"I apologize, dragoness, for the wait. I just saw the message requisition that I contact you," Nixy offers politely, but her blue-hazel gaze is sharp as it takes me in.

Good, she knows something is up. The fact that I have access to a com device now is probably a big giveaway.

"Is now a good time to discuss your dress for your Naming and go over the plan for tomorrow?" she asks, her tone even, with just enough push in it to let me know that she understands we're not alone on this call.

"Yes, I can speak to you now. How's everything coming?" I inquire smoothly, working through my plan of how to tell Nixy exactly what I want and need without outright telling her what I want and need.

"I'm excited for how the look is coming together," Nixy tells me, sounding genuinely enthusiastic. "I struggled at first with a direction, but then it came to me." Her smile shifts from polite to cheeky. "I went with the *caterpillar to butterfly* theme you mentioned at our last fitting. I've still got some work to do, but if you'd like to see it, I'd be more than happy to show you."

I wave her off. "No. I'd rather see it when it's all finished and I'm trapped in it with no way to escape. But if there's a way you can make the dress shoot lasers at anyone who gets too close or dares to ask me to dance, I promise it will quickly become my favorite dress *ever*," I tell her, half-joking and half-hopeful.

Nixy laughs. "Getting some *first dance* jitters?"

"If complete and utter revulsion at the idea of dancing or having to socialize with Horde nobility counts as jitters, then yes, I'm *all* jitters over here."

"Has anyone gone over what you should expect?" Nixy asks, her smile amused but the look in her pretty eyes trimmed with concern.

"Yes and no. I know it's all very fancy and formal. I thought a Naming Day would be more like a birthday. But it's not a celebration at all. It's a weird pageant where all I do is prance around like some show pony on display. It's nothing more than an ancient rite of passage steeped in a bunch of boring history with traditions that no longer seem relevant. But apparently, I get gifts, so there's that."

"Sounds . . . fun," Nixy teases, and I roll my eyes.

"Anyway, while I have you on the line, I was wondering about the loungewear I requested when I saw you last," I tell her, knowing full well we've never talked about anything of the sort. "I'm having trouble sleeping, and I was curious if you found that fabric I mentioned. I'm hoping if I try to sleep in something familiar, I might feel more comfortable and it'll help."

Nixy pauses for a second, and I hold my breath, hoping she picks up on my rudimentary hints.

"Yes, I did find it," she answers after a beat. "But I couldn't find the gray color you wanted; I was only able to track down black, green, and orange."

Relief floods me as she matches my rudimentary code with one of her own. Black is the color of The Scorch. Orange and green are Enslee's and my most noticeable features: orange for our hair, green for our eyes. It's not an unbreakable code, but it'll do in a pinch like this.

"That's fine, they're just for sleeping in. Black, green, and orange are perfect," I repeat, instantly feeling lighter. I'd hoped that the mention of sleep *trouble* and wanting *help* to find something *familiar* were the right clues to get Nixy on the same page as me, but when it comes to improvising this kind of clandestine shit, you never know which way it will go.

"I can get started on those right away. Would you like me to send them up to you tonight, or would tomorrow work better?"

"Tomorrow is fine," I assure her, letting her know my request for help isn't urgent and that she has time to set things up.

Nixy nods with understanding.

"I can pick everything up when I come to get my dress," I add, hoping she can set up whatever tech she used before that allowed us to talk without my guards realizing.

"Actually, dragoness, it's been requested that you be fitted in the keep tomorrow before the assembly," she tells me evenly, but I see the edge of strain in her gaze.

"Oh. But you can't come to the keep," I point out, confused as I try to think why they'd suddenly not want me to leave.

Maybe it's because of what happened last time with the guy and the camera, or maybe it was because of the Tainted. We never did discover any definitive proof, other than that brief whiff of rot we all smelled, that they were even there.

"Not to worry, dragoness. I'll be there via com for the fitting, and Azo will be the one to get you ready. We'll have plenty of time to sort out your loungewear and to make sure your dress for the evening is perfect."

I blow out a tense breath and nod. I would have preferred seeing Nixy in person, especially since the content of the message I need to send to my sister is sensitive. But I can make do with Azo. In the end, it doesn't matter how my warning gets to Enslee, only that it does.

"Don't worry at all, dragoness, we'll make sure you have *everything* you need for tomorrow. Trust me and Azo to ensure it all goes off without a hitch," she tells me pointedly.

Nixy waits for me to say something, to agree or get off the call. I should, but suddenly I don't want to. Maybe today has taken a bigger toll on me than I realized, despite my incredible discovery in the vaults and the progress I made with Lorn. What happened with Aeson after has thrown me, to say the least. Add to that, the last few hours I've spent remembering how to use the Vitric Port—and shaking off the subsequent flashbacks—and I find that I'm feeling overwhelmingly sad and . . . lonely.

It's foolish. I'm closer to answers than we've ever been. I'm out of the cage Wistan and the Tainted kept me in, I'm healing, I'm safe—for now—and yet it all feels like a juggling act that's destined to go wrong any second.

I stare into Nixy's eyes, and all I can think about is how much I miss Ren and wish she were here.

"Can I help you with anything else, dragoness?" Nixy asks cautiously.

"No, I apologize. I'm just tired. I should probably go to bed early. Tomorrow's going to be a long day," I tell her dismissively.

Her features fill with gentle understanding, and for a second, I pretend it's Ren looking back at me through the com screen and not her little sister.

"Hang in there, dragoness. You know dawn is coming, even when the night is at its darkest. It will all be over before you know it."

I nod and give her a half smile. "True. Maybe I've been staring at the dark for too long and it's time to look for the light."

My words tug me back to my earlier thoughts about love and light and what happens when we lose them. Aeson's face pops into my mind, but I quickly brush it aside.

"Spark the flames you need to see by, dragoness," Nixy says evenly.

My answering smile is grateful, and Nixy mirrors it.

"In the meantime, I'll look into what I can do about those lasers you've requested," she teases with a wink, and I laugh. "Get some rest. I'll speak to you tomorrow."

I disconnect the call without saying goodbye, and my stare once again returns to the sky. I should feel better. Nixy's going to get a message to Enslee. Everything went smoothly, and I doubt anything we said will trigger the suspicion of anyone who's listening in. But all at once, I'm fighting the urge to pull up the number pad on my com and call Enslee right now.

I know I can't. I know I'm just being a big baby and feeling sorry for myself. But I've spent too much time in the past today. I can't stop seeing a six-year-old Enslee, terrified, tears dripping steadily down her face as we crept from our father's spelled armoire and looked for a way out of his tower.

A distant roar pulls me from my haunted thoughts. I watch as a small group of dragons dances and dives over the tallest peaks of Talon's Reach. I run my hand down my face as exhaustion presses in on me. I want to talk to my sister. I need to see for myself that she's okay. But the closest I can get right now is stepping back in front of the Syphon Glass now hanging in my room and pretending I'm looking at Enslee and not myself when I stare into it.

I suppose the good news is that I now remember how to use a Vitric Port and what they can do. The bad news is that I don't see my nightmares getting better anytime soon. Not after all the doors and windows I threw open on my trauma today.

I push up from the ground, careful to stick close to the wall as I go. Warmth blankets me when I step through the transparent barrier that fills the massive arched opening. The tall fireplace in my room is blazing, and I don't know if Ogdan lit it the last time he was here checking on me or if it's programmed to turn on when the room drops to a cooler temperature. Either way, I leave it on, enjoying the heat.

I stride toward the large sitting area in the room and grab the controls for the vid screen, turning it on. A loud commercial blares to life, and I cringe at the cacophony of noise that instantly chases away the silence I've been sitting in all evening. I don't bother turning it down. It's the perfect level of loud.

I've been keeping my TV on every night since I got here to help mask my movement, to mute my nightmare-induced screams, and to help condition Aeson's Wing to ignore the white noise always coming from my room at night. I wanted the noise to help cover me in case I needed to sneak out, but now it will be the perfect cloak for what I need to do with the Syphon Glass.

The commercial on the vid screen ends, and a news story about the upcoming Blood Rite fills the room. I tune it out, rubbing my eyes until they're nice and red while I stride to the main door of the room. Opening it a crack, I look out and surprisingly find Ogdan standing guard. I was expecting Blay, but maybe he took a break. Ogdan's gray eyes turn to meet mine, and I notice his hair is braided in the same style it was the first time we met.

I pause. He was wearing his burgundy hair down earlier when we spoke. I've gotten the distinct impression that he only braids it when the Wing is being deployed somewhere. But unless they're going on a last-minute trip, this is for my Naming tomorrow. He must be expecting more trouble than he's told me. I know I am.

"You going to bed early?" Ogdan asks, the question pulling me from my disquieted musings.

"Yeah. Night," I tell him, and he gives me an annoying little salute.

"Gatlin will be on guard tonight if you need anything," he tells me as I step back and start to close the door.

Hmmm, Gatlin, not Blay. I guess Blay's off for the night.

A thought occurs to me, and I lean back out of the doorway.

"Tell Gatlin . . . " I pause hesitantly. "Tell him I might have a few more nightmares tonight than usual. It's been a long day and I'm dealing . . . " I blow out a tired breath. "The Crush was hard. Just tell him to ignore . . . " I gesture behind me at the room, and Ogdan gives me a solemn nod.

"I'll tell him, lass," he assures me softly, the pretty lilt in his voice adding a depth to the declaration that almost makes me want to cry for real.

I give him one more nod and then shut the door without another word. Guilt pools in my gut, but I stomp through it, ignoring the way it splashes around and makes a mess of my insides. I don't know what's wrong with me. The Syphon Glass is exactly what I need to help me move forward with my plans here in Four Tiers, but for some reason, I'm struggling.

I need to get my shit together and move past everything that happened today. I doubt the Wing or any of the Noctises are feeling shitty about the ways they're manipulating me. And they are manipulating me. I'm sure of it. But when I try to do the same, there's this bitter taste in my mouth that I can't seem to get rid of, and the tang of it tastes awfully close to regret.

But as genuine as Lorn might have been in his guilt and wanting to make things right, it doesn't mean I can trust him. And as good as Aeson felt, it doesn't mean he's not playing me. I can trust myself and I can trust Enslee. I used to think there were more people on that list, but what happened with the Tainted has rocked that foundation. Either way, I'm here in Four Tiers for a reason, and it's not to make nice with the Noctises and their Wings.

It's time to get some answers.

It's time to find what I came here for . . . or rather, *who* I came here for.

CHAPTER 32

I change into loose black pants and a fitted top with a hood I can pull up to hide my hair. I'm not sure exactly what I'll find once I activate the Syphon Glass. My plan tonight is mostly to see if it even works and where it links if it does. I doubt I'll port anywhere, but I want to be prepared just in case I stumble across something that might be worth the gamble.

I tie my hair into a chaotic pile on top of my head and move toward the bed to pluck a shard of glass from under one of the pillows. I *accidentally* broke a vase earlier, and this piece should be sharp enough for what I need.

My heart is beating fast but steady in my chest. Adrenaline warms my veins and magnifies an anxious urge to get going already. My gaze darts to the two doors that lead into my room, and I pull in a fortifying breath as I weigh my options. The main entry is a revolving door of random checks from Aeson's Wing. It does lock, but the Wing has a key, and I learned early on that locking the door isn't a deterrent when it comes to them ensuring I haven't flown the coop.

The question I'm wrestling with now is, do I lock it tonight?

If I do, it may give me the few seconds I need to shut down the Port and cover my tracks if someone tries to walk in. However, if I lock it and Ogdan or Gatlin hears it, that might make them suspicious. If I pique their interest, they'll no doubt switch up their schedule and check in on me at all kinds of random times, and I'll be screwed.

I weigh the pros and cons and then decide not to take a chance locking the door. With their advanced hearing, I'm sure it would tip the Wing off, and I think that's more likely to get me caught than the off chance Gatlin wanders in here unexpectedly while he's on watch tonight. Hopefully, my emotionally tortured, red-eyed performance will keep the Wing at bay and give me a little extra privacy for the night.

Before I can change my mind and convince myself to wait a few more days to do this, I step up to the big mirror and slice open the pad of my thumb. Blood fills the tiny gash, and I crouch down and press the bloody digit to the floral crest etched in the bottom right-hand corner of the mirror.

I close my eyes in silent plea for the Port to work, and to stave off the memory that's trying to surge. I can hear the faint rumble of my father's voice in my mind as he tells me and Ens about magic mirrors.

"Do you see that symbol right there, my girls?" Dad asks as he points to a flower with six petals sitting in the middle of six circles that all intertwine until they look like an even bigger flower surrounding the first.

Enslee and I both nod our heads.

"That is what connects all the Vitric Ports, and that also keeps anyone who isn't a Tenebrae from using them," he explains, and I marvel as I take in the symbol and the big mirror in front of us. "As long as two mirrors have this symbol, you can use them like a spy glass, or you can communicate back and forth with them like a com, but my favorite way to use the Syphon Glass is to travel from one Port to another."

"Like the gate we used to come here?" Enslee asks excitedly.

Dad smiles down at her and smooths the hair on the top of her head. "Exactly like that, only the Syphon Glass doesn't let you go as far as a gate does, but you don't need a sorcai to use the Port, you only need your blood."

I shake off the memory, hastily closing the door on our little-girl giggles and the games we played with our dad as he taught us how to use the Syphon Glass and then showed us all kinds of things around the keep with them. I press my bloody finger harder against the symbol that was created and keyed specifically to the Tenebrae bloodline thanks to a favor owed to a long-dead ancestor by a long-dead powerful sorcerer.

Pulling in a deep breath, I open my eyes to see if the blood and the symbol are doing what I need them to. A gasp escapes me when the surface of the glass ripples.

Bloody stars, it worked!

Awe and a zap of excitement replace my trepidation. A blurry image starts to fill the surface of the rolling glass, slowly coming into focus with each second that passes. It takes me a moment to realize what I'm looking at. It's some kind of cover, a dusty drop cloth, maybe. I try to see if I can make out any details beyond the white expanse taking up the entire frame, but I can't tell where this Port might be or what's blocking it.

I move my bloody finger from the center flower and trace one of the concentric circles surrounding it. Suddenly the image floating on the surface of the rippling glass flicks from the white drop cloth to something else, as though I just changed the channel. Which, I suppose, in a way, I did.

A dark office with a desk and empty bookshelves now fills the bronze frame. I study the space for a moment and then change the channel again and again. I connect to several more random Ports, located who knows where, before I land on one that shows people.

I fight the urge to duck and hide when I find myself staring at three women. My pulse thunders in my ears, and I go completely still, worried that they'll somehow be able to see me.

But when they don't start screaming or freaking out and just keep talking like they were before, I blow out a careful breath and tamp down on the smile that wants to take over my face.

Elation bursts through me like fireworks, and I bite back the excited squeal that tries to slip out.

I can see these women, but they can't see me.

The magic mirrors really fucking work. I'm connected to the Port hanging in this room, and they're none the wiser.

"Don't worry, Jess. You two have had an agreement in place for forever. The king isn't going to dishonor that. Whoever she was, it's probably not what you think," a pretty Black woman with waist-long braids assures either the small blonde or the woman with bright candy apple–red hair. Both are sitting in comfy chairs across from her.

"Maybe, but this surprise Naming and the way the royal family has been acting has my father worried. He hasn't said anything, but I can tell," a voice declares, but it must be coming from someone I can't see, because none of the women framed in the mirror are talking.

"My mother thinks something weird is going on too," the pale woman with bright red makeup and matching hair agrees. "She said the king and scions have been cancelling meetings and seem especially tense about something. And my stylist swears up and down that Aeson Noctis has a female staying in his rookery with him."

Her bright red eyebrows almost reach her hairline, and she gives the other females a knowing look. The other person I can see, the one with the platinum-blonde hair, suddenly scoots to the edge of her seat and leans in conspiratorially.

"I heard the same thing as Dasha," the blonde tells the others. "But my uncle saw a woman being escorted through Thrasher Keep by the scion's Wing. He said she didn't smell like anything he'd ever scented before." She leans in a little more and drops her voice dramatically, but I can still hear her. "He thinks she's fae."

Silence fills the room for a beat and then another. Laughter suddenly rips through the quiet as everyone but the blonde starts to cackle and guffaw. I almost join them. The blonde scowls at the others, clearly not pleased at being the focus of their tittering.

"Blair, even if there were fae sneaking around Drameric—which there aren't, I'd like to point out—they wouldn't be escorted around the keeps by the scion's men. They'd be dead and in pieces. Or, in the scion's case, ash on the wind. Your uncle was just trying to freak you out," the beautiful Black woman dismisses.

I listen for a little longer, but when the conversation turns to what the females are wearing to tomorrow's gathering, I change the channel again.

I note that there are more active Ports than I thought there'd be. Lorn mentioned that King Noctis kept some of my father's collection around. From the look of things, I probably have him to thank for the larger-than-expected network. It's hard to tell if all of the mirrors are in King's Keep, as it's nighttime and many of the channels only show darkness at the moment. I'll need to scry through them during the day and catalog what I find and where.

The night I used the one in my father's room, Enslee and I jumped to the first place that looked empty and quiet. We got incredibly lucky when, just a few halls down on the lower decks of the keep, we ran into the group of other Syphon kids and the wyvern guards with them from The Wells. I remember my father telling me and Ens that the longest recorded jump by our ancestors between Vitric Ports was just under five miles. So while the Syphon Glass won't let me sneak out of Four Tiers altogether, it will let me slip in and out of my room and possibly the keep undetected, which is all I need.

I flip through a few more places I can't identify, and then, to my surprise, Aeson Noctis ripples into existence across the surface of the Syphon Glass.

Stunned, I reel back and land on my ass. My eyes dart frantically to the door between our rooms, expecting it to be open and for Aeson to have used it to be standing right in front of me, but the white wood door is still firmly closed. Which means wherever the commander is, there's a Vitric Port in the room with him.

I cover my mouth with my hand, afraid to breathe or make a noise, even though he can't see me.

"What on your com is so interesting that you've been ignoring me since you got here?" Aeson asks as he claims a chair that's positioned in front of a fireplace, judging by the way the light is flickering over his features. "Sit down at least. You're making me jumpy."

Lorn steps into the frame, his eyes fixed on a screen floating above a portable com resting in his palm. He leans against the desk behind him for a long moment, and then the com screen disappears and he tucks the device in his pocket.

"He'll get on you about sitting on his desk if you're doing it when he gets here," Aeson chastises his brother.

Lorn rolls his eyes, but he gets up and moves to sit in a seat across from the commander.

"She got a call from her stylist. I was reading the transcript," Lorn tells his brother.

"Anything good?" Aeson asks, sounding disinterested.

"Something about lasers and dancing, but you interrupted me with your whining, so I have no idea what it means," Lorn huffs, but it's more playful than annoyed.

My mouth drops open when I realize they're talking about me. I lean closer to the mirror, hanging on every word.

"Is Chastain any closer to figuring out what was interfering with his affinity in the wyvern's studio?" Lorn queries, and my stomach drops.

Shit.

"He thinks it was some kind of bastardized magi-tech, but he still isn't sure what. We've been watching Fenox Lael and everyone she employs, but nothing has been flagged as a concern. No calls. No money in any accounts that's unaccounted for. No one that has any family with ties to the insurrectionists. No questionable dealings with anyone. Even her mail is tidy. Everything looks clean," Aeson declares.

"Which probably means it isn't," Lorn adds, and Aeson chuckles.

"My thoughts exactly," Aeson agrees. "But the tech could have been used by someone else to spy on that excursion. My Wing confirmed that they picked up on a strange scent there, the same one the others mentioned in Lairwood with that ambush. Farrow's looking into it."

Lorn nods and rubs his thumb across his lower lip, his gaze thoughtful.

"How'd today go?" Aeson inquires.

Lorn shrugs. "She fought it at first, but I got her there eventually. She wasn't interested in much, which I thought was odd. Every dragoness we know would have tried on every piece of jewelry in those vaults or at least started to reorganize things to their liking."

Aeson looks thoughtful. "Did you talk to her about Novak's secret? Tell her about our suspicions that there might be other survivors?"

Lorn nods solemnly.

"And?" Aeson's hard stare roves over his brother's face, looking for clues.

Lorn's brow furrows. "She lied to me," he answers, but he sounds more perplexed than pissed.

"Selik pick something up?" Aeson queries.

"No. She used my name," Lorn explains, and I freeze. "She said something about Novak misunderstanding things, but then she called me Lorn. She doesn't do that. She calls me Heir, or Scion, or some other derivative, *not* my name."

Flustered by his words, I think back to what happened in the vault and start to comb through it, searching for the part of the conversation he's talking about. My heart starts to hammer even harder in my chest until all I can hear is the resonant clang of it in my ears.

Double shit.

He's right. I did. I used his name when I was trying to redirect him around the *sister* conversation.

Stupid fucking mistake, Ever.

And here I was thinking I was in the clear.

"What do you think it means?" Aeson asks as he runs the back of his fingers against the scruff lining his jaw.

Lorn blows out a contemplative breath. "I think she knows there are others out there. I think she's protecting them."

Slowly Aeson nods his agreement. "She doesn't feel safe here or trust us. She's not going to risk anyone else until that changes. Can't say I blame her. We'd do the same thing in her shoes."

"How many do you think are out there?" Lorn wonders.

Aeson grunts and rubs his cheek. "Can't be that many. If all the Syphon males were able to sire at least one child, we'd be looking at less than forty. But I doubt that's the case. If I had to guess, I'd say no more than twenty, maybe twenty-five if we're lucky."

Fifteen, I correct in my head.

Fifteen of us survived that night.

Lorn nods, his gaze considering. "Anything new on the Oric?"

Aeson lets loose a frustrated sigh. "Nothing. No sign of a struggle anywhere. Her quarters show she left the following morning and never made it home that night. Nothing on any of her devices shows any calls, messages, or anything else even remotely suspicious. Nothing has moved in any of her accounts. She's just . . . gone."

"Running?" Lorn theorizes.

My brow furrows and a foreboding prickle settles over me.

"Maybe, but why? As long as she kept her mouth shut about Ever, she wasn't in any danger, and everything up until her disappearance indicates that she didn't tell a soul. I think she's dead, but if that's true, we have a massive security breach. My best guys can't find anything that would indicate even a whisper of that though, and if it were there, they'd find it."

A cold sweat breaks out on the back of my neck. They're not talking about some random Oric. They're talking about the one that tested me my first night here. Tahir. She confirmed that I was a Syphon, and now she's missing?

Somewhere out of frame I hear a door open and close. Both Aeson and Lorn stop talking and look over at whoever just joined them.

"Sorry I'm late," a commanding voice declares. "Damian Cesarini cornered me after the cabinet meeting." The voice grows louder as the owner moves closer to where the two scions are sitting.

"What did he want?" Aeson inquires with a derisive snort.

"Funny you should ask. He made a fine offer for your hand."

And with that, King Noctis strides into frame, an amused smile on his face while his lined blue eyes survey his youngest son.

My heart can't decide if it wants to stop altogether or kick into overdrive, because, holy fuck, I'm pretty sure the Syphon Glass I'm currently connected to is located in the king's tower.

I have direct access to the King of The Dragon Horde, and nobody knows.

This. Changes. Everything.

CHAPTER 33

My eyes are glued to the king as he claims a seat on the sofa opposite his two sons. He moves with a grace that belies his age, his stature and build just as formidable and intimidating as Aeson's and Lorn's. His silver suit fits impeccably. The collar on the jacket and shirt are a military nod, but the tails that turn into an attached cape and the embroidery on the arms signify his status, not that he needs the help. He could be wearing sand rags and his regal bearing would still give him away.

I look for anything that might support my suspicions that this drake before me betrayed my father, someone he once considered kindred before having my kith slaughtered. But there isn't a neon sign flashing *guilty* above his head, and I'm having a hard time seeing him as the monster I've made him out to be in my mind. Probably because when I look at him now, I see his two sons, neither of whom fit the profile of heartless butcher or evil plotter.

Vids from when King Noctis was younger have him looking more like Aeson. However, now the king's hair and neat beard are a beautiful blend of white and black, making him look like a perfect mix of his two scions. His blue eyes fall somewhere in the middle of Lorn's icy tones and Aeson's sky-blue hue, but they're filled with a paternal warmth and pride as he takes in the two males sitting across from him.

His hard but handsome features soften as he settles into his seat and gets comfortable, crossing one knee over another and resting his elbow against the armrest while draping the other across the back of the couch. He picks up a drink that appears to have been waiting for him on the end table, and I notice that Aeson and Lorn have matching glasses with the same large round ice cube and amber liquid.

I instantly know that I'm peeping in on a personal moment between a father and his sons and not just spying on a king and his heirs.

"An offer for my hand?" Aeson snorts, reminding me of what the king was talking about before I got distracted by his mere presence. "Even if I did fancy males, I wouldn't look twice at that bumbling windbag."

Lorn chuckles and the king smiles around a sip of his drink.

"He's still rather convinced that you and his daughter Claudelle were made for each other and, if I would only facilitate a meeting between you two, that you would see it for yourself."

"It's time for Cesarini to cede his chamber seat if he can't remember that we've met his daughter dozens of times already," Lorn points out, and King Noctis lets loose an amused huff and an agreeing hum.

"I believe he was just trying to get me to admit that Aeson is off the market. It seems the rumor mill has been churning away about a mysterious occupant of a certain someone's mating suite." The king's smile slowly stretches, and a playful gleam alights in his eyes. "How is your little Syphon adjusting?"

Aeson releases a sound that's half groan, half laugh. "She's as cagey and cutting as ever."

I narrow my gaze at the mirror. "I'll show you cutting," I grumble at the commander's firelit profile.

King Noctis chuckles. "Merik was never one to mince words or pull punches. I'm glad to hear that side of him is living on through his little girl. It'll be a treat to go toe to toe with him again, if only in spirit," King Noctis declares, his tone wistful and fond.

An ache starts in my chest at the mention of my father, and as much as I want to condemn the king for everything, the longing in his tone falls in line with what I've seen from Aeson and Lorn when it comes to the loss of my loved ones.

"She definitely doesn't pull her punches," Aeson agrees, purposefully rubbing his jaw.

I huff out a laugh, thinking about what happened earlier in his room when I was trying to get away from him. Then I'm suddenly bombarded with what happened when I *didn't* manage to escape him, and a flush crawls through me while lust starts to simmer and settle low in my stomach. It seems my attraction to the commander isn't something I can ignore or control, even though I'm trying hard to do both.

"I take it things are going well, then?" King Noctis asks.

Aeson shrugs. "As well as can be expected for someone who doesn't trust us and blames us for the death of their kith and kindred. I think she's starting to nest though. She got very territorial earlier, and she took a mirror from the vaults for her room. She may not understand her instincts just yet, but she's giving in to them all the same."

My brow furrows at that declaration, but the king's features suddenly grow serious, and he looks over at Lorn.

"A mirror?" he asks.

Lorn nods and then out of nowhere, the king shifts until he's suddenly looking directly at . . . me.

My mind stalls for a moment as we stare at one another. My heart hammers in my head, and I refuse to blink as Kathal Noctis's intense gaze sucks me in. Instinctually, I start to lean away from the Port as though that will break his hold, and for half of a millisecond, I'm convinced that he can somehow *see* me. His gaze starts to blur as mine dries out. I fight the urge to look away, convinced that he's about to reach through the mirror and pull me through. Then his stare starts to circle where I'm kneeling, and I realize he's not actually looking at me, he's simply studying the mirror in his office.

"Her father liked to collect them," King Noctis mumbles almost to himself, his focus all at once thoughtful and faraway.

"She mentioned that when she opened the vault. I think it was the only thing in the Crush that she felt connected to. She didn't really seem interested in anything else, but that could have been because I was there watching. Like Aes said, she's cagey."

King Noctis looks lost in thought for a moment, but then he nods and turns away from the mirror. I blow out a relieved breath as soon as his attention leaves me and returns to his sons.

"I'm glad to hear she's softening toward you," he tells Aeson. "I know I don't need to remind you how important it is that she accepts the claim. If she's coming around on her own, that's good. It means we won't have to take more drastic measures."

Aeson nods, and I bristle.

More drastic measures?

What in the bloody Bearing does that mean?

"I wish you had more time, son, but after her Naming, the pressure will be on for her to accept you. Once The Horde knows who and what she is, you can expect others to make a play for her. Regardless of the fact that she can't reveal, her political influence alone will be enough to entice them. And that's not even accounting for the ones who will want her dead. Speaking of, are we set for tomorrow?"

A ringing starts in my head, and I sit back on my heels. I knew what they were up to, encouraged it even. So why do their words feel like stones skipping across the still waters of who I am? Why does it send disappointment rippling through me? Why does it hurt?

Am I so bereft of genuine love and affection that I can't tell when it's counterfeit?

I exhale a barbed breath, feeling it rip me apart as it leaves my lungs.

Is Aeson Noctis that good, or am *I* just that pathetic? Because when Aeson kisses me, I don't taste a lie. When he touches me, it doesn't feel like manipulation.

My head bows under the weight of that realization. I stare at the shard of broken vase in my hands and can't help feeling like it's symbolic. The needy, shattered slivers of my soul are making it entirely too easy for the Noctises to play me. All Aeson has to do is bat his lashes and whisper a few filthy words and I come running, ready to call it more. I'm over here steeped in delusion, pretending this thing between us could be everything when really it's as hollow and empty as I am.

I twist the shard, tracing the jagged edges with a finger.

Aeson Noctis stumbled upon the sucker of the century, and I'm barely putting up a fight.

My fist closes tightly around the broken vase until it's cutting into my palm and blood starts to speckle the floor. I release my grip, staring at the cuts on my hand that can't heal because I'm half of what I'm supposed to be.

But that stops now.

It's time to embrace the truth, to see things for what they are. Maybe the Noctises didn't slaughter my family, but it doesn't mean they're knights in shining armor. I need to wake up. No more fawning over pretty scions. No more benefit of the doubt. I'm going to take what I need and do it on my terms.

Fuck everything else.

What they're saying changes nothing. I inhale a fortifying breath and focus back on the Port and the conversation happening on the other side of it. The three Noctises are discussing logistics and security. I listen and let my gaze wander, no longer focused on the scions and the king, but on where they are and how it might help me.

They're either in the king's office or library, judging by the desk and the wall of bookshelves behind it. I'm surprised by the variety of volumes that are on display. Physical books are rare these days. Most everything is digital, but Kathal Noctis must be a collector, because his shelves are teeming with all kinds of treasures from what I can see.

My eyes catch on a set of matching spines taking up the entirety of two shelves just behind the desk. I read *Render Territory Census* on several spines and then *Channeler Territory Census*, *Thrasher Territory Census*, and lastly *Burner Territory Census*. I go still, holding my breath as I reread everything again. Every ounce of my attention hones in on those two shelves as I read all of the spines for a third and then a fourth time.

No fucking way.

I stare at the books, stunned and reeling. Is it possible the sorcai I'm looking for might be listed? The Relacours have burrowed even deeper into hiding as we've mercilessly hunted them over the last several years. But if anyone knows where they are, it would be the king.

There's no way it's that easy, I warn myself, careful not to get my hopes up. I don't even know what years those books are for. They could be older censuses from a long time ago.

But what if they're not?

What if they're current records of the citizens of Drameric? What if Noctis knows where the rest of the Relacour line is hiding? What if the sorcai we've been searching for is listed right there in those censuses, like a treasure map just waiting to be discovered?

X *marks the spot that frees the Syphons from their curse.*

Eager anticipation has my heart galloping with all kinds of possibilities. I doubt it'll be that cut-and-dried. Nothing in my life ever is. But it's possible King Noctis is old-school and likes physical copies of things. And it's possible that he might have records of where the remaining Relacours are holed up. All I need is one, because where there's one Relacour, there's crumbs that lead to the others. And who knows, I just might get lucky and find the bloodline's Conduit on my first go . . . and then it's game fucking over.

"I don't like using her as bait," Aeson growls, drawing my attention back to him and the conversation he's having with Lorn and the king.

Confusion plumes through me. He'll claim me as a mate for political gain but draw the line at using me for bait? That doesn't make any sense.

"I don't like using her as bait either, but what choice do we have?" Lorn argues.

Aeson rounds on him. "She's not yours. You don't understand."

I roll my eyes. Of course it's a territorial thing. The commander doesn't like anyone else playing with his toys. Typical fucking dragon.

Lorn's eyes narrow into a scowl. "I know my draw to her is different than yours, but it doesn't mean I don't care about what happens to her just as much as you do. And last *I* checked, she's not yours either," he snaps.

"Are you challenging me?" Aeson asks, his tone eerily even and soaked in menace.

"Lorn, stop antagonizing your brother," King Noctis commands before turning to Aeson. "No one is challenging you for your Syphon, son—not yet anyway. But Lorn isn't wrong. We have traitors in our midst, and like it or not, Ever Tenebrae is our best bet to flush them out. I wouldn't put her in their path if I could help it—I loved Merik too much to do that to his daughter—but the secrets of the Syphon aren't going to stay hidden forever. She's more at risk moving around in the dark than she would be if her existence was brought to light. Yes, it puts the spotlight on her when it comes to our enemies, but it also means she'll have more of us looking out for her too."

I study King Noctis for a moment. My gaze traces the touch of age in his features, the white in his hair, the strength in his countenance. I can imagine my father and him laughing over a drink, discussing their concerns about Drameric and how to best solve the problems and serve the people. I can see how Kathal Noctis would have been a good friend to Merik Tenebrae; he's still a good friend even though my father is long gone.

Aeson drops his head and pulls in a deep breath and then another before slowly nodding. "Have we made any progress on figuring out how to help her reveal?" he asks, a hint of a growl still present in his tone like he hasn't managed to banish it completely even though he's trying.

I lean closer to the mirror, making sure I catch every word they're about to exchange.

"I have some trusted sources looking into it," King Noctis answers. "They're going to want to bring her in and run some tests, but we'll worry about that after her Naming."

The ice cube in his drink clinks against the glass as he empties it in one last swallow and then sets the tumbler back down on the table.

"Now, I have to be up very early tomorrow, and you two still have another security meeting tonight. You'd best go see to your duties," the king declares dismissively.

Both Aeson and Lorn stand up to leave, but I'm surprised when King Noctis pulls Aeson in for a hug. They embrace each other tightly, like it's something they do often. The king whispers something into Aeson's ear, but I can't hear what it is before they pull away and the king starts hugging Lorn.

I fight the need to fidget, even though none of the affection is aimed at me. I'm both mesmerized and oddly uncomfortable at the exchange. The warm display doesn't fit with any of the notions I had about the king and what he would be like, which, I suppose, tracks when it comes to the Noctises. They seem to be full of surprises, but whether that's a good thing or bad one, I still can't say.

The office empties, and the lights slowly dim before going out altogether. I stare into the dark Port for a long time, wondering what it would be like to be raised with the kind of love and attention I just witnessed. It's clear that the king respects his sons. He speaks to them like they're his equals, but he was also quick to step in when they needed guidance. They all work seamlessly together. A true team, and none of it was for show. They didn't know they were being watched. They didn't know every action was being dissected. This is just how they are with each other. It's humbling, and beautiful, and I want it.

I want what they have.

I want to know a love where it's safe to trust like that, where it's okay to just be. One where it doesn't matter who or what I am, because I'm no longer hunted, no longer coveted, no longer a danger to everyone around me. I want what they have, but what if the only way to get it is to take it from them? What if the only way I'll ever know peace is to steal theirs?

Could I do it?

Would it be worth it?

I used to be able to say yes without pause, without question, but now I'm not so sure.

CHAPTER 34

My tread is silent as I pace in front of the mirror. I make one pass, then another as I once again think through every step of what I'm about to do. I've watched the dark office for the last few hours, and I haven't seen any evidence of a security system. I also haven't spotted any cameras. Not that I'm surprised by that; I'm sure the king isn't interested in a record of the conversations and decisions made in his private space.

I've scrubbed myself raw with a floral-smelling soap that was in my shower. I'm pretty sure Tove put it in there as some kind of jab at the strange way I smell, but joke's on her, because it's about to help me cover my scent trail. I'm saturated in so much flowery perfume I'm surprised I don't start actually blooming.

Regardless of the helpful scent cover-up, I still need to get in and out of the king's office as quickly as possible so all traces of my visit have plenty of time to disappear. It's working in my favor that the king will be busy with council meetings all morning, and then there's the Naming tomorrow night. Between that and the cleaning drones that will hopefully tidy up at some point between today and tomorrow, all traces of my break-in should be long gone by the time he sets foot in his office again.

My stare fixes on the shelf of census records through the Syphon Glass. Their closed covers beckon me closer, and a heady rush of anticipation encourages me to close the distance right this second and give in to the siren song. I ignore the sensation and focus. I want the information tucked between the covers of those books, I need it, but there is zero wiggle room to fuck this up.

I blow out a breath and go over the plan again.

I'm being neurotic as fuck right now, I know I am, and yet I can't seem to snap myself out of it. If Ren were here, she'd be rolling her eyes at me and telling me to get the fuck on with it. But she isn't here, she's dead, and that's on me.

My neck pops as I stretch out. I roll my shoulders and then shake my arms to get the blood flow going and to help calm my nerves. I need to get my shit together. I'm on edge and it has my head and my heart disagreeing on what to do, a surefire way to guarantee everything goes tits up.

My head is telling me I should probably wait. I could watch the office for a while, see what else I can learn, maybe come up with a more secure plan involving suppression suits, scanners, and alternative escape plans. But my heart is thrumming a steady rhythm of *now or never*. It's telling me I'm banking on time I don't have and that this is the best shot I'm going to get at the king's office before I'm wrapped up in all of the political jaw-wagging and showboating that the king and his sons have lined up for me. I need to make a decision before my opposing sides drop the gloves and start taking bare-knuckled swings to see which one wins.

I stop my pacing and square off with the Syphon Glass.

It's just a quick in and out.

No big deal.

I've done it plenty of times before.

I scoff at that thought, because I've never broken into the tower of the most powerful being on the planet, but there was that one time I had to steal an egg from a nest of breeding gorgons. This should be a cakewalk compared to that.

I glance over my shoulder at the door I know Gatlin is guarding. He's already done his checks for the night and shouldn't come in here unless something draws his attention. The keeps are quiet, and there's even a blanket of clouds keeping the stars from spying on what I'm about to do.

If I'm going, I need to go now.

Filling my lungs with a fortifying breath, I banish the last of my doubts. I take one more look around the dark office, but no new cameras have sprung up, and there still isn't any sign of an active security system. I exhale the breath I was holding and move.

Thumbing the cut on my finger from earlier, I watch as fresh blood wells. I press the scarlet drops to the crest in the corner of the Syphon Glass, tracing a pattern that shifts the surface from spy mode and turns it into a Port. The image on the surface vibrates and then bows slightly before rippling back into place and smoothing out.

Before I can talk myself out of it, I step into the pane of magic. Immediately, a glacial rush envelops me. The frigid wash of power is a shock to my senses. It feels like I'm walking through a sheet of slush as I'm magically transported from my room in Aeson's rookery to the king's office.

I don't remember it feeling like this the last time I used a Vitric Port, a realization that has unease solidifying in my stomach. The wasps in my gut should be rioting alongside the settling apprehension, but I'm pretty sure they're frozen solid at the moment.

Adrenaline floods my veins, my heart working double time to prime my system now that I'm finally taking action and not just fretting. My body is no longer beholden to the laws of gravity. My limbs feel stretched to the brink even though I can see that they're still perfectly normal. My labored breaths are plumes of frost, and my lungs are quickly becoming nothing more than icebergs floating in my chest. I can't really see anything around me; my surroundings are a weird blur that makes me want to rub my eyes until my vision sharpens.

Just as quickly as it all started, it stops, and I step out of the Port in King Noctis's office onto a low cabinet that's positioned directly under the magic mirror. The glass surface of the Port ripples and eddies behind me as I'm released, and blessed heat once again kisses my skin.

Out of nowhere, the quiet plink of rattling crystal suddenly fills the room, and I go utterly still. My gaze frantically searches for a source or a threat, and then I notice a tray at the end of the cabinet I'm perched on that has decanters of alcohol and spare glasses sitting on it. I blow out a careful breath and move slowly so as not to disturb the tray more than I already have.

I crouch on the cabinet, sitting long enough that if a silent alarm had alerted anyone to my presence, I'd hear their hurried footsteps heading my way by now. Thankfully, the office is quiet and undisturbed, just like it has been since the king and the scions left hours ago. Cautiously, I press a foot to the ground, and then I wait again to see if the movement or pressure on the floor sets off any other security measures.

When it's clear I'm not setting off any unseen sensors in the king's office, I climb fully off the cabinet and step cautiously into the room. I edge around the back of the sofa the king sat on and ignore the floor-to-ceiling shelves of books to my right and left.

Slipping silently behind the king's workspace, I aim for the census records on the shelf. A trio of monitors lights up unexpectedly across the surface of the desk, and I just barely swallow down my gasp at the jump scare. My heart hammers a pounding rhythm of *oh fuck* against my sternum, and the sudden burst of light in the darkness has me blinking spots from my vision. Slowly my eyes adjust again, and I cautiously study the three glowing, transparent screens. They float a few inches above the wood, and there's an equally diaphanous-looking keyboard waiting to be of use just in front of them.

The setup looks innocent enough, almost inviting, but as innocuous as it seems, I know better than to go messing with tech like this. There may not be cameras or an extensive security system in this room, but I guarantee the king's mainframe is locked down as tight as they come.

I give the desk and computer my back and once again zero in on the spines of the census records. I've already decided to start with the Burner territories, since the other Syphons and I don't usually hunt that far north. The book is lighter than I expect it to be as I pluck it from the shelf, and that makes my stomach start to roil with worry.

"Come on," I whisper, hoping I'm wrong as I open the cover and look inside.

The spine of the book creaks, but it isn't a weathered paper page that greets me, it's a black screen that instantly boots up to show a search prompt.

Fuck.

It's a digital record that's been made to look like a leather-bound tome.

Double fuck.

I grind my molars as my gaze flicks from the digital record in my hands to the off-limits computer on the desk and back again. There's a chance they're not connected. Their networks could be different. The odds aren't great, but it's possible.

My fingers hover over the dim keypad.

Eight letters and a little good fortune is all I need . . .

I close the book. My head drops back and I huff out a long breath laden with frustration. It would be so easy to type *Relacour* in the search bar, but I can't risk it. I've pushed my luck enough simply breaking in here.

I want to throw the book across the room and curse everything to the moon and back again, but I keep my anger in check. Maybe there's something else in this office I can use. My intuition was practically shoving me through the Port to get in here; it can't all be for nothing. There has to be something here that I need, something that will help the Syphons.

A smooth, canorous voice suddenly rings out behind me, and my blood turns to ice in my veins.

"Want to tell me who you're looking for, Ever Tenebrae? Maybe I can be of assistance."

CHAPTER 35

Alarm detonates through me like a PHaSR grenade. Quick as a blink, the book that's not a book is flying through the air, aimed at the intruder who just caught me. I dart for the Syphon Glass, just making out in my periphery that the fucker crashing my break-in is wearing a silver suit with an attached cape.

Shit.

Please don't let that be who I think it is.

I focus on my immediate escape and refuse to let my thoughts circle the fact that I'm pretty sure King Noctis just caught me red-handed in his office. I have no idea where he came from or how he got in here. The door didn't open and I didn't sense any hidden access points, but I'll have to freak out about that later. Right now, I need to run.

I'm steps from the Vitric Port when a wall of white flames surges up from the ground and blocks my way. A hiss rips out of me when my skidding stop isn't fast enough to keep my forearm from brushing against the barricade of fire. Pain flashes up my arm, but I ignore it as I pivot and frantically search for another exit.

Like this is just another day in the office, King Noctis watches all of this while casually leaning against a wall by the entryway. He's holding the census I chucked at him, and his face is surprisingly curious, not angry or outraged like I'd expect it to be. My eyes flit to a window opposite the both of us, but before I can even shift my weight in its direction, another wall of white flames cuts off my access.

Sweat and panic drip down the back of my neck when I realize I have no choice but to turn and face off against Kathal Noctis, King of Drameric.

Fuck.

All of the ways he could torture and then kill me flash quickly through my mind. I close my eyes for all of two seconds and slow my frenzied breathing. By the time I open my eyes, I've dropped my arm to my side, straightened my spine, and promised myself I won't break no matter what.

"Are you done?" King Noctis asks evenly, a surprising hint of amusement lacing the question.

The burn on my elbow painfully thrums in time with my pounding pulse, and I use it to ground me. I steal one more hopeful glance around the dark room, but I'm well and truly trapped. I do notice that somehow the king's fire hasn't so much as scorched or wilted anything else in his office but me. I file that away to think about later, probably between the beatings and interrogations that are in my near future.

The king lifts a dark eyebrow. The gesture is expectant, and it takes me a second to remember he asked me a question. One that continues to go unanswered as I just stand there—a phenomenon, I suspect, he's unfamiliar with.

"I'd like to keep this conversation between us," he tells me when it's clear I have no intention of addressing what he asked me. "If you're not amenable to that, I can call one of my Wing in here. Or, if you'd prefer, Aeson. If asked, either one will tie you to a chair so that we can talk. And we *will* talk. We have quite a few things that need to be sorted out before your Naming tomorrow."

He looks toward the window, his gaze briefly studying the sliver of dawn that's just starting to peek between the summits of Talon's Reach.

"Correction, *today*," he amends. "I planned on meeting you tomorrow, but this works just as well."

Puzzlement immediately permeates my panic. What is he talking about? Why would he want a *conversation* to stay between us? Am I supposed to add whatever he's about to say to this list of things I won't be confessing to midtorture? I move closer to the king and farther from his blistering walls of fire. My instincts flare with warning, but I flip them the bird. If I survive whatever this is, my intuition and I are going to have a serious heart-to-heart. My gut is supposed to be warning me about traps, not leading me straight fucking into them.

The flames behind me instantly die out, and I can't help but longingly glance over at the Syphon Glass still hanging undisturbed on the wall.

"Don't even think about it," King Noctis warns. "I know how that mirror works. Even if you make it through, you'll be surrounded by guards on the other side faster than you can say Vitric Port."

My attention snaps back to the king, his words a sharp, sobering slap.

"How the fuck do you know what a Vitric Port is?" I demand, shock shoving the gravity of who I'm talking to completely out of my mind.

King Noctis smiles, and it's unsettling and reassuring to see both Aeson and Lorn in it. He calmly ambles over to the bookshelf behind his desk and rehomes the digital census that lured me into this elaborate trap.

"When my son mentioned that you'd taken a mirror from the vaults, I wondered if you knew about the Ports. Your father pretended to collect all kinds of mirrors to help hide the special ones. Your decision could have been purely sentimental, but it made me curious."

"Do Lorn and Aeson know about Syphon Glass?" I ask, wanting to know just how much I misjudged this situation.

Was the vault and the Crush a setup from the beginning?

Did the Noctis brothers play me . . . again?

Instead of answering me, Kathal Noctis nods in the direction of the sofa and chairs in his office. The gesture is a silent order to pick my poison and choose a seat.

The king's gaze roves over my face when I once again don't respond. "I am not your enemy, Ever Tenebrae. I suggest you endeavor to keep it that way."

I debate for half a second whether or not I'm going to comply, but curiosity has me cooperating. I move to the chair Aeson occupied earlier, the one in front of a now-dark fireplace, and I sit.

A sliver of a smile lifts one corner of the king's mouth, like he's amused by my choice for some reason. King Noctis selects the same sofa he sat on when I watched him and his sons earlier from the safety of my room. I'm getting the sense that this is some kind of test, one that doesn't start or end with the Vitric Port I took from the vaults earlier, and that means not all is lost. I don't know what King Noctis wants, but he most definitely wants something.

"No, to answer your question, my sons have no idea that Vitric Ports exist, let alone that there's a network of them hanging in the keeps," King Noctis tells me while he makes himself comfortable.

I file away his use of the word *keeps* and settle back in my chair, mirroring his easygoing posture even though I'm strung tighter than a mech bow.

"That's quite the hole you've knowingly left in your defenses," I blurt and then instantly want to punch myself for it.

Nice, Ever. Let's provoke the asshole who just caught you rummaging through his office. While you're at it, be sure to remind him that he should shatter all the escape routes you just discovered.

"It's not a security concern when you think everyone capable of accessing the Ports is long dead," King Noctis counters, and there's a tinge of sorrow in the statement.

"And did you have anything to do with having my family and my people ambushed and murdered so you could take the throne?" I ask point-blank.

His eyes fill with an unfathomable amount of agony, but his features soften. "No, Ever," he answers, his tone laden with emotion. "I could *never* have hurt your kindred. They were my kindred too in so many ways. The crown was the last thing I wanted, but I took up the mantle rather than see The Horde destroyed from infighting and mistrust. I wasn't going to let everything your father worked for die with him."

King Noctis runs a tired hand down his face, and for a moment, I see clearly the toll all of this has taken on him.

"I never wanted the throne, not for me or my boys," he goes on. "I would trade this position and power in a heartbeat if I could have your father, Paloma, and your brothers back. I've done everything I could to honor my best friend's memory. I've hunted those who betrayed him, brought them to justice, or so I thought until you told us there was more to all of this than we knew."

His sorrow is palpable, genuine, and the authenticity of it undercuts everything I thought I knew about the king. I should feel relieved by Kathal Noctis's heartache. My father's love and trust weren't misplaced. And yet, all I can think is that I'm back to square one in my search for who's responsible for all of this loss and pain. Up until now, the Noctises betraying the Tenebraes made the most sense. All the threads lined up perfectly.

But ever since I was brought here, the big picture isn't revealing what I thought it would. Which means I'm once again nowhere close to figuring out what really happened that night. And for the first time, I'm starting to wonder if I ever will. If Kathal Noctis didn't betray the Syphons . . . then who did? And if the King of The Dragon Horde isn't my enemy . . . then what does that make him?

His gaze flits over my face, and the room grows quiet as he takes his time to survey me. I'm not sure how much he can make out in the dark, but it reminds me of the way Lorn and Aeson looked at me in Lairwood when I first told them who I was. I can tell he's looking for my father in my features, and something about the earnestness in his search makes my chest ache.

"I promised your father I wouldn't tell anyone who didn't need to know about the Syphon Glass," he explains, his fingers tracing abstract patterns over the arm of the sofa he's leaning against. "I take my oaths seriously, even when I'm the only one left to do so."

"So my father trusted you enough to tell you about his magic mirrors but not enough to tell you about me?" It's a harsh question, maybe even a brutally unfair one, but I have to ask. My father seemed to entrust this male with so much—why not that too?

King Noctis doesn't get upset. There isn't even an ounce of defensiveness in his demeanor; he suddenly just looks really sad.

"I wish Merik had told me," he murmurs, but I don't know if the declaration is for me or him. "If I had known you existed, Ever, I would have stopped at nothing to protect you."

Steely blue eyes meet mine, and I struggle not to squirm under the weight of a stare that feels far more paternal than I'm prepared for. I'm not sure what to make of that, so instead of analyzing it too closely, I rally my indignation.

I don't want his sympathy, and I don't want to feel sorry for *his* loss, not when my own is so overwhelming. I've spent so much time pitting myself against The Horde and everything that was taken from me, I don't know what to make of these gray areas the Noctises are unveiling in my black-and-white world. I wasn't prepared to have holes poked through my carefully curated anger, not when I can barely keep the underlying chasm of sadness at bay as it is.

King Noctis takes me in like he can see all of that written across my face. I realize with a start that he's looking at me the same way he was looking at his sons, and it unsettles me more than anything else he's done till now. There's a compassion and care in his countenance, neither of which I've earned or know what to do with.

"I tried to get to your father. I was the first to make it to his rookery . . . to see what they'd done . . . " The king's eyes leave mine, and his thoughts drift elsewhere while his words taper off.

He doesn't need to say anything else; we both know what he saw. We both know what he found in my father's tower. That truth drains some of my ire, and a weighted weariness trickles in instead. My shoulders sag and my gaze wanders to the surrounding bookshelves. The king wipes at the corner of one eye and collects himself as he clears his throat.

Watching him carefully tuck his anguish away so he can focus back on the matter at hand does something to me. I can't count the number of times I've done the same over the years. And I realize, in this moment, that we both mourn my father. We both live with the horrors of his final hours. And we both grieve in stolen moments coiled between everything else that's demanded of us. Loss has aligned us and it's also driven us apart.

"Who were you hoping to find in my census records?" King Noctis asks after a long stretch of silence.

With admirable finesse, he circles back to the unanswered question he first lobbed my way. He holds up a hand, like he's already anticipating the lie I'm working to string together.

"Think carefully on what you're about to tell your king, Ever Tenebrae. Like I said before, I'm not your enemy. Not unless you put me in a position where I have no choice but to become exactly that."

"I haven't sworn fealty to you," I counter, but he waves it off like it's a trivial detail.

I study him, and he patiently returns my silent scrutiny. I swiftly flick through everything I heard him talk about with Aeson and Lorn. I could approach the king's question from a lot of angles that are technically true, but which one is going to get me closer to what I want, to what I'm here to find?

My heart hammers hard against my breastbone. I can't tell if it's urging me on or begging me not to do what I'm about to.

"I'm looking for members of the Relacour bloodline," I finally answer after a prolonged, weighted moment.

I can tell instantly that my answer has surprised the king. He sits up a little straighter, and a budding shrewdness blooms in his gaze.

"And why would that bloodline interest you?" he asks, the question a perfect balance of polite interest and nonchalance.

If I didn't already know what I do about sorcai and the Relacour line, I wouldn't find anything amiss in what he's asking me . . . lucky for me, I do. I loose a measured and calculated sigh and relax deeper into my chair.

"I've spent a lot of time thinking about what happened the night of the rebellion. I've combed through every report I could find. I've examined every account on record of that night. And I noticed something. A lot of the sorcai involved in the rebellion were Blood Crafters. More specifically, Relacour Blood Crafters. There were other sorcai that participated, but when I looked into who, I realized that a startling number of them descended from branches of the Relacour line too."

I purposefully fidget in my chair and then thread my fingers together to look like I'm trying to stop my nerves from peeking through. King Noctis's gaze tracks the show I'm putting on, but he doesn't say anything as he waits for me to continue.

"It's a connection that means something. I can't say exactly what, but I suspect Blood Crafters, or more specifically Relacour Blood Crafters, were involved in the curse that kept the Syphons from shifting the night they were killed. That means they know why, to this day, *I* still can't reveal. I want to ask them, but the sorcai involved in the rebellion are all dead. And when it comes to the other Blood Crafter lines, most of them have been wiped out or they're in hiding for fear of being wiped out, like I was. If I could just talk to one of them though, I might be able to figure out how to reverse what they did. That's who I'm looking for. *That's* who I'm trying to find."

I watch the king carefully as he processes what I just said. Every word is true, or true enough to pass muster. He doesn't need to know that I've personally hunted enough Relacours and Relacour relatives to confirm that my theory is correct. The Syphons know that particular line of Blood Crafters is to blame for our broken natures. For the longest time, we thought we had to track down those who initially invoked the curse in order to break it, but thanks to a particularly whiny and motivated relative that I interrogated and then killed, we know there's a loophole when it comes to blood magic.

"If anyone can help me, it will be their Matron." *Their Conduit*, I finish, but only to myself. If the king knows what that is, it's not in my best interest to tell him that I know too. And if he isn't in the loop, that's not my problem either. "Blood magic trapped my dragon, which means blood magic is the way to release it."

I sit back and give him time to consider what I've revealed. Silence stretches between us long enough for the shadows in the room to shift. An unseasoned liar would fight the need to fill the pervasive quiet, but I'm not some wet-behind-the-ears greenling. I know the king is searching for anything that might indicate deception or hint that there's more to the story.

There is . . . there always is. A wise person knows that. But is King Noctis wise? Will he take a leap of faith on behalf of his friend and former king? Will he help me? Or have I misjudged this situation like I have so many times with his sons?

The king's body language and any hint of what he might be thinking are locked down tight. It's an impressive and intimidating poker face, probably the best I've ever seen, which makes sense. As the king, I imagine he's had plenty of practice mastering every tic, blink, and breath.

"What you're saying has merit. I'd probably draw the same conclusions that you have . . . "

I sense a definitive *but* trailing those words, and the flash of relief that just flickered through me morphs into misgiving.

"You're right, Blood Crafters are a difficult ilk to track down, and for good reason. Reasons I'm not keen to ignore or supersede . . . not for just *anyone*, that is."

My brow furrows as I try to pick through the word salad he just tried to serve me. The king drops his ankle from his knee and once again leans back in his seat. It's his power position, one that's easy to recognize because he used it on Aeson and Lorn. And with that, I realize I've just entered a negotiation, only I've been left in the dark as to what the terms are.

"Oookaaay," I hedge, warily studying the king. "And who *would* you ignore those valid reasons for?"

An impressed twinkle enters his blue gaze. His shrug is insouciant, but his smile is predatory. "My sons. I'd do almost anything for them. And of course, that same trusted consideration would be given to their . . . mates."

My breath stalls and the wasps in my stomach fully defrost and begin to buzz with a renewed fury.

Is he serious right now? Is he really trying to leverage my fucked-up curse with an arranged mating?

King Noctis stares at me, a look in his eyes that vaunts victory. My answering glare is fulminating, but I manage to keep my tone even. I cant my head in consideration.

"I did hear something about an interest in aligning with me because of . . . what was it?" I ask absently as I tap my chin. "Oh, that's right, political influence." I shake my head disapprovingly. "I would think a loving father, such as yourself, would want more than just that for their son."

King Noctis chuckles. "Of course I want more for him than just that. I want his happiness above all else. And if you think Aeson's interest in you starts and stops with the political advantages, then you haven't been paying attention to what's been happening around you like you should," he tells me cryptically.

What the fuck does that mean?

I haven't been paying attention?

All I *do* is pay attention. I overanalyze every-*fucking*-thing, and then I plot and plan accordingly. I heard them with my own cursed ears talking about my influence and how important it was that I accept Aeson. So what in the bloody stars does he think I missed when it comes to his son and this *situation*?

I rub my temples, the long day finally starting to catch up with me in the form of an oncoming headache and the disappearance of the last vestiges of my patience.

"Let me get this straight," I snap. "If I agree to mate your son, you'll help me track down the Relacour Matron and break my curse? Do I have that right?"

The king straightens like he knows he has me up against the ropes and he's ready to deliver the final blow.

"Close, but not exactly. I will arrange a meeting with Matron Relacour, but I can't guarantee that she will break the curse. In exchange, you'll agree to mate Aeson, regardless of the outcome of your meeting or whether your curse is broken or not."

I reel back at that, my face scrunching with confusion. "But if I can't reveal, if I'm not a full dragon, I can't bond. The mating would be incomplete . . . it would be deficient from the very start," I argue.

He doesn't look concerned in the slightest by anything I just said. It's almost like he knows something I don't. While really fucking frustrating, that isn't exactly surprising. I wasn't raised by dragons, so what I don't know about my own kind can probably rival the grains of sand in the deadlands.

King Noctis offers me a warm smile that only serves to deepen my glower. "That's my offer. Take it or leave it."

"I want time to think about this," I counter.

"That's fine with me," he surprisingly agrees, and then he suddenly rises from the sofa.

I scramble to stand too, bewildered as to what's going on.

Is that it?

Am I headed back to the warren of dungeons now?

"You should get some rest. Your Naming is going to be here before we know it," he announces with a nod as he gestures toward the mirror. "Are you okay to get back the way you came?"

My head snaps between the king and the Port. "Wait. I can go? Just like that?"

The king's warm laugh fills the room. "Of course. I did tell you that I preferred to keep this visit between us," he reminds me, and that statement triggers all the same alarms that it did the first time I heard it.

I open my mouth to argue, to demand answers, but then it dawns on me that he's actually letting me go. And from the sound of things, he's prepared to continue to honor his vow to my father about the Syphon Glass and keep it secret. I have no idea why, but I'm also not stupid enough to *not* take advantage of it.

I warily move closer to the Syphon Glass.

"Oh, and Ever . . . " he calls when I'm about to climb up on the cabinet. "If you try to break into my tower again, it will be the last thing you ever do. I don't care whose daughter you are or what you mean to my son. Are we clear?" All the warmth and humor has evaporated from his face, and for the first time since I laid eyes on the king, I feel the full weight of his station and immeasurable power.

The hairs on my body stand up in warning. My swallow is audible, and my nod is jerky. "Got it," I chirp.

"You have until your Naming tonight to give me an answer. That should be plenty of time for you to think things through."

With that, King Noctis strides out of his office. He doesn't give me a chance to answer. He doesn't look back as he goes. He simply walks out, the door to his office closing quietly behind him, and I'm left standing by the cabinet utterly gobsmacked.

I waste no time hurrying back through the Syphon Glass to my room. To my surprise, everything is exactly as I left it. Aeson and his Wing aren't waiting for me. No one comes stomping out of the dark with an accusatory shout and declaration of betrayal. The room is quiet and the shadows painted across everything are starting to fade as night gives way to morning.

It should make me breathe easier, help me to relax, but there isn't any part of me that feels relieved.

I broke into the king's office certain I would find answers. Instead, I only found more questions. Now, I have to figure out what I'm going to do.

Strike a bargain with a king? Or bet on myself?

Both are a gamble. Neither is a sure thing. And the stakes couldn't be higher.

CHAPTER 36

Rise and shine, Frills, your . . . uh . . . glam squad is here."

Karis's calm voice plucks me from a fitful sleep, and the ring of uncertainty I hear in it has curiosity shoving back my exhaustion. I teeter between consciousness and unconsciousness for a moment before deciding sleep wins. Curiosity has fucked me over enough in the past twenty-four hours; it can wait a little longer before it starts making doe eyes at trouble again.

"Why is she on the floor?" a rough, unfamiliar voice asks.

"She does that. Don't worry about it," Farrow answers.

"And who is *she* again exactly?" another male inquires, and from the sound of it, this isn't his first attempt at fishing for information.

Great. They have a bunch of Wing wannabes assigned to guard me, but they haven't told them who I am or what's about to go down tonight. I'm sure that bright idea will bite no one in the ass, especially not me.

"You don't need to worry about who *she* is either. You're here to protect her, not write her memoirs. Focus on the task at hand," Farrow rebukes.

I groan irritably at the grating exchange. "Can you gossiping biddies sip your tea elsewhere? I'm trying to sleep," I grumble and then burrow deeper into my nest of blankets.

I'm spent and need way more rest than the few hours I've managed if I'm going to deal with the shit today has in store. A raucous clattering suddenly fills the room, followed by a strange thrumming, and—against my will—I startle all the way awake.

Fuck the fae.

I throw blankets off my head and sit up with a growl. "I swear on the ancestors, I'll throw each of you off the bloody balcony if you don't fuc—"

"Happy Naming Day!" Azo croons from where he's struggling to set up some kind of metal chair and table in the middle of the room.

The human beams at me and then starts to wrestle with the chair again. A small rack with a single covered garment bobs in the air behind him. I eye it warily. I don't know much about fancy dresses, but whatever's hanging on that rack doesn't look big enough to be a dress, fancy or otherwise. Concern prickles through me, exacerbating my crankiness.

Chair wrestled and placed next to the table, Azo grabs a metallic disc from a case on the floor and starts messing with it. My focus drifts from whatever Nixy's quirky assistant is doing to the sun gleaming at me through the window. Surprise whips through me when I realize it's late afternoon. Looks like I slept longer than I thought. Not that I stopped tossing and turning long enough to feel rested at all.

I quickly catalog the details about the five drakes I don't recognize. They have to sense me studying them, but no one meets my eyes. They simply survey the room, tense and ready, like the good guards they're here to be for the day.

"Up and at 'em, dragoness. We let you be lazy for as long as we could," Farrow orders.

"You've been hanging with Tove too much," I harrumph as I shove off the rest of my covers and get up while aiming a scowl at the cheeky fucker.

His grin fades all too quickly and his face scrunches with concern. "Why do I smell charred skin?"

Shit.

I forgot about my burn.

Karis steps closer, his focus aimed on my arm when I take a retreating step and try to tuck the injury behind my back. I didn't get a chance to look at the burn until I was back in my room last night. It's not bad, the blisters will heal in a week or so, but it's there. Proof that last night wasn't some kind of fever dream, it really happened, and somehow I'm alive to tell the tale. Not that I have any intention of telling anyone. If I did, then I'd have to explain about the Syphon Glass, and that's not happening if I can help it.

Karis holds out his hand expectantly. The determined look in his cinnamon-brown eyes tells me he's not going to let me dodge this. I sigh and pull back the sleeve of the shirt I wore to bed, showing the big stubborn Thrasher my injured forearm.

"How did this happen?" he asks, turning my wrist so he can see the entirety of the burn.

I shrug and gesture in the direction of the fireplace on the other side of the room as though its mere presence will help solidify my story. "Must have sleepwalked too close to the fire."

"Lie," three separate voices proclaim at the same time.

Yeah, I didn't think I was going to get away with that one, but I had to try.

I frown over at Farrow and give the two other tattling Thrashers the bird. I glower up at Karis for good measure, because he's a Thrasher too, and try to take my limb back from him. The gentle giant doesn't let me reclaim my arm.

"Tell Pacey he's needed. He can switch out with Daega," Karis orders, turning to a Channeler in olive-green scale armor.

The Channeler nods once and starts typing the command into the com fixed to the top of his hand. His brown hair is short but messy like he just rolled out of bed. The unruly scruff on his face only adds to that unkempt impression. The bump on the bridge of the male's nose has me wondering how he got it and, better yet, why he kept it. The Horde's Healers could have easily mended it, and yet the drake wears it like it's an important part of his personality.

One of the Thrashers—Daega, I'm guessing—leaves just as Pacey strides purposefully through the door. His violet eyes immediately settle on the arm Karis refuses to give back, and his features sharpen with consideration.

I study the prominent dragon mark claiming the Healer's throat, a black sun with flares that stretch into the shaved undercut of his pitch-black hair.

"May I?" Pacey asks, nodding toward my arm as he draws closer.

Karis tries to hand off my limb before I can say anything, but the Healer doesn't take it. He just stares at me like he's genuinely waiting for my answer.

"If you don't want me to heal it, I won't," he tells me when I still don't respond.

The surprise must show on my face, because Pacey takes a moment to really assess the situation. His violet eyes study the way Karis and Farrow are crowding me. Then his gaze drops to the blankets and pillow on the floor at my feet before his attention darts to the made bed off to my left. Disquiet flickers across the Healer's face, but the flash of emotion is gone by the time he looks back at me.

Interesting.

"You can fix it," I tell the Healer, quickly tucking away my observation to look at later. "Thank you for asking."

"Fenox, can you hear me?" Azo asks loudly, and I look over to see the human circling the metal disc he was messing with.

An image strobes above it for a few seconds before blinking out.

"You there, Nixy?" he asks again before he bends and fiddles with the apparatus again.

"I . . . here . . . an . . . you . . . hear . . . me? Nothing's on my screen, Azo, but I can hear you." Nixy's voice suddenly rings clearly through the room.

"The sound is working, but it looks like the projector is on the fritz," Azo tells her before he gives the device a good slap.

A full-sized, semitransparent version of Nixy flares to life, just as the metal saucer that's projecting it rises and starts to float about a foot off the floor.

"I can see you now," the wyvern announces before her gossamer blue-hazel gaze moves around the room.

"We can see you too. Welcome to the party," Azo chirps, and then they both turn to me.

"All set, dragoness," Pacey announces, and I look over just as the Healer steps back.

I didn't even feel him working on the burn. My eyes snap down to the mended skin of my forearm, but before I can thank him, Pacey moves to stand with the other drakes. He says something to the Channeler in the olive-green scale armor, but I can't make out what before Nixy and Azo step in front of me and block my view.

"Let's get started, shall we?" Nixy asks, and I fight the urge to look around her at the two drakes I can see whispering back and forth through the sheer projection of Nixy's head.

"Are you excited for your big day?" Azo asks, practically buzzing with exhilaration.

"Ecstatic," I droll as the human tugs me away from Karis and Farrow, toward the chair he set up earlier.

Nixy's projector drone circles me with a peppy whir as I plop down in the chair. Azo immediately gets to work while Nixy guides him like she's the artist but he's the brush and paint. They toil together, chittering back and forth while I get hydration patches on my arm, my hair combed out and readied for the styler, and bites of breakfast between wearing the makeup machine with its long-lasting dyes that will have me looking like a goddess come to life in no time flat. It's chaotic and impressive, and the next thing I know, Nixy and Azo flit back and marvel at whatever it is they've done to me.

No one hands me a mirror or asks my opinion, which is fine by me. I trust Nixy and Azo to make me look appropriately extravagant and fussy. I might even like it, who knows. There's a lot to be said for being clean, fed, and clothed. I'm not wiping sand from unmentionable crevices or pretending dried meat is a delicacy. I still think dancing with strangers is a form of torture I could live without, but I'm curious about The Horde, about what it will be like to be around them.

"Are we ready for the dress?" Nixy asks, pulling me from my thoughts.

Her blue-hazel eyes are filled to the brim with eager anticipation. I look over at the floating rack, and instantly the butterflies in my stomach start to riot. The mystery dress feels like the final nail in my coffin, and yet it's also the armor I desperately need to survive the night.

Please let it have lasers.

"Everyone out. The dragoness needs to get dressed," Nixy barks with surprising authority.

The guards I don't know glance over at Karis as though waiting for his order. He nods and then they abandon their posts around the room and file out.

"How long will you be?" Farrow asks Azo before he gives one last visual sweep of the room.

"Fifteen minutes, give or take," Azo answers, and both Farrow and Karis nod before leaving.

I turn to Nixy to ask her about the garment bag that doesn't look like it's holding a dress and freeze. She has a finger held up to her lips while her eyes track something that Azo is doing behind me. Alarm kicks my heart into high gear, and I whirl to find the human quickly moving around the room and spraying something around the windows and the doors. He finishes and walks calmly over to the table where he picks up a small silver case.

Four marble-like devices rise out of his hand and then dart in four separate directions until they're about ten feet away. Just as soon as they stop, a square security field buzzes into place, trapping me, Azo, and the projection of Nixy within its walls.

"What is going on?" I demand just as soon as Nixy drops her finger from her lips.

"You have exactly nine minutes," she instructs cryptically.

"Nine minutes for what?" I ask, confused.

"Azo, mark the time now," Nixy tells the human instead of answering me.

My eyes snap back and forth between Nixy's projection and Azo, who starts pressing buttons on his com. Before I can repeat my question, the image of Nixy starts to flicker, and then suddenly it isn't Ren's little sister staring back at me from the drone, it's Enslee.

My breath whooshes out of me at the sight of my twin. I told Nixy that I needed to get a message to my sister, but I never thought in a million years the wyvern would arrange for me to speak to Enslee directly. My throat and eyes fill with emotion. It's so good to see her. I know she's not really here, but even her projected presence momentarily lifts all of the worry and tension that serves as my constant companion these days.

Tears well in her eyes as she takes me in. "You look really good, little sister," Enslee teases, but I feel every layer of emotion and distress woven in those six simple words.

"I always look good," I joke back, though my voice is thick.

Enslee's chuckle sounds strained, and all attempts at humor go flying out the window.

"What's wrong? Are you okay?" I ask, stepping closer to the drone as though I can walk right through the projection and into my sister's arms.

"Hey, that's my line," Enslee counters while her light green gaze drinks me in. "I heard it's your Naming Day today."

My huff is derisive.

"You'll have to drink a glass of champagne in my honor," she tells me lightly, but it's obvious she's dodging my question, which just makes me even more wary.

"Eight minutes," Azo counts off, and my adrenaline spikes.

Shit. How was that a minute already? All we've done is say hi.

"Ens, we have a problem," I tell her, getting right into it.

The faux levity in her features immediately cracks and falls away.

"It's not just betrayal within our walls we have to worry about; someone on the outside is making trouble for us as well," I tell her, and her features harden.

Enslee grasps her hands in front of her and widens her feet, like she's preparing to go blow for blow with whatever I'm about to tell her.

"The Tainted weren't a coincidence, Ens. We didn't start running into them on missions by chance. I think one of our blood bank contacts put them on our trail. They're hunting us. And I think they might know where we are. They can't get in through our wards, so they're picking us off when we leave them. Enslee, I don't think whoever betrayed us and this shit with the Tainted is unconnected. I have no idea how or why, but all of this—everything that's been happening, everything that's been going wrong lately—I think it's orchestrated."

Enslee's already-fair complexion grows even paler, and she closes her eyes like she's hoping it will shut out the overwhelming scale of betrayal I'm unveiling.

Azo steps up next to me and taps me on the shoulder. "Six minutes, and we need to get you dressed while you talk," he tells me.

I nod absently and start pulling off my sleep shirt and shorts while I hear Enslee speaking hurriedly to someone off-screen.

"Step into the skirt," Azo instructs, and I glance down just long enough to see a mass of fabric that looks unsettlingly see-through.

I step into it and then immediately dismiss everything Azo is doing so I can stare down my twin, who looks both pissed and crestfallen as she continues to quietly argue with someone I can't see.

"How could you have known?" the mystery person comforts my sister, and I recognize Amadi's voice. She's a Syphon that's a couple years older than us and the person Enslee trusts the most aside from me.

"Ens?" I ask, pulling her attention away from her hushed conversation. "What couldn't you have known?"

Enslee's gaze flicks back to mine. There's frustration in it, and resolute determination, but it's the regret simmering in her stare that has the blood in my veins congealing with trepidation.

"What did you do?"

The words are half accusation, half plea to be wrong. But I can see in her body language, in her pinched features, that something has happened, and whatever it is, my sister feels responsible. Enslee flinches and her gaze drops like the shame is just too heavy to bear. Instantly my mind conjures all kinds of horrifying scenarios.

"The intel looked good, Ever. I had the information contained within our ranks. I would have never sent them out if I'd known there was more to all of this, but everything pointed at the possibility of the Conduit. You know I couldn't just ignore that. Maybe some other Blood Crafter, but not the Conduit," Enslee rushes to explain.

"You greenlit a mission after I told you not to?" I ask incredulously, and then it hits me, why she looks so distraught, why she looks so . . . guilty.

"Who did you send out, Enslee?" I demand, but I already know. It's written all over her face.

Azo tugs at the dress he's fitting around me, and it suddenly suctions to my skin. I wobble on my feet as the human fusses over the bodice and then the skirt, but I can't focus on what he's doing as devastation and outrage play tug-of-war with my heart.

"Your Flight has the highest success rate and the most experience," Enslee defends, delivering the final blow with her shoulders back and her chin lifted.

It's my turn to close my eyes as though it will shut out the inescapable reality of what she just said. I want to pace, to rage, but Azo pleads with me to stand still or I'll ruin the dress, and it sucks me back into where I am and why. I'm stuck in Four Tiers, hours away from facing off with The Horde for the first time, and my Flight is hunting a Conduit that may or may not be real when danger is at an all-time high. Anger suffuses every ounce of patience I have left.

"*I* told you it wasn't safe," I snap at my sister. "I told you to keep everyone *inside* the wards!"

"I know, and I had every intention of doing just that, but a chance at the Conduit . . . I couldn't ignore that, Ever. You know I couldn't."

"So you sent my fucking Flight? Like they haven't been through enough . . . like *I* haven't?" I shout at the projection.

The square barrier buzzes, making Azo jump and Enslee flash brighter as I work to rein in my runaway rage.

"You knew we had a traitor. Why would you believe any intel coming in after what I told you, after what happened to me and Ren? Just because it's not *your* life on the line out there doesn't mean you can be so fucking reckless! What were you thinking?" I castigate.

Enslee's eyes narrow and she steps closer to the screen. "Reckless? I'm not being reckless, Ever. I'm doing what we always do, capitalizing on an opportunity. We can't all be in Four Tiers, playing dress-up for the dragons. I'm holding things down for all of us, and that requires making difficult decisions in impossible circumstances because they just might be the thing that saves us."

I reel back, the vitriol in her words clocking me so hard that my vision wavers. Stunned, I stare at my sister. I take in the tight line of her lips, the angry flush working its way up her throat and settling in her cheeks, the outrage blazing in her light green eyes. Contempt radiates off her, and for the first time in my life, I feel like I don't know her. And *that* hurts worse than any of the fucked-up shit that just came flying out of her mouth.

We are the same in every way, we always have been. And yet, right now, it's painfully clear that we're not.

I slam an emotionless mask in place and shutter myself off from the one person in this world I've never challenged, never questioned, never doubted . . . until now.

"Shit, Ev, I didn't mean tha—" Enslee starts.

"Are they dead?" I interrupt coldly, addressing the Queen of the Syphons as though the answer won't gut me, as though I'm not already bleeding out at her feet.

Enslee shakes her head, and I don't know if it makes it easier or harder for me to breathe.

"We don't think so. We lost all communication with them three days ago, but it's possible they were pinned down and are waiting for things to clear to make contact or come back. There's a lot of Horde activity down here; it's not as easy to move around as it used to be."

I don't know if she means that to be a jab, but I take it as one all the same.

Three days . . . my Flight fell out of contact three days ago. If Wistan has them, he'll bleed them. I don't think he'll kill them, not that quickly at least, but if he's managed to capture my whole Flight this time, he's got two Syphons and three wyverns at his disposal. How long before he decides the wyverns are of no use to him? How long will any of them last against what I know he's going to do to them?

"Where were they going?" I ask icily.

"Ever, I'm sorry. Things are fucked here. You have no idea what I'm deal—"

"Where did you send them?" I cut her off again, not interested in anything other than facts right now.

"Groton. It's on the other side of the divide in Thrasher Territory."

Azo's com chimes, and he curses as he looks at the message.

"The keep's security system just tagged our signal. You're going to need to cut it short, dragoness," he tells me apologetically, already reaching for the silver case that houses the disruptor shield that's buzzing around us.

"Ever, please. I don't want to end things like this," Enslee calls after me when I start to move away from the drone projecting her image.

I look back at my sister, hurt and fury numbing the impact of her repentant tone and the apology gleaming in her gaze.

"Don't worry, Enslee, I'm only off to play dress-up with the dragons and make a few difficult decisions in impossible circumstances because they just might be the thing that saves us."

The projection of Enslee cuts out, and with it goes the last of my self-preservation and wary indecision. I pinch the bridge of my nose and look over at Azo, who's shoving the silver case into a hidden compartment in the styler that did my hair.

"Azo," I ask with a sigh. "Do you by chance know how to get a message to the king?"

CHAPTER 37

My life is going to shit in every possible way, and tonight is only going to make it worse. But, hey, at least I look good.

I twist and study every angle of my body in the Syphon Glass I'm pretending is just a mirror. The crystal butterflies that adorn my dress glitter with my movement as they catch the light. The dress hugs my torso like a second skin while leaving my back bare. It drapes beautifully to the ground. The fabric the jeweled insects are clinging to is some kind of gossamer, ethereal material I couldn't name if my life depended on it. It's a shade rosier than my complexion, and there's a sheen to it that gives off a subtle glow. It's the perfect canvas for the butterflies of all shapes and sizes that cluster around my bust, flutter down my torso, and gather in droves around my hips. The crystalline creatures cover every private part of me while giving the illusion that they could fly away at any second, leaving me completely exposed.

The gown is a stunning work of art, and I'm not even mad that it doesn't appear to have any lasers.

I lean closer to my reflection and marvel at the beautiful updo my hair has been styled into. There's zero chance I could ever replicate it on my own, but it doesn't stop me from studying every detail. I brush the tips of my fingers across the rosy apple of my cheek. The dye applied to my face has even me questioning if there might actually be a deity perched on one of the branches of my family tree.

I've never looked more beautiful, or felt more doomed because of it.

"Do you like it?" Nixy asks softly as the drone projecting her image circles me.

If she was here in person, she'd be fluffing my skirts and fussing over the jeweled butterflies that have been pinned in my hair, even though they're fine. Her blue-hazel gaze studies my face, but I know the concern I see steeped in her features isn't about the dress, it's about everything that just happened between me and Enslee.

I don't know how Nixy listened in on the conversation, but from the moment the wyvern blinked back into existence and told me that Aeson's Wing should be able to get a message to the king, it's clear that she heard every sniped word.

"It's incredible," I tell her, a hitch in my tone.

I drop my eyes from hers and run my hand over a butterfly near my shoulder. It really is the perfect camouflage I need for tonight. With so much of me on display, people won't know where to look, or where to leer. If the nobles are busy ogling and judging, maybe they'll miss what's not there to stare at . . . like a dragon mark.

Divided attention makes it easier to overlook the enchanted anklet I'm wearing, or keep The Horde from noticing how intently I'm watching each and every one of them while searching for any signs of malice or recognition. They can look their fill while I gather useful intel the Syphons will need when this forsaken curse is finally broken and we once again claim our rightful place.

Arguing starts up behind me, and Nixy and I both turn to watch Azo and a couple of my newly appointed guards locked in a heated exchange. Things have been tense since the guards stormed in here in search of the unauthorized signal being flagged as a security breach. They scanned the room several times and found nothing. Farrow and Karis accepted those results before they left to deliver my simple message to the king. However, two of the initiates haven't been as willing to let it go. A hairy male named Shaw, who looks more lycan than drake, and the Channeler from earlier with the crooked nose and olive-green scale armor, Julian.

Azo shoots a pleading look at either me or Nixy as the two drakes do their best to intimidate him into giving them answers. With a huff, I abandon my reflection in the Syphon Glass and stride to the human's rescue.

"I assure you, the signal the security system picked up on has to be that," Azo affirms, gesturing to the small black remote that Shaw is holding in his hand. "It's the only thing it could be. If you would just allow me to turn it on, you'd see what I mean."

"You'd like that, wouldn't you," Shaw growls at the human. "We turn it on, and boom, you take out everyone in this room in one fell swoop. Is that the plan?"

Azo sighs and deflates with defeat. He put on a good act of being terrified when the guards first started questioning him, but now he's starting to look tired of the endless loop of accusations.

"It's not an explosive," Azo argues. "If it were, the four scans you've already done would have picked up on it. It's for her dress. It arms the butterflies."

"Arms the butterflies?" I ask as I join the keyed-up huddle.

"Yes, it's the security measure Nixy programmed at your request," Azo tells me.

My head snaps in the direction of Nixy's semitransparent visage. "Do the butterflies shoot lasers?" I ask excitedly.

The flat, troubled line of her lips lifts into a smile. "No, dragoness, I couldn't get authorization for that . . . though I did try."

My eyes flare with surprise, and my grin suddenly matches the wyvern's. I can only imagine how that conversation went with the royal planners. If Nixy wasn't already on a watch list, she sure as shit will be now.

"While there are no lasers involved, the butterflies will serve as a dance deterrent once they're activated," Nixy explains.

"Say less," I chirp, and then I snatch the remote out of Shaw's hand before he can stop me.

"Dragoness, don't!" several drakes shout at once, but I'm already pressing the button on the device marked *on*.

Julian leaps toward me and tries to make a grab for the remote, but it beeps and the on button turns green. I can just make out the sound of tearing fabric over the alarmed shouting, and for a second, I worry I've ripped my dress. Then, out of nowhere, a kaleidoscope of butterflies breaks free from the bag still hanging on the rack across the room. They quickly flash my way, and the next thing I know, I'm surrounded by flying, bejeweled magi-tech that starts to dive-bomb and slash at the guards with razor-sharp wings.

I watch in rapt shock as the crystalline butterflies attack. They draw blood and elicit chaos as they push back the small contingent of guards tasked to protect me. One of the Channelers blasts the swarm with air, blowing them away from me and everyone else, but the fluttering little weapons simply regroup and renew their charge.

"If you back up, they'll stop!" Nixy shouts at the guards, her drone joining the melee. "They're programmed for a six-foot radius, but it can be adjusted if you'll just back off for a second so I can fix it!"

I look down at the remote and hurriedly click another button. It starts counting down from six with each press, and I stop when I get to two, resetting the attack radius for the dress. I look up and the butterflies instantly calm. They pull in closer to me, some of them landing and blending in with the others already attached to my dress, while the rest of the kaleidoscope continues to flutter around my body like they're nothing more than innocent animatronic accessories.

Bloody scales, that just might be better than lasers.

My smirk is wide and elation percolates through me as I survey the cuts and scrapes marring a handful of very pissed-off drakes.

"Please don't do that, they're very hard to make," Nixy pleads, and I look over to find a Burner melting butterflies with the blue flames floating in his hand, while a Thrasher works to crush the ones he managed to catch.

"Hey!" I shout, rage and possession surging in time with my dragon as it unexpectedly swells and presses against the confines of my body. "Those are *mine*."

Something in my voice has every head in the room cautiously turning to take me in. The blue flame in the Burner's hand sputters out, and the Thrasher opens his fist and lets two butterflies fly away. I glare at both guards while internally trying not to freak out over the unexpected possessive show of my broken other half.

"What is going on here?" Farrow demands, drawing everyone's attention as he strides into the room, Karis tight on his heels.

Both Wing members look pissed, but that could have everything to do with my refusal to explain my cryptic message to the king before I ordered them to deliver it, and nothing to do with the face-off that's occurring between me and the guards they left behind.

"We leave you alone for ten minutes and come back to this," Farrow barks with obvious disdain.

"It's the butterflies, sir," Shaw rushes to explain while gesturing wildly in my direction.

I bite back a laugh at the incredulous look that crosses Farrow's face.

Karis turns to me and notches an eyebrow. "Explain."

For some reason, that makes me want to laugh even harder, and I press a palm to my mouth to keep it in.

Nixy's projection zips forward a couple feet, and she squares her shoulders. "The dragoness requested a proximity trigger be added to her gown. She wanted to discourage anyone she wasn't comfortable with from getting too close. We were just arming it, and they reacted before we could set the parameters for the tech."

"That's the addition to her clothing that had to get approval?" Karis asks, his eyes tracking the innocent laps the butterflies are now making around me. "Proximity bugs?"

Nixy nods. "Yes."

Karis opens his mouth like he's going to say something else, but then he seems to think better of it and simply shakes his head.

"On a positive note, we know that everything works now," Azo adds cheerfully, as though that makes all of this better.

A guard with a good-size gash on his forehead glares at the human, and I lose the battle with the giggles I've been trying to fight off. It's probably some sort of stress response and a surefire sign that I'm losing it, but there's no holding back the peals of laughter that pour out of me.

"You got your asses kicked by . . . butterflies," I howl, pointing at the guards before bending at the waist to help me breathe between guffaws.

"I'd hardly call it an ass kicking," Julian grumbles as he studies the already-healing cuts on his hands.

"What would you call it then?" I titter. "A butterfly beatdown?"

An amused smile replaces Julian's scowl. "We're all still standing, so it falls miles short of a *beatdown*. And if you hadn't gotten all possessive when Lahar started torching them, we would have had everything under control in no time. I'd say it was a *wing whoopin'* at best."

His brown eyes drop to my dimple when my smile grows even wider. "A wing whoopin' it is then," I agree brightly.

"Enough," Farrow interrupts, a disapproving look fixed on Julian. "I want everyone cleaned up and ready to go. We move out in five."

The order has everyone sobering and snapping to it, including me.

I look over at Nixy. "Any way you can lengthen the proximity to twenty feet instead of two?"

She huffs out a small laugh. "Afraid not, dragoness."

I sigh. "Worth a try." I turn to Karis. "And I definitely have to go to this? We can't pretend I'm sick or something?"

"We move out in five," he repeats, stone-faced and firm.

"Shit. This is actually happening," I murmur, somehow surprised by that fact even though everything has been leading up to this since I got here.

Maybe it was all the time I was convinced someone would kill me before now, or the hours I spent just last night debating if I should try to make a run for it, but somehow, against all odds, I'm still here, and The Horde is waiting.

Azo starts packing up the table and chair into cases and loading them onto the floating rack. Nixy's drone darts in front of me, and we stare at one another for a moment. There's so much I want to say to her right now, but I can't, not with everyone listening.

"Thank you, Fenox," I offer instead.

She risked so much to let me talk to my sister, and I can't help feeling like I squandered all of her hard work and disregarded the danger she put herself in with the way I handled that conversation with Enslee. My anger suddenly feels misplaced, and regret swarms me at how I left things.

Enslee and I don't argue often; we never have. There's always too much to prepare for, too much to do. It leaves no time to get tangled up in hurt feelings and ego. We both let ourselves get dragged down into the muck of stress and pressure today, and what's worse is we did it in front of an audience.

"It was my pleasure to assist you, dragoness," Nixy tells me, the picture of professionalism. "Azo has a clutch for you that will hold that remote. In case you want to disarm the butterflies."

I nod and look down at the device I'm still holding.

"It'll be okay," she whispers. "Spark the fla—"

Nixy's diaphanous image vanishes. I startle at the unexpected departure and look down to find Karis picking up the drone. He must have turned it off. Karis hands it to Farrow, who tucks the device under his arm.

"That was rude," I chide.

Fast as a striking snake, Karis plucks the remote from my hands. The butterflies instantly react to his breach of the two-foot perimeter I programmed them to defend, but as soon as he backs away, they become docile once again.

"That was even ruder!" I snap.

Karis presses the off button, and outrage starts to surge through me until I notice that the butterflies are still flapping around like they're blatantly disregarding the command to stop. The big Thrasher aims the remote at them this time and tries the off button again, but still nothing happens.

"It's keyed to the dragoness's biometrics," Azo offers cheerfully.

I can't tell if that's the human's default personality setting or if this is his passive-aggressive way of saying *nanny nanny boo boo* to the drake that's trying to ruin all of his and Nixy's hard work.

"Escort him out," Karis tells Farrow, and alarm permeates my indignation when Farrow grabs Azo by the arm and drags him away.

"What's your problem?" I demand, growing even more pissed by the second, because I want to stop what's happening, but I'm worried if I try, it will show my hand and make everything worse.

"Aside from your mystery message to the king, your attack butterflies, or the fact that the human and the wyvern facilitated an unauthorized transmission to someone in the southern territories, I don't have any problems. You, on the other hand, have some serious explaining to do. But that's the commander's problem, not mine. Let's go."

My heart drops like a cannonball into my stomach. I lock down every voluntary reaction I have and force myself to inhale and exhale evenly until any involuntary sign of panic or guilt is crushed under the force of my ironclad resolve to give nothing away.

"You're hilarious," I deadpan, desperate to throw him off. "Now answer my question truthfully this time."

Karis gives me a look that makes it clear he's not buying anything I'm trying to sell.

"Are you going to turn those off?" he asks, obnoxiously unfazed as he holds out the remote to me and nods at the winged security system gliding gently around me.

I let my gaze fill with a silent yet unmistakable *fuck you* and cross my arms in answer.

"Yeah, I didn't think so," Karis grumbles before he turns and walks away, the remote to my dress still clutched in his hand.

I have no choice but to follow, my heels clacking annoyingly on the dragon stone floor as I go. I need to warn Nixy, but as quickly as that thought surfaces, I already know it's impossible. Even if I tried, I'd only dig a deeper hole for her and Azo. As much as I hate it, their best bet is for me to pretend like I don't care for now and then set things up so I can fall on my sword for them later.

My mind gets busy trying to spin things into a story that's true enough to stand up to a Thrasher's lie-detector abilities while exonerating Nixy and her assistant. Hopefully, they have contingency plans in place to destroy evidence and cover their tracks in the event something like this happened.

I trail after the big grumpy Thrasher until I'm once again surrounded by guards and being led out of the rookery. The halls and elevators we take are all familiar, but the final destination is not. Everyone is silent as we make our way, either due to vigilance or because they're pissed like I am. When we stop at a pair of towering golden doors, I know my time is up. On the other side of this threshold is the king, The Horde, and the scion I agreed to mate. My past and my future are about to collide, and I have no idea who will be left standing in the wake of the impact. I'm also not sure I even care anymore.

"Ready?" someone asks me, but I don't turn to see who.

I pull in a deep breath, raise my chin, and put my shoulders back as I whisper beneath my breath. "Spark the flames. Ignite the infernos. Ash the embers."

And then, the doors open.

CHAPTER 38

The few times I envisioned what it would be like to walk into a cavernous ballroom filled to the brim with The Horde, I always thought it would be the sheer number of bodies that would intimidate me. Turns out I was wrong, because when hundreds of drakes turn to watch me make my way down a carpeted aisle toward the king, it isn't the quantity that puts me on edge, it's the silence.

I was told about the reverence of a Naming. I knew it wasn't a loud and boisterous affair, but I didn't expect this. I could hear a feather fall in this kind of quiet, and it's beyond unsettling. A group this size shouldn't be this reticent, this subdued. They're drakes, for fuck's sake. Back home, the Syphons aren't even this static and soundless in our sleep.

My ears ring from the stifled stillness the same way they would if someone was howling directly into my ears. Every step I take, every breath I steal, is so loud it's like I'm screaming into an abyss. My pulse sounds more like a drum corps that's playing a final dirge as I march to my end.

Power permeates the room, unbridled, viscous, heavy. The deeper I move into the massive hall, the more it's like I'm wading against the strong current of a stream. My pace slows to accommodate the force, and it looks as though I'm taking a casual stroll, when the truth is I wish I were sprinting down this aisle and right out the fucking back door.

With effort, I move against a tide of riches and finery. I overlook the jewels, the fancy hair, the perusing gazes. I ignore the stunning suits and gowns that appear to be made of sparkling droplets of water, delicate flowers, or bone-charring flames. All of it tries to tease my attention from the dais and the three occupied thrones waiting for me at the end of my yawning trek. But my focus stays on the king.

I walk a gauntlet designed to feel daunting as mute onlookers keenly watch my every move. Most drakes do this as children, although usually they don't do it alone. In the territories, the noble houses preside over a quarterly Naming Day where all eligible children take their turn being Named and Claimed by their clan, kith, and kindred.

Here in Four Tiers, the king lords over the nobles' children and their big reveal. If the failed uprising had never happened and my father hadn't been killed, I would have undertaken this rite of passage hand in hand with my sister, surrounded by the other Syphon children. Instead, I walk this path alone—something that's starting to feel all too common and all too disheartening.

My thoughts want to drift to Enslee, to my Flight and what might be happening to them at the hands of Wistan and his Tainted, but I quickly lock all of that up and shove it as far away as possible so I can focus on the task at hand.

The king's face is like a stoic beacon that I tether myself to. I can feel Aeson's gaze branding me as I draw closer, but I'm not ready to face him. The king would have told him by now that I've agreed to be his mate. The commander could be smug—resigned is an option too—or maybe he's completely indifferent. Whatever his reaction, I'm not interested in finding out just yet.

I tell myself it won't matter if he doesn't actually want me, if he resents the part he played in all of this, a part he played so well that he's stuck with it now . . . stuck with me. It won't bother me in the slightest if I was right all along. But another voice, one buried deep in my chest where it's been trapped since I can remember, growls a definitive and undeniable . . . *mine.*

Shock crawls through me at that declaration, but I quickly slam a wall down to block it all out. This isn't the time or place, and I can't afford distractions right now.

The aisle feels never-ending, but I pretend I'm a link in a chain, one that's being pulled into the depths of the sea at the behest of an anchor—and that anchor is the king. I hope I've read him right. I hope he'll keep his end of the deal. He clearly has a vested interest in my relationship with his son, and even if the Matron can't break the curse, I think the king might help me track down someone who can. After all, as soon as I'm officially mated to his son, my strength becomes the Crown's strength. They'll want to figure out how to break this curse too. If for no other reason than their own interests.

I approach the end of the aisle and note that the king looks even more formidable in the light of day. His suit is pure white with ivory embroidered flames on his pants and suit jacket. The cape he's wearing today is draped over one arm of his throne so it can spill down the steps of the dais in an impressive display. It looks like it's made of the same white fire he conjured in his office to trap me, and my forearm tingles at the sight of it.

Butterflies flit in and out of my line of sight, and finally I find myself standing at the foot of the regal dais. I'm supposed to either bow now or curtsy, then the king will Name me and offer my clan the opportunity to claim me. Once that's done, the party, the dancing, and the gossiping can start. However, I don't bend the knee or genuflect in any way. I simply stand and stare up at Kathal Noctis, my face blank and my spine stiff and unyielding.

I did point out to the king last night that I haven't sworn fealty to him. He waved it off like it wasn't important, but that was his mistake. I don't bow for just any man, and without a sworn vow, Kathal Noctis is not *my* king.

A rustle of unease ripples through the crowd when it becomes clear that I'm going off script. I watch the king, waiting for a flash of impatience or a flicker of indignation, but just like last night, my defiance doesn't anger him. In fact, he almost looks proud of it.

I hitch an eyebrow and offer the monarch a look that says *your move*.

He has every right to burn me to a crisp where I stand, or punish me in any other way he sees fit. But I'm hoping he'll simply carry on with this ancient tradition that hails from a time when clans lived solitary lives in distant territories and only came together to celebrate the coming of age of their young.

Kathal Noctis rises from his throne, and I swear he looks even bigger than he did in his office. The sides of my face prickle from the intensity of both Aeson's and Lorn's stares, but I keep my attention rooted to their father. Only an idiot would look away from the biggest threat in the room.

"Today, we celebrate. A great treasure, once thought lost to us, has been found," King Noctis declares, his voice moving through the massive room like a surging tidal wave. "A gift, a miracle, a token of hope has made her way . . . home."

I want to be annoyed by the king's flair for dramatics, but I'm unexpectedly touched by his choice of words. I know they're meant to hook and entice the crowd, but they burrow and bury themselves inside of me like they're awaiting the day that I might truly become all those things.

"My people," the king commands, and it feels as though The Horde all collectively hold their breath. "Sixty-two years ago, our enemies moved against us, and we lost not only our king and the royal family, but we lost the Syphons too. Today, at this unprecedented Naming, I come before you to decree that not *all* is lost."

With measured, confident strides, King Noctis descends the steps of the dais until he's standing in front of me. He cups my face and looks down at me with so much warmth and acceptance that it sets me adrift. I don't trust it, but I also can't ignore the pieces of me that really want to.

"I Name you Ever Tenebrae, daughter of King Merik Tenebrae, and the last Syphon."

The astonishment that pulses through the crowd makes the hair on my arms rise in warning. King Noctis bends to kiss my forehead, the gesture reminiscent of a Sovereign pressing their royal crest into the malleable wax seal of their latest decree. It dawns on me that my butterflies should be attacking him. He's well within the two-foot parameter they were set to guard, and yet they're still drifting around me like they haven't detected a breach.

Maybe Karis found a way to turn them off after all.

By the time the king straightens, the eerie silence in the room has been shattered by gasps, cries, and a steady thrum of startled murmurs.

I stare up into King Noctis's blue eyes as he drops his hands from my face and grasps my shoulders.

"Are you ready for what comes next?" he asks me quietly, and I'm surprised that he would give me one last chance to back out of our deal.

But as much as I want to run, my missing Flight has forced my hand. If there's any chance of saving them, we need to be whole. The Syphons are broken, and if I have to sell myself to the enemy to fix them, my life is a small price to pay.

I may be nothing more than a pawn to them, but even a pawn can check a king in the right circumstances.

I nod. "I'm ready."

His smile is genuine, and his eyes are alight with that same warm pride that makes my throat get tight. The king turns me until I'm looking out at a sea of faces all belonging to The Horde. He keeps his hands on my shoulders and waits for the room to once again grow silent. The nobles collect themselves much faster than I would have thought possible.

"And who claims Ever Tenebrae, the last Syphon, and the daughter of King Merik Tenebrae?" The king continues like he didn't just drop a bomb and isn't getting ready to drop another.

"I do."

Aeson's voice rings out loud and clear, and I don't need to look to know that he's rising from his throne and moving down the dais toward me. Swallowing hard, I finally lift my gaze to look at him.

His suit is pitch-black velvet that's trimmed in gold. Embroidered flames decorate the lapels of his jacket, his shoulders, the sides of his pants, and the cuffs of his sleeves. The thread used for the flames glints and changes color from gold to amber to orange as Aeson moves and the filaments catch the light. He's clean-shaven and devastatingly handsome, but the harsh look on his face instantly makes me wish I'd stayed strong and kept my eyes away.

The butterflies around me are calm as can be, but I can't say the same for the rioting kaleidoscope in my stomach when I look at the commander's face and see it void of all emotion. He joins me at the bottom of the dais, but he doesn't close the distance between us. I have a feeling it's not because of the security feature on my dress.

"Do you claim her as clan, kith, or kindred, Scion Noctis?" the king proudly asks his son.

"I, Aeson Noctis, claim Ever Tenebrae as my mate," he answers smoothly, and I wonder if they rehearsed this.

More gasps and cries fill the colossal chamber as Aeson's declaration fills it. I swear I even see someone off to the side faint. The commander doesn't meet my gaze despite having just publicly claimed me. I think it's safe to say that he's pissed—the question is over *what* exactly.

The anger radiating off of him makes my stomach drop and my heart feel like lead. Is it the deal in general he's mad about? Did the king tell him about the Syphon Glass? Or did Karis already tattle about the unauthorized call I'm still trying to figure out how to cover up? The possibilities are endless.

"The Crown accepts this claim and thus this Naming is complete," the king declares, pulling me from my thoughts. "Tomorrow I will sit with the heads of state and discuss the details of how all of this came to be. But tonight we celebrate the Named and honor her newfound place among us. You now belong to The Horde, Ever, and The Horde belongs to you. Welcome!"

The approving roar that fills the hall rocks me to my core. Chills ripple through me at the wave of acceptance that blasts over me like a summer gale. The power that felt so heavy and thick before now feels almost . . . comforting.

The aisle I traversed to get to the dais disappears in an instant as The Horde hurriedly converges. Their excitement is surprisingly contagious, and I feel a laugh bubble up my throat as the room erupts with awe and celebration. Before the dais can be overrun, a wall of stone-faced guards moves to stand between the royal family and The Horde.

I turn and see Lorn. He's watching me, concern swimming in his eyes. His jaw is clenched with what looks like frustration, but before I can ask him what's wrong, I'm being herded away.

It's chaos as everyone tries to press closer. I spot Chastain and Sondar in the contingent of muscle keeping The Horde at bay. Other familiar faces from this morning move in and out of my line of sight as I'm hurried to the side of the throne room.

Shouted orders ricochet all around me, and I'm taken through a doorway and into some kind of antechamber. Everything shifts so quickly from silent to raucous and back again that it takes me a minute to notice the guards around me yelping and cursing.

I look around and watch as several of them hurry away from me, or more specifically the butterflies that are viciously attacking them.

What the fuck? I thought Karis turned them off.

And then it hits me. Of course the butterflies wouldn't attack the king; that'd be treason. Nixy would have accounted for that and must have programmed them not to react to the royal family.

"Leave us!" Aeson snarls out of nowhere.

I flinch as the command booms through the long room, bouncing off the white stone walls and floor. I have no idea if this space is used for storage or if it's some kind of pass-through, but it's long, fairly wide, and empty.

Warily, I study the commander from where I'm standing at the opposite end of the room. He surveys me with equal intensity, his eyes bright with anger and his hands fisted at his sides. I'm not sure what to make of it, but there must be something seriously wrong with me because, instead of being scared, an ember of excitement settles deep in my core and starts to simmer.

When the last guard disappears through the door, Aeson slowly and methodically starts to prowl closer.

"Mind telling me what the fuck is going on . . . mate?" he growls, his long strides quickly erasing the distance between us.

I retreat a few feet as he continues to cross the room, but as soon as I realize what I'm doing, I force myself not to give him one more step. My trapped dragon hums its approval.

"You were there, so if you really don't know . . . we might have a problem," I answer, going for light and quippy but only managing startled and uneasy.

"Oh, we most definitely have a problem, because when the fuck did you meet my father, let alone have time to broker a deal with him, *mate*?"

"Stop saying that," I snap, irritation drowning out the caution I should be proceeding with. I don't know if it's his tone or his use of that word that's grating on my last nerve, but whatever it is, I just hit my limit.

"Stop saying what? Mate?" he asks incredulously. "But isn't that what you are? My lying, deceiving, infuriating little mate?"

"I don't know about *lying* and *deceiving*," I lie. "And the second part sounds like a you problem . . . but, yes, I agreed to be your mate, so stop saying it like it's a dirty word."

His eyes flare with both need and fury. It's anyone's guess which one is going to come out on top, but he's more than halfway across the room now and gaining.

"Come now, mate. I thought you liked my dirty mouth," he purrs, and I swear I feel it in my fucking clit. "Now answer my question. When did you make a deal with my father, and more importantly, why? I want every single detail, or so help me, I'll—"

"You'll what?" I growl, more than ready to meet him head-on. "Lock me in my room? Monitor my calls? Control my every move? Oh, oh, I know," I eagerly chirp, a saccharine grin spread wide across my face. "How about you'll manipulate me to get what you want? News flash, Commander, you already do all of that and then some."

The fake smile drops from my face, and I glower at him before continuing.

"And don't pretend that you didn't start this. You put me in your rookery. You locked me up in your mating suite. It was your Wing that told me to play along. So what's your problem? It's all fun and games until the game turns on you?"

He stops a few feet away from me, and for a second, I hold my breath, unsure if I want the razor-winged butterflies to intervene on my behalf or let the scion sidle closer. This might be easier if he wasn't so fucking beautiful. I could fuck him up without also wanting to fuck him if I didn't know how good his hands felt on my body, how soft his lips are, or what he tastes like.

"Everything I did was a necessary precaution. Necessary until we know you can be trusted," he defends. "At this rate, if you don't start leveling with me, they'll be *permanent* fixtures in your life. Is that what you want?"

I bark out a laugh, but there isn't a drop of genuine humor in it. "What *I* want? When has anyone in this forsaken keep given two shits about what I want?" I demand. "When have any of you even bothered to ask? But I'll make you a deal, Commander—and don't worry, we can cut your daddy out of this one. I'll start leveling with you when you do the same with me. Until then, you and your demands can fuck right off."

"I have been straightforward with you from the very— What the bloody fuck?" he snarls when he takes a step closer and the butterflies immediately respond.

One dives through the air and uses its wings to slash the back of his hand, and he snatches another out of the air when it aims for his face.

Shit!

I quickly back up so the winged deterrents disengage. I wince as another butterfly gets in one final shot to Aeson's ear before calmly fluttering my way.

Correction, Nixy programmed the dress not to attack the king, but it looks like the scions are fair game.

I might feel bad if Aeson wasn't being a dick right now.

"What is this?" he demands, holding up the jeweled assailant.

"It's a security precaution I asked for. As long as you stay two feet away from me, you won't activate it," I explain while he inspects the cut on his hand and then studies the crystalline insect struggling to escape his iron grasp. "Beats lasers if you ask me."

"Lasers?" he asks, confused, but then his features turn thoughtful. He's probably thinking about the conversation he had with his brother last night. Lorn was reading through the transcript of my call with Nixy while they waited for their father in his office.

Aeson's eyes meet mine, and the fiery fury that was just there calms to a simmering vexation. "You went behind my back and made a deal with my father. I want to know what it was and how you did it."

I study the sharp curve of his jaw, the angry line of his lips, the blazing demand in his gaze. This is not a male that people refuse, and yet I have no hesitation. I just wish I could get a read on whether it's the deal part that's pissing him off or if he's mad because it happened right under his nose and he wasn't the one to broker the terms.

"You should ask your father these questions," I evade.

"I'm asking *you*," Aeson growls. "*My* . . . mate."

There's no caustic bite to the way he says it this time. Instead, he's laced the title with a lethal combination of desire and promise. He savors the phrase, plays with it on his tongue like he can't get enough of the flavor. It's both a taunt and an invitation, one I'd suddenly like to RSVP to.

My eyes drop to his mouth, and I can feel the ghost of it across my shoulder. The flames of his dragon mark dance as he swallows, making his Adam's apple dip and then rise. His nostrils flare like he's searching for my scent, and when I lift my eyes to his, longing burns in both of our gazes.

Tension crackles and frustration crawls over his face. "I—"

A door on the far end of the room suddenly opens, and Ogdan peeks his head in. "Sorry to interrupt, Commander, but Count Marteen and Lord Proost are leaving. If we want to get tails on them before they clear the gate, we need to move now."

Aeson's eyes never leave mine. The longing between us builds into an insatiable ache, and my feet carry me forward, responding to the undeniable need to be closer. But he takes a step back. He blinks and douses the pyre in his eyes, leaving me to burn alone.

"Coming," Aeson tells him, already turning and walking toward the door.

I watch him as he goes, wondering if this is the only future we'll ever have—one of us tentatively reaching while the other is perpetually walking away.

My eyes stray to Ogdan, and I replay what he said when he interrupted us. Tails? They're tracking members of The Horde? All at once, puzzle pieces fit into place, and I realize this is why Aeson's Wing couldn't guard me tonight. This is why the king gathered The Horde to announce who I am. The Noctises wanted as many drakes here as they could get so they could monitor their reactions.

They set up a sting.

Quickly, I try to fit faces to the names Marteen and Piers, but I don't remember either of those in any of the files the Syphons managed to access and go through.

"You're looking for the traitors, aren't you?" I ask, because what else could it be? I already know from the conversation I spied on that I'm bait tonight. I doubt there would be anything more pressing to the Noctises right now than finding out which dragons were involved in the rebellion sixty-two years ago.

"We're looking for a lot of things," Aeson answers cryptically as he continues to walk away.

That's not a no.

I move to follow, determined not to be left behind when it comes to this. If anyone has earned the right to help bring down the bastards that betrayed the Syphons, it's me. I'm halfway to the door when Aeson realizes I'm shadowing him, and he rounds on me.

"Not a chance, Claws. You're staying right here," he orders, like he has any right.

"You can eat my ass with that bossy bullshit, Commander," I snap. "I can help."

Aeson narrows his gaze at me, but he looks thoughtful for a beat. "You're right, you can help," he agrees, and relief pools in my stomach at the recognition. "Answers, Claws. That's what you can help me with, and you better have them ready when I walk back through this door. I'm done playing around."

He storms out of the room, taking Ogdan with him, and the door slams hard behind them. I'm left staring after Aeson, my mouth open in shock and my temper building into a bonfire of rage.

Is he serious? Done playing around?

"Well, that makes two of us, asshole," I grumble, stomping the rest of the way across the room and grabbing the door handle.

My rage becomes a wildfire. One I have every intention of incinerating Aeson Noctis in when the door doesn't open and I realize he just locked me in here.

Motherfucking dragon.

I pound on the door until my fists are guaranteed to bruise, and then I give it a few heel kicks for good measure, but no one answers my enraged summons. I plot vicious retribution and growl a steady stream of curses as I crouch down in front of the doorknob and examine it. Threading my fingers through my hair, I pull out a few of the pins helping to keep everything in place.

Good thing I know how to pick a lock.

CHAPTER 39

Music and chatter tickle my senses as I survey my Naming party from the shadows of a side entrance no one is paying attention to. Drakes dance in the center of the large ballroom or mill about around its edges. It's all very civilized for a species that can be anything but.

The impressive glass ceiling allows the night sky to look down on us, and it's so beautiful I thought it was a painting at first. I almost wish I could stand here all night under the protection of the stars and the great mythical beasts carved into the columns that border the room. There are snakelike creatures with wings too small to ever ride a current. Great sea beasts with fins and gills. And wingless monsters with heads that look like some mix of lion and leviathan and long ribbons for tongues.

I think they're depictions of dragons, or what some ancient cultures thought dragons looked like, but I can't say for sure. The people who thought such things are either long dead or now know that our kind can walk among them just as easily as we can turn into the great winged beasts of their nightmares.

Well, most of us anyway.

A strand of flame-orange hair falls in my face, and I smooth it back. My updo is a little looser than it should be thanks to all the pins I used to open the door. I'm also a handful of butterflies short, but their wings helped me finally wedge the door open, so I consider their sacrifice worth it.

Slipping a calm, apathetic mask in place, I abandon my hidden perch and step into the ballroom. The Syphons know most of the big players in the hierarchy, but our intel is a hodgepodge of hacked files, gossip feeds, and back-channel rumblings. I can identify all of the dukes and duchesses, probably half of the counts and countesses, but when it comes to every lord and lady, I'm done for. The same can be said for their military leaders. I have the generals and commanders locked in, and maybe a few captains, but trying to identify all of the Wings, Flights, and Squads is impossible.

I study the drakes that I pass while making sure I don't run into any hovering trays holding cocktails and canapés. I skirt the crowd and open my senses, combing through the various scents and sounds for anything noteworthy. All too quickly, I pick up on a murmur spreading through The Horde like fire eating through dry brush. People watch me intently, bowing and curtsying when I pass, and it's plain to see that my days of just being another face in the crowd are over.

Tonight, my anonymity was officially stripped from me. I was willing to trade it for a name and a place amongst the dragons, something I've wanted and thought about since I was old enough to understand the magnitude of what was taken from me. And yet it all feels surprisingly . . . empty.

Maybe it's because I'm here alone and still only on phase one of the Syphons' plans to reclaim what we lost. There's so much left to do before it will be us in this ballroom, together, laughing and prattling on without a single other care or worry.

"We weren't expecting you for another half hour," Lorn declares, and I turn to see him striding toward me.

"Expecting?" I ask, confused, and then quickly throw a hand up to stop the scion just as he's about to invade my personal space. "You need to stay two feet away from me or you're going to set off my dress," I warn.

"What?" he questions, confused.

"My dress will turn on you if you get any closer." I gesture to the deceptively calm butterflies, and Lorn's gaze alights on one that has dried blood on its wings.

"Got it," he murmurs warily, taking half a step back while he studies me a little more intently. "Where are your guards?" he asks after a beat.

I shrug and once again point at the fluttering kaleidoscope. "Best bodyguards I've ever had. Ten out of ten, highly recommended."

A flicker of suspicion moves through the scion's features. "Better yet, where is Aeson?"

"Your guess is as good as mine," I answer flippantly as I resume the circuit I was making around the room. "He has a tendency to run off, but if you see him, feel free to strongly encourage him to stay the fuck away from me."

Lorn snorts and falls into step next to me while carefully staying more than two feet away. "I take it things are going well?"

"Dandy," I deadpan.

Lorn's grin is pure amusement. "He cares for you, you know."

I scoff and roll my eyes. "He's got a funny way of showing it."

"Mm-hmm," the scion hums. "I suspect you both do."

"He doesn't know me well enough to care for me—none of you do," I counter, dismissing Lorn's obvious fishing expedition.

"That's not how it works with our kind, you know that. He doesn't need to know everything about you to form a bond."

I laugh and Lorn's brow furrows. "Bond? That's not what's happening here. I *can't* bond, I haven't revealed."

Lorn reaches out a hand to stop me and then quickly pulls it back before a butterfly can nick him. "You're kidding, right?" he asks, his eyes raking over my face. "Who told you that?"

My grin falters. "What do you mean? Everyone knows that."

"Everyone most certainly does not," he contends. "You can't go into estrus unless you've revealed, but once you've matured, you can absolutely bond. That sort of thing is innate. There have been plenty of cases in our people's history where a dragon took time to reveal but they were still able to bond."

My thoughts stutter, and my mouth drops open and gets stuck as I try to process what he just said. Lorn's eyes flick back and forth between mine, growing more troubled with each pass.

"Ever, you do understand that's what's been happening between you and Aeson since you met, right? It's very serious. You almost sent him into a frenzy the night you got here. He can feel your dragon calling to him. You most definitely triggered a bond."

"I did not," I argue, immediately defensive, confused, and really fucking concerned. I press a palm to my chest as though it will help my racing heart chill the fuck out.

He can feel my dragon?

"Wait, why is it serious?" I demand, bafflement temporarily staving off the rising tide of my alarmed astonishment.

"Because bonds can be tampered with if they're left unfulfilled," he explains. "From the second a bond forms, your instincts go into overdrive. You'll become more possessive, more restless, more volatile, and more vulnerable. The bond will relentlessly push and push until you give in. If you don't, you'll reach a point where your instincts no longer care *who* you bond with, just that you do. Anyone at that point could step in and trap you in a warped bond, and you'd be so crazed with need and driven to the edge of your instincts, you wouldn't stop it even if you wanted to."

I stare at Lorn, completely dazed. I wait for him to crack a smile and fire off a *gotchya* before he starts laughing hysterically at my expense. Instead, he looks just as worried as I feel.

What the fuck? Where was any of this in the Growing Up Dragon *books the wyverns told us covered the basics? I mean, I knew my education was lacking, but I didn't know I could be turned into a sex-crazed maniac who'd settle for absolutely anyone if I didn't hop on the magic dick my instincts decided was* just right.

My chest starts to feel tight. Did it get hot in here, because I'm suddenly roasting. I start to fan myself, my eyes darting around with the realization that far too many people are probably listening in on this very private, very messed-up conversation.

"Don't worry, your dress has its tricks, and my suit has a few precautions of its own. No one can hear us."

Well, thank fuck for that at least.

Lorn looks at me like I'm some kind of enigma. I'm pretty sure he's horrified by my clear lack of understanding when it comes to my own nature, although why he'd assume I know shit about our kind, I don't know. To be fair, I haven't exactly been forthcoming with my ignorance. I was so worried that they might use it against me, I never thought that I might be setting myself up for something like this simply because I didn't know better.

"Your dragon has claimed him too," he tells me, like it should be obvious. "Bonds aren't one-sided. That's the pull you feel. That's why you're territorial of him and your nest."

"That's not fucking possible," I whisper-shout, my eyes flicking around us as I try to school my features.

The drakes around us may not be able to hear what we're saying, but they can still read body language. I don't want it to look like I'm fighting with the scion or like I'm on the verge of losing my shit.

"My dragon hasn't claimed him, Lorn. I don't have a fucking dragon!"

"Ever, you *are* a fucking dragon! Just because you can't reveal or manifest affinities doesn't change what you are at your core. Aeson is your Bonded Mate and you're his."

I shake my head like it will clear it of everything Lorn is lobbing at me and round on him. "Then why in the fae fuck is he so mad about the deal I made with the king? I agreed to be his mate; isn't that what he wants, what will keep us both from going crazy?"

"Yes, but he wants you to agree *willingly*, not be coerced into it," Lorn argues. "No honorable male would accept that."

My thoughts dart back to the conversation I heard the night before. King Noctis mentioned they would take more drastic measures if I didn't accept Aeson's claim, but it wasn't about my political influence and using me, it was about what would happen to us if I kept fighting the inevitable.

I press a hand over my mouth as though it will anchor my reeling thoughts. I'm dumbstruck, and yet . . . the pull, the awakening of my dragon and my instincts, the lust, the way my brain turns to mush the second he gets too close . . . the signs were there. I just didn't know what they were pointing at, so I dismissed them.

Lorn sighs and his features soften. "I know you've been fighting practically your whole life, Ever, but you don't have to fight him. Aeson is the best male I know, next to our father. He'd do anything for you, but not if you won't let him in. I know you think you're doing what's right, that your silence and impenetrable walls are protecting you, but at what cost? You're not alone now. Let your mate help. Let us help, as your new family."

His offer both touches and terrifies me. It sounds so simple, and yet the opposite is true. My mind is a whirlwind of *what the fuck*, and I have no idea what to think, feel, or do right now. I close my eyes, desperate to recalibrate, to let my world shift on its axis so I can make sense of all of this.

Aeson Noctis is my Bonded Mate.

My. Bonded. Mate.

"I was wondering where you disappeared," King Noctis exclaims, and with a jolt, my eyes flash open.

He knew. This was the reason for the deal. It wasn't a political move—he was protecting his son, and maybe even me.

"Oh good, I see you found the lady of the hour," the king declares with a wide smile, his eyes landing on me for a moment before they begin searching behind me. "And where is . . . ah . . . Aeson, there you are!"

I tense and my whole body grows frigid while simultaneously flashing with heat.

Shit.

I'm not ready! I can't face him yet!

Desperate to escape, I start frantically searching for an exit, but the annoyingly familiar faces of Aeson's Wing are spread out all around us. I start tabulating which one of them I might be able to get past, and then I feel a large, scorching palm against my bare back.

"There you are," Aeson rumbles, and I wonder if anyone else can hear the menace in it or if it's just me. "I was just wondering where you *snuck* off to."

He quickly steps away before the butterflies can get more than a few swipes in, and my skin instantly laments the loss of his touch. His presence is all at once overwhelming, even two feet away, and I know it's too late.

I'm trapped . . . in every sense.

My blood is molten lava. My pulse is one continuous beat of *shit, shit, shit.* My body is aware of every shift in weight and intake of breath, and my dragon is demanding I close the distance between us immediately. I almost want to laugh, because how the fuck did I not see it before? It's so damn obvious. I can practically feel the bond snap into place at his proximity, like a tight string on an instrument ready to play the perfect note if plucked, stroked, or caressed just right.

I brave a glance at Aeson's face, and the second our gazes connect, I'm certain he can read every chaotic, confused, carnal thought careening within me.

You don't have to fight him.

He'd do anything for you.

You're not alone now.

Lorn's assertions rebound through my mind, blocking out the pleasantries the three Noctises begin to exchange.

I study the commander, looking at him as though I'm seeing him for the first time. He's no longer just my enemy, my captor, the itch I've been fighting not to scratch. He's now the berth I'll be moored to, the sun my instincts will forever orbit, the future I'm not sure I can ever have.

Lorn wants me to let Aeson in, to solidify this tether between us by giving him my trust, my secrets. But they're not mine alone to hand over. I can't compromise all the other vital connections that make up who I am, not even for my Bonded Mate. And that realization guts me.

King Noctis says something that has Aeson grinning and looking over at me with a curious glint in his eyes. "What do you say, Claws? You up for the challenge?"

"I'm always up for a challenge," I answer evenly, proud that I sound calm and confident when inside I'm a screaming knot of nerves and exhilaration. I have no clue what I just agreed to, but I'm not going to admit that my brain is melting down over this mate shit and I haven't been paying attention.

"Excellent." The king nods and then tosses me a wide smile. "Any particular song?"

Song?

"It's okay, I'll choose one," he dismisses and then strides off before I can respond or figure out what he's talking about.

Puzzled, I turn back to Aeson. "What's going on?"

His features fill with mischief, and he bends at the waist, offering me his hand like some gallant gentleman. "Ever Tenebrae, may I have this dance?"

Well, fuck.

CHAPTER 40

"This is a bad idea," I tell Aeson, who's standing a handful of feet away from me in the center of the ballroom.

The other dancers have cleared the way, and all eyes are on us as we wait for the music to start.

"I thought bad ideas were your bread and butter," he replies nonchalantly. "What's one more to add to the list of many?"

I'm pretty sure that's a dig at my butter knives, but I've got bigger things to worry about right now than defending that decision, *again*, so I begrudgingly let it slide.

"I don't dance," I argue, plastering a fake smile on my face as I look around at everyone watching and try not to spiral. "And that's not my mulish nature talking, I can't. I have no idea how to do this," I squeak, gesturing between us.

His hard features thaw infinitesimally. "If you can fight, you can dance," he assures me, but it's not comforting in the slightest.

Pretty sure if I haul off and hit him, The Horde will hang my entrails from the beasts decorating the columns of this ballroom.

Shit! The butterflies!

I can't let him get near me, or these drakes are going to have my head!

"Treat me like an opponent," Aeson encourages, oblivious to my newfound dread. "Mirror me like you're trying to get a feel for my fighting rhythm and stance, and then counter my moves. I step forward, you counter by stepping back. I step to the side, you follow. I'll tell you with my hands and arms where I want you to go. All you have to do is follow."

"And that's where we have a problem," I start, but music suddenly fills the air and there's no more time to argue.

Aeson bows and then he steps toward me. I do exactly as he said and instantly step back, countering his move. A smirk cracks the facade of the commander's stony mask.

"I need to be touching you before you start mirroring my steps," he tells me, like I misunderstood his initial instructions.

I fight the urge to roll my eyes. "I know how it works. But you can't come any closer."

Ignoring my warning, Aeson advances, and once again I dodge him.

"Claws," he rumbles in warning. "Stop running."

"I'm not running. I'm keeping you from being attacked by my dress and me from being mobbed by The Horde for hurting their precious scion."

"I can handle your sharp edges, Claws. Now be still before you set off my prey drive and we give the audience a very different kind of show."

I trap a whimper in my throat as his words crackle through me like an electrical current intent on lighting up every cell in my body.

"Aeson," I contend as he draws closer. But I don't move. "I'll cut you. I'll destroy your suit. I'll hurt you." I plead for him to listen, but I don't know if I'm still talking about the butterflies or if I'm warning him about . . . me.

His features darken with desire, and his eyes flare with intent as they drink me in, but he doesn't stop walking toward me, like he's all too ready to breach the last of my defenses.

"Cut me. Hurt me. Destroy me. I'll happily bleed for you, Ever. Every drop is yours already."

And then he's in front of me, pulling me against his chest. His palm presses against the small of my back while the other wraps around my hand. The butterflies converge, tearing his suit and slashing at his hands. Gasps and murmurs ring out around us, but Aeson doesn't even flinch, his blazing gaze steadily fixed on mine. He gives me a second to adjust to the press of his body against mine, while razor-sharp wings do their worst. And then Aeson starts to lead me, and for once, I follow.

He breathes me in deeply and holds me like a newly discovered treasure that he has no intention of ever letting go. I get lost in the feel of his body guiding mine as we stride and spin across the dance floor, his bright blue eyes tugging on the tethers between us until the lines blur where he ends and I begin.

Is this the bond?

Is this what surrender could *feel like?*

A butterfly slashes across his cheek, and I tense and try to pull away, but I only manage to put a few inches between us before he stops me.

"I'm ready for my answers now," he tells me, his voice low and paved with gravel. Sensing my immediate hesitation, he strokes a thumb up my spine and holds me tighter. "We'll do this all night until I'm a pile of bloody ribbons on the ground or you've answered my questions."

Distress crashes into dismay as they both rush to the forefront of my mind. Another butterfly draws blood through a cut on the arm of his suit, but I find myself suddenly less bothered by his plight.

"Fine," I concede. "I'd like a few answers myself."

Aeson raises a single eyebrow, the look on his face an invitation and a challenge.

"Why didn't you tell me that we'd formed a bond?" I start, cutting right to the quick.

His full lips flatten as he considers me, and his eyes rove over my face like he's debating whether to answer.

"At first it was because I didn't trust you," he finally admits after he glides us into a small circular pass around the floor that earns him several more rips in his jacket, a small gash on his chin, and half a dozen new cuts on his hands. The startled sputtering and clucking of the surrounding crowd begins to sound like white noise before it fades altogether. "I couldn't tell if you were pretending not to know what was happening or if you genuinely had no idea. I decided to let it play out."

"Is that why you put me in your rookery, or was it really just for my protection?" I ask as I stare into his now-stormy blue eyes. I'm pretty sure I already know the answer to this question, but I want to see just how forthcoming the commander is going to be.

"I knew from the second I tasted your blood in Lairwood," he confesses. "That's why you're in my rookery and in *our* mating suite."

Shocked, I draw back and stare at him. I thought my injuries in the dungeon were what set things in motion, but Lairwood? I study every inch of his face as he weaves and twirls us across the floor. He doesn't let me stumble or overthink what I'm doing. In his hands, I look like I've spent a lifetime in ballrooms doing nothing but this.

I sigh. He's gorgeous, capable, and cunning. It's a lethal combination I wish I didn't find so fucking enticing.

"I didn't request a meeting with your father or try to broker any kind of a deal," I tell him, deciding it's best to get ahead of the questions he's already asked me. This way I can offer him enough slices of the truth to make him think he has the whole pie. "He just showed up. It was completely unexpected and I have no idea where he came from, but he wanted to talk. So we did."

"And where were your guards?" he asks, evidently troubled by the possibility that one of his Wing kept something from him.

"I was in the keep alone; they weren't with me."

Aeson draws back this time. His eyes are wide with shock but banked with fury. "And how the fuck did you manage that?" he all but growls.

"That, I'm not going to answer," I tell him calmly but firmly.

His beautiful blue eyes narrow on me, and he pulls me even tighter against his body. A sharp crackle fills my senses and then a tinkling crash draws my attention. I track the noise and find several crystal butterflies on the ground, each with a small trail of smoke rising from their now-inert bodies.

I glare up at Aeson, my pique rising even further at the satisfied smirk stretching wide across his face.

"And what do I get to *fry* when you don't answer one of my questions?" I ask, virulent syrup dripping over every syllable as I fight the possessive need to safeguard my remaining fluttering protectors.

He contemplates the question for a second. "For every question I don't answer, you can have one weapon of your choosing," he offers, and I almost stumble in shock.

"Done," I immediately agree, and he laughs at my overeager display. If it gets me weapons though, he can laugh at my expense all the way to the armory.

"Why did you make a deal with my father?" he starts, but I shake my head.

"No, it's my turn."

He gives me a conciliatory nod and makes a show of closing his mouth. A mouth I find myself transfixed by until he clears his throat, and I shake off my sudden stupor.

"How is a bond completed? Is it just fucking, or is there more to it?"

Aeson chokes on air, and our steps slow briefly while he collects himself. His eyes are like shimmering aquamarines when he looks back down at me. His entire countenance begins to smolder, and he makes a noise somewhere between a growl and a purr as his gaze drops to my lips.

"Tell me you're mine, Claws, and we'll leave right now and go somewhere I can show you, at length, exactly how a bond is completed." He nuzzles my neck, brushing his lips up the side of my throat and skimming them across my jaw before he pulls back to avoid losing an eye to a razor-winged assailant.

Desire pools between my thighs, and I bite back a whimper. If he keeps this up, blood isn't going to be the only thing dripping all over the floor by the time this dance is done.

"Answer the question," I demand breathily, ignoring the ache in my core and the fire in his eyes.

Aeson inhales long and slow, scenting me, and the low groan he releases is slightly pained, entirely too satisfied, and edged with possession. His hand on my back dips lower until the tips of his fingers caress the tops of my ass cheeks. My nipples become stiff, sensitive peaks against his chest as we spin and slink into a third pass along the dance floor. Warm blood trickles from his cuts onto me, and it feels like a sensual caress as it drips slowly down my back and arms.

"Fucking is part of it," he finally answers. "Blood also has to be exchanged. There's a magical aspect to it that our dragons have sole control over, and there are vows, although those are more ceremonial than essential. But once you've done all of that, you're bonded for life."

I nod in understanding and grow contemplative. When I agreed to mate Aeson, I thought there would be time before I'd have to fulfill my end of the bargain—at least as long as it took to plan the ceremony—but this connection between us changes things. If the drive to bond progresses as quickly as Lorn said, Aeson and I need to mate sooner rather than later, which means I need to rethink the timeline for phase two with the Syphons.

I focus back on the scion and answer his question.

"I thought your interest in me was based solely on political advantage," I explain. "I was willing to trade that currency for something that I wanted, something that only your father could help me access. I thought it was nothing more than a mutually beneficial arrangement. I didn't know about the bond or what it meant. But knowing doesn't change my decision. I gave my word and I stand by it."

"And what is it that you wanted so badly that you were willing to trade yourself for?" he demands, and I can't tell if his question is laced with indignation or intrigue.

I swat away a butterfly that's aiming for the dragon mark on his neck. I study the lines that come together to form flickers of flame and trace one with the tip of my finger until it disappears under the collar of his slashed shirt. Goose bumps skitter up his throat, and a pleased hum sneaks out of me. I like touching him like this, even though I shouldn't.

"I'll answer that question, but not here. I know your suit keeps everyone outside of a certain radius from hearing what we're saying, but I won't risk it. Ask me again when we're back in the rookery," I tell him, and he dips his chin in understanding.

"What does my dragon feel like to you?" I ask offhandedly.

"Ah, ah, ah, you didn't answer my last question, so it's still my turn," he contends.

I huff out a laugh and gesture for him to proceed. We stop dancing and Aeson looks down at me, his countenance reverential and his stare earnest.

"Ever Tenebrae. Will you accept my bond and become my mate?"

Surprise jolts through me at his words. I stare up at him, confused. I just told him I stand by my agreement with the king, meaning his question is unnecessary. But as I study his fervent stare, I realize this gesture isn't about that. Our relationship so far has been rooted in mistrust, posturing, and testing the waters, but we don't have to continue down that path, not if we don't want to.

He's giving us a chance to recalibrate and move forward from a place of mutual understanding and sincerity. He's giving me the illusion of choice, even though we both know it doesn't really exist, and it warms the dark recesses of my broken little heart.

I smile up at the commander, but he must see the tinge of sadness in it, because a flicker of apprehension alights in his gaze.

"I will accept your bond and become your mate. But you shouldn't fall for me, Aeson," I both confess and warn in the same breath. "Things would be easier for both of us if we just stayed enemies."

He considers me for a long moment, studying my face like he knows it well enough to follow its clues to help uncover what he wants to know.

"We were never truly enemies, Claws," he tells me gently, and his fingertips whisper just as gently across my back as he traces the ridges of my spine.

I fight off a shiver and blink away the spell his intense gaze is trying to cast on me.

"Maybe not," I agree with a shrug. "But give it time. I'm sure we'll get there."

The music stops and the crowd around us begins to applaud. A drop of blood from Aeson's cheek spills onto mine, and it slips down my face like a tear, which feels oddly symbolic.

"That doesn't scare me, Claws. I like a challenge," he professes, the glint in his gaze eager and determined.

"I'm counting on it," I murmur, and then I step out of his arms and walk away.

CHAPTER 41

I need to get out of here. There's a conflagration of lust trying to consume every inch of my body, and if I don't find somewhere to cool off, I'm going to go up in flames any second now. It's ridiculous. I shouldn't be this hot and bothered simply from being pressed up against Aeson Noctis for only a handful of minutes, and certainly not while I'm wearing an alarming amount of his blood. But it's as though acknowledging this bond between us has somehow strengthened it, and now my head and body are a tandem riot of lascivious longing.

His touch, that smug smile he favors, the way his eyes become a deeper blue when he's digging between the lines of everything I say—I can't get any of it out of my head. I'm fixated, which is really fucking inconvenient, because I have enough shit to worry about. I don't need Aeson Noctis and this bond trying to weasel their way higher up on my list.

My vision tunnels toward the exit I used to sneak into the ballroom earlier. I just need to make it past the columns, and then I'm free. Free to question everything that I'm doing here. Free to lock myself in my room, get myself off, and scream my release into a pillow so no one can hear me. Free to freak out about the fact that the commander is my Bonded fucking Mate.

Someone calls my name, but I ignore them. I can't stop or I'm going to spontaneously combust.

Escape is fifteen feet away.

Twelve feet.

Nine.

I've set one heel in the shadows of the columns when, out of nowhere, I'm tackled from behind. Shock slows my reaction, and a large palm over my mouth stifles my cry of alarm. I start to fight back, but the next thing I know, my back is plastered to the cold stone of a column, and Aeson's there, looming over me, his eyes blazing with hunger.

His chest rises and falls with quick breaths, the motion teasing my nipples as he wedges a muscular leg between my thighs and drops his head until his lips skim the shell of my ear. His hand moves from my mouth and wraps possessively around my throat.

"I believe I was clear what would happen if you kept running from me," he growls in my ear.

I gasp as he nips my earlobe, and I automatically grind down on his thigh in search of friction, frantic for relief. He purrs with satisfaction and pulls back to look at me. The cuts on his face and hands have healed, leaving only lines of blood as evidence that they were ever there. His suit jacket is sliced up beyond saving, and the few butterflies that I have left around me get to work destroying it completely.

"You may not know this about me yet, Claws, but I'm a man of my word. I do not make idle threats, and I do not back down . . . ever."

He presses his lips against mine, but instead of kissing me like I'm suddenly desperate for, he sucks my lower lip into his mouth and bites it just hard enough to coax a little whimper out of me before he lets it go.

"You think your ominous little warning is the end of our discussion?" he asks me as his other hand drops to my thigh and starts to slowly work its way up. "Think again, Claws. I'm nowhere near done with you."

"Aeson," I pant, and I have no idea if I'm begging him to stop or begging him not to.

He's too close, too hot, too all-consuming. If I was a blaze before, I'm a raging inferno now. I writhe against him, and that maddening, self-satisfied smile of his is back.

"What do you need, Claws?" he purrs, like he doesn't already know. "Tell your Bonded what he can do for you."

Like a match to dry kindling, I ignite and then I burn.

"Kiss me," I command. "And then take me somewhere so I can fuck you and no one will hear me scream."

Fast as a flickering bolt of lightning, he claims my mouth, and I claim his right back. His lips are supple and soft, but his mouth is hard and demanding. His tongue teases mine, luring me deeper until I'm lost to the heady taste of him. I thread my fingers in his hair, needing more, needing him everywhere.

My heart races to catch up with the frenzy building between us, and my blood sings a carnal ballad as every nerve in my body flares with need. The vicious butterflies diving and darting all around us match our insatiable fervor and once again draw Aeson's blood. His hand drops from my throat and he grabs my ass and lifts me. I wrap my legs around his waist and devour him.

He sucks my tongue as he pulls back, breaking our kiss, and I mewl an objection. But then my eyes fall on a tendril of scarlet that's just started slipping down his throat. I don't know what comes over me, but I lean in and lick it up, my tongue stroking over the new wound like Aeson's blood is my favorite flavor of ice cream.

I greedily swallow my little taste of the commander, and his desperate groan is all the salacious endorsement I need to trace the lines of his dragon mark with my tongue before I lick the line of his cut again. Fuck, he tastes good. It makes me instantly want to drop to my knees and test the flavor of his cock down my throat.

"I need to be inside of you, Claws. Can you make it to the rookery? I want your cum all over our sheets and your screams embedded in the walls of our rooms."

"Anywhere closer?" I pant and roll my hips against the hard bulge in his pants. "Because if you're not fucking me in the next minute, I'm going to start fucking myself. Where in the keep that happens is up to you."

His answering moan is both pained and encouraging. His eyes dart toward the shadowy exit behind us, and then we're moving. He doesn't put me down, and that's fine by me. I take the opportunity to familiarize my lips with the line of his jaw and the curve of his ear while I let my hips bounce against his with every confident stride he makes.

In a blink, we're racing down a dark hallway, and then all at once the last of the butterflies attacking Aeson go crashing to the ground. Outrage pours through me, but then Aeson pins me against another wall and kisses me until my indignation burns to ash and my white-hot desire is soaking his pants.

Aeson snakes a hand between us and finds his way under my skirt. His fingers immediately caress the seam of my pussy, and he hisses and jerks his face back with shock.

"You've been bare this whole time?" he demands, the look in his eyes wild and hungry.

My answering smile is sultry as I ghost my lips over his. "Bare and dripping down my thighs even before you locked me in that room."

I bite his lip hard to let him know exactly how I feel about that shit.

The vibration in his answering growl works its way through my body and settles deliciously in my clit. I wiggle against Aeson's fingers, and he parts my lips and slips the tip of one inside of me.

"Fuck, you really are dripping," he moans. He trails his finger up to my clit and starts to slowly, methodically circle it. "All this for me, Claws?" he purrs as he plays.

I'm pretty sure this asshole is trying to edge me, but joke's on him, I'm so turned on right now, I can probably come from just this. Like he can read my mind, and he refuses to allow it, he pulls his hand away and continues down the hall.

"Aeson," I beg, but there's a distinct note of a snarl in it.

"Ever," he counters innocently, like he has no idea what my problem is.

"Fuck me here," I order impatiently. "I need you," I whine, hoping the declaration will help push him over the edge I've been teetering on for entirely too long.

"Give me two minutes, Claws. I know a place, it isn't far," he counters, and I groan with frustration.

"Then give me your fingers. Let me ride your hand until I can ride your cock."

He squeezes my ass cheeks harder and grinds me against his shaft, which is annoyingly still tucked into his pants. "You can have my fingers another time. I want you screaming my name while you're impaled on my dick, not my fingers."

I whimper at the visual that teases my imagination and clench my inner walls around nothing.

That's it. Time to take matters into my own hands . . . literally.

"I warned you," I snap at him, every ounce of reason and patience sapped by the overwhelming drive to have him in me, under me, on top of me, and dripping out of me everywhere. But if I can't have that right now, I can at least take the edge off.

I snake my own hand between our bodies as Aeson slips through another one of those side hidden doors that I had no idea was there until it's opening.

"Claws, what do you think you're doing?" he demands, and it's *his* voice now that rings with a subtle note of hysteria.

My only answer is to moan as I dip my fingers inside myself. I get them nice and wet and then I pull them out and start stroking my clit just the way I like it. I put a little extra oomph in the satisfied sounds I start making, and a string of very colorful expletives spills out of Aeson's mouth before he starts down a flight of stairs at a breakneck speed.

"Don't you fucking dare, Ever," he barks as I plunge my fingers back inside my pussy and wiggle them around a little so he can hear how obscenely wet I am. "I swear, if you come on your own hand instead of my di—"

An extra loud moan cuts off his threat, and I throw my head back like I'm on the cusp of a life-shattering orgasm. "This could have been you, Spare," I taunt as I ride my own fingers. "Don't worry, I'll send a *wish you were here* postcard to your blue balls when I'm done."

I press my tits harder against his chest and pant hot, staccato breaths against his shoulder. I have no idea where he's taking us. The stairwell is dark, but there's a faint glow to the smooth gray stone all around us that washes us with enough light that I can still make out every detail of Aeson's pained face and taut body.

Another exaggerated mewl slips out of me when I start back on my clit, and I notice a strange sparkle of light ripple through the surrounding stone in an unmistakable wave that quickly fades.

The beginning of an orgasm starts to take root, and all my attention is sucked away from wherever we are and zeroed in on the building release my fingers are eagerly coaxing from my body. My muscles start to tense and I rub my clit even faster, chasing release.

Out of nowhere, Aeson spins us. I yelp and am forced to try to grab onto him with both of my hands when my weight shifts back and I'm pretty sure I'm about to fall. Strong arms keep me pinned to Aeson's chest, but then the smooth edge of the stone steps cuts into my back, and I realize he's now pinning me against the stairs.

Aeson hovers over me, and the look on his face is menacing. He snatches my hand so fast I flinch and brings it to his mouth, while his fiery blue eyes do their best to sear me. His lips close around the two fingers that were just inside of me, and his face morphs into a look of pure ecstasy. His groan is sensual satisfaction in its rawest form as he sucks my arousal from my skin, tonguing my fingers like he's giving me a taste of what his mouth intends to do in other places. He meticulously licks every last drop of desire from my digits, and then he pulls them out of his mouth and looks down at me with a punishing glare.

"From now on, you will only come on my cock, my fingers, my hand, my mouth, and my tongue. Every orgasm, every moan, every gasped word, and every drop of cum is mine. And do you know why that is?" he asks as he pulls the tatters of his jacket and shirt off.

My mind stalls as I take in the wide expanse of hard muscle that's intersected by the black flames of his dragon mark on his chest, shoulders, and upper arms. He reaches for the clasp on his pants, and I'm all but drooling from multiple places as muscles flex and strain in time with his hurried, jerky movements.

My chest heaves even faster and my heart pounds excitedly against my sternum in anticipation of what I know is coming. Desire floods my core, and every inch of me grows hot and sensitive. I suddenly want my dress off, but as I run my hands across my chest and down the sides, I don't feel a zipper or a clasp or anything else that will help me get it off.

"You asked me what your dragon felt like, but I didn't answer the question. Ask me again, Claws."

I tug on my dress, my movements growing more and more frantic, but it still doesn't budge. Aeson lifts his hand, and a small orange flame flickers to life in his palm. At first I think he's trying to illuminate the stairwell to help me figure out how to take this thing off, but then he flicks the flame at me. I yelp and try to scramble back in panic.

"It's okay, it won't burn you," he hurries to assure me as he keeps me pinned against the stairs. "I control the flame. I decide what it consumes and what it doesn't."

"Burners can do that?" I ask, aghast, my wide eyes jumping frantically from his calm face to the flame that's flickering on my stomach like it's waiting to be given orders.

"Not all of them, but I can," he tells me evenly, like it's no big deal.

I shove at his chest, but he doesn't move so much as a centimeter. "How 'bout you clue me in to the whole *I'm not trying to immolate you* thing *before* you start chucking flames at me next time."

"I can agree to that *if* you agree to my previously stated terms."

My brow furrows with confusion.

"Your pleasure is mine. Your orgasms are mine. If you play with yourself, it's either because I want you to or because I'm not there and you're thinking of me."

His demands are ludicrous. He's being domineering in the most absurd way. Who agrees to hand over the reins of their pleasure like that, especially to someone they barely even know? So why am I dripping on the steps below me at the thought of it?

"You want to own my orgasms?" I dispute. "Then earn the privilege. I'm not agreeing to shit unless I know I'm in *good* hands. Then we can talk."

He smiles like I just said exactly what he was hoping I would. With a flick of his hand, the stationary flame on my stomach starts traveling up my torso, and I realize it's burning the gossamer fabric of my dress away as it goes. It's hot but not painfully so. The solitary flicker of fire doesn't hurt me as it trails its way up my body, but I still hold my breath, worried I'll feel a bite of pain seconds before my skin starts to scorch. However, Aeson's control on his affinity must be second to none, because the fire doesn't so much as singe a hair on my body; it only burns a line up my dress like a fiery zipper.

Aeson kicks off his pants and lifts me off the stairs. My dress falls away with the motion, and the flicker of flame dancing across my chest instantly dies out. We're skin against skin now, and there's something about it that's so intimate and erotic that the haze of manic lust clears for just a breath, and the impact of what we're doing registers.

I'm about to fuck my mate for the first time.

Not too long ago, the thought of a mate, let alone the reality of being bonded to Aeson Noctis, second son of King Noctis and Scion of The Dragon Horde, would have made me laugh my ass off, because *fuck no*, that would *never* happen. I know this will change things, shift things, and as stupid as it is, as selfish as this choice will undoubtedly be, I'm making it.

Aeson carries me into a large room that's made up of the same smooth gray stone as the stairs. He lays me down on what feels like a floor made of sparring mats, and I hiss at the cold touch of the semi-spongy ground. The noise makes flashes of sparkles detonate like glittering fireworks on the ceiling, and I pause to watch.

"Where are we, and what is that?" I ask, and several places in the room light up at my voice.

"A training room, and that's Flare Moss. It reacts to sound. Our tutors used this space to train stealth. As younglings, we had to execute all of our forms without triggering any of the moss. Most programs use magi-tech to do that, but our instructor was old-school," he answers absently, and I look down to see that his eyes are tracing a path down my body and he's pumping a fist up and down the thick shaft of his cock.

He catches me watching him, and that arrogant smirk makes an appearance. He guides his big hand up and down once, twice, his eyes watching every eager, wanton, needy flash of emotion that flickers across my flushed face.

"I'm dripping for you too, Claws," he murmurs as a glistening bead of precum spills from his tip. "Now ask me what your dragon feels like to me. Ask me what right I have to demand dominion over your desires and pleasure."

I lick my lips and pull my enamored gaze from his cock and look up into his scorching blue eyes.

"What does my dragon feel like to you?" I half whimper, half sigh, spreading my legs as wide as I can to make room for his massive frame.

A possessive heat banks in his gaze, and he leans over me until our noses are almost touching. "Your dragon feels the same way that you do . . . like you were made for me and me you. Like the metric of my happiness rests solely on yours. Like I could never be complete without you by my side."

He kisses me then, and his lips and tongue walk a fine line between feral and fervent. It has all the edge of wild abandon, and yet it's deeper, more profound, utterly life-changing. It's reverent and resplendent, and I voraciously accept every promise I feel on his lips, every covenant I taste on his tongue, and every oath our mouths make.

My lungs begin to scream for air, and he pulls away, dropping his mouth down my throat, descending my chest until he's claimed a nipple in his hot, wet, talented mouth. He sucks and toys with his tongue, and I gasp desperate breaths between moans while I writhe under his massive frame. His hips rest in the cradle of my thighs, and I roll against him, borderline distraught with how much I need him inside of me right fucking now.

"You're so beautiful," he whispers against my sternum as he focuses his wicked mouth on my other breast.

"No," I bark at him, and he looks up at me, confused. "None of that sentimental tender shit," I breathily scold him, needing to draw the line somewhere if there's any hope of maintaining dominion over my heart.

His scowl is indignant. "Oh, right. We're supposed to be enemies," he deadpans, like it's the most asinine thing he's ever heard.

"Exactly," I agree. "Now fuck me like you hate me."

My kiss is bruising, vicious, demanding, and he growls his approval into my mouth and lines himself up between my thighs. He palms my ass and tilts my hips up, and then he thrusts into me, seating himself fully in one smooth drive. I throw my head back, my deep, satisfied moan lighting up the walls in time with his.

Finally! I scream in my head as my body adjusts to the delectable intrusion of his cock.

"Fuck, you feel so good," he rasps. "I knew you would, but this . . . "

His words get lost as his lips once again claim mine, and he drinks me down like I'm the elixir of life and he's fighting his way back from the brink of death. I need more, more of his mouth, more of his cock, more of all of him.

He pulls out of me to the tip and pistons back in. We both swallow each other's moans, and then Aeson stops holding back. He fucks me hard, fast, and deep. Exactly the way I've been craving for longer than I'll ever admit. I tear my mouth from his as desperate breaths pepper my sonorous moans.

He touches places inside of me I thought were more myth than truth.

Each thrust is punctuated with a roll of his hips, and my clit sings praises to his technique while my vagina starts buying merch that says *Property of Aeson "Fucks Like a God" Noctis.*

All too quickly, the tingling in my limbs begins to coalesce at my core, and I know this orgasm is going to be one for the record books.

"I'm going to come," I mewl as he starts driving into me even faster.

"Soak my cock, Claws. Give me what I need," he growls in answer as he nips the top of my shoulder.

White-hot pleasure detonates through me, and I wail my release as I almost black the fuck out from the rush of it. Aeson stills inside me as his name bounces off the stone of the room. The echoes sound fittingly like a hymn that might be sung at the foot of the shrine I now have to build for him. Light flares on the other side of my closed lids, and I bite back a laugh at the thought of the Flare Moss getting off on what we're doing just as much as we are.

I lie back, sated, sweat dotting my skin, and my body completely boneless. I have no idea how I'm going to get up off this floor, let alone walk, but that's a problem for later, when I'm not still twitching with the aftershocks of the best orgasm of my life.

"If I'd have known it was going to be like that, I would have fucked you in Lairwood right after you tackled me in the street."

I laugh and then sigh happily. Aeson's quiet, probably recovering himself, but I realize he's still inside of me, and I wiggle my hips to signal he can pull out now.

He doesn't move.

I open my eyes and find him staring at me, and something about the determined look in his eyes makes me pause. "What are you doing?" I whisper warily.

"Waiting," he answers matter-of-factly.

Confusion trickles through me. "For what?"

"For you to be ready to continue."

I reel back with surprise, my gaze jumping down to the cock that's still inside of me. I roll my hips once, and, yep, he's still hard.

What the fuck?

"We're not done?" I query, like the thought itself is beyond my comprehension.

"Oh, Claws," he croons at me, punctuating his saccharine-sweet tone with a firm thrust of his hips. "We're just getting started."

A larger flame than the one he threw at me last time alights in his hand, and I don't freak out this time when he sets it gently on my chest. As soon as the fire kisses my skin, it splits into half a dozen smaller fireballs, which then shoot off into different directions down my body. I gasp and goose bumps skitter across my bare skin as the chill in the room wrestles with the heat of the flames roving over my torso.

I moan, and my startled gaze snaps up to Aeson's when two little fireballs start to circle my nipples. His gaze is like a hot brand against my skin. It stamps ownership all over me while his affinity helps him stake his claim.

The flickering flames darting down my body are hot enough to leave a tiny sting in their wake, but they don't hurt exactly. Instead, they seem to make everything they touch infinitely more sensitive. The fireballs on my nipples almost feel like Aeson attached heated nipple clamps to the tips of each of my breasts. I've never felt anything like it and, while unusual, I quickly succumb to the sparks of pleasure it's stimulating.

Just when I get used to the naughty flames plucking at my nipples, two others slip between my thighs. I gasp, and my spine bows as one flame starts bouncing on my clit, while the other begins to slowly circle the base of Aeson's shaft where it's pressed against me. It's like he's rubbing a hot finger around my entrance at the same time I'm stretched to the brink and as full as I can possibly be with his cock.

The final roving flame makes me yelp when it dips down my ass and settles between my cheeks. It starts to pulse in time with the one flickering at my clit, and I'm instantly a puddle of sensation and need. My murmurs are incoherent. My mind can't figure out which sensation to focus on, so instead, it seems to misfire, holding me hostage in this weird state of limbo where everything feels like too much and yet somehow not enough.

Aeson wraps his arms around me and then sits back on his heels, bringing me with him. We're now upright, still chest to chest, and he's still settled deep inside of me. I anchor my arms to his shoulders and start to slowly, languidly rock against him.

"Mmmmm." Aeson hums his approval as I start to ride his cock in time with the throbbing heat of his fire. "You light up for me so beautifully."

I lick up his throat, and then he takes my mouth again, searing me with a bone-melting kiss. I rub myself against the hard planes of his mouthwatering body, and I suddenly want to lick and claim every inch of it. The black flames of his dragon mark dance in the flickering glow from the flames lighting up every erogenous zone I have.

Flare Moss glitters on and off all around us as our moans grow louder. Aeson starts meeting my bouncing hips with hard thrusts of his own, and something untethered and feral starts to build within me.

My dragon fluxes through me, pressing against the barrier of my skin as though eager to feel everything that I do right now. It's a sensation I have no words for. This being inside of me is both everything I am and yet not. It's like coming home while also feeling completely foreign and new.

Aeson's flames all suddenly sync up in time with his pistoning cock, and the inferno I was combusting into earlier is now a supernova intent on wholly consuming me—mind, body, and soul.

The gray stone room all around us blazes to life as my ecstasy sets off the Flare Moss. Suddenly it's as though we're suspended in deep space, floating amidst a sea of endless stars.

It's the most beautiful thing I've ever seen, next to the drake fucking me like he was created to do nothing else.

"Give me one more, Ever," Aeson commands, and my body submits instantly, giving me no choice but to shatter into a thousand pieces as a screaming orgasm claims my fucking soul.

Tears slip down my cheeks as he drives me over the edge again, and this time, he follows me with a roar that has the stars all around us swelling into the suns. His hot release fills me, one more flickering flame hell-bent on fracturing me with pleasure beyond all repair.

I float in a pool of euphoria, distantly aware that Aeson's gently caressing my body and kissing me softly as my mind tries to make sense of all the ways he just ruined me. I cling to him, like I'm afraid of what will happen if I let go. I told myself I couldn't belong to him, that this curse corrupting my blood would also taint the connection we'd have and I'd be safe from ever falling.

But I was wrong.

Because I can feel his dragon.

It's coiled in the center of everything he is, and somehow . . . wrapped around everything that I am too.

Realization falls into me, stealing my breath.

I don't think Aeson Noctis is my Bonded Mate.

I think he might be my Soul Tied.

CHAPTER 42

My thoughts wind in and around two words, scrutinizing every angle of them, mulling over what they could mean.

Soul Tied.

It can't be, and yet, I've never heard of another connection that would explain what I think is happening—what's already happened, if my suspicions are correct. I need to get back to The Scorch, and I need to look through my mother's books that we recovered from The Wells. It's the only place I've ever seen the term referenced as a link between dragons that died out when the Surgers did.

When Lorn mentioned that Aeson could feel my dragon, I chalked it up to the bond, because Bonded Mates have been known to sense one another's emotions or feel a strong connection to their mate's source of power. But what I'm feeling with Aeson is different. It's not just a sense of who he is at his core or reading how he's feeling in general; I felt his dragon within me. I felt it like it was my own . . . and it wasn't the first time.

I didn't realize it then, but after the dungeon, when I was Source drunk, I felt the same thing. I wasn't thinking about mates, or bonds, or anything like that then because I had no idea that I could trigger any kind of connection without revealing first, but now . . . now I think there's more at play here than should be possible . . . unless . . . shit . . . but that would mean . . .

Out of nowhere, I trip. With a gasp and a squeal, I go careening forward. The only thing that stops me from faceplanting is Aeson's quick reflexes. He grabs me, sets me on my feet, and holds me until I regain my balance. I tear the blindfold off my face and chuck it at him.

"This is bloody stupid," I snap, bending down to rub my stinging foot. I have no idea where I lost my shoes, but somewhere between the ballroom and the training room, they disappeared.

"No. What's stupid is you stubbornly insisting on *walking* when I offered to carry you," Aeson argues.

I throw my head back and groan with frustration. "You were just *inside* of me. How are you okay with that level of trust, but the second you tuck your dick in your pants, it all disappears? Make it make sense! Why is it okay for me to see all of your *secret passages*, but the ones winding through King's Keep are off-limits?"

I pull at the hem of his torn-up shirt to make sure it hasn't climbed up my thighs too high. Lucky for me, the back of his shirt was mostly intact, thanks to the protection of his now-shredded suit jacket. I just threw the shirt on backward, and so far I'm not flashing anything I shouldn't be. Aeson's pants aren't in the best shape, but at least we're semi-clothed as we make our way back to his rookery.

"Do you really want to get into a discussion about trust, Claws? Because I have some questions about other Syphons that I'd love your *honest* and *trustworthy* opinion about if you're up for it."

This motherfucker.

I roll my eyes and level him with an unamused glower.

"Ask away, Spare. I'll tell you exactly what I told your brother when he brought up his own suspicions. It's possible others have survived just like I did, but I can't say one way or the other if it's true or simply wishful thinking on your part."

"Oh, so we're back to *Spare*?" he asks with faux indignation. "What happened to *Aeson, you feel so fucking good, yes, right there, fuck me like the god you are*," he mimics in an exaggerated falsetto that sounds nothing like me.

My cheeks heat.

Crap.

Did I really say all of that . . . out loud? I mean, I know I hit a point where I went half-catatonic and fully incoherent, but I didn't think I'd let the god *shit spill out.*

I shove away my chagrin and cross my arms over my chest as though the power stance will protect me from any more embarrassment. "My bad, I didn't realize we were switching up the pet names this early in our relationship. I'll be sure to call you exactly that in front of your father the next time we're all together."

Aeson laughs. He closes the distance between us and presses a soft kiss to my lips. I freeze, unsure what to think about the casual and yet intimate act. My insides squirm while also feeling oddly giddy, and the rest of me can't decide if I'm dubious about this development or into it.

He opens his arms to me. "Come on, I'll carry you the rest of the way," he offers while trying to hand me back the blindfold.

My answering look shouts *you have to be kidding me.*

"Thirteen strides that way." I point directly behind us. "Take a left, fourteen strides, another left, five strides, a right, two strides, a left, eighteen strides, another right, thirty-two strides to get to the stairwell where I'll take eight flights down, swing a right, take thirteen more strides down before I hit another set of stairs, and then I'll be back in the hallway that leads to the ballroom," I recite.

Aeson's stare fills with surprise and then indignation. "How the hell did you do that?"

"It's called counting, Spare. Not all of us can be wealthy scions who get by solely on their looks," I taunt with exaggerated exasperation.

It's probably better to keep things lighthearted instead of pointing out that I was held prisoner for months by the Tainted, often with my senses being spelled to make it difficult to figure out where I was. I got creative in trying to decipher things, especially potential escape routes in case the opportunity ever presented itself.

I turn to continue to make my way down the rest of the corridor, but I'm scooped off my feet and thrown over a wide, hard shoulder. I shriek my protest and a large hand slaps my ass in response.

"I'll show you counting . . . One," he calls out and then spanks me playfully again. "Two . . . " Spank. "Three . . . "

I shout an objection, but it quickly morphs into a squeal with each palm against my ass cheeks. I try to flip off Aeson's shoulder, but he has a firm hold on my legs, and I can't dislodge myself.

"Four," he taunts, and I squirm to get out of his hold, but my laughter is sapping me of my strength and making me easy prey.

"Welcome home, Commander Noctis and Ever Noctis," I hear a robotic feminine voice greet, and I look up and realize that we must have exited a hidden passage that put us right by Aeson's rookery.

The door to the tower unlocks, and I can tell by the displacement of air and the gentle breeze against the back of my thighs that it's swinging open. I study the walls around us, but I don't see evidence of a hidden panel in the wall or even a seam in the stone that would tell me where we just came from. He carries me into the main room of his quarters, and I decide I'll have to look for the hidden door in the hallway another time. Maybe it has that same kind of tech that hides it like Aeson's trove does in his room.

"Put me down, you brute," I snap before slapping the commander hard on his ass when I realize I have a pretty good angle to do a little of my own spanking.

He chuckles and sets me on my feet. I pull at the hem of my shirt to make sure everything is still covered and turn around, my smile faltering when I find all of Aeson's Wing spread out around us in serious-guard mode. My gaze lands on a stranger's as he rises from a couch, and I instantly realize why everyone looks so tense.

He's a member of the king's Wing.

Aeson comes up behind me, and I feel the exact moment he spots the visitor, because he goes stiff.

"Raeger," he greets tersely, and I look back to see him offer the Channeler a nod.

"Scion," Raeger acknowledges just as curtly. "I'm just dropping off a missive," he explains, which is when I notice the gold disc in the drake's hand.

Aeson steps around me and approaches the male, his arm stretched out expectantly.

"It's not for you, Scion. It's for the scioness," Raeger announces, bypassing Aeson so he can hand me the golden disc. "The king passes along his wishes for a safe and expeditious trip," the Channeler informs me, and then without another word, he proceeds to walk toward the door and promptly leave.

Aeson's stare moves from the front entrance to me, all lightness and humor in his blue eyes replaced by wariness. One of his eyebrows lifts in question.

"Trip?" he queries flatly.

I look down at the disc in my hands, and surprise trickles through me. I didn't think King Noctis would arrange the meeting tonight. I thought it would take more time than that.

Instead of answering Aeson, I compress a button in the center of the disc, and four holographic documents blink into existence directly above the device. There's a royal authorization from the king, allowing me limited access to a restricted area that's not named. From the look of things, the pass is good for exactly four days, and based on the activation time, I'm expected to leave as soon as possible. There's a packing list that consists of warm clothing, temperature packs, and instructions not to bring my com. The third document is encoded and meant to be deciphered only by my escort, and the last image is a note from Lorn, offering to take me if Aeson refuses.

That gives me pause. Why would Aeson refuse?

I release my thumb on the disc, and the documents all disappear. I stare off at nothing for a moment. Why would I need to meet the Matron in a restricted area? Was that at her request or the king's? Someone clears their throat, and I'm pulled from my thoughts and focus back on Aeson and his Wing, who have closed in around us.

"I think it's time you answer my question now," Aeson declares as he grimly looks from the disc in my hand back up to me. "What did my father agree to give you as part of your deal?"

In answer, I toss Aeson the disc and watch as he reads through the documents. As soon as he gets to the encoded destination, anger and suspicion flash through his features. He's quick to banish them, but there's an undeniable tension now radiating off him while he moves on to read Lorn's note. When he finishes, he studies me intently, and it's as though I can see him fortifying his defenses breath by breath, brick by brick, until the sexy, easygoing male I've spent the last few hours with is gone, and in his place is the hard, unyielding commander I know all too well.

My heart lurches, and the moths in my stomach are threatening to crawl up my throat as unease and hurt wash through me.

"Why, of all places, would you ask to go here?" he asks coolly, holding up the golden disc, and I feel the icy bite of his accusing tone nip at me.

I recoil and study the scion as he hands the missive to Ogdan, who quickly surveys it, his demeanor growing just as stiff and stony as Aeson's.

I scowl, unsure what to make of this. Is it still the deal that's pissing Aeson off, or is it something else now?

"I haven't been clued in to exactly where we're going, but I requested a meeting with the head of the Relacour sorcai, and whatever is encoded on that disc is where your father saw fit to host it," I answer, ignoring the ache in my chest that's throbbing in time with the one starting to hammer inside my skull. It's been a long night.

Aeson looks over at Farrow and Karis, and then both Thrashers move to flank him. They stare at me with that blank look that tells me they're ready to comb through everything I say in search of lies or any hints of deception.

I reel back, looking from the Thrashers to the commander. Even now, after everything, he's still trying to catch me in a lie. I shake my head, disappointment mixing with my anger and dejection. I was worried that tonight would change things between us, that everything would be different after being with him. But it never dawned on me that accepting Aeson's bond would change *nothing* at all. And yet, as I'm met with the same mistrust and skepticism that I've been up against from the first second I laid eyes on the scion in the streets of Lairwood, I realize I've made a glaring overestimation about what tonight meant to him.

"And here I was thinking we were past this," I tell the commander flatly, a bone-deep weariness and heartache suddenly weighing me down.

"Why do you want to meet with the Relacour Matron?" Aeson asks instead of acknowledging any aspect of what I just said.

Fine. If this is how he wants things to be between us, cold and disconnected, then he'll get exactly that. I can do frigid bitch with the best of 'em.

"Because Relacour Blood Crafters played a major role in the wyvern and sorcai rebellion, and I strongly believe that they are the ones responsible for the curse on the Syphons. If there's anyone capable of fixing what was done to me, it will be the Matron," I answer smoothly.

"And if she can't break your curse, is your deal with my father void?" Aeson queries, his intonation flat but the anger in his eyes cutting.

I scoff and look at him like I'm seeing him for the first time.

Maybe I am.

"Wow. So eager to torch every ounce of goodwill we just built, aren't you?" I lob at him.

"Answer the question," he growls back.

My answering glare is blistering, but he's not cowed in the slightest.

"My agreement with your father was for him to arrange a meeting with the Matron, but don't worry, regardless of whether or not she can break my curse, you and I are still a *thing*. And before you try to make this more about you than you already have, let's get one thing clear: This has nothing to do with you, Aeson. I wanted a chance to be whole, to free my dragon, to take back what was stolen from me. Your father promised me a shot at that, and I took it, because it's a fuck ton more than anyone else has ever given me."

My chest heaves with the effort it takes to reel in my emotions. I showed Aeson enough of my vulnerability tonight; he doesn't get to see any more.

"I've been here for weeks, and not one of you assholes has bothered to *ask* me what I want out of all of this, or even how I feel about it. You've ordered me around, lectured me, made decisions on my behalf, treated me like I'm nothing more than a pawn or a puppet, and then had the audacity to get mad at me for protecting myself, for ensuring that I get what *I* need from this fucked-up situation."

I angrily gesture at the commander, his Wing, and then to the room all around me.

"If you want to be pissed, go for it, but aim that shit at each other where it belongs. I'm doing what I've always done. I'm surviving. I'm looking out for myself because no one else is. Now, if you'll excuse me, I have to pack . . . and call Lorn."

I turn to leave, rubbing at the anguish in my chest and quickly blinking back the emotion welling in my eyes.

"Lorn won't be taking you," Aeson calls after me.

"Since I prefer him over you at the moment, I disagree," I shout back as I head toward my room. If I turn around, I'm going to get vicious and that's not going to end well for anyone.

"It's either me or you're not going," Aeson threatens, and I stop and slowly turn to face him.

He's still only wearing his diced-up suit pants. His muscles and dragon mark are on full display, as is the tension that's rolling off him in waves. "We'll be ready in thirty," he states before crossing his arms like he's preparing for a fight.

Any other day, I might have been up to giving him one. But right now, I don't give two shits about squaring off with him or his bruised ego. I care about meeting with the Matron and breaking this curse. If I have to put up with his surly ass to do that, then so be it.

"Fine," I bite back. "But Aeson," I call as he turns to leave, "you're my mate, not my master. Be sure you don't get those two mixed up, or you'll be nothing to me at all."

CHAPTER 43

I storm into my room, glaring at everything in the mating suite like it's personally offended me.

What a fucking asshole.

They think I'm untrustworthy? I'm not the one that shifts from playful and flirty into a distrustful douchebag in the blink of a fucking eye.

Restless and beyond frustrated, I pace back and forth in my room. I can't tell if I want to rage or cry, which pisses me off even more, because the king just secured a meeting with the Matron. The fucking Matron. The Syphons and I have been searching for her forever, and now it's somehow happening, and instead of being happy about that, I'm reeling over Aeson Noctis's mood swings.

I rub at my temples, suddenly so fucking tired. I want to sleep for a week, but I have a meeting with the leader of the Relacour Blood Crafters, and I need to get my head on straight and focus on what's important.

Something on the long coffee table in the sitting area catches my eye. Several somethings, I realize as I move closer and find a few stacks of wrapped boxes.

Did Nixy send me something? Usually her deliveries go straight to the closet, but maybe these are the pajamas I requested to cover for wanting to get a message to Enslee. I pick up a box from one of the stacks and examine it. When it doesn't look, sound, or smell like anything dangerous, I sit on the couch and begin to open it.

I get the paper off and cautiously lift the lid. I stare down at the contents, my mind slow to catch up with my eyes, because I'm staring down at a case that's marked with the magical brand of the weaponsmiths from the Bone Isles.

My lungs fill, but my breaths stall as I reverently open the case and find two exquisite bone blades nestled within the safety of emerald-green velvet. The handles have the swooping clouds, jeweled stars, and crescent moons found on the crest of the Renders. I run a worshipful finger gently across the ivory blade, and I can't stop the smile that slips across my face.

I take in the boxes in front of me, and excitement has me reaching for a second package, which contains two stunning lock sheaths for the bone blades, the kind that you can attach to any surface and know they're not going anywhere. A stunned breath whooshes out of me, and I start frantically opening every wrapped box in front of me.

I discover a pulse bow and harness, two fourth-generation XD pistols and the thigh holsters that go with them, a belt of PHaSR grenades and a case of refills, six batiirien spikes, and a grappling gauntlet.

There's a disc attached to the last box in the first pile, and I press down on the button and a recording starts, zooming in on all the smiling faces of Aeson's Wing.

"Happy Naming Day, Frills!" everyone enthusiastically offers—well, everyone except Tove, who rolls her eyes and looks the exact opposite of enthusiastic, but she's there, so I guess that's something.

"This is everything on your list, and one extra-special present we hope makes you think of all of us every time you look at them," Chastain excitedly explains. "Happy Naming Day, from your favorite Wing," he adds, batting his lashes coquettishly at the cam before he starts making kissy faces at it.

Everyone groans at his antics, and someone shoves him out of frame before Ogdan steps up front and center.

"We're glad we found you, lass," he declares warmly. "We know you're more than capable of guarding your front, especially with your new arsenal, but know we'll always be here to help guard your back. Happy Naming Day."

The recording cuts off, and I blink back the swell of emotion Ogdan's words have stirred within me. Reverently, I open the last present in the stack and then throw my head back and laugh when I see what's inside.

My cackle rings off the wall of the room, and laugh-tears quickly start to stream down my face. I reach inside the box and pull out a glass case housing two viciously sharp daggers almost the length of my forearm. The silver metal of the blades gleams in the light, but it's the hilt and the cross guard on the daggers that has my stomach hurting from laughter and my cheeks sore from the grin stretched wide across my face.

The face of a lizard looks as though it's biting down on the base of the dagger's blade. Just behind the lizard's head is a frilled neck that serves as the dagger's cross guard. The body of the fabricated reptile makes up the handle, and its tail spirals around the body to create a surprisingly comfortable grip.

These fuckers gave me frilled lizard daggers.

I shake my head, my body still vibrating with amusement as I expertly twirl the lizard blades in my hand and test the weight and balance. Aside from being hilarious, the daggers are expertly crafted and perfectly balanced. They're light but solid, and there's a button at the base of the handle that makes the frilled neck of the cross guard lie flat, so the daggers are easily wearable, and I find two more lock sheaths nestled underneath the glass case.

There are three boxes left, and I quickly open them. One is from Nixy and contains a gorgeous armored bodysuit that will fit perfectly under the holsters, sheaths, straps, and belts of all of my new weapons. It's dark gray with lines and vortexes that resemble the dragon marks that Syphons often have. It's like she was trying to give me my own version of scale armor, and I'm touched by her effort and thoughtfulness.

Lorn gave me fang breakers, along with a vid message declaring it was the best of both worlds: a weapon that looked like jewelry. I study the jewelry that's designed to hook around your neck like a necklace and then sit across the top of your shoulders where it fastens under your armpits. I press a button at the back, and sharp spikes shoot out all across the glimmering defensive device.

A small squeal slips out of me, and I do a little happy dance like a kid in a candy store as I look around at my trove. I spot one last box under scraps of wrapping paper, but inside I only find a message telling me to "Look behind me."

I stare at the blank wall at my back for a second, confused, and then it dawns on me what it could be. I rise from the couch and approach the innocuous-looking stone. Sure enough, as I get closer, the wall in front of me disappears and reveals a glass cabinet filled with empty shelves and a large rack to house all of my new weapons and then some.

I gasp and press a hand to my mouth when my eyes catch on something sitting in the center of the cabinet meant to house the greatest treasures of my trove—it's Aeson's constellation lily. I approach the stunning one-of-a-kind flower cautiously, as though I'm afraid it will disappear at any moment. There's a note tucked under the petals of the precious lily, and I tug the paper free and read what's written in a masculine but surprisingly neat script.

Ever,

My grandmother was right. Every dragon deserves to fill their life with treasures that they'll cherish, revere, and protect. This flower was the most breathtaking thing I'd ever laid eyes on, until I saw you. It feels fitting that you should have it now. A great treasure for the greatest treasure of all.

Yours,

Aeson

I read the note for a second, third, and fourth time, and then realize I'm crying as a tear falls and wets the paper. I have no idea how to reconcile the male who wrote this note with the one I was just raging over when I walked into this room. Our bond has barely even formed and it's already in shambles. Maybe it's better this way. Things were always going to be complicated between us; maybe it's for the best that things came to a screeching halt before they could get even messier than they already are.

As much as it hurts, I needed to see the reality of what I've gotten myself into. Now I can treat my arrangement with Aeson like exactly what it is—a deal, a means to an end, and nothing more. It doesn't matter if we're Bonded or Tied if neither of us will ever trust the other, and it's clear that's off the table.

My dragon rumbles a disagreement, but I'm obviously more pragmatic. Indifference keeps us safe. I try to cling to that fact, even though it's proving harder this time than it should.

A hard knock on my door jolts me from my thoughts.

"Fifteen minutes," Farrow calls out, and I realize I need to clean up and pack.

Quickly, I put away the pulse bow, the extra grenades, and half the batiirien spikes on the rack designed to house the weapons. I set Aeson's note next to the constellation lily and move back from the cabinet until it rearms itself and once again returns to looking like nothing more than a stone wall.

I race for the shower, needing desperately to clean the night off of me, and wonder offhandedly if the tech these cabinets use to camouflage themselves can be used on people. Is that how the king kept himself hidden in his office?

My mind is a mess of anticipation for what's coming and a tumult of emotions I don't know how to make sense of. The wasps are back in my stomach, dancing around with the butterflies because I can't figure out how I feel about anything.

I dress quickly in the bodysuit Nixy gifted me and hurry to pack. I start strapping on my new weapons, my heart calming with the familiar movement and muscle memory of gearing up for a mission, although I've never been armed with this caliber of weaponry.

My thoughts wander to my sister, my Flight, and the other Syphons. I give myself a moment to miss them, to hope that this meeting will be the thing that turns the tide for us, and then I push all thoughts of everyone out of my mind. I can't be worrying about them and stay focused on everything I need to do now.

I scan the room one last time when I'm ready to go. My eyes drift over to the hidden cabinet, and in a hasty, last-minute decision I decide not to question, I march over to it and pluck Aeson's note from the safety of its confines. I tuck the slip of paper into a hidden pocket in my armored bodysuit, where it should be safe, and turn my back on the room and leave.

A forlorn feeling grows with every step I take away from the room, but I refuse to examine it. I've gambled with the king to save my people; now it's time to see if that gamble pays off.

CHAPTER 44

A huff escapes me when a sorcai offers to let our party skip to the front of the line waiting to travel through the jump portal, but Aeson waves them away, telling them we're happy to wait our turn. It's polite and considerate of the other travelers but annoying as fuck. Especially since the only reason he's doing it is to irritate me and prolong our leaving.

I wave away my irritation and look up at the night sky through the peaked glass ceiling. I don't know if the transparent roof is a design feature or if it's easier to replace glass in the event a dragon reveals and blows out the ceiling, but I'm not mad at this common feature in the buildings here. I like being able to see the sky at any time of the day; it reminds me of home and grounds me in a way I need right now.

For a moment, I let myself get lost in the unknown galaxies and worlds hiding within the night's darkest depths. The peaks of Talon's Reach loom over us like shadow-clad giants that could either protect or destroy depending on their mood. There's a hum of quiet chatter all around us as other travelers prepare to depart or gossip about the presence of Scion Noctis and his Wing.

The travel station we're standing in is stark, sleek, and designed to move large numbers of Arcs in and out as quickly as possible. Two of the four available jump portals are up and running at this hour, and I marvel at the large, arched openings that are about fifteen feet tall and wide. A border of stones with sorcai runes etched into them surrounds each bright white pool of magic. They're a more refined version of the makeshift portal I was shoved through in Lairwood.

Absently, I observe the sorcai manning the tall desk near the jump portal we'll be traveling through. They scan travel documents, upload destination coordinates, and answer questions with a bored yet practiced ease. Several covens of licensed Span Crafters maintain this and the one on the west side of Talon's Reach. They rotate who resides at the stations themselves to ensure the portals are always operational.

My attention wanders to the travelers all around us, mostly to keep from staring at Aeson and overanalyzing everything he's doing and saying and everything he's not. It's been crickets since we arrived at this portal station on the east side of the mountain range, and my frustration grows with every breath I take.

Thankfully, the line we're in moves fairly quickly, but I'm surprised there are so many people traveling this late, or rather, this early in the morning. Aeson, Ogdan, and Sondar are called to the side to provide the Span Crafter the coordinates for our jump, and I'm tempted to follow them just to see if I can get a clue myself.

Chastain nudges my shoulder with his and wags his eyebrows at me. Coming from him, the gesture could mean anything from *I want to discuss my latest conquest* to *I have to shit*, so I simply stare at the cheeky Channeler and wait for him to tell me what he wants. He nudges me again and offers me a goofy smile and a nod.

"Nice daggers," he finally tells me, and it's the exact tool he needs to crack my stoic facade.

A smile slips across my face, but I shape it into a coy smirk and shrug my shoulders. "They're no butter knives, but they'll do," I tease, and Chastain's grin morphs into a beaming smile.

"I know we gave you shit about wanting weapons, Frills, but if I'd known you'd look like that wearing them . . . wooo eeee, I would have gotten on board a lot sooner," Blay proclaims as he exaggeratedly starts fanning himself.

I bark out a laugh, unable to stop myself. When I walked out of my room earlier, I was ready to thank all of them profusely for my new treasures. But the commander and his Wing were all being very solemn and guarded, and it was obvious there'd been some sort of conversation about me. So I tucked my gratitude away and just kept my mouth shut, wondering once again if my gifts were less gift and more warning.

"Hear! Hear! Biscuit, I don't know if I want to eat or be eaten," Herm chimes in as he exaggeratedly clutches at his chest and appreciatively rakes his eyes up and down my body.

Tove throws her hands up in exasperation and grumbles something to Farrow about *acting like they want to be beaten with their own severed arms*. Farrow just smiles and shakes his head. I instantly feel lighter now that they're no longer looking at me like I'm the enemy, but I know this won't last either.

"Who's eating my *mate*?" Aeson inquires from behind me, the heat of his body suddenly lapping against my back as he stands as close as he can without touching me.

All I would have to do is lean back to breach the barrier of suspicion and mistrust that's once again been erected between us, but I don't. Some walls are there for our protection and better left alone.

"We're up," Ogdan announces, and I look over to see two sorcai feeding magic into the jump portal.

What's odd, however, is that several guards have blocked access to this jump portal, and now they have their backs to it as though they're prepared to stop anyone, by force, who might try to follow us. I haven't used these portals other than that one time I fell out of one into the sky, so I don't know if this is normal protocol when a royal travels or if this is something else.

"You're awfully subdued for someone who's about to get what they want," Aeson observes, his mouth close to my ear—too close.

I fight off a shiver that wants to quake through me as his breath tickles down my neck and move to put more distance between us.

"In my experience, it's never a good idea to get your hopes up; life proves to be less disappointing that way."

He doesn't respond, but I can feel his stare burning into the back of my head. It makes me wonder if he's sorry, if he regrets putting distance between us. Or maybe he's just trying to read between the lines of everything I do, like always.

I search for our connection, for any hint of his dragon or mine present in this exchange, but there's nothing there. It makes me wonder if I actually sensed what I thought I did. Maybe this is just a run-of-the-mill bond. What do I know about any of this shit anyway?

When we're given the all clear by the Span Crafters, we walk up to the archway of glowing white magic and step through. It's cold, but the suit Nixy gave me has thermal sensors, and it automatically grows warm to combat the sudden change in temperature.

My second trip through a jump portal goes much better than the first. Instead of careening through the sky like last time, my feet immediately touch solid ground when I step through the frigid wash of magic. Wherever we are, it's also night outside, but everything here is covered in snow, and it makes the dark feel brighter.

My heart drops a little. It was a long shot, but part of me hoped we'd step out into Thrasher Territory. Somewhere near Groton, where my Flight was headed in search of the Conduit. I knew the chances were low, and yet I couldn't help but hang on to a small sliver of hope that maybe they were on the right track and hadn't been betrayed again. But we are most certainly not in Thrasher Territory.

"Permits," a monotone voice demands, and Aeson moves toward the front of the group and presents his forearm.

The guard greeting us scans Aeson's com patch and then starts flicking through the documents that just uploaded on his tablet. A cutting, icy wind whips strands of my hair free from the slicked-back bun I styled my mane into. My breath fogs in the chilly air, and there's something strange about the smell of wherever we are, but it's not what I scent that's worrying me, it's what I don't.

Aeson and his Wing are busy with the guards, and I slip a few inches to the right so I can study our location. Unfortunately there's not much to see. We exited the portal into a rocky inlet. I look down and disturb the snow at my feet to try to see what the vegetation is like under the icy fractals. But the snow floats oddly around as I kick it up, which I don't think is normal.

Puzzled, I lean down to get a better look, and freeze.

No fucking way.

It's not snow . . . it's ash.

My head snaps up and I frantically search for something, anything, that will tell me I'm wrong. There are no trees, no bushes, no foliage of any kind. The only living things that I can see are us and the guards still checking everyone's documents.

My shocked stare skims across the light gray ash that's dusted over everything. It's what the wind is kicking up. What's choked the life out of the very land beneath our feet. With a start, I realize we're in the Ash Barrens.

As soon as the thought registers, all the pieces fall into place. The restricted airspace. The time limit. The way Aeson freaked the fuck out. There's only one possible reason why we'd be here . . .

"You're all set, Scion Noctis," a guard declares with a respectful nod. "Welcome back to the Fae Gate base camp."

Bloody fuck.

Disbelief jabs me right in the chest, and a chill slithers down my spine. No wonder Aeson freaked out. I didn't think anyone was allowed up here for any reason other than to protect the Fae Gate and ensure that it stays closed. But if that's true, then why would the Matron of the Relacour Blood Crafters be allowed anywhere near the Fae Gate? Her bloodline was one of the main covens who participated in the rebellion; they can't be trusted.

I look around, searching for the gate itself, but the inlet around me hides its location.

"Captain Zhao will escort you to your quarters. Would you like us to wake Matron Relacour now?"

"No, it's late, we can wait until a more reasonable hour later today to meet with her. But per sections forty-three through forty-nine of secondary security protocol, please keep the jump portal open," Aeson orders, and the guard nods and then his gaze jumps back to me.

Another guard approaches the group, and we follow him away from the gate, my thoughts racing a mile a minute. Why didn't the king tell me this is where I would be going? Is this some kind of a weird test?

Glacial wind wails at us as we make our way through a rocky maze. I start to question whether or not we're being led in circles when we round a bend and there it is, the Fae Gate that almost destroyed our world.

It sits at one end of a valley, and I sense a hum of ominous power vibrating steadily from the massive ring that's bordered by tall cliffs on each side. It has to be well over a hundred feet tall and wide, with edges banded in metal. A metal that doesn't naturally occur in this world, and one scientists haven't been able to replicate no matter how many times they try. The surrounding border is covered in glyphs that look similar to sorcai runes, but these markings are different and can only be read by the fae. The whole thing is bigger and far more intimidating than I could have ever imagined, not that I would have thought in my wildest dreams of being here one day, staring up at it.

At the base of the gate is a small town that's reminiscent of something that could be found in an ancient black-and-white Western. One- and two-story buildings line a single road. There appears to be housing, a canteen of sorts, and a small supply store for the Squads and leadership stationed up here. There's also an army's worth of defensive tech and monitoring systems built into the surrounding cliffs to protect the gate itself—and us from the gate if needed.

We're led toward a two-story building that sits opposite the Fae Gate. I don't spot anyone moving around, probably because of the late hour. Not that this is the kind of place where people just mill about.

A line of vehicles are parked off to the side of the building next to ours. They look like modified ourocycles, but the front and back rotors are horizontal instead of vertical. They appear to be more machine than magic, sort of like the frankensteined creations we have back home, but these aren't welded-together death traps. They're top-of-the-line and pristine.

"You've been here before?" I ask Jori, the closest guard to me.

"A couple times," he answers but doesn't offer anything more than that.

The guard leads us to a building and we pile inside. It's surprisingly spacious and comfortable-looking, with a bottom floor that appears to be some kind of rec area with several tables to sit and eat at, a lounge space, and some game tables. Our escort explains that there are a few private quarters toward the back of this ground floor, while the rest of the rooms are located upstairs.

"As a reminder, please be mindful that no weapons will be allowed outside these premises. You can wear them when you depart, as you did when you arrived, but they are to be stored in your room for the remainder of your stay here or they will be seized." Captain Zhao looks pointedly at me.

I sigh, figuring the *but I just got them* argument isn't going to cut it with him. I'm probably lucky they haven't already confiscated them. If I were traveling with anyone other than a member of the royal family, they probably would have.

"Noted," I acknowledge politely.

With that, Captain Zhao leaves, and it takes exactly three seconds for Aeson to turn to everyone, arms folded across his chest, with an expectant look fixed on his face.

"Get some rest. It's been a long day," he orders, looking around as though he expects someone to argue with him.

No one does.

Karis hands the commander his bag, and then he gives him my pack too—the one he stole from me earlier when we were leaving the keep. Aeson's unreadable blue eyes meet mine, and my pulse instantaneously spikes.

The commander turns to stride down a hall, calling back over his shoulder, "Let's go, Claws. You're with me."

CHAPTER 45

Aeson drops both of our packs onto the large bed that's pushed up against the far wall. He starts to look around, peeking behind the door we just entered through before he wanders over to a solitary armchair that's sitting in front of an unlit fireplace. From there, he strides into the attached bathroom like he's clearing it of potential attackers. I have no idea why he's doing any of this; if there were someone in here other than us, he'd hear or smell them, but I keep my mouth shut and take in the view of the Fae Gate from the window. It looks so innocuous right now, so deceptively dormant. How could something so simple be responsible for so much desolation and destruction?

I can't even imagine what it would have been like for this gate to appear out of nowhere and then release an army intent on destroying everything in its wake. The number of humans that were lost in the waves of the first strike were staggering. More than two-thirds of their total population perished before the dragons and the other Arcs were able to best the fae and send them back where they belong.

Aeson finishes his search, and I watch him in the reflection of the glass as he tosses a fireball into the fireplace. A small pile of wood that's already been stacked within quickly becomes a cozy crackling fire, and then the commander fixes his attention on me.

"Want to tell me what your plan is with the Blood Crafter tomorrow?" Aeson asks.

I turn to face him. "Want to tell me why you have a Blood Crafter residing at the base camp of the Fae Gate?"

"It's classified," he answers, walking over to the window I'm next to and tapping the glass twice until it shifts from transparent to opaque.

"Classified?" I challenge, studying the scion. "So I'm allowed to stand in front of the fucking Fae Gate, of all places, and have a meeting with this mysterious Matron Relacour, but I'm not allowed to know what she's doing here?"

"Sounds about right." Aeson shrugs and then nods toward a side table near the head of the bed. "You can keep your weapons there."

"Is your father hiding her here or protecting her?" I ask, disarming myself of my arsenal and setting everything neatly on the table while I try to make sense of what's going on.

If the king was trying to hide the sorcai, this place would be the best option for it. It's secluded, fortified, impenetrable. But why would he be willing to do that?

"He's not protecting her, just the gate," Aeson surprisingly answers.

"So she's connected to the gate somehow?" I question, even more confused.

"Not her specifically," he supplies cryptically from where he's leaning against the wall, watching me.

I throw my hands up, frustrated. "I have no idea what that means."

"Because you're not supposed to. It's *classified*," he repeats, and I fight the urge to chuck a dagger at him.

"As your *mate*, shouldn't I know what the fuck is going on?"

Aeson is suddenly in front of me. I jerk back, but the wall behind me makes it so there's nowhere to go. His muscular arms cage me in and he leans down until I'm hopelessly locked in his gaze.

"Yes, you should, but I don't think you want to play that card right now. Not when I know you're not telling *me* everything. And don't bother denying it; I know you're up to something, I can fucking *feel* it."

"Of course I'm up to something, I'm trying to break this stars-forsaken curse. Why is that so hard for you to believe?" I snap, beyond fed up. "I want to be whole. I want what was stolen from me. I don't know what else you think I'm doing here, but you're wrong. This is about the curse. It's only ever been about the bloody curse! And don't look at me like that," I snap when his eyes narrow at me and that tic in his jaw pulses from the effort of biting back an argument.

I try to move out from the cage of his arms, but he traps me once again.

Fine. Here we go.

"You have no idea what it's like to be half of yourself," I thunder up at him. "To feel the power searing through your veins but never being able to reach it. To know that vital parts of who you are, who you're supposed to be, have been stolen from you!"

My voice cracks as I press a palm over my heart. I hate the hurt and vulnerability visible through my fissures, but he needs to understand. I need him to see all the ways I'm broken, that I will never stop trying to fix what's been done to me for as long as I fucking live.

"Every time my dragon reaches for you but can't get to you, it crushes me. When I watch my own kind soaring through the skies, when they reveal but I can't, it kills me. I can't heal. I can't manifest an affinity. I can't fucking protect myself," I yell, a tear spilling down my cheek. "I walk around wearing a charm to hide what's been done to me because I couldn't stop it. I should have been able to stop it! I'm half of what I should be, fractured in a way you refuse to see or understand. I don't give a fuck about the Fae Gate. I don't have an ulterior motive. I want to be a Syphon, not a shadow of one. I want to be *me*."

Anger slips from Aeson's features, and his eyes soften. He wipes at the tears trickling down my cheeks, and then he pulls me to him, wrapping himself around me and squeezing me tightly to his chest. My arms automatically go around his waist, and I hold him just as hard. I press my face into his chest, burrowing against his warm scale armor, breathing him in, letting his presence, his scent, and his touch soothe me.

We stand like that for a while, neither of us speaking, neither of us letting go.

"Is this all we'll ever have? Secrets and mistrust?" I murmur, breaking the silence, the sadness, and the uncertainty that's wrapped around us. But I don't know if the question is aimed at Aeson or if I'm asking myself.

"I don't want that," he confesses quietly, placing a soft kiss on the top of my head. "But every time I think we're getting somewhere, there are more secrets."

"I'm not trying to hurt you, Aeson," I whisper, meaning it. "I don't *want* to hurt you," I add, because the distinction matters too.

"Then let me in, Ever," he pleads, and I close my eyes against the ache in his voice.

I look up at him, needing him to see the truth in my eyes. "I'm trying. It's not that easy, not for me, but it has to go both ways. I'm not the only one holding back."

He sighs and places a kiss on my forehead. "Okay," he concedes. "I can accept that. We don't have to figure everything out tonight. I don't know about you, but I'm exhausted." A cheeky smirk slips across his face. "Fucking like a god really takes it out of you."

I bark out a laugh and then groan, pressing my forehead to his chest in mild mortification. "You're never going to let that go, are you?"

His laughter vibrates through me, and I can't help my smile. Carefully he starts deconstructing my bun. He pulls the band free and runs his fingers through the twisted tresses. I bite back a moan and lean into him while he rubs my scalp and finger combs tangles from my hair.

"Not a chance. I'm adding it to my business cards," he deadpans.

I snort and playfully slap his hard stomach. "You don't have business cards."

His hands drop to my shoulders and then move to the back of my neck. Deft fingers find the hidden zipper on my bodysuit and start pulling it down.

"Are you one of those guys that will become pure marshmallow fluff when it's just the two of us, but the minute anyone else is around, you're an asshole?" I ask as I step back and pull my arms out of my suit but hold the loose top to my chest.

His blue eyes flare as they trace the planes of my shoulders. "Was I an asshole?" he rasps, reaching for me, but I sidestep his grasp and move toward my pack.

"From the minute you saw Raeger in your rookery," I answer, pulling out my sleep shirt and sliding it over my head.

His scale armor slowly begins to recede, the plates slipping back into his skin until his upper body is bare. I stare at every delectable curve and dip and completely lose my train of thought.

"You have your ways to protect yourself, I have mine. I wasn't trying to be an asshole; I was just trying to figure out what you and my father were up to," he defends.

"We're not *up* to anything."

Aeson's smile makes the butterflies in my stomach swoon.

"That's where you're wrong, Claws. My father is always up to something. It's often for the good of his family, The Horde, or Drameric in general, but *cunning* is an understatement when it comes to him."

"I see where you get it then. Always ten annoying steps ahead of everyone at every turn," I observe and pull off the rest of my suit so I can slip my shorts on.

Aeson groans. "Why are you never wearing underwear?" he demands, and I laugh.

"Makes it easier to fuck with you."

"Fuck *with* me or *fuck* me?" he counters huskily.

Grabbing a blanket and a pillow off the bed, I shoot him a wink. "Both work for me when you're not being a dick."

He clutches his chest like I just struck a wound. "You know you like my dick," he argues with a cocksure grin.

I snort out a laugh and move over to the chair in front of the fireplace, pushing it out of the way so I have more room for my bed. I lay the blanket down and then the pillow.

"What are you doing?" Aeson asks, his brow furrowed with concern.

"Uh . . . going to sleep," I answer cautiously.

"On the floor?" he objects, striding closer like he's going to snatch my bedding away.

I step in front of him, blocking his access. "Yes, on the floor. I have an issue with beds. I'm sure I'll get over it eventually, but right now, the floor is the only place I actually get some sleep, and I really need rest. I'm running on fumes. Turns out being fucked by a god really takes it out of you."

Aeson laughs, like I hoped he would, and some of his shock and indignation deflate.

"Fine," he sighs, walking over to the bed and pulling off the rest of the bedding and the other pillow.

"Wait, what are you doing?" I protest as he stomps over and lays everything out like I just did.

"What does it look like? I'm sleeping with you," he explains, like it should be obvious.

"But . . . I don't . . . I'm not a cuddler," I supply awkwardly.

"Then we won't cuddle, but I'm sleeping next to you, Claws. Get over it."

I let loose a resigned sigh and lie down, pulling the blanket over me and settling in. Aeson follows suit, and then he snakes an arm under my head and pulls my back to his chest, making himself comfortable all around me.

"I thought we addressed this and reached a *no cuddling* solution?" I complain as he relaxes around me.

"We're not cuddling. I'm just holding you for a couple minutes."

I huff out a laugh. "How many minutes are we talking here?"

"It'll be over before you know it. Five minutes tops."

I snicker, but I don't push him away. As much as this changes nothing between us, I need the reprieve more than I can say. Later we can go back to the battling and omissions and wariness. But right now, we can just be Bonded Mates lying together with no complications, no mess, no distrust.

I relax against him and close my eyes.

I can do this. No biggie.

Five minutes won't kill me.

CHAPTER 46

A ripple of awareness moves through me. It draws my somnolent attention to a quiet but steady droning noise. My mind nudges me to do something about the grating sensation, but the rest of me is warm and content and not so eager to abandon sleep. I nuzzle into the sturdy warmth blanketing me and try to drift back to oblivion. Shockingly, my blankets start to move. A pair of arms tightens around me, and the comfy nest I'm lying on sleepily mumbles something.

I wake all the way up, confused and disoriented.

Floor pallets aren't supposed to move.

My eyes adjust to the dark room. The slight change in the angle of the shadows tells me I've only been out for a couple of hours. I look down and see that the bedding I'm lying on isn't a sheet or blanket at all, but a commander. I'm splayed half on top of him like he's my own personal body pillow.

So much for not being a cuddler.

Embarrassment plumes through me, but I wave it away.

No one has to know.

I shift so I can roll over and put some distance between me and Aeson, but then I notice that strange hum again. I keep myself still, drowsily trying to figure out what it is or where it's coming from. For a split second, I wonder if it's the Fae Gate outside, but when I try to zero in on the sound, I realize that it's coming from me.

Understanding pistons adrenaline through my system, and I sit up and immediately start scanning the shadows. There's nothing there, and yet my blood continues to buzz in that unexplainable way that tells me there's a Relacour nearby.

The first time it ever happened, I didn't recognize the sensation for what it was. I thought it was the high of the hunt, the intoxication of finally getting answers that was buzzing through me. But after the third and then the fourth time, I began to recognize that something odd was happening. It wasn't the euphoria of trying to reclaim my destiny that was singing in my bloodstream, it was Relacour magic.

I could feel the Relacour Blood Crafters, sense them.

All of the Syphons could.

It was proof that our hypothesis about the Relacours was right. Our blood recognized the Blood Crafters because it was their magic that was polluting our veins; it was their blood dripping down the bars of the cages trapping our dragons.

Carefully I untangle myself from Aeson and move to get up. He grunts his displeasure and reaches for me.

"Where you going?" he sleepily murmurs.

"Bathroom," I whisper.

He mumbles something incoherent and wraps himself around my pillow, shoving his face into it and breathing deeply until he's out again. Warmth settles in my chest as I watch him succumb to sleep.

I eye my weapons as I move, debating what to take. I don't want to wake Aeson up by strapping everything on, and I don't want to put the Matron on the defensive right away. Silently, I swipe four daggers. My frilled lizards and my bone blades. I press their lock sheaths to the skin of my back under my shirt, concealing them as best I can.

The polished wood floor is frosty against my bare feet, but it thankfully doesn't creak or do anything else to give me away as I pad silently across it. I hold my breath, cracking open the door and only daring to exhale when I'm safely on the other side before I quietly close it. I take a second to scan the dark hallway. There's probably a Wing member on patrol somewhere, but I don't see or sense anyone.

The buzz of my blood remains steady despite the way my heart is hammering. My quick breaths match my quick steps down the corridor. I reach the main room and instantly feel the all-too-familiar staticky sensation that indicates a magical barrier is nearby.

I go eerily still, my eyes darting around the room in search of the source of the magic. I don't see her, but the buzz in my blood is even more insistent, and I know the Relacour Matron isn't just close. She's here.

I'm surprised that she decided this introduction should take place inside the dragons' temporary quarters. It's audacious as fuck, but that tracks when it comes to the Relacour sorcai. They always think their magic is unbeatable, but I'm counting on that.

I fill my lungs with a fortifying breath and try to talk my adrenaline down, but it's not budging. Everything the Syphons have been working for hangs on this moment, and every cell in my body knows it.

Wasting no more time, I step through the barrier, quick to shake off the uncomfortable way the magic crawls across my skin. As soon as I'm inside, the dome of magic all around me hardens into a thick, transparent blockade perfect for keeping me in and everything else out. Cautiously I scan the dark rec area, running my gaze over the dining tables and benches, the chairs set out for lounging, and focus on a dense swatch of darkness directly opposite me.

Just as soon as I clock the anomaly, a svelte form separates from the shadows, and a cloaked figure steps forward.

"Now, what do we have here?" a husky yet melodious voice asks.

She pushes back the cowl of her hood, and I'm met with dark eyes, platinum hair, and a face that looks entirely too smooth and dewy to belong to the leader of an entire coven, or someone as old as I know the Matron is.

Her eyebrows dip with confusion.

"You're not sorcai," she observes, surprise registering across her features. "And yet your blood sings for me."

Anticipation surges through my limbs at the sight of her, but I keep my cool and offer the sorcai a casual shrug. I pretend like I haven't done this song and dance a ridiculous number of times with all the ones that came before her.

"I don't know if I'd call it singing," I tell the Matron as she continues to survey me. "It's less melody and more of an incessant buzzing to me."

Surprise flickers through her features. "You can sense me as well?" she asks, her head canting to the side as she tries to solve the puzzle that's been placed before her.

Her eyes dart to my ears, but they're covered by my mussed hair. I don't know why the Relacours always look there when they're trying to piece things together, but it never fails.

"I must admit, it's been ages since I've been this stumped. I can feel my people's magic, but you're not one of us. I don't sense dragon, although you keep company with them. Wyvern is off the list," she declares, her face scrunching with distaste. "And you're not one of *them*," she murmurs as she fills her lungs with a deep inhale.

My brow furrows at that.

One of them*? What does that mean?*

She moves silently closer, pausing mere feet away. I force myself to stay calm and relaxed despite the overwhelming urge to move that floods me. The Matron stares intently into my eyes like she can enchant me with just a look. If I were anyone else, it might be possible; some sorcai possess the ability. Some vampires too.

"Would you bleed for me, child?" she asks, her eyes roaming over me like I've already agreed and now she's deciding the best place to draw from. Avarice alights in her dark eyes and she draws even closer. "I'd love to see what creation your blood confesses to," she whispers covetously.

Blood Crafters are so fucking creepy.

Why do they all do this?

I fight the instinct to step back and put space between me and the predatory look in the Matron's eyes and stop myself from reaching for my knives. I need to time this perfectly.

"I'll tell you what I am," I offer politely, my smile wide and sweet. "Technically you had a hand in my creation, so it's only fair."

I extend my hand, offering to grasp forearms in the customary greeting often exchanged between sorcai. I relish the moment her brow twitches with confusion.

"Hello, Matron," I greet in encouragement.

After a moment, she steps forward and grasps my arm. Her eyes dart back and forth between mine as she continues to search for hints as to what I am, which is when I reach behind my back and unsheathe a dagger. Her eyes flare with concern when my grip suddenly tightens on her forearm and the friendliness in my face dies, but she doesn't retreat.

"I'm Ever Tenebrae," I offer, my voice low, my eyes boring into hers, suddenly heavy with decades of hate. "I'm one of the Syphons that's been hunting down your bloodline. It's so good to *finally* meet you."

Alarm detonates across her face, and she rips her arm from my grasp, tripping over her feet in an effort to get away from me. Impressively, she doesn't fall, but she does quickly cast a red barrier between us. Her hands lift sharply in the air as bolts of magic flare from her palms. The power disperses through the air like a cloud of glittering pollen until it forms a new protective dome around the Matron.

"Impossible," she gasps as she watches me from within the confines of her own power.

She doesn't attempt to run, which is too bad. I always like it when they try. Then again, it's probably best we keep things contained within the lovely soundproof barrier she previously erected around the room.

I begin to circle the Matron. Absently, I tap on the power encasing her, like I'm looking for weak spots. This new barrier is roughly ten by ten and see-through, just like the outer barrier still encasing us. However, this cast is fresh and the magic still has a red tinge to it.

"What do you want?" the Matron snaps, more annoyed than genuinely concerned as she tracks my slow circuit around her.

"What all the Syphons want—our dragons back," I tell her simply, and I welcome the bloodlust as it starts to build in my veins.

I've been at a disadvantage since I was collected by The Horde. I've been playing catch-up with the Noctises from the moment I met them, always on the defense. But not anymore, because this—hunting the Matron, drawing things out so I can get the answers I need—this is what I do.

This is what I'm good at.

Too bad for the Matron, I don't need any more answers. I've found exactly what I'm looking for. She's standing right in front of me.

"Your dragon?" the Blood Crafter huffs, like I'm some whiny child demanding something I'm not entitled to. "I can't lift the curse on your dragon. It would have to be done by the sorcai who cast it, and they're all dead."

I tsk and stop pacing in front of her barrier like some caged lion. I level her with a look so loaded with loathing and steeped in vengeance it makes the hairs on her arm rise with alarm.

"Wrong," I snap, and then I walk through her barrier like it was nothing more than a soap bubble and wrap my hand around her throat.

She gasps in surprise and tries to fire off another defensive cast at me, but I brutally slam her back into the hard magic of her red barrier. In a panic, she shoves raw power into me. It sizzles and scorches, and pain blasts through me as she breaks my hold and then works to incinerate me from the inside out. I grit my teeth through the electric shocks she feeds through my system. I've met one other Blood Crafter capable of doing this, but the bite of the Matron's power is truly unmatched.

Good thing I'm no stranger to pain.

Her dark eyes fill with hate and satisfaction as she pours even more power into me, but it all bleeds into shock and then fear when I start to laugh.

"How are you still standing?" she shrieks at me, both shocked and outraged. My only answer is to spring for her.

I split her eyebrow with a well-placed hit, and we start to grapple, slamming one another back and forth against the walls of her protective dome. I get in a few more hits, and she tries to kick my feet out from under me, which makes us both start to lose our balance. She presses a hand to the red barrier to keep from falling, and I slam a dagger through her palm, pinning her hand to her own magic.

Except it isn't her magic anymore, it's mine. She just doesn't realize it yet.

The Matron's scream is music to my ears. Crimson magic pours out of her hands like blasts of boiling water, and she tries even harder to fry me where I stand. She coats me in what should be a lethal amount of power and then watches in horror as my body absorbs the magic and I'm left standing without a mark on me to show for her trouble.

Horror-struck, she quickly abandons the fight and starts trying to escape. She attempts to yank the dagger out of her hand, but it doesn't budge. She tries to drop the red barrier around us once again so she can dislodge herself that way, but the magic in the barrier doesn't respond to her.

"How are you doing this?" she cries, pure panic now bright in her eyes.

"Didn't you know?" I purr. "Thanks to the curse the Relacours put on us, your magic now runs in my veins," I inform her casually as I pull another lizard dagger from behind my back. "It lets me do fun little things like this . . . "

Grabbing her other hand, I press it against the barrier and slam my other dagger through it, pinning her with her arms outstretched as tears begin to drip down her face and she screams with all of her might for help.

I grab her throat and press her hard against the barrier at her back. "My kindred screamed that night too. When your people stole their dragons and helped slaughter them. Nobody came to help them either."

"I can't break your curse, you stupid bitch!" she snarls and tries to spit at me.

I dodge the glob and smile viciously at her. "Now, now, *Conduit*, yes, you can," I cluck, and her eyes widen with pure, unadulterated terror. "Oh yeah, I know *all* about that little loophole. Only the sorcai that casts a curse can break it, right? Wrong. There's one exception you magical fucks like to keep to yourselves, isn't there? If you kill a bloodline's Conduit, everyone in that line dies, and when that happens, their magic dies with them."

"You can't," she gasps through panicked breaths.

"Watch me," I snarl in her face.

She starts screaming and thrashing, but just like all the others that came before her, it's not going to do shit to stop what's about to happen. The other Syphons and I have been hunting the Relacour Conduit from the moment one of the other Blood Crafters confessed what it was—or rather, *who* it was and why they were special.

Turns out sorcai are kind of like vampires. They're all linked back to a sire or a creator. Kill the master vampire and all of their progeny goes with them. Kill a Conduit, and they take out their coven in exactly the same way. It's a closely guarded secret, one offered in exchange for a life that I ended up taking anyway, because no Relacour will ever find mercy at the hands of a Syphon again.

Out of nowhere, one of the daggers pinning the Matron's hand to the barrier goes flying away. My head snaps to follow the trajectory of my blade, and I find Herm on the other side of the first barrier with his hand outstretched. My lizard dagger flies toward him like he's a magnet.

I guess I know now how he stole my butter knives.

Fucker.

Aeson's Wing comes streaming into the room, spreading around the rim of the outer barrier. I watch them shouting orders at each other, the two sets of magical domes between us blocking the sound, but I don't need to hear them to know my time is running out. Herm holds up his hand again, and I turn to see my other lizard dagger start to tremble like it's fighting the force of the Stormer that's trying to steal it.

Shit.

The Matron's shrieks and wails become louder as she sees the scramble of activity around us. She starts begging for help as tears and blood spill freely down her face and off her hands. My remaining lizard dagger loses its fight against Herm and goes flying out of the Conduit's other palm and out of the inner barrier. I hurry to unsheathe a bone blade while keeping the Matron from crumpling to the floor.

Done with drawing things out, I line up my new dagger so it can enter between the Matron's ribs and pierce right into her heart. In one swift and practiced move, I sink half the blade into her chest before she grabs my hand with surprising strength and fights me from delivering the final blow. Warm blood spills from the puncture and coats both of our hands, and she slowly starts to lose her grip.

"Wait," she begs, tightening her grasp on my hand when I win another inch. "Don't you want answers?" she rasps, her eyes desperate as they flick between mine.

"No," I growl. "Your death is the answer."

I gain another inch.

A thunderous boom sounds off around me, and my head whips in the direction of the sound to find Aeson. His face is filled with rage and he pounds on the outer barrier, intent on getting my attention. He shouts something angrily, pointing at me and then the ground. I can't hear him, but I'm pretty sure he just ordered me to drop my weapon and step away from the sorcai.

I glare an unmistakable *not a chance* his way and then focus back on the Matron. Aeson punches the barrier again with a resounding bang that sends a chill skittering up my spine.

"If you kill me, you'll weaken the Fae Gate," the Matron gasps, her mouth filling with blood as I shove the dagger even deeper, drawing closer and closer to her heart as her strength wanes and mine prevails.

"I wouldn't believe a word out of your mouth even if every Thrasher in existence vouched for you," I snarl at her, and she whimpers.

Despite my declaration, I consider her words for a millisecond. She is here at the Fae Gate for reasons I don't know, but Aeson himself said that it wasn't the Matron specifically that had something to do with the gate, so fuck her mind games and stalling tactics.

Suddenly, a pulse of power tears through the room with a thunderous clap of sound. I'm thrown away from the Matron, and she collapses to the ground. I sit up, a steady ringing now in my head, and I work to shake off the momentary shock of whatever just happened.

Aeson is suddenly in front of me, tinged in red from the only magical barrier that still separates us. He and his Wing must have just ripped through the other one. The Matron coughs, choking on her own blood as she tries to crawl toward her hopeful saviors.

"No, you don't," I croak, grabbing her leg and pulling her toward me.

"What the fuck are you doing, Ever?" Aeson shouts at me, and I'm surprised I can hear him now.

I look down and find my bone blade still lodged in the Matron's chest. Blood pools underneath her, and she's pressing a bloody hand to the barrier next to me like she's still trying to drop it so Aeson and the other drakes can get in.

She doesn't understand that the minute I touched her protections, I seized control of them. I have no idea how it works, but the Relacour magic in our veins allows the Syphons to withstand Relacour casts, null their control, and claim their protections at will.

I reach for the handle of the dagger that's sitting in the sorcai's chest.

"Ever, stop!" Aeson commands, pressing a hand against the barrier like he can will me to obey. "You need to listen to me, you can't kill her!" he shouts, and I hear the fury and betrayal in every word.

I close my eyes for a moment to help stave off the rush of emotion I unexpectedly feel from the hurt in Aeson's voice. He calls my name again, and I press my hand against the barrier where he pounds his fist.

"I don't know why you're doing this, but there has to be another way," he growls at me, and I bow my head, because there isn't.

I know he's furious, that he doesn't understand, but there's nothing I can do. The Relacours started this, and now it's time for the Syphons to finish it. If there were a way to belong to both Aeson and my people, I would take it. If I could fix what was done to us without hurting him, I would. But it's not possible. I won't choose him over the Syphons. I won't choose him over me.

"Claws, listen to me, I need you to trust me," Aeson tries again, calmer this time, like he's hoping he can talk me down from the ledge since he can't order me off of it.

Resolved, I drop my hand from his and wrap it around the dagger in the Matron's chest. Aeson starts frantically pounding on the barrier again, shouting and barking orders as I unsheathe my final bone blade from behind my back with my other hand and press it against the Matron's throat.

She's on the brink of death, blood pouring freely from her chest, mouth, and hands, but she still manages to look up at me with pure malevolence. "You think this will save you, but it won't," she rasps, choking on vitriol as it spills out in time with her life force. "The fae will come for you, and I don't mean the ones on the other side of the gate. I'm talking about the ones that are already here."

Ice spills into my veins at her words, but I'm already drawing my blade across her throat while I shove my dagger into her heart. Aeson roars and it echoes all around me as death finally claims the Matron, her coven, her bloodline, and her magic . . . forever.

Sixty-two years of suffering, planning, hunting, and clawing our way back from the brink of annihilation, and it's done. The Syphons are finally free.

Tears spill down my cheeks. Relief and sorrow churn in my chest as I sit back on my knees, wiping the blood from my blades on the matron's cloak. Aeson's face is a mixture of rage and betrayal. I'm whole again, a Syphon in every sense now that the curse is broken, and yet the way he's looking at me threatens to shatter me all over again.

I open my mouth to explain, to help him understand, but my blood all at once flash boils in my veins, and my bones become molten. My dragon pushes against the bars of its cage . . . but they suddenly fracture and crumble. Power surges through me, filling every cell in my body and purging every drop of foreign magic from my blood. The inferno in me builds, and blinding pain is quick to follow. My body bows, a silent scream pouring from my mouth, and then the well of power that's rising and expanding inside of me . . . explodes.

CHAPTER 47

AESON

A groan spills out of me, and I roll onto my side, disoriented and sore. I'm on the floor.

Why the fuck am I on the floor?

Ash floats in the air above me, and it takes me a second to figure out where I am. Then it hits me like a fist through my chest . . . Ever . . . the Fae Gate!

I sit up with a pained growl, feeling like I just went ten rounds with the entirety of The Horde, but I shove all thoughts of my battered body aside.

"Ever?" I shout, and I hear a moan come from underneath what looks like a chunk of fallen roof.

I scramble over to the debris and find Karis and Tove lying next to it. They're already stirring. Frantically, I scan the room for the rest of my Wing, and relief rushes me. Everyone is here; they're okay and coming to.

Everyone except her.

I stumble over to the Matron's dead body and try to figure out what the fuck just happened.

Ever killed her.

In cold blood, she just . . .

Horror overcomes me and I sprint to the shattered window that looks out at the Fae Gate. I huff out a soul-deep sigh of relief. The Gate's not down. No alarms are blaring through the base camp, and the same wards that were churning in place before appear to be intact. The question is though, for how long?

"I need security status on the gate," I bark, looking over to Ogdan. He's just sitting up and I hurry to help him to his feet.

"Stable," he grunts while rubbing the back of his head. "Contingencies state that an outcome like this should only weaken protections, not dismantle them altogether, but we'll need to shore everything up until we have a fix in place. We need to get another Relacour Blood Crafter up here, and we need to get one now."

I pinch the bridge of my nose, my head already throbbing. "Contact my father, tell him what's happened. Have him send Lorn up here with a new Blood Crafter," I tell Ogdan, and he nods. "Anyone have eyes on the Syphon?" I call out.

"I think she's gone," Sondar rasps as he approaches. "I'm splicing the security feeds now. Give me a sec. There's no sound and they're glitchy from the explosion, but it's the best we've got."

"That fucking bitch," Tove groans as Herm helps her off the ground. "She just killed a fucking Matron. The Relacour covens are going to lose their shit. How are we going to explain this shit?"

My heart hammers in my chest, and my thoughts are troubled and angry. Why the fuck would Ever do this? She said she wanted to break her curse, but how is she going to do that by killing the Matron? I'm obviously missing something here, but I have no idea what.

"Got her," Sondar announces as he rushes over, pressing buttons on his com until he's transferred the security feed to mine.

My shoulder twinges with pain when I lift my arm to watch the playback. I ignore the ache and grit my teeth as I witness, for the second time, my mate stabbing and slitting the throat of the Relacour Matron. I speed the feed along until she pulls her daggers out of the body and wipes them clean, which is the last thing I recall her doing. A flash of blinding light suddenly fills the screen. That must have been what knocked everyone on their ass and ripped the barracks up.

Slowly the light fades, until it blinks out altogether, and I find my gorgeous, deceitful, lying little mate standing at the center of the room. She looks dazed, and she staggers a bit but manages to stay on her feet. Ever glances around, seemingly confused, and then she registers the damage to the barracks. With panicked steps, she rushes through the room and starts pulling my Wing from the rubble. One by one, she checks everyone's pulse and breathing while scanning the wreckage.

Suddenly, she dashes toward an upturned table and shoves it to the side. She drops down next to my prone body and checks my vitals and airway just like she did with the others. I watch as she sighs with relief, brushing ash from my face before she clasps one of my hands between hers. Ever says something, but I can't hear or make out what.

I lie there unresponsive, my chest slowly rising and falling, when she leans over me and presses her head to my chest like she's seeking comfort. She stays just like that for almost a minute before she sits up, kisses the inside of my palm, and then rests it against my chest. I look down at my hand as though I can still feel the press of her lips there, and then I watch on the feed as my mate stands up and walks out of the frame of the camera.

I rewind it and rewatch everything again.

"Is that what I think it is?" Blay asks, pointing to Ever just before she disappears.

"What?" Chastain asks, leaning over Blay to get a look at what he's gesturing to.

Shock, fury, and pride fight for dominance of my thoughts when I zoom in to confirm that I'm seeing what I think I am.

"Ever has a dragon mark," I murmur, and everyone goes still, stunned by my declaration.

Zooming in even more, I study the grainy still shot of the feed. At first I think Ever has flames climbing up her throat like I do, but the closer I look, the more I realize the lines of her mark look more like calligraphy. Inky strokes of varying thicknesses highlight the feminine angles of her jaw and shoulders. There are some daintier lines flowing between the broader ribbons of black, and there's a star shape—or maybe it's a rhombus—on the front of her throat. The dragon mark flows under the neckline of her top, and I suspect it continues down her back and across her chest.

It's beautiful and perfect, and I want to trace each line with my tongue, but only after I throttle her until she explains what the fuck she was thinking. She could have altered the wards on the Fae Gate and subsequently fucked all of Drameric with this stunt, all because she wouldn't listen, wouldn't trust her own Bonded.

"What are your orders?" Karis asks, shaking ash out of his hair and pulling me from my furious thoughts.

"As soon as my brother gets here and the Fae Gate is resecured, we're moving out."

"Where to?" Farrow asks, pulling up several maps on his com so he can start preparing logistics.

My scowl deepens and my features grow hard. "Syphon hunting."

ABOUT THE AUTHOR

Ivy Asher is an international bestselling author of paranormal and fantasy romance. She loves snowstorms, swearing, drinking chai, and writing epic stories that feature badass women and leave readers begging for more. When not planning her next tattoo, reading, or generally being a menace, she's daydreaming about new characters and worlds. Asher resides in Bengaluru, India, with her husband, daughter, and three fur babies.